Mountains Piled upon Mountains

Mountains
piled

Appalachian Nature Writing
in the Anthropocene

pon
mountains

Edited by **JESSICA CORY**

West Virginia University Press · Morgantown 2019

ISBN

Paper 978-1-946684-90-5

Ebook 978-1-946684-91-2

Library of Congress Cataloging-in-Publication Data

Names: Cory, Jessica, editor.

Title: Mountains piled upon mountains : Appalachian nature writing in the anthropocene /
    edited by Jessica Cory.

Description: First edition. | Morgantown : West Virginia University Press, 2019.

Identifiers: LCCN 2019010275| ISBN 9781946684905 (paper) | ISBN 9781946684912
    (ebook)

Subjects: LCSH: Appalachian Region–Literary collections. | American literature–
    Appalachian Region.

Classification: LCC PS554 .M69 2019 | DDC 810.8/0974–dc23

LC record available at https://lccn.loc.gov/2019010275

Book and cover design by Than Saffel (WVU Press) incorporating illustrations by
Sko Olena (Shutterstock).

To those who see themselves
as extensions of the natural world.

Contents

DESTROY

PRESERVE

PROTECT

EVOLVE

CELEBRATE

Introduction

Jessica Cory

———

Let's be clear: Appalachian nature writing is nothing new. Recently a colleague, the wonderful Dr. Mae Miller Claxton, declared that "every Appalachian writer is an environmentalist"—and she's right. With roots in the oral histories of the indigenous peoples who resided in these mountains and continuing on with the explorers and naturalists who found themselves in the region, nature writing has a rich and developed history in Appalachia. William Bartram's *Travels* is often credited as the seminal work of Appalachian nature writing, and Horace Kephart notes in *Our Southern Highlanders* that "William Bartram of Philadelphia came plant-hunting into the mountains of western Carolina and spread their fame to the world"; he goes on to refer to Bartram as "the botanist who discovered this Eden." Kephart's admiration of Bartram struck a chord, too, with Edward Abbey, who is best known for his musings on desert life. In one of Abbey's lesser-known works, his "Natural and Human History" essay in Eliot Porter's *Appalachian Wilderness: The Great Smoky Mountains*, Abbey quotes Kephart's praises and expands on the ideas first put forth by these pioneers of the genre. *Mountains Piled upon Mountains* continues to develop this understanding of the importance of Appalachian nature and human engagement with it, as well as further examines the definition of "the nature focused text" as "a cultural-literary text."[1] The popularization of the term *Anthropocene* over the last decade to describe our new epoch as one marked by human influence only serves to further these connections between nature and culture and, as such, the texts that spring from this relationship.[2] By bringing together both well-known and emerging Appalachian writers to explore Appalachian nature in the Anthropocene, this collection shows that nature writing in and of the region continues to flourish and evolve centuries after Bartram's legacy and the continuation of human involvement in the natural world.

Certainly, collections of nature writing that focus on particular areas of Appalachia exist. Excellent examples include George Ellison's two-volume *High Vistas*, which examines western North Carolina and the Great Smokies; *The Height of Our Mountains* by Michael Branch and Daniel Philippon, covering the Blue Ridge Mountains and Shenandoah Valley of Virginia; and Neil Carpathios's *Every River on Earth: Writing from Appalachian Ohio*. However, as Heike Shaefer notes, nature writing is often a regionalist endeavor.[3] Consequently, these collections, while helpful in understanding and appreciating the human engagement with Appalachian nature, offer a limited scope that diminishes the similarities of Appalachian areas and reduces the broader voice that the region as a whole can uplift, adding to the larger conversation of Appalachia and its natural (and, in some cases, man-made) environments. Regional place-based writing certainly provides those familiar and unfamiliar with the area with an "ecologically informed [redefinition] of human identity and cultural practices."[4] However, it's my hope that a compilation of nature writing representative of the entire Appalachian region provides readers with a more comprehensive scope and understanding of Appalachian nature, culture, and people.

When selecting the works to be included in this collection, I considered the public perception of Appalachia, particularly by those who may live and work outside of the region. Often there is the misconception that Appalachian authors (and, indeed, Appalachia itself) are simply rural, white, and male. Though the latter part of that assumption has begun to fade with the fame of Kathryn Stripling Byer, Ann Pancake, and others, the perception—and to an extent, the reality of Appalachian literature being largely white—still persists. As Althea Webb reveals, "Appalachia has always had a racially and ethnically diverse population that has been significant and influential. Migration and mobility has shifted patterns of diversity within sub-regions and particular counties, but many areas recall traditions of inclusive collaboration unlikely to have taken hold outside the mountains."[5] Fortunately, there has been a recent effort to include and incorporate Affrilachian and Native American authors in the study of Appalachian literature. As these authors help to create the ecological history of the region, it's important that we consider their works with the same, if not more, appreciation with which we approach more demographically homogenous Appalachian texts.

By having a better understanding of the history of nature writing in Appalachia and by gaining insight into the motives of writers who engage with nature, we're encouraged to analyze our own ways of interacting with the natural world, especially as human engagement has become the marker for our current epoch. Are we activists fighting in the war against mountaintop removal? Do we shop at our local farmer's market? Perhaps some of us garden or raise animals for meat. Or maybe we enjoy sipping our coffee on the front porch and watching the hummingbirds flit in and out, sipping their sugar water from the red glass ornament hanging from the hook beside the butterfly bush. All of these methods of interaction are important, as they shape our worldview and impact our human experience.

As evidenced in the works of Kephart, Bartram, Abbey, and many others, nature writing is almost always created with one or more of a few select purposes. These objectives include to recount an event tied inextricably to the natural world, to contemplate or appreciate a facet of one's natural environment, to express outrage and raise awareness of environmental destruction, to encourage others to preserve or protect part of the natural world, to explore potential benefits and drawbacks as humans continue to evolve within and beside nature, and, finally, to celebrate the wonders and bounty that nature provides.

Meditation on aspects of the natural world, as the section on contemplation evidences, whether in simply appreciating nature's beauty or being enthralled by its capabilities, can have an amazingly therapeutic effect on both the meditator and the reader. Many Appalachian writers throughout the ages have contemplated either the infinitesimal or the overwhelming. From Annie Dillard who in *A Pilgrim at Tinker Creek* describes the minute evolution of caterpillar eggs to Barbara Kingsolver who rhapsodizes on the positive effects of local food production on the region's landscape and economy in *Animal, Vegetable, Miracle: A Year of Food Life*, Appalachian writers are hoping to create in their readers a similar contemplation or at least to help readers see nature's relevance. Perhaps changing the mind of a single reader is all it will take to change the larger man-versus-nature narrative.

In Taylor Brown's "Harper," we see a young man's contemplation and engagement with nature play a pivotal role in his coming of age and understanding. A similar importance of contemplation as part of one's journey can be found in Jeanne Larsen's "At Goshen Pass, the *Search*" wherein entering nature without the extraneous "necessities" of modern life is "like . . . going into rehab." Echoing the role of nature on one's journey, David Young and Lisa Ezzard ponder in their works how nature and their experiences within it affect their thoughts and thought patterns, and how nature shapes the people we become. Continuing the inward focus that contemplation often takes, Scott Honeycutt and Felicia Mitchell use nature as a touchstone to contemplate human impermanence, as Mitchell muses on a "name I'll forget / before I forget why I wanted to remember it all" and Honeycutt reflects on "the silence of hills and returning to / nothing that beauty of lost hours." The internal dialogue that the natural world facilitates can be pivotal not only to writers but also to the rest of us as we struggle to fit in moments of self-reflection amid our busy schedules and demanding societal pace.

It's important to note, however, that nature-based contemplation isn't all inward-focused navel-gazing; often an aspect of nature will spark a curiosity that puts nature itself in the place of the role of the protagonist. G. C. Waldrep and Stephen Cushman, for example, channel plants in their poems "White Trillium" and "Green Zebra," wherein the tomato realizes it "had evaded human improvement." Gene Hyde's "Shooting Rivers and Smoldering Churches: Fire and Rain in Appalachia" examines the role of water, specifically rainfall, in the region, as does John Robinson's "Evening Storm." This placement of nature at the forefront of contemplation, rather than simply the medium, allows readers to notice the ways in which their perceptions of nature are shaped by human interaction.

Recounting an experience is another common way for writers to engage with nature and help their readers connect to a particular place. Many times, we find something in nature that an experience or memory is tied to. Perhaps it's berry picking with an older cousin or eating one of grandpa's tomatoes, fresh off the vine. Maybe it's the wafting scent of lilac or honeysuckle that reminds us of our childhoods, playing barefoot with the cool, slick blades of grass sliding between our toes. By describing a particular setting, writers are able to reenter their experiences and take the reader with them, as we see in the section that focuses on this purpose. In Sarah Beth Childers's "Beaver Pond," we see the narrator recounting her trips as a young girl to Beaver Pond with her father and uncle, a place she returns to in order to find solace and remember her uncle after his passing, but all that's left are "a few dried-out sticks, gnawed to sharp white points" with no pond in sight. These themes of recollection and loss can also be found in Jesse Graves's "Our Mother," whose speaker is reminded of his loss by the "blackberry-scented" air. In Ellen Perry's "Joni and Jesus," we see the changing seasons parallel Joni's relationship with her brother, Jackson, and her reflection on the loss of that relationship. Finally, Scott Honeycutt's tragicomic "Reverie with Chestnut Trees" paints a portrait of a deceased loved one encountering the changed landscape of modern-day Appalachia. By using nature to channel the memories of their loved ones, these writers are able to maintain a sense of connection to their beloveds despite their physical absence.

However, recounting doesn't have to involve a physical loss. In Bill King's "Going for Tadpoles in My Son's 18th Year," the speaker not only recounts an experience that he shares with his son but also rhapsodizes on how quickly childhood fades into adulthood. M. W. Smith also attains a sense of nostalgia in "Spring Box," which recalls a simpler time when "Drinking, tying flies, laughing" reigned, but now remain "only a vague narrative." These writers show that by fully immersing themselves in the experiences and reveries provided by the natural world, they are honoring not only nature but also themselves.

While meaningful contemplation and engagement with nature can be enjoyable for its own sake, it can also lead to the discovery of larger issues, exemplified in the section on destruction. In modern-day Appalachia, rife with hydraulic fracturing (or "fracking"), injection wells, logging, mountaintop removal, contaminated water, and continued underground and strip mining, the exploitation of Appalachia and those who call it home is palpable, as is the destruction such practices bring to the natural world. As many residents and nature lovers try to resist, fight, or perhaps even cope with the damage being perpetrated on their landscapes, writing is often a tool that they use, as Susan Deer Cloud notes in "Mountaintops, Appalachia." In addition to Deer Cloud, this collection also showcases many other writers taking to task the destructive measures of energy companies and other corporations. Julia Spicher Kasdorf's speaker narrowly avoids confrontation with energy sector workers in "American Bittersweet," and Lisa Hayes-Minney discusses the dangerous side effects of fracking, which companies continually dispute. Madison Jones in "At Heaven's Dirty Riverbank" echoes Hayes-Minney's concern about the impact of environmental peril. In order to halt the environmental degradation taking place in Appalachia, additional action is necessary, and it's clear that many writers hope that their works can be a catalyst for such action by bringing attention to these exploitative systems and measures.

Sometimes larger-scale destructions, such as long-term effects or systemic destabilization, occur long after the immediate danger appears to have ceased. One classic example of destruction can be found in Kathryn Stripling Byer's "Just before Dawn," based on the debris flow, or mudslide, that occurred in Maggie Valley, North Carolina, in 2003 when a woman died as mud engulfed her home. Heavy rains and a faulty retaining wall were blamed for the event. Debris flows can often be expedited by human infrastructure or interference. As we are shown in Ben Burgholzer's "Border Waters," Julia Spicher Kasdorf's "They Call It a Strip Job," and Byer's "On Waterrock Knob," exploitative land practices can result in irrecoverable damage to the environment and to those who depend on it for survival. In addition to destruction of the land to gain access to natural resources,

Heather Ransom's "Stockholm State: A History" exposes how the systems at work in the region can damage the region's own citizens.

Clean drinking water and uncontaminated air are a necessity for everyone, including those with occupations that endanger the very land they inhabit. While it's easy to associate destruction with exploitation, the other side of the argument brings about the issue of destruction of one's way of life. In Ed Davis's "Making Paradise," the locals are terrified of losing their livelihood as loggers and paper manufacturing workers. Destruction can also be so simple that it becomes commonplace, as Michael McFee takes notice of in "Devil's Rope." It's important to note that even destruction that appears to be nominal can wind up having a serious impact, and often the impact isn't felt until intervention becomes a complicated and arduous matter.

When writing about environmental destruction, many authors choose to champion preservation. Preservation, in one sense, involves taking care of the environment rather than defending it from those who wish to exploit it for their own means. In this section, Brent Martin brings our attention to the history of conservationism and preservation in "Appalachian Wildness and the Death of the Sublime" by noting a historical issue that continues in many parts of Appalachia today: "Urban and industrial America called for conservation and preservation, while rural Americans, as well as corporate America, saw the vast expanse of publicly owned land as either a common space to be utilized or as a natural resource base to be exploited for profit." Laura Henry-Stone discusses preservation in her essay, "Hemlocks, Adelgids, and People: Ecological Learning from an Appalachian Triad," showing how even small-scale actions can make an impact.

Preservation in another sense can be seen as an action taken to avoid erasure of memories, customs, and histories. In this view of preservation, Gail Tyson's "Man Talk" and "Frog and Tadpole," and Julia Spicher Kasdorf's "Home Farm," portray the struggle of preserving one's way of life. In these poems, we see how family and community members uphold traditions. Such writing of preservation has a lengthy history in the region. Much of Appalachian culture, including the indigenous cultures of the

Ani'yunwi'ya (Cherokee), Shawanwa (Shawnee), Coyaha (Yuchi), Chikasha (Chickasaw), Lenape (Delaware), and Mvskoke Etvlwv (Muscogee/Creek), was, and still is, passed down through oral tradition. Unfortunately, as families and lineages are separated by forced removal, diaspora, migration, or simply death, these oral histories are not always passed on. Recording, by writing or other means, allows the continued existence of these histories and provides a way for future generations to learn about the cultural heritages of the Appalachian region. Emma Bell Miles's *The Spirit of the Mountains* is one such example of writing to preserve the mountain culture, as are the narratives of Sarah Gudger, Dan Bogie, Harriet Mason, and many other former slaves, whose recorded experiences help add to our historical and cultural knowledge of the Appalachian region. In my essay "Uprooted," I both preserve what I know about my family's history and argue that the tradition of farming in Appalachia needs to be preserved and handed down as well. Preserving these stories of Appalachian individuals and communities allows us to understand and honor the full range of Appalachian experience.

While some community members may band together to preserve their livelihoods, other Appalachians may feel the need to protect themselves and their landscapes from these community members. Protection in Appalachia can look very different depending on which side you're on. Since this collection focuses on nature, understandably the vast majority of works in this section center on protecting the natural world from the man-made forces that jeopardize it. In Katie Fallon's "Forest Disturbance," the vulnerable forest is put at risk by privately held mineral rights below its humus. In George Hovis's "Your Mee-Maw vs. CXP Oil & Gas, LLC," a grandmother takes a stand to protect her land from the effects of fracking. Rick Van Noy's "Take in the Waters: On the Birthplace of Rivers, West Virginia" and Kathryn Stripling Byer's "Waynesville Watershed" remind us of Wilma Dykeman's warning in *The French Broad*: "Water is a living thing; it is life itself," and if the water quality suffers, "all the network of creatures that live by water, including man himself" are in danger. Thomas Rain Crowe also echoes Dykeman's sentiment that "if the fundamental ingredients of living [are] sound and good, the furbelows [can] be done without." In his essay, "In Praise of Wilderness: Getting What You Give Up," Crowe suggests that in protecting the land, we are truly protecting ourselves. What these writers convey is a theme often found in Appalachian literature: that to survive on the land, one must protect it.

To close the section, Rosemary Royston takes us in a new direction: protecting oneself and one's family by natural (and, save the death of a blackbird, largely nonviolent) folkloric methods. These poems and the suggested protection methods are based on Royston's recent research from "Edain McCoy's *Mountain Magick: Folk Wisdom from the Heart of Appalachia*, along with stories shared with [her] by those who've lived the majority of their lives in Appalachia." Her poems both remind us of the region's cultural heritage as well as how the region is ever evolving.

Evolving views on folkloric protection methods are just one way Appalachia has changed over the centuries. However, what comes to mind more immediately than myths when transformation and Appalachia are discussed is the industrial presence in the region. As industry progresses and changes the landscape as well as the way of life for many residents, uncertainty and anxiety creep in and are often expressed in the essays and poems in this section focusing on Appalachia's evolution. The discussion of nature versus industry, or what some may tout as "progress," particularly in Appalachia, has long been a source of fuel for writers. In an 1899 issue of *McClure's Magazine*, Sarah Barnwell Elliott contributed a piece called "Progress," centering on the feared changes of a widespread railroad industry. Concerns about change, whether largely unfounded or based on science and economics, continue today in the nature writing of Appalachia.

This section begins with Ann Pancake's "Letter to West Virginia, November 2016," exposing us to the contradictions and evolutions both the land and its people endure and the hopeful idea "that tearing down clears an emptiness for opportunity." Writer doris diosa davenport's "cycles and (scrambled) seasons" echoes this complex and often cyclic evolution of both nature and our own lives. In "High Water," Mark Powell presents the transformation of numerous characters against a natural world that moves from foreground to background and back again in a sort of ethereal evolution all its own. Stephen Cushman's "Love in the Age of Inattention" and Felicia Mitchell's "Towhee" bring to light the effects of technology not only on human relationships but also on human relationships with nature. As Mitchell notes, "I am complicit here / . . . Without thinking, wasting electricity / I can disturb the universe." While the effects of humans on nature cannot be negated, Libby Falk Jones, Larry D. Thacker, and Jesse Graves focus instead on the evolution of nature itself, particularly the signs of seasonal transformation, such as the "Bush budding white, crocus unfolding" in Jones's "February Springtime in the Mountains" or the way in which "the first cold nights have curled / the edges of forest-floor ginger" in Graves's "October Woods." In many ways, these seasonal transitions shape our everyday lives.

These changes in season are more than just beautiful; they're often reasons to celebrate. Just think of the way the natural world plays a role in many of our own celebrations. Many of us marvel at the first snow of the season or carve pumpkins for our front porches in late autumn. We spend time swimming in lakes and rivers at summertime get-togethers and hunt morels in the late spring. As prominent a role as nature plays, it's no wonder artists and writers invoke its beauty in celebration. In this section focusing on such celebration, Jane Harrington's "Settling" revels in the relief Cornelius is able to experience when met with opportunity in a difficult landscape. "How to Avoid the Widow Maker" by Jim Minick may not seem to be celebratory at first read—the speaker is felling trees, after all. However, triumphing over a widow maker certainly is celebratory, as knowledge and skill aren't always enough to avoid a falling tree. These examples display the harmony that can arise when humans and nature are truly integrated.

The natural world can often remind us to celebrate those who mean the most to us as well. In Jeremy Michael Reed's "In Tennessee I Found a Firefly," the speaker's time in the yard, alone except for fireflies, causes him to reflect on the love he shares with his partner: "the way love bends / over time, the way a hushed phrase / creates flash of lightning." M. W.

Smith's speaker is also reminded to celebrate his loved one—a deceased grandfather—by the "eight hundred acres" this "unofficial town mayor" left behind. Whether it's a hiking trail that we've trekked with a spouse or a fishing hole where we caught our first trout, nature is full of small reminders to honor our loved ones and experiences.

While the themes of honor and respect for nature are present in Susan Deer Cloud's "Clingmans Dome Before Thanksgiving" and Lisa Ezzard's "Wine Is the Color of Blood," the respect is very much earned, as the speakers wrangle with the natural world. By juxtaposing a celebratory tone with surprisingly intimidating imagery, Deer Cloud's "Spanish moss hanging like lynched ghosts / in the mists" and Ezzard's "I spit and feel the sharp edge on the palate" may seem at odds initially. This combination, however, makes the celebration seem much more deserved, hard won. When Deer Cloud's "lovers" are "lit to bedazzlement" among "frozen trees, broken weeds, limp grasses," the reader knows that a journey through the natural world can be just as difficult as many of the other journeys we face, but just like the more mundane sojourns, the view at the end is often worth it. These pieces also serve as reminders that reasons to celebrate are perhaps not always easy to identify; it's by excavating through the "gnarled vines" that we find true joy.

In whole, this collection represents a wide swath of Appalachian engagement with nature during a time of great environmental change. The natural world in Appalachia is incredibly significant for a variety of reasons—its obvious beauty, its ample biodiversity, and its struggle, the latter of which is indelibly tied to the Anthropocene. On a more national or global scale, the immense exploitation and degradation of the Appalachian landscape is both cause for concern and reason for hope: if people here can learn to live in balance and harmony with nature, then it's possible anywhere. The writers in this collection seem to share the goal that, while it may not be easy, such a future is possible. While the spectrum and experiences can vary widely, as do the writers' understandings and encounters with the natural world, they also implore us to explore the role nature plays in our own lives and communities and to deepen those connections in light of what the Anthropocene might mean for ourselves, our communities, and our world.

NOTES

1. Karla Armbruster and Kathleen R. Wallace, *Beyond Nature Writing: Expanding the Boundaries of Ecocriticism* (Charlottesville: University of Virginia Press, 2001).
2. Paul J. Crutzen and Euguene F. Stoermer first introduced the term *Anthropocene* to describe a new geological epoch in "The 'Anthropocene,' " *International Geosphere–Biosphere Programme (IGBP) Global Change NewsLetter*, 41 (May 2000): 17, http://www.igbp.net/download/18.316f18321323470177580001401/1376383088452/NL41.pdf.
3. Heike Schaefer, *Mary Austin's Regionalism* (Charlottesville: University of Virginia Press, 2004).
4. Schaefer, *Regionalism,* 66.
5. Althea Webb, "African Americans in Appalachia," Oxford African American Studies Center, 2012, http://www.oxfordaasc.com/public/features/archive/0213/essay.jsp.

Contemplate

On the Verge

David R. Young

———————

Stevie ran down the sloping hillside. He'd been to the border of the woods more than once, but this was the first time he'd wanted to go farther, maybe out of boredom, of needing to get away from the small farm and the only family he had known for the last five months, the family he'd even begun to call his own in moments of despair, the three old people who vexed him.

He climbed over the barbed-wire fence and entered the woods. Until the past week or so, there had been merely the faintest green or purple aura around the trees in the distance, but now small bright green leaves provided a canopy, so that light filtered quietly down where he walked in the forest. Tiny yellow warblers appeared briefly, out of nowhere, and vanished as quickly.

Soon he heard the sound of a creek, full to its banks with spring rains. He walked beside the small waterfalls and rapids and stooped to drink from a spout where water rushed over a rock. Violets grew on the banks, and the wind moved in the impossibly green grass.

Farther along the creek was a small dam of rocks and branches. Upstream, a shirtless boy sat almost motionless on a flat rock by the little pool, shivering, his skinny arms crossed over his bare chest. With his feet in the water and his wet blue jeans clinging to his legs, the boy looked as though he had just got out of the creek at Stevie's approach. The boy's dark, slicked-back hair curled around his ears.

Stevie stared. He had not seen this boy before, not at school or around the square in Pendarvis. When the boy gestured toward him, as though a game of frozen tag had been called off, Stevie ventured closer. The boy might have been fourteen or fifteen. Tall and wiry, he had a downy mustache on his upper lip.

"What you looking at?" he asked.

"I'm not looking at anything," Stevie said, turning his head away.

"Just who are you?"

"I live with my grandparents up on the ridge," Stevie replied, "up on Barrows Road. You can see the Waller strip mine from there."

"I know that road," the boy said.

"I'm at Garfield School."

But Stevie did not plan to go to Garfield School next year. Once his dad found reliable work, Stevie would be sent for. He would return to the East.

Still perched on the rock, the boy leaned over to retrieve a flannel shirt, which lay on top of what appeared to be a buckskin jacket. It was too warm for this sort of clothing. But taking a pack from the shirt pocket, the boy asked, "You want a cig?"

Stevie had smoked his dad's Kools on a few occasions back in the neighborhood. His dad liked to smoke, especially at Mets games where he could watch the smoke drift up into the huge new grandstand. Stevie's mother hadn't allowed his dad to smoke at home, but after she'd gone away for a while, to recuperate, his father left his nearly empty packs around the apartment.

"I've smoked menthols," Stevie said.

The boy said, "My name's Dennis." He put two cigarettes in his mouth, struck a safety match on the box, and handed Stevie a lit cigarette. Then he threw the match in the creek and the matchbox back into an open canvas rucksack on the ground. "The last name's Brady," he added.

"I'm Stephen Hartley." He coughed after inhaling the smoke and sat down on the grassy bank of the creek. "I go by Stevie."

"These ain't menthols," Dennis said, laughing. "These are real ones. That's my sister back there, Nora. She don't smoke."

Stevie turned around. A small girl about his own age had appeared out of the woods. She stood alone upstream by the creek, staring back at them. Nora wore blue jeans like her brother, though hers were dry and the cuffs were rolled up above plain brown shoes, the kind boys wore to school in Pendarvis. She had stringy, dark red hair that touched the collar of a dirty tan corduroy jacket.

"That's okay, Nora," Dennis said. "He won't bite."

But Nora remained at some distance, watching the two boys smoke their Pall Malls. Stevie had never smoked an unfiltered cigarette.

"She's shy," Dennis said, "like a rabbit."

But Stevie was shy, too, and the kids at Garfield School made fun of his black glasses and wavy blond hair. His mother had never allowed him to get a crewcut, instructing him instead to get a "regular man's haircut" at the barbershop. And so far he had resisted his grandfather's urging that he look like the other boys.

"Where do you go to school?" Stevie asked. "I've never seen you or your sister before."

"We don't go," Dennis said, stirring the water with his bare foot. "We live down by the Little Muskingum now. There's no road, so Daddy says there's no way for us to come to school. He says maybe we can go next year, when we move back to town. I went all the way through fourth grade over to Mineral City."

"I'm in fifth grade now in Pendarvis," Stevie said. As much as he couldn't wait for the end of the school year—three more weeks—he couldn't think of anything much worse than a boy and a girl not going to school at all. Besides, they looked like tramps, like the stranger in that poem his grandmother read to him, "The Raggedy Man." His grandmother wouldn't let Stevie wear blue jeans to school, and even now in the woods he was wearing green cotton Dickies instead. Dungarees were for farm work, she said. Some of the boys wore blue jeans to school, but their families didn't know any better. Almost all of the girls wore dresses.

Nora walked slowly toward the boys. When she stopped to take off her jacket and hang it on a branch, Stevie saw she was skinny like her brother, with small pointy elbows protruding from her short-sleeved shirt. It had once been a long-sleeved shirt, cut off with scissors.

"We need to be getting home," she said. She had a round, pretty face under her stringy hair. If his mother had been there, she might have said that Nora's face was "the map of Ireland."

"Daddy's going to kill us, Dennis," Nora added. "He don't like us talking to people."

"We're not talking," Dennis said. "We're smoking. Anyhow, you should let Steve hear what sound you can make." He turned toward Stevie. "Nora's good at this."

"I don't want to," Nora said.

"Go ahead," Dennis said. "He won't tell nobody."

Nora looked at the two boys doubtfully.

"Come on, Nora," Dennis said. "Do this for me."

Nora lifted her head, cupped her hands to her mouth, and let loose a fearsome, high-pitched cry. It was really a series of cries, one echoing after the other, like the screech of a hawk. It seemed to come from deep within the cavity of her small body.

"Let's go," Nora said, breathlessly.

"I better be going too," I said. "I can't be late for dinner."

"I want to show you something," Dennis said. He got off the rock and waded into the creek. Stevie followed him along the bank, upstream from the little pool, to a place of tiny rapids and swift water. Nora followed a few steps behind. Stevie's nostrils were assaulted by a rank odor as Dennis pointed to a large turtle, partly decomposed, lying on its back. He said it was a snapper.

"Dead three or four days," Dennis said. "It's a beauty. I'll come back for it later on."

Next to the turtle were small castles of mud, unlike anything Stevie had seen before.

"Those are crawdad holes," Dennis said. "I can't believe you never seen them."

"Never," Stevie said.

Nora said, "Let's get out of here, Denny. It smells bad."

Returning to their spot by the pool, they sat cross-legged on the bank together. Now that she was closer, Stevie marveled at Nora's bright green eyes.

Dennis reached into the rucksack and pulled out the shell of a box turtle and a small, desiccated bird.

"It's a wren," Dennis said. "There are other things in the bag. Maybe I'll show you someday." He struck another wooden match and lit another Pall Mall, inhaling twice before passing it to Stevie.

Dennis added, "If you smoke the same cig, you're blood brothers."

As Stevie took his turn smoking, Dennis, until now bare-chested, reached over for the flannel shirt that seemed large enough for an adult man. Over the shirt he placed the buckskin jacket, with tassels on the sleeves, the kind cowboys wore on TV. Stevie wondered if Dennis and Nora had a TV, or had ever seen TV, but he wouldn't ask. Anyhow, it seemed too warm for a buckskin jacket, though Stevie could understand why a boy would want to wear it always.

"You look like Daniel Boone," he said, exhaling. Stevie took another puff, offering the cigarette to Nora. "Are you going to be a blood brother?" he said, aiming for a laugh.

"You can't see too good," she said, reaching for the cigarette and taking two small puffs, coughing as she did. She handed the cigarette back to Dennis, who stood up to leave. He fumbled in his jeans pocket and produced a small, football-shaped plastic coin purse. Dennis opened it by pressing on the ends.

Stevie also stood up.

"I think she likes you," Dennis said. "I never seen her smoke before." He took something from the coin purse and held it out for Stevie. "You keep this for now and swear to come back same time tomorrow, here by the dam. That Indian penny's worth a lot of money," he added, "so don't lose it."

"I promise," Stevie said, but he wasn't sure he'd be able to keep his promise. He got up to leave. Upon reaching the place where the path angled back toward the farm, Stevie turned around. He saw Dennis and Nora standing together by the little pool as before, holding hands and watching him.

Stevie held the Indian Head penny tightly all the way through the woods to the edge of the fields, fearful it would slip out of the loose pockets of his Dickies. He crossed over the barbed wire. As he began to climb up the slope across the green fields to the farmhouse, he thought he heard Nora's distant wild cry among the many sounds of the woods. By this time, his friends may have made their way back to the place where they lived with their father by the river.

He didn't say anything as he pumped water from the wooden handle in the sink and washed his hands. He sat down to join his grandparents and Aunt Ruth at the table in the small, hot dining room. They were already finishing up, but Aunt Ruth went to the kitchen to get him a plate of food. The room was suffocating because the only window was shut tight. His grandparents wouldn't open it until they were sure the cold weather was behind them for good.

"We waited for you as long as we could," Aunt Ruth said, putting the fried chicken and mashed potatoes in front of him. Her gray hair, usually pinned in a bun at the back of her head, was loose and unkempt, like that of a child grown old unexpectedly.

"Shit, you were gone a long time," she said.

"Ruth, there's no need for that kind of language," the boy's grandmother said. Her wrists were so thin, at the end of buttoned sleeves, that Stevie wondered how she could even lift a trowel. "That kind of vulgar language is used in town," she added.

He toyed with his food but wasn't able to eat much. Maybe the two cigarettes had upset his stomach. Or maybe he was nervous. He didn't want to tell them anything about the children he met in the woods. Finally, Stevie said he couldn't eat any more, and his grandfather angrily repeated grace, punishing Stevie for being late to the table.

"You won't be going back to the woods anytime soon," he said.

On weekends he would help his grandfather with planting and weeding, and once school was out, he'd spend long days in the hot sun. By late July, his grandmother had started to fail, and his father arrived to drive him back to New York.

Back in the apartment, he got the cigar box down from a shelf. When it was opened, the picture of a white owl with blue eyes stared back at Stevie from inside the lid. He put the Indian penny in the box, and though the box has moved many times over the years, there the penny has remained.

Three for My Trail Guide

Kathryn Stripling Byer

———————

for Jim

1
Ascent

Before I can catch
my breath you right away
start to identify

Wild Ginger,
Mayapple,
Bloodroot.

I'm dizzy with switchbacks
I see rising into
the hardwoods you hail

Sarvis
Sycamore
Tulip Tree.

Trillium sweeps down
the hillside like angel wings
come to rest creekside.

You chanting *hepatica,*
stonecrop, anemone,
we climb until

we reach the summit,
where underfoot
some stubborn lichen

you can't name
has already claimed
the best view.

2
Star Grass

You name it
and there it is
at the edge
of the outcropping
over the gorge.

Not to worry,
I placate the ravens
that harry us,
we won't be lingering
long in your aerie.

See? Even now we are
striding away
into star grass,
its small spikes of clear
recognizable light.

3
Galax

Squatting behind bushes,
I smell it nearby, neither bear scat

nor carrion vine, to which naturalists
liken its scent, but the breath

of an old woman lowering herself
to her chamber pot, sighing

as I heard her sigh while I tried
not to listen. Hoisting my backpack

I leave her behind in the underbrush,
glad to be back on the trail

with you, sidestepping tree stump
and blowdown, splashing through

creek bed, striding from switchback
to switchback toward sky we see,

step by step, open its window,
when, almost to summit, I stop.

Breathing hard. The scent
of her following me.

Landscape with Shoes, Stewarts Creek

Felicia Mitchell

————

One day the wind will blow the leaves away,
and every twig away, and the dried mud,
or maybe time will turn it all to a fine dust:
even this grass as green as any patch of grass
and the black shoes that are stepping on it,
gingerly, avoiding trout lilies underfoot.
Not much lasts, not the sound of water rushing
or a vireo singing in a tree whose name I'll forget
before I forget why I wanted to remember it all:
the leaves, the twigs, the mud, the grass,
skin and bones inside a simple pair of shoes.

Dried-up Earthworms

Michael McFee

———————

This hot sidewalk's
their no man's land,
its pale concrete
a killing griddle
frying the juices
out of live bait
trying to squirm
to cooler grass,
desiccated bodies
curled like commas
or question marks
on pages emptied
of watery prayers:
no quickening rain
could ever light
these mislaid fuses.

Shooting Rivers and Smoldering Churches: Fire and Rain in Southern Appalachia

Gene Hyde

———

I. RAIN (SUMMER 2016)

> I remember seven floods, the worst
> In 1946 when the sluice-gates burst
> And logs came blundering from the paper mill,
> Choking Pigeon River below Smathers Hill,
> Clanging culvert pipes and headfirst fast
> Into Fiberville Bridge.

—Fred Chappell, "Dead Soldiers," *Midquest*

Appalachian flooding often begins, benignly enough, far out in the Gulf of Mexico. Moisture flows upward from sea to sky, forming clouds that head inland until they meet the Appalachian Mountains. The same thing happens in the Atlantic, where similar clouds gather and journey until they also bump up against the Appalachians. This long mountain chain, with its northeast-to-southwest orientation, creates a natural barrier of continental proportions, just waiting to confront sea-soaked, moisture-laden clouds. When the clouds meet the mountains, they lighten their load by dumping rain and snow, sometimes in biblical proportions.

The streams and rivers that flow through these hills ripple and rage with water that came from the Atlantic and the Gulf, oceans which, in turn, are constantly being fed by the waters that flow from these mountains. As a collective drainage basin, the Appalachians are a critical component of the great water cycle. Through this aquatic catch-and-release system, the mountains disperse water in this part of the globe, and this ability to channel water on a planetary scale is part of the greater geological purpose of the Appalachians. A quick visual inspection shows that this has been the case for some time. The vertical contours in any mountain are evidence of an ongoing, gravity-fed flow of water.[1]

As the eons marched on, this flow of water eventually eroded the Appalachians—from tall alpine peaks resembling the Rocky Mountains to the heavily wooded drainage system we live in today. Unlike those upstart Rockies out West, the Appalachians are old folks when viewed through this geological lens, seemingly mellowed and long inhabited by a dazzling mixture of flora and fauna, with humans being the most recent visitors to the scene.

Living in Appalachia entails dealing with heavy rain at times, and my first experience with prolonged drenching came a year or two after I moved to Boone, North Carolina. I was in my midtwenties and working part-time for a small weekly newspaper. My rental lease was abruptly terminated when the landlords kicked us out so they could burn the house down and attempt to collect fire insurance. They succeeded at the former, but the state police put an end to the latter part of their plan. I scrambled to find a place to live, quickly signing another lease. The new rental wouldn't be available for six weeks, and since it was summer, I planned on camping and spending the occasional night on the couches of different friends.

The first day of my six-week sojourn started with a heavy summer thunderstorm. It was too wet to pitch a tent and retain any semblance of dryness, so I went to the newspaper office and spent the night on the couch. That pattern continued every day for the entire time I was between houses—heavy rain would start early to midafternoon and continue most of the night. I never pitched my tent, but I did spend many nights on the lumpy couch at work and learned a lot about rainfall in Appalachia. It can be sustained and heavy, and if you're in a low area, it's potentially dangerous. I gained respect for mountain rainfall that summer, learning the value of waterproof boots and a good raincoat. A few years later, I lived in a cabin in Blowing Rock and we had similar rainfall all summer. My wife often commented that it was so humid that her nylon bathing suit would never dry.

Over the years I've lived in three different regions in Appalachia—at first high up in the Blue Ridge near Boone, North Carolina, later moving to the Allegheny range in Virginia's New River Valley, and finally living on the western slope of the Blue Ridge just north of Asheville, North Carolina. In each place I've repeatedly heard some version of this statement: "If you don't like the weather now, just wait an hour." A variation could also be: "If you don't like the weather here, just go over the ridge." This often holds true, as weather systems can move through rapidly, and places near one another can have dramatically different weather patterns.

For instance, just down the road from Asheville is Transylvania County, which has the highest recorded rainfall on the East Coast. The area is a temperate rain forest averaging over eighty inches of rain annually. All this water dumping on the eastern slope of the Blue Ridge creates a massive amount of runoff, to the extent that Transylvania County calls itself the "Land of Waterfalls." The "wettest weather station" in North Carolina is at Lake Toxaway in Transylvania County, which receives on average ninety-one inches per year. The highest annual rainfall ever recorded in North Carolina also occurred in Transylvania County, when the town of Rosman recorded nearly 130 inches in 1964.[2]

Drive back to Asheville, a mere forty miles or so, and it's a completely different story. In contrast to the wettest place in the entire state—Lake Toxaway—Asheville is the driest weather station in the state, averaging just over thirty-seven inches annually. Just north of Asheville, where I live, is the town of Weaverville, which was originally known as Dry Ridge.

Despite this overall dryness, when it rains it can be hard and heavy, sometimes resulting in flash floods. Last summer was particularly wet in Asheville, which recorded 6.65 inches of rain in August, more than 2.2 inches greater than the average August rainfall of 4.4 inches. The heaviest rain occurred August 9–10, when 1.64 inches fell. "August was found to be the most active month in terms of flash flooding across the southern

Appalachian Mountains, but flash flooding is a problem throughout the entire year," according to a National Weather Service study, adding that this is "mainly due to the steep topography characteristics of the southern Appalachian Mountains and their proximity to the Gulf of Mexico and Atlantic Ocean moisture source regions." Dump a lot of rain across steep terrain in a short period of time and it quickly drains off into the low areas. When that happens, it floods in Appalachia.

A century ago last summer, in July 1916, the southern Appalachian bioregion was dealt a one-two climatic punch when two hurricanes (anonymous storms, as it were, for the National Hurricane Center didn't start naming storms until 1953) traveled over the mountains, one after the other, dumping record amounts of rain. The greatest twenty-four-hour rainfall in North Carolina's recorded weather history occurred during the second of these hurricanes, when Altapass, on the Blue Ridge near Spruce Pine, received over twenty-two inches on July 15–16. All that water poured downhill to ground that was already saturated and into streams that were already flooded.[3]

Asheville, which sits at the confluence of the Swannanoa and French Broad Rivers, was inundated. The French Broad was nearly a mile wide at the crest of the flood. Dams burst, every bridge on the Swannanoa River between Black Mountain and Asheville was destroyed, scores of houses and buildings were washed away, and the industrial area that had developed along the rivers (much of it now repurposed as the River Arts District) was laid to ruin. There were reports of houses floating along in the rushing waters with desperate people huddled on top. Estimates put the death toll at somewhere between ten and forty people.[4]

Even as the centennial of the 1916 Asheville flood was covered in the local news, leaving historic images of the surging French Broad River in public memory, another series of storms was pounding the mountains a bit further up the Appalachian range. In July 2016, West Virginia was hammered by a so-called train of severe thunderstorms that rolled in one after another, dumping over a foot of rain in some areas over the course of just a few hours. The toll was steep, with twenty-three deaths and the loss of over 1,200 homes, with forty-four of West Virginia's fifty-five counties declared disaster areas. Those who monitor mountaintop removal mining in West Virginia believe that the floods were exacerbated as a result of the extensive amount of mountaintop removal strip mining in the state, which significantly alters drainage and erosion patterns.[5] As one West Virginia resident said, mountaintop removal makes "monster funnels of our villages," opening the door to extreme runoff and heavy flooding to the extent that what the National Weather Service calls "nearly a one in a thousand year event" seems to be occurring far more frequently than this millennial moniker suggests.[6]

II. FIRE (NOVEMBER–DECEMBER 2016)

Holocaust, pentecost: what heaped heartbreak
The tendrils of fire   forthrightly tasting
foundation to rooftree   flesh of that edifice . . .
Why was sear sent   to sunder these jointures,
the wheat-hued wood   wasted to heaven?
Both altar and apse   the air ascended
in sullen smoke.

—Fred Chappell, "My Grandfather's Church Goes Up," *Midquest*

It rained and rained, and then it stopped. As I pick up this narrative in mid-November, about two months after my last entry, the air outside is hazy with gray smoke. While Appalachian summers are often wet, autumn in the mountains tends to be dry. It's rained very little over the last eight weeks, and there are now over two dozen wildfires burning in the mountains to the south and southwest of Asheville, wafting smoke through the passes and along the river valleys.

The smoke is thick at times, stinging the eyes and giving the back of the throat a rough edge that coughing doesn't seem to cure. State air-quality monitors issued a red alert for the Asheville area, meaning that breathing the smoke particles is deemed "unhealthy." The far western mountain counties are under a purple alert, the most severe rating of "very unhealthy." It looks and feels unhealthy outside, and I go out by necessity: dogs must be walked, errands need running, and my job beckons that I attend. I tote a bandana in my pocket and use it as a temporary mask. I can barely see across the valley through the smoke where the town formerly known as Dry Ridge sits in the haze.

My first experience with mountain drought came while camping in Linville Gorge during my college years. I was a frequent visitor to the Linville Gorge Wilderness, which offered a rugged solace from city life in the hot North Carolina piedmont. On the spur of the moment, three of us headed to the gorge to go backpacking. Based on limited empirical knowledge from a handful of previous trips, we decided that because freshwater springs were so common along the trail in the gorge we could rely on them for our water supply.

We didn't factor in the drought. We drank all our water on the hike down, then looked for the springs that weren't there. Being young and naive, we didn't bring a water filter, so fixed were we on the idea of drinking only pure mountain spring water, kind of like that character in the movie *Dr. Strangelove*. We started scouring for springs in the thick foliage with no luck. Our mouths became so dry it was difficult to speak. Finally, after several hours scrambling up and down the walls of the gorge, we found a spring. We drank deeply, filled our water bottles, and noticed the irony of suffering parched throats while a torrent of (unfiltered and untreated) water loudly rushed and roared in the Linville River a few feet away. Water is fickle in the mountains, coming and going with little regard to human needs. Ye best plan ahead.

Historically, fires in the southern Appalachians were considered "a pervasive presence." From the eighteenth century well into the twentieth century, both accidentally and intentionally ignited blazes were so common that nearly three-fourths of the land in some locations showed evidence of having been burned. Early European travelers to the region noted the "fire landscapes," often the result of intentionally set fires that cleared out forest undergrowth, making it easier for livestock to graze in the open "free range" that was the Appalachian forest. It's been estimated that as many as five million mountain acres may have been regularly burned to make the forests more conducive to free-range grazing. Fires were also set to clear woods to create cultivable fields, to open up grassy areas to attract game, to make it easier to gather chestnuts or ginseng, and sometimes for the "simple purpose of making it easier to travel through the woods."[7]

By the early twentieth century, however, the development of professional forestry in the southern Appalachians led to different ideas about fire. While farmers and livestock owners favored the burned forest floors, foresters wanted the forest unburned, viewing "the fires that helped to sustain the lives of mountain people as anathema, a scourge to be stamped out, a universal negative that impeded the growth of valuable timber trees, facilitated erosion, and disfigured the landscape. If Southern mountain forests were to be preserved, fire must be suppressed." Burning bans replaced seasonal burning as part of the life of Appalachian residents.[8]

Autumnal dryness is normal in this part of Appalachia—in fact, rain is less likely to fall in October than in any other month of the year.[9] Conditions in October 2016, however, were unusually problematic, as persistent high pressure cranked up temperatures while relegating rainfall to little more than something everyone longed for but, day after day, failed to see. The woods were so parched by November that a state climatologist noted that it had been dry since May, and several counties were recording "one of their top driest years based on more than 105 years of records."[10] These conditions turned forests into tinderboxes, and by Thanksgiving more than one hundred thousand acres had burned in southern Appalachia, hundreds of homes were evacuated, and several hundred people were hospitalized for smoke-related respiratory problems.[11]

Even more alarming was the fact that this is becoming the new normal. "Wildfires, once a seasonal phenomenon, have become a consistent threat," noted the *New York Times* in an article about the Appalachian fires. The *Times* also placed the blame partly on climate change, which has "resulted in drier winters and warmer springs, which combine to pull moisture off the ground and into the air." When that moisture flees skyward and fails to fall back down as rain, conditions are ripe for conflagration.[12]

Conditions became catastrophic near Gatlinburg, Tennessee, on November 28, when the combination of extreme drought, low humidity, and high winds turned a small fire into a fast-moving inferno. The fire dashed across rough mountain terrain so quickly that a Great Smoky Mountains National Park official said "none of our firefighters [had] ever seen a fire hop like that in the Southeast in such a short time."[13] It roared into Gatlinburg as people scrambled to get out, with reports of folks driving down fire-engulfed roads to escape. Over 14,000 people evacuated, and more than 2,000 buildings and homes were destroyed. Fourteen people died and nearly 200 were treated for injuries.

In Gatlinburg, the fire skipped around town, destroying some buildings while leaving others unscathed. The damage to churches reflected this randomness, as some were left intact, others were partially charred, and a few—altar and apse, pew and pulpit—succumbed to the tendrils of fire and were burned to the ground, leaving a legacy of holocaust, pentecost, and sullen smoke.

III. WHAT MEN CHOOSE TO FORGET

I do not know much about gods; but I think that the river
Is a strong brown god—sullen, untamed, and intractable,
Patient to some degree . . . the brown god is almost forgotten
By the dwellers in cities—ever, however, implacable,
Keeping his seasons and rages, destroyer, reminder
Of what men choose to forget.

—T. S. Eliot, "The Dry Salvages"

The severity of rain and fire during 2016 is a sign of significant change in seasonal weather patterns, a constant threat to life and property in the mountains. The Union of Concerned Scientists notes, "This pattern of intense rain and snow storms and periods of drought is becoming the *new normal* in our everyday weather as levels of heat-trapping gases in the atmosphere continue to rise."[14] While hotly debated in the political realm, where the deep pockets of industrial heat-trapping gas emitters fund the climate-change denial community, there is a remarkable 97 percent consensus among climate scientists that climate change is a direct result of human activity.[15]

So what do we do in southern Appalachia, given the high likelihood that we'll be dealing with more frequent and intense floods and fires now and in the future? The Union of Concerned Scientists suggests adapting to the effects of climate change through "efforts such as modifying local infrastructure to withstand floods, adjusting agricultural patterns to account for droughts, as well as establishing emergency planning in our homes," noting that such remedial and preventative measures "would be far less costly to implement when compared to the costs of responding to washed out bridges, deluged homes, or loss of life."[16]

Encouragingly, people in my own backyard are working on such preparations. The National Environmental Modeling and Analysis Center (NEMAC), based at the University of North Carolina at Asheville, examines climate data in order to create tools for coping with climate change. They document stories and models of successful strategies from around the country and post them on an award-winning website (https://toolkit.climate.gov/). For Asheville and Buncombe County (which, you might remember, has the driest weather in North Carolina), NEMAC works with local emergency responders and long-term planners to develop response and mitigation plans in case of fire, flooding, extreme storms, and other climate-related calamities. With pentecostal images and allusions of Noah bearing frequent witness, we'll be forced to adapt as the wind blows, the fires rage, and the rain falls.

Or, perhaps, one could seek insight in poetry, adapting a more aggressive stance to climate change like that of Virgil Campbell, the drunken flood-killer in Fred Chappell's poem "Dead Soldiers." When the rain-choked Pigeon River engulfed his house, Campbell took matters into his own hands:

"You can't goddamnit shoot
A river."
He spat. "I'd like to know why not."
And so he did. Loaded, then started pumping
Slug after slug at the water rising and thumping
His house like a big bass drum."[17]

As floodwaters kept rising, the inebriated Campbell picked off empty liquor bottles that emerged from his flooded basement. When the roaring water started to take down the Fiberville Bridge, Virgil lifted his .22 Marlin, took drunken aim at the wavering metal span, and fired upon it a single shot, grumbling "better put it out of its misery." As the iron bridge collapsed, the cause of its demise was uncertain: were the raging floodwaters to blame, or was it Campbell's well-placed shot that did the trick?

When fires and floods rage in Appalachia these days, it's sometimes hard to determine if they are the result of divine intervention or if they are caused by the shaky hand of a metaphorically inebriated man. As naysayers ignore how humans are affecting the planet's basic elements—air, water, and fire—they are waking the intractable and implacable riverine god in Eliot's poem. While once patient to a degree, this strong deity will roar out of the mountains into the flatlands, Shiva-like, imposing its will upon distant city dwellers, reminding men of what they foolishly chose to forget.

NOTES

1.   David Rouse and Sue Greer-Pitt, "Natural Resources and Environment of Appalachia," *A Handbook to Appalachia,* ed. Grace Toney Edwards, JoAnn Just Asbury, and Ricky L. Cox (Knoxville: University of Tennessee Press, 2006), 51–52.

2.   Jennifer Frick-Ruppert, introduction to *Mountain Nature: A Seasonal History of the Southern Appalachians* (Chapel Hill: University of North Carolina Press, 2010); rainfall records from the State Climate Office of North Carolina, http://www.climate.ncsu.edu.

3.   Rainfall data from National Weather Service Forecast Office, Greenville-Spartanburg, South Carolina, http://w2.weather.gov/climate/index.php?wfo=gsp; "A Precipitation and Flood Climatology with Synoptic Features of Heavy Rainfall across the Southern Appalachian Mountains," http://www.srh.noaa.gov/mrx/?n=heavyrainclimo.

4. Nan K. Chase, *Asheville: A History* (Jefferson, NC: McFarland, 2007), 85–88.

5. Jason Samenow, "West Virginia Flood Was 'One in a Thousand Year Event,' Weather Service Says; More Heavy Rain Forecast," *Washington Post*, June 27, 2016, https://wapo.st/292xzPR?tid=ss.

6. Frances X. Clines, "Flooding in Appalachia Stirs Outrage Over a Mining Method," *New York Times*, August 12, 2002, http://www.nytimes.com/2002/08/12/us/flooding-in-appalachia-stirs-outrage-over-a-mining-method.html.

7. William M. Jurgelski, "Burning Seasons, Burning Bans: Fire in the Southern Appalachian Mountains: 1750–2000," *Appalachian Journal* 35, no. 3 (Spring 2008): 170–217. The article is an excellent overview of the history of fire and fire prevention in southern Appalachia.

8. Jurgelski, "Burning Seasons," 182.

9. Frick-Ruppert, introduction to *Mountain Nature*, 161.

10. Bruce Henderson, "Drought Deepens, Feeds Wildfires in North Carolina Mountains," *Charlotte Observer*, November 10, 2016, http://www.charlotteobserver.com/news/local/article113887983.html.

11. Nsikan Askpan, "How Big Droughts, Forest Fires Could Be the New Normal in Appalachia," *PBS Newshour*, November 22, 2016, http://www.pbs.org/newshour/updates/widespread-forest-fires-claims-may-signal-new-normal-appalachian-mountains/.

12. John Jeter, Jonah Engel Bromwich, and Niraj Chokshi, "Gatlinburg Wildfires Force Evacuations: 'It Was Like Driving into Hell,'" *New York Times*, November 29, 2016, https://www.nytimes.com/2016/11/29/us/gatlinburg-tennessee-wildfire.html?_r=0.

13. Don Jacobs, "Park Didn't Heed Gatlinburg Firestorm 'Call to Action,'" *Knoxville News Sentinel*, December 30, 2016, http://www.knoxnews.com/story/news/local/2016/12/30/park-didnt-heed-gatlinburg-firestorm-call-action/95797456/.

14. "Is Global Warming Linked to Severe Weather?," Union of Concerned Scientists, revised June 17, 2011, http://www.ucsusa.org/global_warming/science_and_impacts/impacts/global-warming-rain-snow-tornadoes.html.

15. John Cook et al., "Consensus on Consensus: A Synthesis of Consensus Estimates on Human-Caused Global Warming," *Environmental Research Letters* 11, no. 4 (April 13, 2016), http://iopscience.iop.org/article/10.1088/1748-9326/11/4/048002.

16. "Is Global Warming Linked to Severe Weather?," Union of Concerned Scientists.

17. Fred Chappell, "Dead Soldiers," in *Midquest* (Baton Rouge: Louisiana State University), 25.

Who Would I Be without the Fear of Early Budbreak

Lisa Ezzard

I feel the sap rising in my vines, awake midnight, a frostless winter
daffodil in bloom, blueberries in swell, and the Sun so full of himself

with the trickery of light and air, that first blast of tenderness,
the hormones, the skin, and the limbs adolescent

warm whispers arouse the vines to bud and to flaunt,
to bulge and to flirt, to sprout shoots into the green goddess

But my midwife is up on the porch, in her rocker drinking nettle tea,
scanning the horizon, the late frost down in her bones

she cannot force back the crowning or take life pushing forth back into
        herself
she cannot draw from her medicine chest to dampen the season's desire

Still. She breathes a long exhale across her sucklings and opens her palms
to the many gnarled bodies in their umbilical universe,

each a Mary in holy labor, gods birthing too soon all over the hillside,
she cannot hold them back

But what would she do without this fear of budbreak,
this passion for every hue?

Voice

Jesse Graves

———

This is where your parents walk,
around the family cemetery,
your mother's people buried
in land your father tends.
You have come to join them,
this late September evening,
first cool winds of the season
blowing heavy clouds between
you and the bright blue above.

Gravestones bear the names
of your personal history,
so many who came and went
before your time began.
In the soft voice of your mind
addressing itself, the interior
sound only you ever hear:
someday I will come here
and never leave.

At Goshen Pass, the *Search*

Jeanne Larsen

---

and Rescue Squad, 3 vans of *State Police,* drained, fill
the riverbank picnic shelter, all wet suits and grim
red vests. Precarious boulders [400
     million years back, a beach]. *It's like
I'm going into rehab*: me to friends, before
this state park camping trip. I laughed. They
veered. I edited: *Or a sweet few days in a sensory
     deprivation tank.* Entirely false. Mostly
I'm sober, and wide open now, like the mountain
biker rolling off a crash-down trail
along Blue Suck Falls who [kite-high] pumps
     his fist and whoops. The hollow across

the lake *gives birth* [Wang Wei] *to clouds.* White-pink
laurel discloses how the sandstone strata lie. Down
here, kids net fidgeting salamanders. Their shape
     -shift young will fidget too. Crying *mid-wood*
[Frost or Dante?] near the dam, an ovenbird [olive
-gray, crowned orange] cripple-circles. Her wound
is a fake. Protective. From a bench *In memory
     of Harry "Sonny" Reid* beneath dense branches
I guess what pocks the water. Small bugs landing,
fish snatching air? [Bashō: *learn about the pines*]
The rain [*from pines*] picks up. Each day a gateway.
     Chorus frogs [*the Hyla breed*] kick in.

Harper

Taylor Brown

———————

Ryan scaled the wall of slick, gray stone first. His bare feet gave him a sort of natural friction against the falls. The remaining five of us stayed seated, roughly two stories below. Where we sat, our damp swimsuits created moist spots on the hot, mountain rock to eventually shrink and evaporate under the June heat. From early morning to sundown, we climbed all over those rocks. We jumped from the highest ones, tanned on the sun-bathed boulders, and cooled off once more in the wading pools before racing to beat sundown and refueling with trail mix and light snacks from our day packs. It was a forty-five-minute uphill hike from the head of the trail and thirty minutes downhill.

Ryan meticulously checked his footing and continued to advance up the slippery face of Harper Falls. We watched and waited for a cue to panic or celebrate. Young boundary pushers like us were airlifted out of Wilson's Creek all the time. Nearly every year the creek flooded and sometimes people drowned. Other times, rockslides blocked roads. If the trail didn't catch you, rattlesnakes and black bears were always close behind. Before the trip, my dad told me, "Be careful. The landscape is constantly changing and adapting like the people that hike up there."

Those risks were deemed "survivable," for the most part, and since our first trip four years ago we continued to admire and adhere to my father's code of conduct. No mishaps yet, and as I approach the second of two landmark graduations, my friends and I have continued the commitment. All of us tried to regroup at Harper in western North Carolina every summer. Scattered across the state, each of us drove back home from our respective universities, community colleges, and jobs in a feverish effort to stay connected and continue our tradition.

Ryan eventually reached the summit, and though we all held our breath, no one was surprised. There was a sort of quiet wisdom that floated about Ryan, the kind of aura only emitted by a plethora of experience. "I just natured so hard," he proclaimed from the top of the falls. He clenched his fists and reacted to what I assumed was a mixture of adrenaline and rope burn. I had seen similar heights from the second story of the local shopping mall, and after watching my friend's expression of strength and persistence, I decided to try my own hand at "naturing." I had to first deal with the pounding current at the bottom of the falls, but I had confidence in my competitive swimming skills. Back then, I still had plenty of time before adult responsibilities and frequent ramen dinners affected that confidence.

The system of large creeks and rapids were like varicose veins cutting through the comparatively dulled, rolling landscape of Pisgah National Forrest. The summit of Harper pursed water almost horizontally from the edge like the end of a garden hose half-blocked by a sturdy thumb, but at a rate of hundreds of gallons per minute. "Men's, fifty meter, freestyle," mumbled the buzzer operator in the back of my head. It wasn't a race won by pace. The only way to cut through the force of the falls was to sprint; my slender teenage figure had to extend from toe to fingertip. "Keep your head down. No drag," echoed the voice of Coach T in my head. Any other time, my head would have been down, but for whatever reason I chose to look straight up as I dove from my rocky perch. The warmth on my face lasted mere seconds before my body hit the water and began to operate solely on muscle memory.

The rush of Harper's natural liquid courage pushed against my bare chest, and the world flowed freshly through my fingertips. But instead of staring at a dark blue strip of ceramic tile centered at the bottom of my lane, I kept my eyes closed. The roar of the falls churned louder and louder as I swam. *One, two three, breathe; one, two, three, breathe.* Eventually I tried to look down for some sort of guidance. I only saw dull green hues. Dark grays and black at the very deepest region. When I kicked, I only felt the breaking water tension as the top of my feet slapped the surface. No rocks. Just ghost-cold water.

I listened past my own heart. It pounded against the back of my ribs; I tuned back to the sound of the falls now above me, a peculiar meditative white static that I gradually welcomed in place of dad's warning. Times before, at smaller falls we frequented, I heard drops of water exploding on the rocks below, like Fourth of July cherry bombs. Here, they all blended together.

I had become porous, ubiquitous even. My mind wandered to the possible interactions between my less adventurous (or more intelligent) friends. *Will he make it? What if the two of them get stuck up there? Pass the trail mix.*

Finally. The rope.

At the base of the Harper, I looked up to see Ryan already on the move toward something more interesting than a friend about to scale a waterfall. I paused and listened for any word of doubt or encouragement from the rocks behind me, all I could hear over the falls were faint mutterings about dinner and how many beers would be "demolished" when we returned to our campsite.

I wrapped the scratchy nylon cord around my pruned hand and took a warrior's stance; flat, pale feet spread wide across the cold gray of weathered stone. That was the only time to date that I felt the Earth pulse.

As I climbed, I was lost to sight in the branches of oaks. The green leaves hovered above me in the canopy, slightly allowing the near daunting sun to shine through. The small gaps in foliage casted lines of light like golden arrows. I focused on one spot of sun in particular, fallen across the last length of cord as I approached its origin.

A tree seemed to grow directly from the face of the rock, and in the branches, an end to the nylon cord, wrapped ten or twelve times around the first thick branch near the base. I'll always remember the neon green contrast against the earthy, fresh green of surrounding leaves. The cord had been wrapped so tightly that the stocky tree began to grow around the nylon. The rope had been absorbed as part of the natural fauna and accepted its role in our afternoon adventures.

I start down Connelly Springs Road after getting off exit 113. A classic commercial from the dealership across the exit screams into my head, "For the best deals on Fords and Hyundais, come on down I-40, exit 113, *Valdese!*" For the past four and a half hours, the sun has shone without the intrusion of meandering clouds. Five minutes down the road, cement replaces asphalt as a bridge stretches over Lake Rhodhiss. My small community of Baton, home, is just over this bridge. I look to the right as I reach the middle of the winding, slender lake. Four cement slabs, almost taller than the bridge, tower in the water like guardians ensuring Baton residents' safe passage to the rest of the world. They are the support slabs of an older bridge from before my time and travels.

Flourishing on top of one slab, swaying slightly in the light summer breeze is a tree.

Growing out of the concrete, the small sapling welcomes me home, and after hours of nothing but highway, my eyes become greedy. Like a siren singing to me from beyond the edge of the bridge, I steal glances while keeping the car centered in my lane. Down the sides of the giant slab are cracks in the rock coursing with the tree's roots. Crawling down and over, the roots finally reach water.

Exhausted and rejuvenated in the same instance, I stood on top of Harper. My arms shone beet-red and my hands bore impressions of the worn nylon rope. Looking down at where I had been, I marveled at how the climb looked a lot more intimidating from the top than it did from below.

After catching a quick breath and some farewell waves to uninterested friends below, I made my way to Ryan. As I closed the distance between us, his body grew from the action-figure form I witnessed just a few minutes earlier from on the face of the falls.

He squatted by Harper's crest in a sort of upright fetal position. Resting on the heels of his feet, chin on knees, he watched the water foam as it poured over the shelf of rock to the pool below. His hairless, round face focused contentedly and yielded the appearance of a child. Longer black hair and brown skin brought to mind Disney's animated vision of Mowgli from *The Jungle Book*. I assumed a similar form beside him and asked, "What now?" Ryan comforted me for a moment with an encouraging smile before revealing what I already figured on my own.

Green Zebra

Stephen Cushman

————————

Live in each season as it passes; breathe the air, drink the drink, taste the fruit, and resign yourself to the influences of each.

—Henry David Thoreau

Help, Theophrastus,
or you, lewd Linnaeus,
with classes for plants and Sexual System

that borders on porn, "nine men in the chamber
of only one bride" sounds pretty wild
and might keep her happy, that passel of stamens
for only one pistil,
            but where is the wild
found anymore, what's the vicinity
that hasn't been tilled by husbandry wholly
to nothing but cult, -ivated, -ivar;
                     take Adoration,
cocktail hybrid, or flat-globe Celebrity
or even Enchantment, all engineered
one way or another,
            while here we were thinking,
when madly monandrous
                  and mounted like wolves

howling full moon beyond the tame pale,
we had evaded human improvement,

                  only to find

in ancient love manuals
            we might as well be
a Cherokee Purple, another Big Rainbow,

or this zingy beauty with flavorful flesh
striped green and yellow.

Evening Storm

John Robinson

———————

July's balmy atmosphere, a darkened horizon
      as tensioned stillness fills the land.
            At first a breeze and distant rumble,

      enticing echoes through quiet, profound, mutely grand;
a silence, a presence before presence
      found first in drifting, thoughtful,
            a dreaming ungrounded,

      before thought repeats its search in mind.
Clouds change swiftly over the hollow,
            like waves, leaves and limbs in undulation,

      a kind of faint, modulated thunder.
The wind-lashed rain becomes quiet rhythms of itself.
            This knowledge over the ground-ward delves,

      and shimmered thought you discover not—
only elusive evocation of allusions caught.

White Trillium

G. C. Waldrep

———

in memoriam Gustaf Sobin

as comet, clone
the wheel's
impenetrable

sine; will's
mercy-
blade. I

& reef—this
commandment

spoken-
to, from depth

if not
of *field*, then
calling

out into
night's
gentle mania,

emblem-crux
devoid

of honey's
strict in-
temperance but

no less
silent cellos
braise

this scarred
& heavy

Ave, this
gelded plight—

Poem Written in a Stairwell, Descending

Scott Honeycutt

———————

And so, after death, we get them back:
dogwood petals that dropped in the spring of '93
or whispers just before the bullet clipped bone.
All those other moments too,
hints of reconciling light that float the years between,
all of them ram back—present now and full of lungs,
bleating hearts like animals unaware of slaughter, unaware of angels.

Just this morning, I walked along Clark's Creek
in some obscure notch of Tennessee. I'm always alone.
Just like you,
alone in the hum of April with those insect hatchlings
that seem surprised to be alive as they horde, two hours old,
above pellucid water.
"Where's the bone," they ask, "to fill our tiny baskets?"
"Where's the blood," they plead, "to carry to our queen?"

All was blooming today,
so much so that even now, in the stairwell of a house
that forts its chin toward dark streets, I can almost
feel the dogwood flowers close in around them,
killing with the silence of hills and returning to
nothing that beauty of lost hours.

Recount

Beaver Pond

Sarah Beth Childers

———

"I love winter for the textures," my dad said. I followed his eyes to neon patches of moss, plush clumps of dead grass, a leaf shining under a puddle. We were walking the trail to the Beaver Pond in Lavalette, West Virginia, two years after my dad's brother Mark died.

An early daffodil stopped us in our tracks, domestic yellow between wild green lichens. Until the 1970s, when the state claimed the land for a park, this trail had been somebody's farm. "Look," my dad said, stooping toward the petals, "some old lady's flowers are still alive."

My dad and I walked the Beaver Pond trail with Mark when I was five years old, more than twenty years before. I know, more than remember, what we looked like. My pastel blouse, Mark's jogging shorts and T-shirt, my dad's worn-out work clothes: scuffed black dress shoes, threadbare oxford shirt, khakis worn at the cuffs. The three of us trudged down the sizzling asphalt to the trailhead, jumped from stone to stone across the stream, dodged caterpillars that dropped from June leaves.

A copperhead lay coiled on the path, and my dad moved it with his walking stick, his tan arms wielding that carved pine with the power of Moses's staff. I complained I was hot, so Mark knotted the corners of his white cotton handkerchief and dropped it on my head. "That'll keep the sun off you." I felt better immediately, tamping down the dirt in my explorer's hat.

Finally, we reached the Beaver Pond, a thirty-by-fifty-foot watering hole a farmer had created by building a dam across the stream. The pond lived up to its name. Beavers slapped the water with their wide, flat tails. Beavers whittled tree branches with their teeth. Beavers lounged in a swimming hole they'd built with their own wall of sticks and mud. They looked like teenagers soaking in a hot tub.

When we reached the pond, I sat down on a rock to watch the beavers while my dad slid a chunk of night crawler onto my fishing hook. Dragonflies—red, violet, bottle green, zebra striped—dive-bombed gnats, their lacy wings humming inches from my skin.

Mark carried his tackle to the far side of the pond, probably taking a breather from five-year-old me. I asked my dad if I could fish beside my uncle, and he told me I could if I was quiet. "Mark doesn't like anybody to scare off his fish."

Pole in hand, I crept along the bank until I stood beside Mark. He kept his eyes on his red and white bobber. "Hi there, Sarah Beth," he said softly, and I beamed. He didn't cast my line for me like my daddy would have, but he didn't tell me to go away. I sat in Mark's shadow and tried to keep still. Maybe I wiggled. A startled beaver scurried up the hill behind the pond, less than fifty feet from our fishing spot. I was spellbound for those seconds by the beaver's full, round body, hidden until now in the murky water. All four paws hurrying, its tennis-racket tail bouncing between the trees.

I held my breath as my dad and I neared the end of the trail, waiting for the pond to burst into view as we rounded a bend and emerged from the tree canopy.

But when we rounded that bend, the pond was missing. The farmer's dirt wall and the beaver dam had washed downstream, leaving the rocks where little girls used to sit and puddles barely large enough for frogspawn. We searched for beaver relicts and found a few dried-out sticks, gnawed to sharp white points.

My dad and I stared across the invisible pond, and I knew we both saw Mark on the opposite bank, whistling softly and casting. Maybe we hadn't buried him twelve miles away, under six feet of West Virginia dirt. Maybe he'd just needed a couple of years to go off and fish by himself. My dad and I walked for Mark, straight across the pond bottom, avoiding the puddles, stepping between clumps of weeds that looked like sheaves of wheat.

The bank was empty when we got there, so my dad looked ahead to the hill, the one the beaver had scrambled up twenty years ago. "Sarah Beth, do you remember that no trapping sign?" I wasn't sure, but said *yes*. "Look at that speck of orange behind that tree. It's gotta be the sign. Let's climb up and read it."

He wanted to see if the sign still said the same thing now that all the beavers were gone.

Our Mother

Jesse Graves

———————

We lived in the clouds those years,
sepia-tinted, blackberry-scented,
between the devil, the devotions,
and such deep blue fractures of sky.
It was good that we could float,
and breathe the ether-air.
Our mother was the mountain
that swaddled us in deciduous arms,
cradled us above her ragged cliffs,
gave us the voices of nesting birds.

Going for Tadpoles in the Spring of My Son's 18th Year

Bill King

———

Each spring we go for tadpoles, and find them,
this time, in a pool beneath a culvert
clogged with coke cans and plastic bags;
in a tire track in the turnout, the stink of dumped
deer and motor oil rising on late April air.
With old haunts shorn of their ghosts, we head for home—
a white box beneath maples buzzing with ten thousand
flowers in a valley between two mountains and the sky—
and pour them into the little blue-eyed pond we dug
by hand. They shoot like tiny black comets into the dark
muck below—and while we wait for the heavenly mirror
to repair itself, a brief wind blows: O Earth, be merciful
to us; wash us; for we have sinned against you
and have been evil since the day we were born.

Spring Box

M. W. Smith

———————

Sycamore-lined river,
stone cabin, a wood stove,
and a spring box where the bass
we caught were kept until supper.

Drinking, tying flies, laughing—
only a vague narrative remains
of fishing trips at dawn,
old johnboats, and misty water.

Joni and Jesus

Ellen J. Perry

———————

Dear Jackson,

I thought of you today when the first yellow leaf fell on my patio. Right there in front of me as I was swinging, watching the neighbor's cows graze, minding my own business: here comes this ratty old dead leaf. Fall always was your favorite season, and I wondered if you miss it way out there in Los Angeles, California. Do you miss the seasons? Do you miss us? I sure miss my little brother. Everybody asks about you, says tell you they're praying for your big break. I don't let on to the church people that I mostly pray to Joni Mitchell, hoping she'll be the one to help you somehow. Problem is, Joni and Jesus both seem sort of reclusive these days.

Well, you know how much I love summer. I long for it all winter, live for it when the first spring dogwoods bloom, and by June I'm finally alive and happy in my skin. Though I was born in November under the heavy sign of the stinging scorpion, light sweet summertime was made for me. It's August now, though, and I can feel the blues start to hover around like a lion (Leo!) stalking its prey, like the empty shadows that shift on my lawn. I breathe in those sad shadows, taste their bitterness, and I want to run away. That yellow leaf taunted me, though, when it fell. It said, *Here I am, lady, like it or not: summer's over.* And I knew it was so.

Even if I never looked at a calendar again, I'd always know when August creeps up. William Faulkner talked about the daylight in Mississippi being different for just a couple days in mid-August. He said there was a "luminous quality to the light," something about it being like the olden times. I can tell you that's true not just in Mississippi. Every year in this little mountain valley town of Gladson, North Carolina, where unlike you I've lived all my life, the light in August makes me feel old. And afraid. This year especially, being a new single mom to a ten-year-old, I'm afraid because I found out the hard way my old tricks don't work anymore. Wonder what Joni Mitchell would say about that!

Here's what happened. Last weekend Mama and Pop-Pop agreed to watch Silas for the weekend so I could meet up with my friend K. D. at one of her art shows, west toward Lake Ryan about half an hour out of town. I helped her with sales, or tried to. It was fun just to be in her company and get a change of scenery despite the August fog and damp air. On Saturday afternoon it rained something terrible but we rushed to cover up the paintings and closed ourselves up in her tent, talking fast and crazy like teenagers at a slumber party. It thundered and lightninged and flooded everything outside, but nothing bothered us. We were two souls sheltered in a womb-like tent with our various torments and victories and shadows weaving around us, moving under the table and around the paintbrushes, stirring up laughter and mischief.

By the time the rain let up, we were starved. Deciding to keep K. D.'s artwork covered for a while, we ventured out, reborn, into the soggy grass and drove to the main road to see what we could find. Lord, we found something, all right: a little dive bar that featured a cast of characters that even Faulkner himself couldn't have made up. We were greeted by someone we thought was probably a regular, a twenty-something man with more charm and tattoos and testosterone than he or anybody knew what to do with. Because his energy couldn't be contained, it overflowed—the charisma, the fun, rolling wild and fast like a toppled bottle turning faster and faster, spilling beer off the long table where the man and his biker friends sat, the overflow making its way to us. I thought, oh yes. This man has rough edges and a great smile. Just the kind of trouble I want to get into for a weekend. I could resuscitate that girl I used to be when I was also twenty-something and carefree, before marriage and child and divorce and disappointment.

K. D.'s a photographer so she got her big camera out, and we sat down at a corner table to take in the view. The man slammed back a PBR and called over to me in what sounded like a Tennessee or Arkansas accent, "Hey, I'm

Tommy. Let's act like we just got married and the honeymoon ain't over yet!" He moved in close and wrapped his tattooed arms around me, gazed into my eyes like people do in happy-couple wedding photos, and K. D. got her camera ready to capture the moment. I said to Tommy, flirty, "I don't believe in marriage." He said, "Me neither, honey. Now let's do this!"

When K. D. sent me the picture a few days later, I realized I was smiling but not returning Tommy's gaze at all. I was looking up, to the side, past him, at what? Maybe I was remembering my own wedding photo, the forced poses and all the brassy red and gold at the autumn wedding Stephen insisted on. Even the cake had yellow leaves on it. Remember that damn cake? Stephen had said NO to a July 4th beach wedding, which was what I wanted. Too crowded and hot and muggy, no way, he said. So we recited our vows in October like robots and I was chilled to the bone, not just because of my strapless dress. I was so cold, and that's about all I remember of my wedding day.

I must have been thinking of all that when Tommy grabbed hold of me in the bar, his long dirty-blond hair curling around my shoulders, and K. D. snapped the photo. It must have been the memory of my wedding because even though the bar was sticky-hot, I felt like ice.

I know you don't like to hear your sister (a nice, upstanding church-goer and middle school language arts teacher) talking like this, so I'll spare you the rest of the details except to say we made it back to Tommy's motel, some awful thing along the interstate with dirty carpet and a tiny pool, and I found out he wasn't a local after all. He was from Memphis and in town that weekend for the bike rally where K. D. was showing her art. I wanted to have a harmless fling, ease the loneliness, escape into my old world for a while. I'd never see Tommy again after that, which I knew would be fine with the both of us.

We were good to go until I caught a glimpse of myself in the bathroom mirror and bolted a little before midnight. I just up and ran out of the motel room like Cinderella-gone-bad, half-clothed; I shouted "Sorry!" and then jumped into my car, threw on a jacket, drove off, and called K. D. I figured Tommy would just shrug, drink another PBR, and head back out to a different bar to try his luck with a different lonely woman. Seemed to be lots of us around, and we were all making a variety of choices. Some stayed till the wee hours in cheap motels; others avoided the biker guys altogether and focused on the art show with their girlfriends; some went home to their families, for better or for worse.

K. D. had stayed late at a reception for the artists but met me at Waffle King after I left Tommy's room.

"What happened?" she asked as the waitress brought our coffee. "I thought you were going to live it up!"

"I don't know," I said, and I meant it. "I don't know what happened. I just couldn't do it. It wasn't like it used to be. I've got Silas now, and I thought about him asleep at his grandparents' house."

"That's the problem," K. D. laughed. "You were thinking too much. Just be in the moment. God knows you've earned the right to cavort around a little after putting up with Stephen for as long as you did. Isn't that right?" K. D. asked the waitress when she came back for our order. "Tell my friend here to have a little fun now that her weirdo ex-husband is out of the picture."

The waitress looked us over, her face lined and weary. Though her nametag read "JOY," she'd probably not known much joy in her life, and I was embarrassed that K. D. brought her into the conversation. This woman likely had real problems, not dumb ones like this Tommy thing. But Joy just smiled. She was one of us.

"Well," Joy sighed, "it's like Joni Mitchell said. We love our lovin', but not like we love our freedom. Lord, the men would kill us if we wasn't so tough! Hey go be free, hon," she said to me, "but figure out what kind of free you want. They's all kinds of ways to do it."

Ever since then, Jackson, I've been thinking about the different kinds of freedom: the kind I might want, the kind you found out in California, and how Joni sang about that too. *Will you take me as I am?* She knows everything, Joni. Even though she said she doesn't know life at all, she gets it. If she were here right now, sitting with me on the patio swing, I'd ask her: Is there only one kind of freedom for me? Do I have to limit myself to just one? But Joni's not here and you stay gone, Jackson, so I have to write these letters, even though you say I'm old-fashioned to do so. I can't ask these questions in a text or an email.

It's late August, almost September, and I'm still blue. But Silas and I rake up the first few dead leaves together, and every day I get a little closer to the sun somehow, every day I feel a little more summer, even as she goes.

Love,
Crystal

P.S. I was just about to put this letter in an envelope when Silas came over and asked, "When can we go see Uncle Jackson?" Maybe he and I could use a little adventure in the big city. Let me know if you'll take us as we are.

———

Crys,

I forgot how much you like to write letters. Nobody much does that anymore, but getting yours last week made me feel so good I decided to leave my phone in the hotel room and drive to this hipster coffee shop in Santa Barbara so I could write you a letter back. We had a gig here late last night but yesterday I went shopping and wound up buying a notebook. It's wide-ruled, as you can see, since that was all they had at Staples.

People are drinking cappuccinos and looking at me funny, like why do I have out a pen and paper. I bet they think I'm a foreign spy taking notes on California coffee house customs or something. Everybody's on their laptops and smartphones, and I look like a fool for handwriting (my hand's already cramping up). But I don't care because my mind is on Silas and fall weather back home in Gladson and how much I miss you two. Yeah, please come out here to see me. I sure could use the company. Joni Mitchell hasn't showed up yet and my buddies keep laughing about how I need to give up on folk and country and Americana, but I'm going to stick with it till there's nothing left to stick, like the boxer who leaves town in defeat but the fighter still remains. You always liked the Emmylou Harris version of that song.

Which reminds me, the guy Tommy you talked about in your letter makes me think of Shane Little from home. I hadn't thought about him in years. It was so funny because he was this big old farm boy with a bulldog tattoo on his arm, tall and tough, on the football team, but everybody called him "Little." You remember when we were in high school and he put up all those handmade signs around town saying "Small Town Throw Down 2-Nite"? You didn't go, but I got in trouble with Mama and Pop-Pop for sneaking out and heading up there to his party that weekend. Little's parents were gone somewhere and everybody followed the wooden signs toward his curvy dirt road. (Don't tell Silas about me sneaking out. I want my nephew to act right and not do like I used to, ha ha.)

Anyway Little had that party and a bunch of us went up there. I brought my guitar but nobody wanted to play at first, they were too busy drinking and trying to get girls to go with them out in the woods. Well, close to midnight Little got to swigging too much moonshine that somebody'd brought up there and even though he was tone-deaf he started belting out Johnny Cash songs and weaving around. All of a sudden he took his pants off and then his underwear before his brother Mickey could get to him. Little was right in the middle of "Ring of Fire" (burn, burn, burn) when Birdie Lawrence said, "Well I guess now we know why everybody calls him Little."

I can't quite figure it but that scene strikes me as funny and sad at the same time. Fact is, though, the best part of the night was to come. Mickey got Little back in the house to sober up and I took out my guitar, and we all gathered around the bonfire and I'll never forget how peaceful that felt, to sing and play way out there on the farm where nobody told us to keep it down. That dirt road just kept winding, up and around, and people kept coming, and I kept playing. Birdie and her friends had girly drinks they were passing around, something like wine coolers. They asked me to play some Vince Gill, so me and Birdie sang the duet "When I Call Your Name," which was a big hit then. We hollered that high-lonesome chorus together, Birdie doing the Patty Loveless part. Birdie always could sing, and we sounded perfect together that night. We had big plans. She was going to come to LA with me and we'd be rich and famous and in all the magazines, she said.

Whatever happened to Birdie, Crystal? Is she still in Gladson? What happened to us all? There's a man next to me in a suit holding a stylus in one hand, like it's the key to heaven, and a latte in the other. He looks real important, but all I can think about is how bad I want to see you and Silas and, by God, Birdie Lawrence who went off to the woods with me later that night at Shane Little's throwdown.

There's times out here on the West Coast when I want to forget the South for good but it keeps coming back up, in my songs. I don't even know it half the time and my bass player, T. J. who's from Mississippi, has to point it out to me. "The past ain't never dead," he says to me when we can talk together like home, "it ain't even past." John, our drummer who was an English major before he dropped out of college and broke his mother's heart, says that's something from William Faulkner. I don't know about Mr. Faulkner like you and John do, but for sure I know that even if I went to Australia or the Maldives or Siberia, I'd still really be in Gladson NC with Birdie and Little and the rest, even though they don't answer when I call their names.

Love y'all—
Jackson

In the Time of the Small Frogs

Carol Grametbauer

————

At the season's dim dawn they set out,
  trekking from their winter hibernacula
    through rainy twilights to the wet-weather

ponds that beckon with their eons-old
  imperative. Even as winter's
    dying breath still rings the water's edge

with patterned ice, and light snow
  lingers on last autumn's fallen leaves
    in shaded places, from everywhere they come

to sing: wood frogs quacking in the reeds
  like miniature ducks; the incessant
    creeeek, creeeek of chorus frogs

echoing off the March-brown hills;
  finally the peepers, with their bell-like piping,
    crystalline voices chirping *liebesliederen*

in the low damp places. Earth's first springs
  must have sounded like this, a multitude
    of small amphibious voices trilling

from the ancient waters across the vast
  lonely land, proclaiming their resurrection,
    strident in their insistence that life begin again.

No Historical Marker, Pocosin Mission (Shenandoah National Park)

Stephen Cushman

———————

Good Lord, Lord,
just what pit have we slipped into?
they could have whimpered, cringing in that cabin,
little more than lean-to, the Towles sisters,
Florence and Marion, Bishop-commissioned
into brute wilderness, ogres howling
blind with moonshine, she-wolves tight
with stunted superstition, bad luck to brush,
after baby's born, hair for nine days,
if baby has thrush, find a seventh child
to blow into its mouth, baby born at midnight
can see and talk to ghosts, good Lord, Lord,
two spinster missionaries must have been tough
to tough out an outpost thrown to the mountains,
nothing left of chapel walls but mossy rocks
and four green stairs to sing ascent
through frosty air, arise, shine, Christmas Day
again today, how could their way, native to Asia,
ever take hold where few people probed
farther from home than one day's ride,
kingdom of snakeroot, bloodroot, trillium,
if not for its weedy, expedient genius?

Night Falls on the Mountain

Libby Falk Jones

————

Now it is that time of evening
when pink wisps shade
unmoving clouds.
The half-moon hangs
like an empty basket.
A whippoorwill calls,
an owl murmurs.
The crow of the afternoon
is silent, but the creek
tumbles on. I can hear it,
faintly, like my mother's
voice. Now it is time
to go within,
lower the shades,
turn up the heat.

Another birthday next week, same sneaking episode

Larry D. Thacker

———————

as last year. A familiar creature's whistled stalk of a tune
creeping around corners, soulful invite, like greening grass
yawns finding the warmth of lath work in the walls.

It rests in the emergence of late March songbirds,
repetitive and bright. Routine. Familiar. But too much time
has passed to tell if these are the same songs as last year.
Or the same language. Or the same birds for that matter.

But it's the same message in the end, isn't it? I think so.
In the end, the same metaphor, same analogy, reliable
and eventually dreadful. Another birthday next week,
same stalking bird as last year. I am no better prepared.

Early Sunday, the last "last" cold front wanders through,
unbothered with spring's growing voice. I can't tell if it's
sprinkling rain again, or the ground is smacking its lips
competing with the dandelions. The dirt seems thirsty.

Mockingbird runs its list of languages, perched high,
practicing over a parking lot left empty by spring break,
though traffic's reminder blends its hum from the highway.
A semi's rattling air brakes vibrate the ground and air.

Crows counter robin and starling. Bird of darkness
and snow and shiver, not giving up easily, over-watching
the arrival of concerted reminders. Crocus, come and gone,
doubling their carpet from last year, almost wholly purple.

Holy Purple. The time is near. The crow lights on a barely
greening tree, its gutturals friendly and curious, bowing
its neck and shivering. We banter, as flurries chorus up
into heavier voices, until we no longer see each other.

He calls out. I call. But the snow falls thick like wetted
powdered sugar, jetting sideways and coating everything,
clovers and onions caught off guard too fast to protest.
The crow calls a last time, gone as the sun breaks free.

Another birthday next week, same reunion with time
as before. An unfamiliar creature's hummed lullaby of a tune
curling about the corners, soulful and inviting, too much
like the yawns of Easter lilies, or the warm willing ground.

Reverie with Chestnut Trees

Scott Honeycutt

————————

For Kevin O'Donnell

Uncle Billy, killed in World War One,
Rowed back from Beyond last spring,
But he didn't ask about his sons or wife,
Or the progress that time did bring.

Instead, as he glared at the greening hills,
He spat and settled a question down:
"Where, my friend," he paused and asked,
"Where have all the chestnuts gone?"

Destroy

At Heaven's Dirty Riverbank

Madison Jones

———

Let the rude, unreasonable
      water cleanse me with its murk and filth.
The celestial rivers are polluted, running green,
foul, beautiful. Plastic bags hang in the roots

of the tree of heaven, streaks of sunlight snag
its branches, choking the young sycamores,
          bringing the quarry into view.
May a long drink leave me ignorant and grateful.

Making Paradise

Ed Davis

————

Maggie got to the church early and sat in back so she could watch everyone file in. It was the usual Bear Branch congregation, plus an older man in a suit and several young people she'd never seen before, probably college students. Then it hit her: they were the Edenwood "board" Olivia had spoken of, here to support their leader. She didn't envy her friend's mission: telling southern Ohioans how to use their land.

Latham's truck had been missing when she passed the house, and, sure enough, as soon as she'd entered, she saw her employer sitting in his usual place, three rows back in the middle. He sat up even straighter than usual. He must've left Lily in the care of his former sister-in-law, hopefully not to guzzle pop and wolf down candy bars.

Maggie waved to Sophie Thomas and her kids, heading up the aisle beside her husband. The woman widened her eyes and mouthed: *What are we doing here?* Maggie smiled and shrugged. What would the woman say if she told her, "I'm here for the trees"? (And the entire Lost Creek watershed.) Maybe someone as big-hearted as Sophie would understand, but then again, maybe her new friend would think her insane for believing that a five-hundred-year-old oak had communicated with her. Only a few months ago, she wouldn't have blamed her.

Someone plopped down on the other end of her pew. Peeking, she glimpsed Wayne Estep. Of course. The man loved scandal and controversy (and trees, or so he said). Oddly, Maggie found herself glad to see him. Despite his penchant for finger pointing, he was at least outspoken in a community where taboos made it hard to hear your own conscience. Warmth crept up her neck. Things didn't bode well if she were aligning herself with Estep and against the man who'd given her a job. It hadn't been easy to sever ties with the suburban lifestyle she'd known and move into her late father's getaway cabin and homeschool Lily, a difficult six-year-old by any measure.

She shivered, recalling her parlor chat with Latham yesterday. Why did he want her *upstairs*, where he and his brother slept? Why not find himself a wife? Latham had made zero effort in that department, although he was an attractive man, wealthy by Marshall County standards. *Upstairs*. It chilled her. Was she overreacting? Latham had been a perfect gentleman—he had loved and cared for her father, buying for him precious time on the ridge during his last days. Latham was the natural, necessary heir to the land on which his ancestors had lived for generations. If he were set in his ways, a little righteous and intolerant of the new, who could blame him? Just turn on your TV and you'd see all that he and his kind were up against, even President Bush and his "thousand points of light." Latham was the last of a dying breed and, according to her father, worthy of admiration and empathy. And though Latham made no bones about wanting a woman to care for his daughter, he didn't seem eager to replace his late wife, Anna Lee, except maybe wanting Maggie inside his house. Well, she would never live there, and that was that.

Now that the portals of suspicion had swung open an inch, she went a step further. Maybe her father had conspired with Latham to—she resisted saying the words, even to herself. Suddenly the packed room seemed overheated, making her squirm. She may as well admit what she'd been denying ever since Latham had stood inside her door, humbly and without wrath, the first day she'd met him. He'd acted completely unconcerned about the beautiful walnuts he'd lost due to her hiring a meth-head contractor who'd clear-cut the whole hillside. Later, Latham had welcomed her into the congregation, entrusted her with his daughter and pretty much given Maggie free rein.

She laced her fingers in her lap to keep them still. If the widower thought getting her into his house was the next step to getting her to the altar, he was crazy. Within a month, she'd be as oppressed as poor, doomed Anna Lee. So far as she'd seen, Latham, though principled and kind, was a typical Appalachian male. Did her father know her so little that he'd actually conspire with a man so completely unlike her? She'd no more be a kept woman than she would allow Lily Clair to be barefoot and pregnant when she came of age.

So worked up had Maggie become that her armpits were damp. By the time a hush descended over the congregation, not only was her rejection of Latham Langdon as a suitor complete, but she also found her decision extending to politics as well: she was not going to let Latham's loggers cut down any more trees than absolutely necessary to make overpriced furniture for tourists to buy.

Glancing left, she found Estep looking at her with a bemused grin, almost as if he'd been reading her mind. When he lifted his hand in a perfunctory wave, she nodded and smiled tightly. Wayne Estep had never sucked up to King Latham and apparently lived his life on the ridge as his own man. She directed her gaze toward the front where Eunice stood, hair in a tight bun, hands clasped at the waist of an iron-gray dress. Her head was tipped slightly back so that she could see better through her bifocals, but it made the matriarch look like she was glaring down her nose at them. When Eunice glanced sharply right, then left, even the babies quit babbling.

"We'll not waste time," she began. "We've come to hear Olivia Rankin of the Edenwood organization tell us about their plans. You've all heard the rumors about Westco pulling out and doing away with the few timbering jobs left. And you've heard about what her and her bunch have been doing over there at the Strange Caves property. But you've not heard it from the horse's mouth. I invited Olivia to come and tell us the truth. Some of you know her already. Her people's from around here, but she went away to college then worked out West. Now she's come home. Come on up here, Olivia."

While Maggie watched, Latham stared straight ahead, seemingly impassive. She'd expected to see his granite glower and crossed arms, as he steeled himself for battle. Then it hit her: he *was* readying himself, was no doubt in parley with his Lord at this very moment.

Eunice sat down in a folding chair behind the silk-draped lectern. The Queen Mum was not about to surrender her pulpit entirely to any tree hugger, whether her people were natives or not. The older woman's eyes seemed locked on Latham. Was she daring him to question her authority to share the congregation with this woman? Olivia rose from the first pew and faced them. Gone was the smile she'd worn in the woods the day Maggie met her. And she looked taller.

"Good evening, neighbors," she began. "I know you sacrificed to come here tonight. Supper had to be rushed, dishes washed quickly, kids cleaned up. You know more than I do about sacrifice. You know what it means to try and support a family on less and less, to try to make a living while jobs dry up. And then you hear about a group like ours that's buying up land." She stood up straighter and raised her chin. "Land that we want to take out of the economy. *Forever.*"

Maggie's legs tensed as if she sat on an airplane awaiting takeoff. Peeking at Estep again, she wasn't surprised to find him frowning. She wondered whether it was conceivable for him or any other ridger to listen with an open mind to such a message, threatening in the extreme (at least in the short term). Maybe because of where she'd so recently been traveling inside her own mind, she was amazed at her willingness to believe that, of everyone in this room, this man probably could.

"I want to be absolutely honest with you," Olivia continued. "You've had enough snake-oil salesmen come through over the years. I'm here to tell you about the plan that lots of Ohioans have bought into—including a few politicians in Columbus—to help this part of the state transition into a new way of life that's good for the future. And despite how mad you might be at Westco Paper, they might be one of the first to do what every business in America needs to do, and that's to quit using so much paper."

She stepped closer to the center aisle, shut her eyes a second and inhaled deeply. When she exhaled, Maggie did too, realizing she'd been holding her breath. "Westco foresees a paperless business office. I don't know about that, but with computers, I guess it could happen. There'll still be plenty of need for wood to build houses. Still, if you reduce the need for paper even five or ten percent, that means fewer trees need harvesting around here."

And fewer jobs, Maggie heard Latham silently shouting. *More reasons for young people to leave.* Estep stared straight ahead, arms crossed, chin lifted, mouth slack, while Olivia smiled a small, tight smile, nothing like her full wattage. "In our heart of hearts, don't all of us want fewer trees cut down? I don't know about you, but I'd much rather look at those old beeches out in front of your church rather than see warehouses full of school tablets. What do you think, kids? Could you make do with fewer tablets?"

There were a few giggles from the younger children.

"Well, Westco is contemplating letting go of Serpent Ridge, and we want to buy it to go along with what we've already bought down at the caves. So let me tell you what we'll get for our money."

She paused, waiting for the kids to go back to playing hangman. Maggie breathed easier. Olivia had hit the controversy head-on, hoping to disarm her neighbors—and so far it seemed to be working. Maggie glanced over to see Estep squeezing the knuckles of his left hand with his right, his face still blank while Olivia began speaking.

"You all live in Marshall County because it's the best place in the whole world, right? You don't want to leave the ground of your ancestors, the land where you played, grew up, met your husband or wife, married and started raising your family. You want to stay right here on your blood ground.

"Well, you're right: this *is* the best place—that's why I came back home—but let me give you some other reasons. Appalachia is the only place in Ohio where there's any remnant of the uninterrupted forest that once covered North America, the great temperate forest mostly cut down by our forebears that brought unlimited growth. Trees were cut, swamps drained, buildings built, and pavement put down. Go to any city, large or small, and there it is: the same old same old. Paradise was paved a long time ago."

She let it soak in. Murmuring and whispering had ceased.

"Okay—I know we've got to make a living—but at what cost? Well, here's the cost, folks: the loss of the greatest biome that the earth has ever known. I love that word *biome*. It includes everything alive that's found on this land. We've got waters here that are home to the most diverse species anywhere. We're the heart of the Big Woods. When the cave land came up for sale, I thought that, with so much land given to other purposes all over America, we might be able to preserve just this small corner."

While a trace of her initial smile lingered at Olivia's mouth corners, mostly it was gone; her face was now dominated by eyes, which, like Eunice's, maintained the grip on her listeners. Maggie felt grateful she wasn't close enough to see Latham's jaw tightening. All too soon the questions would begin, but for just this one moment, Maggie basked in Eden.

Olivia stepped into the aisle between the two sets of pews, interlaced her fingers and closed her eyes for a bit longer this time. When she opened them, she began to speak in a quiet but firm voice that sounded something like a memorized poem but also like one of Reverend Higginbotham's spontaneous prayers in Grandma's church.

"By removing a certain amount of land from the economy, Edenwood wants to bring back the mystery of wilderness to the eastern landscape. To restore large blocks of unbroken forest where the trees are allowed to mature to their fullest potential. To return to the landscape the native old-growth forests. To remove a percentage of our native woodlands from working timber-production forests and return them to working ecosystems. To protect the freshwater rivers that still shelter what remains of the highest aquatic biodiversity to be found in the entire temperate world.

"And, yes, we'd still need jobs, and protecting our greatest resource would provide them—maybe not all at once but eventually. Lots of places have retooled themselves for ecotourism. We'll need rangers and guides, bed and breakfast and hotel operators, nurses, doctors, and teachers, construction workers for the infrastructure that such retooling of the economy requires."

She paused to let her vision soak in. Midway through Olivia's recitation, Maggie had imagined Lily wading in the creek at the bottom of the hill. Then, superimposed on that image was a picture of herself, seven years old, heading down the bank behind her parents' home toward the towering sycamore whose branches had comforted her. She realized with a pang she'd never taken Lily up to see the old oaks with her—surely the child knew and loved them. Maggie must do so, and soon. Olivia's voice, a bit louder now, brought her back to the sanctuary.

"This would be paradise, would it not? This is a home where we could live joyfully and feel hopeful for the future. Those of you who have supported the goals of Edenwood understand that paradise is not something that can simply be found, at least not outside our own souls. If you don't find paradise, then you have to make it."

"That's blasphemy!"

Maggie started at the sound of Latham's voice. When he rose to stand, he looked as huge as one of the walnuts she'd accidentally had cut down.

"God created man in his *own* image and told him to be fruitful, multiply, and replenish the earth—and to subdue it. Ms. Rankin, you would undo the order of the world our Lord created."

"And yet, Latham Langdon," she replied softly, "we have not obeyed the Lord's injunction to replenish. We have befouled our very nest as well as those of other species."

Latham gripped the back of the pew in front of him and leaned forward. "But if we do as you bid, we'll be watching squirrels play in the trees while our children starve."

Maggie now saw full flowering of the emotion he'd suppressed, waiting for the right moment that God would provide. Beside her, Estep scowled, but whether at Latham's interruption or Olivia's vision, she couldn't be sure.

"Or," Latham continued, "while we wait for 'ecotourism' to show up, you would have us leave and go to the city, to live in crowded apartments and work in factories making junk that people don't need, just for money— and wait till holidays to come back and visit. The only way we'll be able to stay on our land is to work on the land. The land don't have a soul, Ms. Rankin; *people* have souls. God provides, *has* provided—and you and your people want to take away good land so tourists can come down here and see pretty scenery."

When he sat down, Maggie exhaled. Olivia spoke quietly.

"Thank you, Mr. Langdon—and thank you all for letting me come here and share with you what we hope to accomplish. Friends, you have now heard both sides and can decide for yourselves." She smiled—sadly, Maggie thought. "Latham has his vision; I have mine. But he's right: they are quite different. If you want to help us make paradise, please help by—"

Maggie's heart lifted. It was almost over. It would not be a war after all, could not be if Olivia would not argue.

Latham leapt to his feet again, turning to gaze angrily around him like Christ among money changers. "*People!* She pretends she's not selling anything, but she is." He pointed. "Olivia Rankin, you're not only as bad as the others who come down here to tell us what we should do for ourselves; you're worse because you say you're one of us! I say, leave the land right where it belongs, *inside* the economy. And I say to you—what I'm sorry but I have to say, the Lord has put it upon my heart—go back where you came from, to Columbus or Colorado or—"

Eunice stood abruptly. "Sit down, Latham."

There was stunned silence for a long moment. My back felt like it was locked in a vise. I'd dreaded this inevitable showdown between Latham and his former mother-in-law; Olivia, I now realized, was the perfect spark to set ablaze the tinder left lying in plain sight following Anna Lee's untimely death. There was much unfinished business between them.

"I will not," he said. "This is as much my church as it is yours."

"Not if you aren't enough of a Christian to honor our guest. 'Treat all as if they are Christ.' This woman has a voice that, win or lose, deserves to be heard. If not, it's ever' bit true when outsiders call us poor, ignorant hillbillies too dumb to see the future when it's staring us right in the face."

Latham swept one arm to his right to include the folks on the opposite side of the aisle, then looked left. "Who is with me?" There was not a sound in the room as he waited. Maggie expected Estep to rise, but he stayed put. "Then I will go."

Maggie watched Latham ease past people to make his way to the aisle and stride toward the door, his limp making him list to one side. Gone were her suspicions, resentment, and fear. She wanted to look fully into the face of the man who'd loved her father and given her this chance at a new life by hiring her. But she knew as soon as she did, her distrust would resurface and she'd be right back to questioning the motives of this complicated, infuriating man she wanted, *needed*, to get along with.

She heard the door at the rear of the church open and slowly close. After a couple of heartbeats, two men followed him. Beside her, Estep continued to stare straight ahead. She bowed her head. *God help me* was as much of a prayer as she could muster before she stood up on newborn calf legs.

"My name is Maggie Absher, and I'm new here. I moved to Marshall County from Dayton four months ago. I live on a little piece of land over on Bachelor Ridge that's been in my family for a few generations. As an outsider, I've watched and listened. There are many good people here. And I've also met some really fine trees."

And as she described the ancient oak in the woods above Dad's cabin, she saw knowing nods, as folks saw in their mind's eyes *their* old-growth trees tucked away in their own woods. Glancing his way, she saw Estep sitting tight-lipped, arms crossed. ("Do you hate every living thing?" he'd hissed into the receiver the day he called to report the devastation wrought by the druggie she'd hired.) Did he think her a hypocrite, liar, or worse? But then she saw Sophie, several rows up, glancing back at her, nodding and smiling. Maggie forced her mind away from her harshest critic.

"I've found this . . . *connection* exists," she continued. "It's like these trees talk to each other." She took a breath. "And to us."

She couldn't believe she'd said it. People hushed and sat up straighter. Did they think she was crazy? She was seeing Lily high in the branches of the ancient oak. The image would either sustain her or it wouldn't.

"I mean, it's not the way you and I talk, but I think trees around here know what's going on, and they know it's not good, that a lot of what humans think *they* need—more cutting, more lumber, more money—isn't what's best for *them.*"

"Bull*shit*," said a man in a loud, harsh baritone. "Did you come down here to tell us that we should listen to crazy outsiders like you go on about talking trees, while our children ain't got enough to eat? It's trees or people, simple as that."

Her heckler was a guy wearing a John Deere cap in the second row. *Outsiders like you.*

"No, sir." Maggie was surprised to find herself still standing. "It's not simple. And that's not why I came down here. I came to teach one child.

I want Lily to have the best of what education, good food and health can give her—but I also very much want her to let the land, including trees, teach her how to live . . . down here." Thank God she hadn't said *anywhere she might choose to go.*

As chatter erupted, a loud voice erupted nearby. "Shut up and listen!"

It was Estep, Maggie realized. Now Sophie was on her feet. "Go on, Maggie," the woman said loudly, eyes narrowed as she scanned the congregation, no longer smiling. "We want to hear what you have to say." After a few moments, satisfied there'd be no more interruptions, the woman sat back down. Maggie found her hands no longer trembled.

"Well, like you said, Ms. Rankin, we can begin shifting from something unsustainable to sustainable. If we maintain the land the way our ancestors did, there are a lot of people who will want to come see it and buy products and services. Some might even want to stay here. For good . . . like me."

She was stunned to hear herself admit it until, closing her eyes, she was revisiting her first night on the ridge, when she'd answered the mysterious call and stood in the clearing high above the cabin. *Stay*, the old oak had seemed to say. Should she tell these folks that? Before she could decide, the man in the John Deere cap rose, squeezed to the end of the aisle and huffed out, cursing loudly. A couple of other men followed. In another minute or two, the meeting was over and Olivia was hugging Maggie to her ample bosom.

"I know now," she said, standing back, holding both of her forearms, "that trees can talk."

Maggie opened her mouth to speak, but before she could, Olivia touched her lips with her finger.

"They talked through you."

NOTE

Excerpt from the unpublished novel tentatively titled *Old Growth*.

Just before Dawn

Kathryn Stripling Byer

———————

When the mountainside came tumbling down
on her, where could she run? Darkness
outside and so much rain, had she prayed too hard
for it, her garden turned graveyard, tomato vines
curling into themselves like old women,
beans letting go of their river cane stakes?

She hears the torrent of oncoming mud
from the neighbors so far uphill
she's never laid eyes on them,
dug into slopes where nobody but hunters
once camped, tracking bear
or before her time wolves
she remembers her grandmother
claimed she could hear singing.

She'd seen the logging trucks clearing
the slope of its timber,
the ugly machines come to make way
for dwellings with such pretty names
they sounded like wildflowers
strewn on the hillside around her.

Rank strangers, she called their inhabitants,
singing along with the Stanley Brothers
at night when the radio still worked
and she could still hear every string
on the banjo and mandolin quivering.

Now she hears only the voice of this mountain
folding her inside its blanket of mud.
No Stanley Brothers to sing her to sleep
with their harmonies, promising
The Darkest Hour Is Just before Dawn.

American Bittersweet

Julia Spicher Kasdorf

———————

In the bramble between Possum Hollow and Beaver Road,
between my thirty-years-ago school bus route and PA 136:
a torn mattress heaved into the ravine, diapers, soup cans.

At the sight of burnt-orange berries in the tree limbs,
I pull over, pull a knife from the glove box, walk
the gravel access road past *No Trespassing, Columbia Gas,*

brine tanks, petroleum pipes, *Dominion Transmission,*
to pull vines from branches while compression sheds hum
upwind from the trailer park where poor white kids

boarded the bus. Come fall, Mom stopped the car anywhere
to tear bittersweet from trees and fence rows. She arranged it
on the mantle; later swathed the candles and crèche in crows foot.

Whatever beauty we found in the woods or roadside, we took
like the shotgun shells we shoved onto our fingertips,
red and green plastic shafts with clackety brass caps.

When a white pick-up drives by, I walk to my car, casual.
Somewhere, someone spotted me on a monitor. I pull
away before the truck turns around. He follows me out

onto Edna Road, where rows of company homes
line short streets beneath a boney dump from Edna No. 1
and Edna No. 2. Here the bus picked up black boys

who excelled at wrestling. We never called Edna a patch.
We didn't know that term, or that sharecroppers
driven north by the boll weevil took jobs in the mines

to break up strikes. Growing up, taking whatever we could
from that place, we didn't recognize history or anything
out of the ordinary.

Devil's Rope

Michael McFee

———————

Four barbed wire strands
a hand's-breadth apart
lassoed this sturdy trunk
at the corner of a pasture

who knows how long ago,
cinching it as the bark began
swallowing the prickly fence
until the host tree died,

black as if it had burned,
reduced to a shadow-ruin
guarded by paired horns
stapling the air around them,

waiting for a careless mammal
to stray against their lifted tips
then backpedal away, gored,
bellowing and bleeding.

Water Tank

Meredith Sue Willis

———————

In 1963, before mountaintop removal, but in the full flood of its ugly little brother strip mining—when automation of the underground mines was accelerating and taking away more and more of the miners' jobs, we lived on the highest paved street in Ransomville, West Virginia. There were houses on either side of us, but directly behind us was the steep field of an abandoned farm, and higher than that, the town water tank. When we were little, my friends and I, and my younger sister Janie, played up there. We picked bittersweet to dry and sell to our mothers, we released milkweed fairies, and we took hikes out of sight of the houses. We made up adventures about living off the land in the mountains. We pretended we were wild and free like the hills.

But we weren't, as I thought that evening when Janie and I went up again. We had just been little town girls who hadn't hit puberty yet. This seemed meaningful to me at that moment, like it might make a good college application essay. There is no wilderness anymore, I thought. You can never really escape people and expectations and judging eyes.

I don't remember exactly when I stopped going up on the hill. Certainly by the first year of high school. I think my sister went up by herself for a while, but she had stopped too. She was in eighth grade and as tall as I was, with broad shoulders and full-size breasts that she tried to hide by pulling her shoulders in around them. She also insisted on cutting her own hair, badly. Her unhappiness bothered me, as if it were catching.

I had enough of my own to worry about. I would be applying to college soon, and I was determined to get a scholarship and go out of state. I dressed as if I liked being a girl, but I had never made cheerleader and this year, for the first time, I had some real competition for the lead in the play. I had also broken up with my boyfriend for vague reasons that had to do with planning to become an actress in New York City, but I was feeling lonely and stupid for doing it. Also, there was a test the next day in Algebra II.

So after we did the dishes, when Janie said, "Let's go up on the hill, Leigh," I said okay.

We went out the back door into the dry winter cold and climbed through the barbwire and started up. I leaned forward to stretch the back of my calves. The high sky and cold air were a major improvement over the stuffy, too-warm house and classrooms and the close competition and striving of school.

Janie said from behind me, "This is the first time you went hiking with me since you started high school."

I said, "Well, I'm here now, so don't complain."

We went up the steepest part with dead weeds, flattened by the snow that had disappeared in the January thaw.

Janie passed me, and said, "We can climb the tank."

"It's too cold," I said, but kept walking toward it.

Our town had two water tanks on opposite sides of the river. Ours was the East Tank, and it was shimmering in the sinking sun, except for the huge dark spaces that spelled out RANSOMVILLE WV. The tank was always closer than I expected, looming large and swollen.

Janie got to it first and shook the ladder till it clanged and some rust floated down.

I said, "It's a wonder kids don't get killed all the time fooling around up here."

"Let's go up."

"You do it," I said.

"Both of us," said Janie.

I looked up, deep into the blue, but the color was fading toward the horizon. I had a giddy instant of gravity reversed and falling up. "The ladder's rusty and it's freezing cold and windy. No thanks. And besides, Janie, you always chicken out halfway."

"I won't this time."

"Good, I'll watch."

"I can't do it unless both of us climb."

I felt a little curl of excitement. It really was dangerous, and we'd neither one worn gloves. Janie stepped back, wanting me to go first. I made fists around the rails of the ladder. They cooled my hands quickly, and I could feel scales of rust. I climbed two rungs. I glanced back and the hill fell away so steeply that it was like hanging out of an airplane. I climbed two more rungs and looked out again. I wondered if people who lived in other places felt inspired by the landscape. What would it be like to live in a flat place? What would it be like to live in a city where you could die on the street and people would just step over you? Why had I stopped coming up here anyway? It was a good place to get a perspective on life.

I had to move very deliberately because my hands were stiff and clumsy. It had been a long time since I had climbed so high; climbing the tank was a thing you did when you were twelve, not sixteen. I stopped halfway up, saw the top of Janie's head just below me, staring into the side of the tank, never looking back or down.

I leaned my head back, thinking it would be so much better to fall up into the blue than be sucked under the garbage of teachers and grades and who was going to vote for you and would you get the part and was it better to have a boyfriend than not?

"Don't do that," whispered Janie.

I shook the ladder until it wavered and clanged along its whole length. I waited for Janie to whimper, but she didn't. She pressed her forehead against her rung. She's going to make it to the top this time, I thought.

That felt like pressure too.

The one thing I had never done was step off the ladder onto the roof of the tank. The roof was rounded, but there was a narrow rim along the edge where you could hook your heels if you kept your weight back. A couple of my athletic friends used to do it.

Making no promises to myself, I moved over so that my back was to the dome, keeping my right hand firmly around the ladder rail. I leaned back, and there was nothing but air, steep hillside, and roofs in front of me.

My breath speeded up and I started sweating. I arched with the dome of the tank, and it wasn't hard to stay balanced. I didn't let go of the rail, though, and slowly looked up again, out to the purpling hills with their bumpy tree-topped silhouettes.

"Look at the view, Janie," I said.

She had come all the way, but now she clutched the ladder and squeezed her eyes closed. She shook her head.

"You really should look. It's so beautiful you may never see anything as beautiful. I mean, wherever you go, you could go to the Grand Canyon, anywhere, no place in the world could be so beautiful."

I heard the childish enthusiasm in my voice, for my landscape, for home, but for that moment I didn't care. It was hills upon hills, each rank laid close against the next, a few fields nearby, but the farther out you looked, the more it was only trees, magenta tipped, amber patches of leftover leaves. There were other towns out there, and mine tipples and slag heaps and all the piles of human waste, but for this moment I couldn't see them.

Overhead still this uncanny azure, although at the edges, the purple was turning gray.

I finally looked down at the town. Sorry it was there, spoiling the landscape. Sorry I had become embedded in it. Cutting through the middle was the green and orange West Fork River, which ran north to merge into the Monongahela, which merged into the Ohio and then the Mississippi and then started south again to the ocean. I wanted to explain to Janie about the bigness of things, and how everything connected and that meant there were opportunities out there, other places. But my thoughts seemed overblown, grandiose, and embarrassing.

I said, "You ought to look Janie. You came all the way, so you ought to at least look."

Janie kept her forehead pressed against the top rung. "Tell me."

"The hills look like they'd feel stubbly if you touched them with your fingers. And more hills behind them. The only thing that isn't beautiful is town. I'm looking at all those houses on stilts down by the river on the

West Side, and there's washing hanging out and junky old refrigerators on the back porches."

"Tell me about the hills," said Janie. "Not the houses."

I felt a sliver of cruelty. If she wasn't going to look for herself, she'd see what I wanted to describe. "I'd like to just run my thumbnail along the bank and scrape those houses into the river. The cars too. Just chuck everything that isn't beautiful into the river." Chuck the high school and teachers and all the kids there too, I thought. Chuck the play and all the ways you could be humiliated and rejected by the other kids even if you succeeded, and chuck boyfriends who wanted you to touch this and do that and it was okay because you were so soft and they loved you, who cares if you loved them.

My sweat heat was gone, and my hand that held onto the ladder was a dead lump on the end of my arm. I had to look at it to know it was still there. A gray film was dulling the sky; the sun was down.

I said, "If I did it, if I scraped all the houses away, it wouldn't hurt the river. The river is a mess, it's nothing but sulfur from the mines and whatever comes out of people's toilets."

"I thought you said it was all beautiful."

"I didn't say town was beautiful. It used to be beautiful everywhere, back when it was farms and Indians. Even when Daddy was a boy, you know, they used to fish and swim in the river. But it's poison now. Daddy said he stopped swimming in it when a big turd floated by one day."

"Why?" said Janie. "Why are they allowed to dump in the river?"

"And strip the sides of the hills," I said. "It's because people are disgusting. The hills would be better off without the people."

Janie said, "Do you remember your story about the monster in the tank?"

I remembered. "The water giant. This one, the one in our tank was friendly."

"Sometimes."

"But the one on the other side was always evil." It had been one of my best stories. The other monster came swinging across the valley to attack us, and we called out our monster, and it saved us, and then went back to its home inside the tank.

I rapped hard on the dome, and an enormous distant boom spread through it. "There it is," I said. The creature roused, dripping and thrashing. Konng, konng.

"Leigh," whispered Janie, "what if there was a crack in the tank?"

I laughed. "That's a great idea. There'd be a flash flood. The water giant would rise up and burst out, and see all the ugliness, and wash away the sulfur and sewage. It would knock the houses out from under their roofs, uproot the trees and telephone poles." I imagined people clinging to floating sofas. "In one fell swoop," I said, "Ransomville washed away! One out of every three persons missing! And the river clean enough to swim in once again."

"There wouldn't be anybody left to swim."

I tried to keep myself laughing, but the laughs turned into shivers and I remembered that sometimes there really were flash floods that killed people and dogs and babies. I don't mean it, I said to the monster. I don't mean you should explode and drown us all.

"There isn't enough water anyhow," I said to Janie. "I was just fantasizing. It might wash away one house."

"Our house."

"Yes, maybe just our house, but it wouldn't drown the town."

"Imagine something good," said Janie.

I wanted to do what she asked, but I couldn't imagine how you could fix the river or stop them from stripping the hills. I said, "Start down, Janie. I'm too cold."

Janie started down the ladder, one rung at a time. I gave all my attention to making sure my clump-hand still held on while I worked my way back onto the ladder.

When we got to the bottom, I felt exhilarated by our accomplishment. "We did it," I said to Janie. "You climbed it, and I went out on the roof for the first time."

Janie said, "But what about imagining something good?"

"I can't. People are just too evil."

Janie said, "I'm going to. Imagine a way to clean the river. With filters or something. I want it all back like it was."

"It can't be." I was feeling angry that Janie was so brave and optimistic. "It's just a mess. Everything."

"No," said Janie, who could be very stubborn. "If you can imagine it, then you can do it."

I was going to say, Don't be silly, or that's childish, but I remembered that I had imagined the water giant, and the water giant saved us.

Kudzu

Jeremy Michael Reed

———————

climbs
the hill toward the house,
undeterred.

Terre,
dirt, mud, exist under
green arms

reaching
skyward, stuck to earth,
weighted,

married
to the host. It kills
what remains:

trees,
grass, brush, suffocates,
supplants new skin.

The plant

covers hillsides like memory,
coils, kinks in.

Kudzu

covers everything,
leaves the shape.

Sitting, Scurrying Forward, at Astounding

Jeanne Larsen

---

speed toward Ingles Mountain in the east: a square
koi pond, shadow-scored, of window light slips
off from me on Charles and Ellen's reed-mat
-colored wall-to-wall. Sun climbs sky. The planet,
like a bowl-eyed goldfish, spins. This second-growth
suburb rec room Zendo too. Toward

spring, and I can't
wait. Later, neighbor Wayne [my age, stage
IV], who might go to Duke for marrow, says he hopes
next week [despite the migrants in his body's streams]
he'll feel up to dancing. Then tells

about the wreckage:
that old house behind his mama's, pine boards under
tarpaper, and rotting? *Yeah, we brought a big old front
-end loader in. Took the bucket up and dropped er down.
Smashed that dump to nothing.* Grins.

After, it scraped the red

dirt level *with them metal teeth. Mama didn't
mind much.* [He picked for her a last few early
daffodils from the usta-be-a dooryard first.] *Yeah, squashed
er flat. 3–4 hits was all it took.* How he laughs and
laughs and says, a moment

past [miles closer to the hungry swimming all
-bemusing equinox, the global tipping point, the great
submerge], *Yeah, I surely love to cut a rug.*

Mountaintops, Appalachia

Susan Deer Cloud

———

Took her decades to realize why she hated
driving on Pennsylvania's Route 81
past Honesdale, Scranton, Wilkes Barre
and other towns whose inhabitants
looked as if they ate dirt and their eyes
were made of dark mica.

"The coal, the coal," it shocked
her brain like an eclipse one day
when she couldn't escape taking 81
on her way south, which meant she
couldn't avoid the trucks, constant
construction, and strangely shaped
hills left along the highway after
the coal mines closed.

All that digging up of Mother Earth,
that long rape of the land, the endless lie
of mountains really an ancient plateau
worn down to what can pass for beauty.
A slash of loneliness between
the bereft earth and ghosts who spent
decades digging for coal, buried
when alive, buried again when dead.

And then there was West Virginia
southern sister to her Catskills,
both filled with people a crazy quilt
of nationalities with Indian mixed in,
born to be free-spirited. But hunger
can drive even the most defiant to be
low, to go underground and shovel coal,
just takes children crying, cold in rags.

Then the mines there started to close
and the CEOs in shiny shoes
and polished offices in faraway cities
chose to blow the mountaintops off,
more coal higher up once the machines
took over and rich men were happy to blast
apart all that Appalachian beauty.

She had seen her share of mountains
dynamited so roads could go through.
How would she feel if men came north
and stole away the mountaintops,
what would it do to the trout streams
and the people who were singers
and storytellers and spoke in soft voices?
She had known the tattered dreamers
who left for the cities and never returned.

She signed the petitions protesting
the removal of mountaintops, called
representatives and senators, all
the usual that seemed to end up
where wool socks and mittens go.
For a while it even looked hopeful
until the 45th President barged in,
his view towards Mother Earth
the same as his view towards women.

Poor poet that she was, she understood
desperation and depression. Nothing
against those people down there
in that sister place like the Catskills
only farther south. She knew how
it took the top of her heart off
when men, women, and children
shuffled by with heads hung low,
looking like their eyes were dark mica
and they'd been forced to eat shit.

Stockholm State: A History

Heather Ransom

———

Stockholm Syndrome, captor-bonding, terror-bonding, the ultimate survival mechanism.

Whatever you want to call it, psychologists have been studying it for years. Though many questions surrounding the phenomenon remain, it gained fame back in the early 1970s when a bank robbery in Stockholm, Sweden, turned into a five-day media-frenzied hostage situation, after which one of the victims accepted a marriage proposal from one of the perpetrators. It sounds bizarre . . . until it doesn't.

Prisoners of war and victims of incest, kidnapping, child abuse, and domestic violence are all known to sometimes develop strong emotional ties to their abusers. So strong that they defend their captors against law enforcement, family members, and anyone who tries to intervene. This behavior is completely irrational to those on the outside looking in. How can people hold such violent, evil abusers in such high esteem?

In some ways, symptoms resemble those of post-traumatic stress disorder: nightmares, increased distrust of others, confusion, inability to enjoy life. I've been fortunate enough to acquire my own insomnia and nightmares the good ol' fashioned way—I was born with them. Still, I can't help but feel that I'm stuck on the wrong side of an ever-evolving picture of what Stockholm Syndrome might look like on a large scale. What if an entire colony of people were held captive for years on end? What if the symptoms of Stockholm Syndrome, once held inside individual psyches, seeped out and consumed entire communities, if one person's nightmares and distrust morphed into an entire region's culture of fear?

What if that robbery in Sweden didn't look like a robbery at all? What if it had taken place in the middle of an often-forgotten state in Nowhere, Appalachia, and occurred, not over five or six days, but across decades, in the shape of something else altogether?

The Appalachian Mountains are thought to be the oldest mountains on the planet, born some 480 million years ago—millennia before anything that resembled a human ever evolved.[1] Their steep slopes were carved out by encroaching glaciers, vicious rivers, various explosions of rock, and upheavals of tectonic plates in the Earth's subterranean crust. The land fought against itself for centuries on end, crushing and squeezing its own edges until one side of a fault would collapse and allow its nemesis to rise high above it—a serious power struggle. For something that happened so slowly, that would have been invisible to our eyes had they existed back then, it all seems quite violent.

These mountains of antiquity course through many territories throughout North America, but West Virginia is the only state in the country that falls entirely within the Appalachian region, from border to crooked border. The aptly named Mountain State was born, like the earth she rests on, of conflict, established through presidential proclamation during the heart of the Civil War in 1863. By then, locals had already been chipping away for several decades at the coal formed inside the great mountains some three hundred million years prior.

Around the time West Virginia achieved statehood, her miners, farmers, and other struggling survivalists caught their first glimpse of large-scale coal operations. The traditional family-owned mines that sprinkled the region, that used horse-drawn scrapers and left minimal scars on the mountainside, quickly succumbed to industry, and the coal baron was born.

There are four conditions that must be present in order for Stockholm Syndrome to occur.

Condition Number 1: There must exist a real or perceived threat to one's physical or psychological survival.

Early settlers of West Virginia must have been drawn to the adventure and romanticism of endless peaks and valleys blanketed with maples, American chestnuts (long since wiped out), and virgin soil. At least, I imagine that's what lured my own ancestors from the Black Forest of Germany and rolling hills of Holland. Like their fellow European immigrants who chose not to remain on Staten Island or wherever else they may have landed in the mid-1800s, they welcomed the freedom and independence promised by unchartered land, even in the face of daily threats to their very existence. Disease, accidents, exhaustion, the occasional copperhead. I don't know if they were fully aware of the demands of the mountains, the severity of the obstacles they would face, but these first West Virginians were definitely met with leathery skin, broken spirits, and shorter life spans.

A few generations later, in the early 1900s when my great-grandparents were growing up in the state's southern counties, most of these threats had shapeshifted, but they were no less severe. America was industrializing. Mountain culture was being swept away, overtaken by outside interests whose investments in West Virginia's extraction industries had quadrupled in the fifty years since the state's establishment. Families, oblivious to the real worth of their mineral rights and powerless against the wealthy politicians and businessmen who wanted their land, were essentially robbed of the earth that once sustained them, driven underground into the mines.

About 80 percent of miners and their families lived in company-owned houses at that time.[2] *Company-owned* is an ominous, faceless term, but it can almost always be traced back to a man with a green palm, big ego, and ties to these hills as thin and meaningless as the coal seams left running through them today. The livelihood of most West Virginians was entirely controlled and manipulated by these companies, their coal barons, more than 70 percent of whom lived outside the area they so completely dominated.[3]

Workers were paid in scrip, money created by the company and usable only at company-owned stores and businesses. Miners used the company's equipment, which had to be leased. And the workers' coal tonnage, which determined their pay, was doctored by company men to reflect lower production numbers. When the people of Matewan and other parts of the coalfields tried to buck this system, they were met with violence unparalleled by any other bloody story in modern Americans' history. It was the largest labor uprising the nation had ever seen and ended only after a proclamation by President Harding sent the US Army to intervene. There are no reliable records about how many lives were lost in West Virginia's Mine Wars, but some estimates reach three hundred.

Soon after the Mine Wars concluded, Prohibition began, chased by the Great Depression. West Virginia's already-impoverished population fell further down the metaphorical food chain. I don't know how other families survived, but my great-grandfather made booze in the only bathtub that he and my great-grandmother and their ten children shared inside a tiny home in Nitro, West Virginia. He then sold his bathtub elixir (illegally, of course) to neighbors who were just as hungry as he was for food and amnesia, while the oldest son, great uncle Freddie, learned (by the ripe old age of five) to pick the pockets of passersby as they sulked their way down Main Street.

Thirty years later, great uncle Freddie was tramping across the country on the C&O Railroad, and Appalachia was so destitute and hopeless that even President Lyndon Johnson took notice, reaffirming his commitment to the War on Poverty during a 1964 visit to the southern coalfields. Despite the efforts of Johnson and decades of presidential successors, West Virginia continues to show up close to the top on every bad list and last on every good list. The state has some of the highest rates of smokers, teen pregnancies, obesity, drug overdoses, heart attacks, cancer, you name it. The economic climate is pathetic, we were recently named the most "Unhappy State" in the nation by Gallup-Healthways, and life spans are still shorter here than elsewhere in the country.

Through all of West Virginia's history, including the present day, when has there not been a very real, very unique threat to the physical or psychological survival of her people?

Condition Number 2: The victim is isolated from perspectives other than those of the abuser.

In 1973 Loyal Jones published an essay called "Appalachian Values" that famously, and quite accurately, traced why and how Appalachian culture came to be what it is. In it, he identifies "individualism, self-reliance and pride" as some of the most notable traits of mountain people and suggests that while these attributes were beneficial for those earliest settlers, they are also partially responsible for keeping Appalachians isolated from progressive ideologies as they evolved throughout the rest of the country.

These self-reliant traits can still be detected in my family. My Papaw, stubborn and independent like his older brother Freddie, is one of the most intelligent, knowledgeable men I've ever known. He was an expert chemist and model builder who worked for NASA at one point, despite having dropped out of school in the eighth grade. He taught himself everything he needed to know just as, I imagine, his father did when learning to make home brew and moonshine years prior. On the other hand, Papaw clings to antiquated ideas (to be put mildly) and intolerant ways of thinking about race, equality, and other social issues, so I see what Jones meant about the dual nature of these traits and their ability to isolate.

There are other forces, too, working to keep the people of the Mountain State in literal and philosophical isolation. The most obvious obstacle is the land itself. The rugged terrain makes building and maintaining highways and other vital infrastructure more costly and complex than in many other states. It's not uncommon for a fifty-mile trip, as the crow flies, to be a three-hour drive in West Virginia. And some counties still don't have a single mile of four-lane highway.[4]

Today our disadvantage is in the form of communication: high-speed internet rather than roadways. Broadband was not wired to my parents' house until 2015, and some families in the state are still waiting. At my house, albeit a bit of an anomaly, there are three TV channels when the wind isn't blowing. Cable, satellite, and unlimited internet are luxuries reserved for folks who live closer to town. I'm thankful to have cell phone service.

Poverty, of course, is another factor. Nationally, only 9 percent of poor students complete a four-year degree; more than 75 percent of wealthy people do.[5] West Virginians have fewer bachelor's degrees than people of any other state. I was the first in my family to get one. And yet poverty isolates in ways beyond educational attainment. It makes it hard to do things like visit New York, San Francisco, and other places of "culture." These things just aren't important when you're struggling to pay the electric bill. You know, the one that's kept so cheap because of our coal production.

Always, it comes back to coal. Its barons have done their part to ensure Appalachians are isolated. In fact, when large-scale coal operations began in the nineteenth century, they intentionally segregated their immigrant workers from one another to keep them from rallying together. As long as there were language barriers between workers and the Italians looked down on the Irish who looked down on the African Americans, none would shift their angry gaze to the company itself. None would, or could, share their experience or knowledge or discontent with another group. Divide and conquer, as the saying goes.

West Virginians are still feeling the effects of intellectual isolation, a great deal of which continues to rest on the shoulders of the energy industry and their cozy relationship with state lawmakers. In one recent election year, coal, oil, and natural gas companies contributed around eight hundred thousand dollars to political campaigns in the Mountain State.[6] In turn, representatives who'd been elected with that money attempted to pass legislation that would have repealed federal education standards for public school children—including one such standard that teaches the science of climate change. Some representatives and state school board members maintain that students should debate whether global warming is actually caused by humans, since "supporting evidence remains inconclusive." Yes, a school board official said that. And these are the people who set the curriculum.

Somehow in this interconnected world we live in, West Virginia's collective perspective remains isolated, twisted, and controlled by its captor.

Condition Number 3: The victim maintains a belief that the abuser provided him or her some small kindness, proving that said abuser is not entirely evil (even though the perceived "kindness" actually benefits the abuser in some way).

Around 1950, West Virginia's coal industry hit its peak. There were still five hundred company towns in the state and about 125,000 miners.[7] That's roughly 10 percent of the workforce. This was just a decade before Johnson's War on Poverty declaration, so anyone who could provide jobs—lots of jobs—was a saint. Period. Rational thinking tells us that coal companies were not in the business of altruistically giving jobs to poor Appalachians; they were in the business of making money, and they needed someone to do the heavy lifting. Still, jobs are jobs and people were thankful to have them. Most people, at least.

Papaw and his brothers refused to spend their days and nights underground and, like everyone else, they wanted better lives for their children. They followed other opportunities and wound up in Michigan sometime in the late '50s. This was during the great exodus from West Virginia when coal jobs started disappearing and thousands of families left right along with them. Papaw eventually brought his family back, unable to forget his love of the mountains, but uncle Freddie never really returned from life as a vagabond.

Since that time, the number of people employed by the coal industry has continued to drop drastically for a number of reasons. For one thing, there simply isn't as much coal as there once was; it's running out. There have also been developments in cheaper, more sustainable forms of energy across the country. But a big reason for the decline—that goes unmentioned in a mainstream West Virginia that insists the problem is "Obama's War on Coal"—is because the industry has embraced practices that require fewer laborers. Practices like strip mining and mountaintop removal (MTR), unidentifiable cousins to the ways of my ancestors who would have worked the mines with mules and pickaxes.

Thanks to these "advanced" industry methods, a mountain that has stood strong and proud for billions of years, since long before man arrived, can be frivolously wiped away in minutes. Companies and legislators keep promising that these MTR sites will be "reclaimed." They will be used to house strip malls, airports, and other structures that will result in jobs founded in something other than coal, supposedly. This is clearly an act of kindness, right? Unfortunately, it assumes that West Virginians prefer to be surrounded by high-rise buildings rather than high-rise mountains and trees. And it fails to explain why only 10 percent of these sites are actually reclaimed for economic development.[8]

All of that aside, I concede that coal employs around eleven thousand West Virginians today.[9] As insignificant as that number might sound, politicians, media, and business leaders continue to refer to it as the "lifeblood" of West Virginia's economy. Somehow this reminds me of the idea that man-made global warming is a debatable concept. Even so, coal miners in West Virginia can make almost eighty-five thousand dollars a year.[10] The average salary for workers in other industries is less than forty thousand dollars—and in a state where almost 20 percent of the population lives below the poverty line, a state that's poorer than all but nine others, money talks.[11] When someone's paying you almost six figures, it's easy to forget how you ever wound up poor in the first place.

Still, mining is dangerous and I have to wonder at what price should one risk his life in the name of fossil fuel? It's true that mine safety has improved tremendously since the days of company-owned towns and coal camps when as many as two hundred men might die each year. And to some extent, West Virginia deserves credit for that. Workers who succeeded in unionizing in the years between the Mine Wars and the anti-union movement of the 1980s are probably most responsible, but I can see why it is perceived as a kindness from the industry. For more than thirty years, West Virginia's annual mining fatalities have consistently been less than twenty, with just a few exceptions. Twenty is definitely better than two hundred.

It is this manipulation of information that leads some to wonder: how can coal companies be all bad if they once provided jobs to so many people, if they still provide good paying jobs to some, promise to "reclaim" the land they destroy, and typically kill only twenty people a year?

There's your perceived kindness, though deeply rooted in the industry's best interests.

Condition Number 4: There exists a real or perceived inability to escape the situation.

It isn't impossible for West Virginians, as individuals, to escape the grips of coal—people can, and do, simply leave the state. Great uncle Freddie did without looking back. His children stayed where they were raised, one in Michigan and one in Colorado. To them, Appalachia is just a distant memory in their family history, perhaps like Germany or Holland is to me. Their only remaining ties to this place lie in Papaw and a few of his sisters, a couple branches of the family tree that grow increasingly further from the roots we all share.

I can understand the appeal of leaving. It is expected that in the next decade or two, when other places are growing and recovering from the recession, the population here will drop by about twenty thousand.[12] Some of this is due to the outward migration of younger people caused by the lack of jobs and opportunity, coal related and otherwise. Wal-Mart has been the state's largest private employer for almost twenty years. I don't even need to editorialize that. It's depressing.

But moving across state lines costs thousands of dollars, an average of $5,600.[13] Plus, some families have occupied the same farm or hollow for generations, forming bonds that transcend monetary value. These familial and spiritual ties to Appalachia are why I write these words from within West Virginia rather than someplace else. I left once for almost a decade, but like Papaw, the ancient mountains (or what's left of them) called me back. So for those of us who can't or won't be parted from these hills, what escape is there? As a state, is it possible to break free?

A 2014 *Grist* magazine article said that West Virginia is "less a fully functioning state government than a resource-extraction colony."[14] As sad as that statement is, it rings true, as does the article's greater sentiment that hope for change is miniscule. Right now it looks like King Coal, when and if he falls, will be replaced by an emerging gas fracking industry that's almost as frightening. Maybe it's the lesser of two evils, but in a place where everything from taxes and political systems to public opinion and school curriculums has been built and manipulated by the extraction industry, it's a future that feels inevitable.

History agrees. Before coal reigned over the state's economy, it was the timber industry, and timber didn't hand the power over to coal because the citizenry demanded it. The shift occurred only when every acre of land that could be clear-cut had been clear-cut (eliminating those grand American chestnuts) and wealthy capitalists recognized for themselves that profits were coming from beneath the ground rather than above it. So far, coal companies haven't completely thrown in the towel, and it's pretty clear they will relinquish control only on their own terms, when they decide it's time.

Does West Virginia have the ability to escape coal and resource extraction industries? It sure doesn't feel like it.

Four conditions must be met in order for Stockholm Syndrome to occur:

1. Threat to physical or psychological survival.
2. Isolation from opinions other than those of the abuser.
3. Perceived kindness that actually benefits the captor.
4. Real or perceived inability to escape.

For years I've struggled to understand how a population can relentlessly defend an industry that's been so blatantly abusive and destructive to the land, culture, and people.

Finally, through this lens of Stockholm Syndrome—the ultimate survival mechanism—I've begun to make some sense of it, to absolve myself of the frustration and anger I once directed toward my fellow Appalachians for their stubborn denial of our true history and to reassign that anger to the actual perpetrator—King Coal. Unfortunately, to convince others to shift the blame would require them to admit West Virginians are victims. Around here *victim* is a dirty word. Remember the "individualist, self-reliant" traits that Jones wrote about? Those values translate the victim concept into what is perceived as weakness, and that's hard for us mountain people to swallow.

Generally speaking, I don't think the rest of America realizes that Appalachians are victims either, which is why we are still collectively portrayed in a negative light, judged by outsiders on behaviors and ideas that seem irrational. Society is finally realizing that victims of violence, rape, and other abuse don't always behave rationally and that the resulting illogical behaviors cannot be blamed on the victims themselves, yet we can't change the outside perspective or our state's narrative, not to mention our own future, until we admit to the abuse.

Once we accept that we're damaged, perhaps we can stop blaming the victim (as I once did) with questions like "Why do you keep bowing down to the industry?" And begin instead to ask things like "How do we recover and what will keep this from happening again?" As the gas fracking industry replaces King Coal, these and other similar questions are increasingly urgent. Perhaps once they're answered, we can begin to heal and do more than just survive. Perhaps just maybe, for the first time in billions of years since the birth of the mountains themselves, we can live in an Appalachia that's free of such violence and conflict.

NOTES

1. US Department of the Interior, US Geological Survey, "Geologic Provinces of the United States: Appalachian Highlands Province," April 21, 2017, https://geomaps .wr.usgs.gov/parks/province/appalach.html.

2. State of West Virginia, "Company Towns," *National Coal Heritage Area*, 2016, http://www.coalheritage.org/page.aspx?id=19.

3. Ronald D. Eller, "The Coal Barons of the Appalachian South, 1880–1930," *Appalachian Journal* 4, no. 3/4 (1977): 195–207.

4. Gabriel Trip, "Penetrating a Closed, Isolated Society in Appalachia," *New York Times*, April 23, 2014, https://www.nytimes.com/times-insider/2014/04/23/penetrating-a-closed-isolated-society-in-appalachia/.

5. Melissa Korn, "Big Gap in College Graduation Rates for Rich and Poor, Study Finds," *Wall Street Journal*, February 3, 2015, http://www.wsj.com/articles/big-gap-in-college-graduation-rates-for-rich-and-poor-study-finds-1422997677.

6. Omar Ghabra, Laura Clark, and Sarah Davis, "Natural Gas Industry Challenges Coal's Dominance in West Virginia," *Mountaineer News Service*, WVU Reed College of Media, April 4, 2013, mountaineernewsservice.com/natural-gas-industry-challenges-coals-dominance-in-west-virginia.

7. Stuart McGehee, "A History of Coal in West Virginia," *Friends of Coal*, https://www.friendsofcoal.org/education/a-history-of-coal-in-west-virginia.html.

8. Natural Resources Defense Council, "The Myth of Mountaintop Removal Reclamation," *NRDC*, May 17, 2010, www.nrdc.org/media/2010/100517.

9. "Coal Mining Employment in West Virginia from 2009–2016, by Mine Type," *Statista*, https://www.statista.com/statistics/215786/coal-mining-employment-in-west-virginia/.

10. US Bureau of Labor Statistics, "Annual Coal Mining Wages vs. All Industries, 2013," *National Mining Association*, July 2014, http://www.truevaluemetrics.org/DBpdfs/Wages/Annual-Wages-by-State--Coal-Mining-vs-All-Industries-2013.pdf.

11. Center for American Progress, "West Virginia 2014 Report," *Talk Poverty*, 2018, https://talkpoverty.org/state-year-report/west-virginia-2014-report/.

12. John Deskins Christiadi and Brian Lego, "Population Trends in West Virginia through 2030," *West Virginia College of Business and Economics*, March 2014, http://busecon.wvu.edu/bber/pdfs/BBER-2014-04.pdf.

13. US Government Accountability Office, "Troubled Asset Relief Program: Treasury Could More Consistently Analyze Potential Benefits and Costs of Housing Program Changes," *Report to Congressional Committees*, July 2015, https://www.gao.gov/assets/680/671649.pdf.

14. David Roberts, "Is There Hope for West Virginia As It Moves Away from Coal?" *Grist*, October 20, 2014, https://grist.org/climate-energy/is-there-hope-for-west-virginia-as-it-moves-away-from-coal/.

They Call It a Strip Job

Julia Spicher Kasdorf

———————

this stretch of Route 219—old road out of West Virginia
they call the Mason-Dixon Highway—

which widens and divides at the Myersdale bypass.
Tonight the right lane's closed, drowned by a mound

of inside-out hillside, so I drift to the left lane,
which now runs two ways, and the scent of mud floods

in through the vents. All my growing up among
men who skinned hills to scrape their seams,

I never saw a strip job this deep, or trucks this big.
No one works the job tonight, which stays light

long after the moon rises, no one hears me cuss
at this site. Remember *Stripease*, the goop mom

painted onto antiques, how it burned your skin
and buckled varnish? Feel hot wax stroked

on the bone beneath your brow, the sharp flick
of a stylist's wrist. Think of Ms. Woitek,

turquoise eyelids and coral lips, who danced
on stage at the Silver Dollar out on Route 30

everyone said, but who had seen? Her specialty:
one semester of creative writing for eleventh graders.

She must be dead by now. O, let her rest beneath green
hills someplace. Let the light hold until I make it

home from the job where I sat in a clean, quiet room,
third floor of a brick hall built in the century that built

railroads to haul coal from hollows and logs
from mountains to prop open the deep mines

or to make the ties that held the rails that became
roads to walk out of those towns. O, how did I come

to get paid to sit in a clean, quiet room and listen
to lines written by grandchildren of miners, listen

until we find the spots that smolder and shine?

On Waterrock Knob

Kathryn Stripling Byer

————————

we greet the sunrise
with ragas from
tape players, fog drifting
over the parking lot.
Belly breath,
belly breath,
the yoga instructor
reminds us,
focus on what
you see waking
inside. (If you look out,
you'll see dying
trees, you'll see how
rain never stops
scrubbing rock
down to sea level.)

Shaken Foundations

Lisa Hayes-Minney

I was reading in bed one early Saturday morning when Daisy, our beagle, jumped up from her peaceful nap at my side and looked at me as though I had pinched her.

Then the entire house shook.

At first, I thought something had hit the house. Something immense. Something huge—a plane or a truck. My second thought was more accurate: an earthquake. I could easily guess the cause—fracking was currently underway at the new Marcellus gas well nearby. Though the drilling company denied any correlation between its fracking and the three earthquakes that shook our small community in July and August of 2013, those who felt the quakes knew better.

The quaking only lasted a few confusing, rattling seconds. It wasn't that extreme; carnival rides have tossed me more harshly. Windows rattled, connections creaked. Nothing collapsed, nothing broke, nothing tipped over. Nothing much more than a tremble and shake. Still, I was frightened and deeply disconcerted. I felt as though the world might vanish beneath me, and I would fall into oblivion. My fear did not dissipate when the trembling subsided, and Daisy still gazed at me, awaiting answers.

Neighbors reported seeing the early morning dew shake off the trees. Pocket change stirred in silver bowls, glass trinkets tittered, hanging plants swayed slightly; wind chimes rang out a quiet chord or two. Aluminum siding on hillside trailers popped like buttons. A single log rolled off our neatly stacked woodpile.

We found cracks in the cement block walls of our home, sunlight shining through from the outside. Our well water—once crisp and fresh—now tasted of sulfur and, as if slightly carbonated, was clouded with bubbles.

I began decanting our tap water, letting it sit to allow the bubbles to settle, and we bought ice by the bag and dumped it into our freezer's ice dispenser.

I have since learned that West Virginia sits above the Marcellus shale, a gas deposit that the oil and gas industry has been targeting heavily in recent years. Shale is a flaky rock. Marcellus is a layer of this black rock, 3,500 to 8,000 feet below the earth's surface, and in West Virginia, the average vertical depth of this layer is approximately 150 feet. Our region sits over one of the thinnest sections of the formation, which also stretches into Pennsylvania, New York, Ohio, and Virginia. I've been told the hydraulic well in our community was one of the first drilled this far south, where the Marcellus formation is so thin.

A quick Google search will lead you to learn that 90 percent of all new onshore oil and gas development in the United States involves some form of hydraulic fracturing. Typically, wells are drilled thousands of feet down to access natural gas (methane) trapped within layers of shale. Then, the drill bit moves horizontally across the layer to create a small shaft. The hydraulic fracking process begins when workers detonate small explosive charges along this shaft to open cracks in the rock. Next, to widen the cracks and release the natural gas, they inject a mixture of water, sand, and chemicals, all of which flow back through the well to the surface.

Though they were fracking at the time, representatives from Noble, the drilling company, denied any connection between their active fracking and the local earthquakes. The senior research geologist and head of the Geoscience Section of the West Virginia Geological and Economic Survey said, "I do not suspect there is a connection to human activity." I wondered whose payroll he was on, wondered who was funding his grants.

The epicenter of the July 20 earthquake in Normantown, West Virginia, was less than a mile from the company's cement slab drilling pad, two miles directly beneath their permitted active drilling path in the Marcellus shale. A local surveyor created a map overlay, the epicenter of the quake over the site's permitted maps and drill path (which he found online). The epicenter was directly under the hydraulic fracturing, the second of eight holes and paths permitted for that one pad. He made me swear to keep the map to myself, not to share it or use it in any public argument. He made respectable money surveying for oil and gas businesses, but his house shook just like ours.

West Virginia is not a state prone to earthquakes. I never imagined I would ever experience one in my life. The Appalachian Mountains are the oldest on the planet, and thus, the most stable. For the most part, the Appalachians did all their major nestling and settling millennia ago. While Californians may think it no major concern when the earth moves beneath their feet, the earthquakes in West Virginia rocked my world, literally and psychologically. The first quake may have only been a mere 2.7 on the Richter scale, but my notion of the world beneath my feet was drastically changed.

"The earth moved," I kept repeating to myself and others. "They MOVED the EARTH." While not so familiar with earthquakes, West Virginians are accustomed to disasters and messes created by corporations that capitalize on our natural resources (chemical spills, coal sludge floods, train derailments, traffic accidents, air pollution, sound pollution, light pollution, water pollution, ground pollution, and the general rape of the land). So, like others affected by such unnatural disasters, we ranted, raved, wrote nasty letters and emails, posted accusations and complaints on social media. . . . Then we patched the cracks in our walls, started researching water filtration systems, and went back to tending the gardens, working the farm, and making a living.

My family donated to help a community elder replace the ceiling that fell in her living room, then saved for a year to install a water filtration system in our own home. In the meantime, we purchased drinking water and ice. Our natural gas supply weakened. The gas pressure in the lines became less dependable, so when our free gas began tripping off that following winter with wearisome regularity, we bought a propane stove to supplement our unreliable gas heat.

The second earthquake hit July 30, waking us Tuesday morning around 2 a.m. when we were worn tired from the harvest activities in the gardens and the fields. My husband and I reached for each other instinctively, waiting to see if our bed would plunge from beneath us, or the ceiling collapse upon us. When the shaking stopped without any raucous crashes, we cursed the name of the drilling company, rolled over, and returned to sleep. This second quake was slightly stronger than the first, a 2.8, but was five miles farther away from our home.

The next morning at breakfast I wondered aloud if our surveyor friend was creating a new map, if he would make it public since the second quake was closer to his house. My husband responded, "He still needs a paycheck."

Then we drank our coffee and added "repair new wall cracks" to our to-do list for the day.

The third quake, a 2.6, rattled us on Friday, August 16, around 7 a.m., waking me earlier and leaving me more jangled than usual. In an instant, I was up and standing in the bedroom doorway where the added framing was reputed to provide additional protection if the ceiling fell. My survival instinct had kicked in, and I did not know if I was conscious or having a nightmare. My husband rushed from the kitchen to check my status and laughed to discover me in the doorway, hands pressed white against the doorframe.

We could laugh about it then, but my basic knowledge of tectonic activity had formed an alarming concept in my mind. Pressure was shifting among the ancient rock slabs beneath us, and tectonic plates are nothing more than a house of cards on a planetary scale. A shift here could result in a consequential settle, which could initiate a shimmy over there and another shake. A ripple effect could actually produce collateral adjustments in the region's earth surface for years. Continued shifting of pressure. Sink holes. Aftershocks. My lingering apprehension was an aftershock in itself.

How long would this instability continue? Would the quakes persist through the six additionally permitted drilling paths? How many weeks, months would that continue? How many cracks could our walls endure? Would our water well become flammable from the spigots like those in pictures we had seen? Could the company's new well completely suck away the natural gas from the aged well that heats our home in winter? The Marcellus well activity was affecting us on all levels. How long would the foundations of our lives be shaken, and how much could we take?

In the meantime, our community was dividing. Friends and family employed in the oil and gas industry publicly followed the company's lead in denying any link, explaining how a connection between the fracking and the quakes could not be scientifically possible. Local business owners increased and adjusted inventory to cater to the temporary influx of the employed population—temporary customers from Texas, Pennsylvania, and New York who paid in cash. The local bars, hotels, stores, and restaurants made great efforts to help the workers spend their per diem money. No overlay map showing the epicenters in relation to the active drilling path ever made it to the public.

But we knew. In our hearts and in our minds the link between the drilling and the earthquakes existed. To us it was—however unscientifically—obvious.

A group of environmental organizations (local chapters of national groups and communities already significantly fracked) held a public meeting in the local school gymnasium—a roasting, sweaty gathering with bad PowerPoint presentations and an almost worthless sound system. Their message was even more chilling than the earthquakes.

Hydraulic drilling requires generators, drilling machines, and pumps going twenty-four hours a day, seven days a week. A horizontal Marcellus well uses two million to five million gallons of water every time it is fracked—that's 550 to 2,500 tanker truckloads of water—plus tanker trucks for the sand and chemicals. Wastewater impoundment ponds can be as big as football fields and store millions of gallons of water containing chemicals, radium, and toxic metals that rise from shale wells. Considered proprietary information, the ingredients in fracking chemicals and waters are protected from public knowledge.

I also learned at the meeting that air pollutants released include volatile organic compounds (VOCs), such as benzene, formaldehyde, polycyclic aromatic hydrocarbons (PAHs), and other toxic substances. Benzene causes cancer at high exposure, and exposure to formaldehyde causes nasal cancer in rats. Long-term exposure to PAHs causes decreased immune function, cataracts, kidney and liver damage, and abnormal lung function. Naphthalene, a specific PAH, breaks down red blood cells if inhaled or ingested in large amounts. The hydrogen sulfide released by flaring and venting diesel or natural gas is fatal at high levels.

The meeting organizers clearly intended to terrify us with the realities of drilling and fracking, to motivate us with fear. Wastewater, drainage, radioactive ingredients, air quality, road damage, traffic accidents. They wanted us to take action, to support their cause, to enlist, to donate. The monstrous drilling company fracking in our tiny town did not even send a representative to the foray, but even so, a large number of oil and gas industry employees also attended. I left early, before the yelling started.

The uproar received minimal coverage in the local newspaper, nothing more. The meeting served its purpose, though; it certainly stirred the pot. The frightful presentations fanned the lingering flames of fear and frustration in our community. The drilling company's absence and lack of any real response heightened our feelings of disruption, violation, and dishonor. Rumors regarding the causes of the earthquakes began to circulate: human error in oversight of the water supply, mistakes in the site construction, miscommunication due to lack of a cell phone signal in the area. If there were ever to be any reproach, it would be linked to human error, not industry practices.

Arguments and heated discussions sprang up at the counter of the local general store, neighbors exchanged cross comments at the gas pumps at the local station. Drilling company representatives (readily available before the quakes to promise responsible behavior and tout economic benefits) no longer returned emails or phone calls. A local oil and gas service business owner, who lived less than a mile from the new well pad, took his profits from moving dirt to the well—and then moved to another county. His vacant house later burned to the ground.

Without ever admitting any connection or making any further statement, Noble Energy decided not to drill every path permitted for the local well pad (at this time). Normantown's well is an experimental well after all, the first of its type so far south in the Marcellus, where the shale is thinner, and apparently less stable.

The fracking ceased and the earthquakes ceased. But the effects still linger.

The low-water creek crossing that the drilling company installed for access to their right-of-way (three large culverts covered with dirt and gravel) washed out twice. The company replaced it, quickly and quietly, with a bridge. The company upgraded the local station that processes the gas and wastewater the new well would produce. The upgrades stand on more than three acres of fill dirt deposited in the Steer Creek waterway, not far downstream from our local elementary school. The rotating series of out-of-state workers who came to construct and frack the well has dwindled, the cash flow in the community dwindling with it. The anger and resentment in the community has settled again, just like the ground beneath us.

I think about the gas from that well, running through the upgraded processing plant. I imagine the high-pressured fumes, spewing through the aged transmission line that runs through our property, through our side yard. Just one of many lines that run across the state of West Virginia, the same ancient line that has spouted at least two leaks since we moved here fifteen years ago, half-ass patched each time. I think of a similar gas line that exploded in Sissonville, West Virginia, last year—how it decimated houses, projected flames a hundred feet in the air, and smelted eight hundred feet of guardrails and asphalt on Interstate 77.

I am not opposed to oil and gas. I actually need my SUV and I enjoy electricity. I love my friends and family who make a living in the industry, and I appreciate some of the community perks provided when these big companies need a tax deduction. And though I support alternative energy, I have no illusions that our state will ever turn away from our dependence on fossil fuels.

But I do not like denial, lies, and irresponsibility. I certainly do not like being dismissed. I realize now how corporations prey on communities, how they consider our lives no more than the lives of the fish and salamanders in the streams they suck water from, no more than the lives of skirting water bugs. No corporation should have the right to rattle homes repeatedly, then shrug it off as nothing. No company should be permitted to alter the water in our wells, collapse an elderly woman's ceiling, or even shake the morning dew without consequence. No business should be sanctioned to disturb the ground under our town while they line their pockets. We should have a right to live without the threat of a manufactured earthquake damaging our homes and our lives.

Three earthquakes shook Normantown, West Virginia, in late summer 2013. In spring 2014, the Ohio Department of Natural Resources publicly announced that earthquakes near Youngstown, Ohio, were directly related to drilling operations. Two years after the Normantown earthquakes, a geophysicist came forward to publicly declare a connection between drilling and earthquakes in Oklahoma and Missouri. Two years after that, scientists released a report detailing how fracking affects and pollutes drinking water. There *is* a connection, though it should not require the courage of a brave geophysicist to make that clear. In Normantown, we knew from the moment the earth first moved.

I do not expect instant changes in the world. I cannot imagine this scientific proof, this proven connection between drilling and earthquakes, will stop fracking. I do hope it changes the industry, changes regulation.

I do not expect anyone to pay for our water filtration system or for the woodstove, necessary for supplemental heat, though both are things we can barely afford. I just want the company that drilled here to admit their responsibility, to let their permits for further drilling expire. I want them to acknowledge that they rocked our world, treated us disrespectfully, lied to us—and that they were wrong.

I expect an apology, and a stable future. I am still waiting.

The Glassy Places

G. C. Waldrep

Pickens Co., SC

God made them to drink. Meanwhile we have hair in both likely
and unlikely places. I have replaced all my vowels: Selah.
Men never sing, not really, unless they're thinking
about women is a thought I had while eating a plate of chopped
barbecue in Easley, SC. Like most thoughts it is likely
temporary. I hear my lost vowels on the radio and remember
my mother young and carefree at the granite lip, skirt
flaring, beside her mother and her mother's mother. It had already
occurred to her that she could be dead. But then my body
relaxed into the molded blue plastic in ways it hadn't
in years. I take drugs that keep me from dreaming the sky
opens out like an incandescent bulb. Dear friends, what is there
left to apologize for? I have tried to read all the scars
of my body, both visible and invisible. Once again in the cemetery
where my people are I take a seat. Neighbors profile me
like the thief I must be. It—the cemetery—is the cleanest
I have ever seen it. It is entirely possible that my desire to die
began in this place, against which the May sun strops its day-razor.
I'm deaf to painting's burlapped flame and paraphrase.
But I want slavery not to have happened yet, I thought
I heard the little girl say. O mysteries of eternal recompense.
O NALLEYs and ROPERs and BALLENTINEs and DAYs,

a highway runs through the final exam some oaks are taking
on the periphery of your rest. O SHECKs and OATESes,
mark me present, a biological fact tarted up in synthetic polymers.
Which of us is more radioactive, I wonder. Preach,
play me a hymn, a shoal. What I know about you would fit
inside a stone smaller than your banjo and less precious.
Without drugs I dream I'm in the hospital, in no pain
or other obvious distress but unable or unwilling to speak.
It's not a bad dream to wake from, or into. I couldn't caption
all the graves left by children if I tried, which begs
the question of trying. "Remember the Days of Old, Consider
the Years of Many Generations," Deuteronomy 32:7
on its ragged teat of land. This is one of the first places I visited
before my mother ever saw it, that I came to first. I leave
strands of my hair in the leaf litter. What is most obvious now
is the absence of a church, so I dream one. Welcome
to the Church of the Living Vowel. I am taking up a collection.
I am holding my hands up to the sun so that I can see
my finger bones, their concave semaphores. We could call this
praise. It's possible we have to call it something. Almost
everyone who is going to be buried here is already. A pear
rests in the breath's apse, slits the oak's ark and pawl.
Heat ripples like vintage acetate that's been left out to decay.

Border Waters

Ben Burgholzer

———————

I walk through a field of grassy hills in Pennsylvania heading toward the West Branch of the Delaware in the Catskills. I walk and imagine that these hills are burial mounds, full of bones and buried items the dead intended to use in the next life. I wonder how deep beneath my feet these remains would be, the remains of small villages hidden by dust and time. I wonder how long it would take to dig deep enough to remove the hills and resurrect the villages, to expose them all to open air, and how much deeper beneath them lay the pockets of natural gas, pressurized and silent.

The number of hydrofracking wells in Pennsylvania has erupted in the last decade, some 7,788 currently active wells out of the 1.2 million wells nationwide in 2016,[1] each requiring about three to five million gallons of freshwater to operate[2]—most of the water left irreversibly poisoned and polluted.

The Iroquois, who once lived in this region, lived by the Great Law that urged them to consider the impact of every decision on the seventh generation into the future. They believed that every action should make the lives of the following generations easier rather than harder. I think about how different things would be if that philosophy were adopted by world leaders, CEOs, and politicians.

The grassy hills roll like a green sea in the wind as Tom and I walk. It is June, and the sky is so blue and the air so warm and humid that it feels as though Tom and I are at the bottom of a clear blue ocean that has swallowed us whole. I wonder what one million gallons of poisoned water might look like and think of the way I had poisoned my own body with dope and needles. Now I find peace in places like this, on rivers and streams.

Grasshoppers and other bugs jump over and around me as I move through the grass, interrupting the sound of the heat in the air with their song. My shirt is soaked with sweat, but the breeze is cool on my back.

Tom turns to me. "This is where you're going to get your first twenty-inch brown." I nod as I walk. A brown trout over twenty inches is a small milestone, a good marker of a fisherman who's put some time in on the river. Bigger fish behave differently, and you have to fish for them differently. The Upper Delaware system is full of fish over twenty inches. Most of the river is catch and release/artificial only, which allows the fish to grow much larger and in greater numbers than in most of the other Catskill systems, but it is highly pressured, meaning that many people fish its waters. The fish get smarter and more difficult to catch every year. A biologist may say fish only retain information for a few seconds at most, but I don't know if they've ever seen a trout nose a dry fly enough to see how it sinks or watched a fish rise to the surface only to pause and swim away quickly when it sees the shadow of your .004" 6X tippet.

There is a small swamp after the field of hills toward the river. My boots sink a few inches into the soft mud with every step as we move and duck around branches and trees. Through the trees, I can see the river now, tucked between the worn mountains.

We pause near the river bank to watch the fishermen and the rising fish. At this pool in particular, known for its slow-moving, dry-fly water, I count six guys, all older, lined up next to each other with their hands folded waiting for the fish to start rising. It's common to spend all afternoon working one fish, throwing thirty or forty different flies at it, and then missing the hook set if it finally does take the fly. The best and worst thing about using dry flies is that you can see it all happening. You see the fish rise from the depths and toward your fly, sometimes quickly, sometimes slowly. It comes up, opens its mouth and sucks down the fly—or it turns away and returns to the river bottom.

"I love catching fish on dries, but fuck all that," Tom says and starts to walk upriver toward faster-moving water. "We'll go way above these guys. Faster water and less time for the fish to think about whether or not they want to eat the fly. Nothing quite like the streamer bite."

We walk upstream about a half mile. The river here serves as the border between New York and Pennsylvania and much farther downriver between New Jersey and Pennsylvania. Its fourteen-thousand-square-mile watershed supplies the drinking water for about fifteen million people and is a major investment for the Department of Environmental Conservation and Department of Environmental Protection to keep the water clean and drinkable.[3] As of 2015, hydrofracking is illegal in New York State; some fifty feet across the river, several other states are following suit.

"This is a great spot," Tom says and points into the river. "Walk out into the middle and cast toward the banks. We'll work our way back down to where we came in. Here." He hands me a leech pattern about four inches long. "Big flies, big fish," he says as I study it in my hand. "I'll let you get a few casts in first. We'll fish our way back down to where we came in. Hit the banks."

I tie it on and wade into the water toward the middle of the pool. When I get there, I begin to cast, straight toward the bank.

"Good. Now strip it hard and fast," Tim says from the river bank.

I see the leech go limp beneath the water. I strip the fly in.

"Faster next time! Don't wait when it hits the water. Don't give him time to think about it. Put a big meal right in his home and make him think its swimming away."

I cast again, this time to the New York side. There's an eagle's nest nearby in the tallest tree, which is used yearly by the birds. They were almost extinct here some forty years ago from the DDT that was hailed as a miracle for farmers. The pesticide seeped into the water and into the fish that the eagles ate, causing their eggs to become so brittle and weak that they were destroyed by their own mother during incubation. They have made a great recovery and are no longer on the endangered species list.

I look around but don't see any eagles nearby. The trees, green and bold, are lined up to watch me fish on both sides of the river. There are small mountains up and down the river, old and weathered peaks that once were double, triple the height they are now and carved by the water, broken down by time, by wind, by rain.

The watershed comes together in this river, all 14,110 square miles of it, allowing seventeen million people to have clean water to drink.

"Faster! C'mon!"

I cast to the Pennsylvania side. Fracking is legal and practiced in Pennsylvania. One doesn't have to drive far to see the wells. This has created many much-needed jobs for the area but leaves many drinking wells poisoned. Some link the carcinogens in the fluid used to free the pockets of gas deep in the shale to increased rates of cancer and death of wildlife in the areas. Studies claim hydrofracking is safe because these chemicals are pumped about a mile beneath the aquifer where water flows. The full lists of chemicals often are not disclosed—and they don't have to be, thanks to an amendment to the Safe Drinking Water Act championed by former vice president Dick Cheney when he was Halliburton CEO; the amendment holds that the chemical solution used in fracking is a trade secret, much like the ingredients in Coca-Cola.[4]

I look at my arms, once covered with track marks and scars that have now all healed. My nose bled daily, and I weighed 112 pounds—70 pounds lighter than I weigh now. When things started to get bad, I moved to Dingmans Ferry, Pennsylvania, from New Jersey to get away from all the drugs and try to start over. I was addicted to OxyContin, the next logical step from Percocet and Vicodin, and a half step away from the heroin that would ruin me. I thought this move would fix me. My dealers all lived in West Milford at the time, and I wouldn't drive the hour and a half each way to get more drugs.

It had only been five days when I started doing the drive after work, washing dishes at another dead-end nursing home. It started out as every few days, then every other, then every day, sometimes twice a day. It seemed as though I could do it forever, as long as I could feel nothing.

Even though my job was in the kitchen, I had plenty of contact with the residents in the nursing home. We had to fill big carts with trays and bring them to each wing. I had worked at another nursing home, but there was something different about that one. There was no illusion that people weren't coming there to wait for death. Many were abandoned by their families and hadn't received a visit in years. I always wondered how someone could leave a family member in a place like that, tossed aside like a broken toy. I was high constantly then, my pupils pinned and skin pale, but I loved to talk to residents and listen to their stories.

There was one woman everyone called the Dover lady. She had Alzheimer's and walked from one nurses' station to the other, down the same long hallway all day, back and forth trying to get back home to Dover. When she reached one end of the hallway, she would ask the nurse what way it was to Dover, New Jersey, which happened to be where my grandparents were from. The nurse would promptly answer, "Oh, at the other end of the hallway," to which she would smile, and say, "thank you," and walk down to the other hallway. By the time she got there, she had forgotten where she came from, and this would continue for most of the day.

When I caught on, I asked the nurses why they sent her down the hall and commented that it just seemed cruel.

"Not as cruel as explaining to her that she's in a nursing home and that her life in Dover is far behind her, sweetheart." She smiled. "Plus, she's getting plenty of exercise."

"She ever get visitors?"

"Not in the eight years I've been here."

I talked to the Dover lady sometimes, always the same conversation. My grandfather was the mayor of the town for a few years and ran the local diner for many years. Her eyes always lit up when I mentioned his name, and she spoke of him and assured me that she voted for him years ago, and that he was a very good mayor, the best even. She smiled and asked me if I remembered how to get back there. I hesitated before I pointed and said it was at the other end of the hallway. She thanked me and started walking.

I think about the constant drives back and forth to get more drugs as I stand in the middle of the river. I did that drive every day until it became a part of the day, as routine as eating or sleeping. The sickness seemed to grow with every drive. It got easier and harder at the same time to convince myself that this was normal, until finally there was no more convincing, just a necessity to keep going until there was nothing left.

I think back to the wells and how at first they look as foreign as a needle in the Pennsylvania dirt, and how after some time both begin to transform into part of the landscape, as normal as the trees and the sky.

I take a step and hit the bank with the fly. My casts from bank to bank are no more than twenty feet; the river is narrow and easily crossed. As I cast to the Pennsylvania side I can't help but imagine gas and oil floating atop the water in magnificent rainbows. The explosion of life on the river banks no longer green but brown. It may not be legal to hydrofrack this close to the river, but it only takes one or two mistakes for one of the 416 tributaries of the river to become infected, a nightmare made true by some unforeseeable error, despite the never-ending assurance by gas and oil companies that it will never happen, that fracking is perfectly safe.

I cast to the New York side and think of all the hours I spent driving, creating endless schemes and stories to explain why I was always so late coming home. Plans that never happened, movies I never saw, people I never hung out with. Fictionalized relationships, friendships, houses, and outings. All of it was spent driving, back and forth, wishing I could get there sooner to make the fire in my bones stop burning.

I cast to the Pennsylvania side and think of North Dakota. The one million barrels of oil a day that surge from the Bakken shale beneath the dirt of the old prairie towns that lie in ruin.[5] I see trucks covered in dirt and mud and small Halliburton logos, loaded with chemicals and secrets, and the polluted ghost town it will become when the gas is gone.

I think of the Dover lady and wonder if she's still alive and if she's still walking back and forth between the two wings of the nursing home and at what point in the walk she forgets where she's going or if she's going to make it there.

I cast straight toward the bank in front of me and strip the fly as soon as it hits the water.

"Oh man, that's the cast. I've caught a ton of fish just like that." I have forgotten about Tom behind me.

I strip hard once and see the golden flash of a brown trout and feel the pull on the line as I set the hook.

Tom laughs and claps his hands as the fish takes off downriver. "Told you! Just like that!"

The fish rips downriver. I can feel it death rolling at the river's bottom. Every time he runs, the reel screams, but I can tell I have a good hook in the fish. Every time I try to move him out of the current, he fights harder; his head faces me and violently shakes. After a few minutes, the fish stays in the middle of the current. I'm able to hold him there long enough to net him.

"Awesome fish! Not quite twenty, but we'll take it," Tom says.

I smile and nod and take a picture of it in the water. Tom takes one too before I release it, and he disappears back into the water.

We fish until dusk, but neither of us catches another fish. The mayfly hatch is heavy in the evening, and there's a good amount of bugs on the water, but we decide to head back before sunset.

When we get back downriver, the same guys are still casting to the same fish in the same pool. Two, it seems, have given up and are eating on the river bank while they watch their friends miss fish after fish.

"The fish win today," an older man says to me as I walk by. His friend laughs and takes a puff of his cigar. I smile at him and hope that when I'm his age, I will still be fishing here.

On the way back to the truck as I walk through the green hills, I think again about the gas beneath me. I know that some people view this gas as a miracle, creating jobs to save families in areas where jobs and careers have turned to dust, but what happens after the gas, the companies, and the wells are gone? What happens to generations that come next?

They will be left pacing, back and forth forever, killing time looking for another impossible, fleeting solution to an unsolvable mess so much bigger than them that they won't even know where to start. That's what those six generations will inherent, and that is what they, too, will look for, because there is no other way, because that is what they have been given, that is what they have been left with.

The wind blows as we walk, and I feel again that I must be walking at the bottom of a clear blue ocean. I close my eyes and hold my breath and imagine myself diving deep into the ground below me. It is illuminated by an unseen light. As I swim through the layers of dirt and rock, I imagine a great village. There are bones and spearheads, arrowheads of warriors next to decaying bows, pieces of pottery that took a lifetime to create. I sort through it all with my hands and kick free to dive deeper and deeper. Beneath the village lie porous rock and the smooth layers of shale stacked and woven over one another. I search for something to hold on to, but I smell only gas, and there is only smoke and fire.

NOTES

1. Sam Rubright, "34 States Have Active Oil & Gas Activity in U.S. Based on 2016 Analysis," *FracTracker*, March 23, 2017, https://www.fractracker.org/2017/03/34-states-active-drilling-2016/.
2. "How Much Water Is Used?" *Explore Shale*, Pennsylvania State University, 2014, http://exploreshale.org/.
3. Delaware River Basin Committee, "Basin Information," April 13, 2017, http://nj.gov/drbc/basin/.
4. "The Halliburton Loophole," *Earthworks*, https://earthworks.org/issues/inadequate_regulation_of_hydraulic_fracturing/.
5. US Energy Information Administration, "North Dakota Field Production of Crude Oil," May 31, 2018, https://www.eia.gov/dnav/pet/hist/LeafHandler.ashx?f=M&n=PET&s=MCRFPND1.

Preserve

Appalachian Wildness
and the Death of the Sublime

Brent Martin

———

The passion caused by the great and sublime in nature, when those causes operate most powerful is astonishment; and astonishment is that state of the soul in which all its motions are suspended, with some degree of horror. In this case the mind is so entirely filled with its object, that it cannot entertain any other, nor by consequence reason on that object which employs it. Hence arises the great power of the sublime, that, far from being produced by them, it anticipates our reasonings, and hurries us on by an irresistible force. Astonishment, as I have said, is the effect of the sublime in its highest degree; the inferior effects are admiration, reverence, and respect.

—Edmund Burke, *On the Sublime and Beautiful*

Jewelweed shakes in the late September breeze, pale and wavering within the electric red wands of cardinal flower. Dark purple stems of pokeweed, heavy with seed, bend in arcs of contrast against the many fading greens, while ruby-throated hummingbirds flit through the afternoon light—all of this contained in my narrow field of vision from beneath the lemon yellow of fading catalpa leaves. Bucolic Cowee Valley seems under the spell of shifting autumn light, and the words that come to mind for this moment, or at least for the desire of this moment, are transcendent and sublime— words that arise from imagination and history—anachronistic today, but adequate and relevant to the desires of my cynical and overwrought twenty-first-century consciousness. It wasn't always this way. The eighteenth-century British statesman Sir Edmund Burke spent a good part of his life pondering the word *sublime*, in an attempt to understand the human range of senses and emotions and to create a proper response to what he and others considered to be the intellectual staleness of the Enlightenment. Burke's 1757 *A Philosophical Inquiry into the Sublime and Beautiful* helped usher in the Romantic movement, with its emphasis on emotional truth and its attempt to understand nature through art, literature, and religion. Arriving here in western North Carolina's Cowee Valley in May of 1775 was the first eighteenth-century American to immerse himself in these ideas—the writer, artist, naturalist, and horticulturalist William Bartram.

Bartram traveled to Cowee Valley in May of that year on the eve of the American Revolution, alone and on the prowl for plant specimens to ship to his English patron, John Fothergill. Based on his 1791 publication, *Travels*, the word *sublime* was on his mind quite a bit. When he entered Cowee Valley, capital of the Middle Town Cherokees and site of my old mountain home, he sees the mountains with "grandeur and sublimity" and the valley itself as situated "amidst sublimely high forests." When he reaches the crest of the nearby Nantahala Mountains, he "beheld with rapture and astonishment, a sublimely awful scene of power and magnificence, a world of mountains piled upon mountains."[1] Historian Roderick Nash, author of *Wilderness and the American Mind*, credits Bartram with introducing the word into American literature and for being one of the first Americans to describe the American landscape in such terms. This was contrary to the settler zeitgeist, which saw the American wilderness as a place to be conquered and subdued, along with its native inhabitants.

Cowee would be brutally destroyed the following year, and the settlers would soon pour in, their ancestors today now hanging on to remnants of the large parcels that many of them acquired for nothing, or next to nothing. The once capital of the Middle Town Cherokees is now but a ghost of itself, though its ceremonial mound is permanently conserved and back in tribal ownership after two hundred years. But the ghost is a powerful one. Cherokee place names dot the landscape, along with ethnobotanical and cultural artifacts. Except for the mound and the roadside historical marker, there is no other visual reference. Our most valuable descriptions of Cowee prior to this, including descriptions of the Appalachian plant world, theretofore unknown to science, can be accredited to Bartram. He was here for only a couple of weeks, but he nonetheless devoted a significant portion of *Travels* to this period. He describes Cowee as "one of the most charming mountain landscapes perhaps anywhere to be seen,"[2] and his time spent with the Cherokees is one of compassionate cultural observation, demonstrating a unique sensitivity to their customs and traditions. I once heard the Cherokee scholar and language expert Tom Belt present a possible Native American perspective on Bartram's time spent among them here in Cowee. For Belt, Bartram was the first white man who didn't have a gun, a Bible, something to trade, or papers for them to sign. He was simply curious and open to knowing them and the natural world they inhabited.

When Bartram arrives in the Cherokee town of Watauga, several miles upriver from Cowee, he is greeted by the chief, whom Bartram describes as a man "universally beloved" and "revered by all for his exemplary virtues." He describes his time there as one of "perfect and agreeable hospitality," and bestows the highest compliments upon the people for their happiness— undefiled and unmodified by artificial refinements. *O Divine simplicity and truth, friendship without fallacy or guile*[3]—this was his emphatic reaction to this brief visit and a subtle criticism of what he considered to be the utter lack of such values in eighteenth-century society. Subsequently, *Travels* was lukewarmly received by American critics upon its publication in 1791, and nowhere near so appreciated as it was with its European counterparts. America was still full of revolutionary pride and still in the throes of Native American conquest across the country. Bartram's argument for the shared humanity of those southern tribes like the Cherokee was unpopular, and even after the Cherokee adopted Christianity and Western ways, they were still brutally removed and their property stolen. The heirs of this legacy surround me here in far western North Carolina today, where antifederal government sentiments of all sorts reside, along with resistance to local government regulations, planning, and outside influence of any kind.

Much like the trade paths that crisscrossed the mountains here at the time of Bartram's visit, *Travels* was a major intellectual intersection of sorts.

Scientific in its Linnaean nomenclature and romantic in its effusive emotional response to the landscape and people he encountered, it reveals Bartram's struggle to integrate the two into a coherent rendering that captures the best of the Enlightenment era and the beginning of the Romantic. But what strikes me most about his reaction to the people and landscape of these mountains is his humility. This was not a popular emotion at the time, when thoughts of revolution, conquest, and subjugation were on the general public's mind, but if there is one word that perhaps captures the spirit of his writings, *humility* is it. It can also be argued that it was the beginning of an American natural history tradition. Historian Phillip Marshall Hicks says in *The Development of the Natural History Essay in American Literature* that Bartram was "the first genuine and artistic interpretation of the American landscape," and that "*Travels* was the first combination of accurate observation, aesthetic appreciation and philosophical interest in the realm of natural history literature."[4] Bartram's humble approach to humanity and nature would take hold among a core group of American and British writers in the late eighteenth and early nineteenth centuries with the Romantic movement, which laid the foundation for what was to become one of the core principles of the late nineteenth and early twentieth centuries' conservation movement. It might be a stretch, but given *Travels*'s impact on the development of the Romantic movement and the fact that it was rooted in the southern landscape, it can be claimed as another piece of the southern influence on American literature.

Bartram's sympathetic views of Native Americans and artistic treatment of the American South were highly influential with the early nineteenth-century English Romantic writers Samuel Taylor Coleridge and William Wordsworth, who borrowed heavily from his imagery and who, in turn, influenced early American Romantics such as Henry David Thoreau and Ralph Waldo Emerson. This link is often ignored in the history of America's Romantic movement, but it's a clear one, and significant. America at this time was industrializing in the Northeast, conquering the West, converting my native Southeast to slave-based agriculture, and cutting the forests down here with unbridled rapaciousness. The subsequent effect of this in the coming decades was a national call for the conservation of our last wild places, along with the further divide between those who would as soon continue exploiting them. It was also the beginning of divisions in America between rural and urban perspectives with regard to the land. Urban and industrial America called for conservation and preservation, while rural Americans, as well as corporate America, saw the vast expanse of publicly owned land as either a common space to be utilized or a natural resource to be exploited for profit. This early national divide is a significant piece of what would later become the more multifaceted political divide of what we now call red and blue places.

Here today in the deep politically red country of Cowee, Bartram's legacy is mostly unknown, and were it not for a trail given his name and the efforts of a few local writers and organizations, it would go largely unnoticed. Yet his legacy is profound for those of us who spend time with his writings, puzzling over his routes, and creating a palimpsest from his details and descriptions. It adds wonder to the place, as well as an important historical dimension. I need this wonder, as I once held Appalachia on a pedestal, a place in my young imagination where the people and customs documented in the voluminous *Foxfire* series represented a type of freedom and way of life that I admired and longed for. These youthful romantic notions led me here eventually, where I pursued a career of conservation and sought to live a life that I hoped would in some ways mimic the simplicity and independence of the people, my own included, who also moved here for the same reasons some two hundred plus years ago. My own family line left the southern Appalachians to find work in the late nineteenth century, but their ways remained, and perhaps this is what was lodged somewhere back in my genetic memory. I was a victim of my own romanticism in many ways, as it has never been the place of *Foxfire,* though the landscape and the spirit of this place still speak to me as powerfully as ever. I'm an outsider, though born just two hours away, and with a southern pedigree that dates back to the early eighteenth century. My wife and I moved here imbued with what we thought was humility toward the people and the place, but we have learned from over two decades of living here that, with the exception of a minority of newcomers and open-minded locals, only the landscape—with its world-class biodiversity, spectacular beauty, and cultural history—is worthy of it. And, of course, its connection to William Bartram.

Two years ago at a celebration in Albuquerque honoring the fiftieth anniversary of this landmark legislation, I participated in a panel discussion on the history of American wilderness. Bartram was my subject, and when I asked the group of fifty or so people whether they'd heard of William Bartram, only three or four raised their hands. However, when I asked how many people had seen or read the book *Cold Mountain* and remembered the strange book (*Travels*) that Inman kept close by and referred to as he made his way back home to the mountains, almost every hand in the room shot up. Inman quoted Bartram's descriptions of Appalachia because they are the most passionate renderings of the region's magnificence to this day. Plodding his way home, Inman describes the lowlands with disdain—the muddy rivers, bad roads, mean people—and Appalachia, much as it was to Bartram, is elevated to the sublime. I don't mean to imply that this feeling isn't shared by most locals and newcomers residing here today but only that this is no longer the landscape of *Foxfire* or any other number of publications exalting Appalachian culture—real or imagined.

Aldo Leopold, famous for his shift in thinking after seeing the fierce green fire in the dying eyes of a wolf he had shot, said of the founding of the Wilderness Society in 1935, "The Wilderness Society is, philosophically, a disclaimer of the biotic arrogance of *homo americanus*. It is one of the focal points of a new attitude—an intelligent humility toward man's place in nature." But humility is one emotion that is increasingly in short supply in the recently defined geological epoch, the Anthropocene, where we now dominate and control nature, and where wilderness and past ideas of the wild are considered outdated, irrelevant, and destined for the dustbin of history. Nature, once the romantic construct that grounded the conservation movement in both its science and emotion, is being deconstructed and reconstructed to define us in this new geological era as gardeners and ambitious utilitarians who must manage and restore, as we are now completely in control. Humans are the dominant species, and nature is ours completely. Humility is for losers.

As someone working to conserve our last wild places in the southern Appalachians, these ideas are making the effort increasingly challenging. Bartram's idea of wilderness as sublime and the evolution of this idea into wilderness legislated have already suffered the effects of academic deconstruction, but couple this with the dull ideology of the Anthropocene, along with the growing wave of those who want no limits when it comes to human activities, and advocacy for these ideas takes place in difficult terrain. Here in western North Carolina, where over a million acres of federal public lands make up almost a quarter of total ownership, a new management plan is being created that will determine their future for the next fifteen to twenty years. Wilderness is a piece of this, as new wilderness areas can be recommended as part of this plan. With only about 6 percent of this current acreage designated as such, it seems reasonable that we would protect more, yet advocates seem less and less enthusiastic while opponents seem to grow in rancor and numbers. Humility and sublimity have no place at the planning table, for management advocates on all sides of the table want all land open always to whatever activities they see appropriate to meet human desires—whether it's restoration or the need to be able to access and manage game species. Arguing with these values for the protection of nature at this table places one in a camp of outdated romantics, out of touch with Anthropocene reality, and unwilling to move on.

So what does *wild* mean anymore, and why trouble myself with these heady thoughts of the sublime, here in the cynical twenty-first century? Maybe if nostalgic views of wild nature are truly bound for the dustbin, where ideas and viewpoints sometimes rightfully go, I should just get over it. But if these ideas no longer have a place at the table within the modern-day discourse of the Anthropocene, what does this mean for art and poetry, both of which draw from the human constructs of beauty and which enrich and humble us before nature? And what can the Anthropocene offer in return? Beauty in our engineering and technology, our final and ultimate conquest? Maybe we need this idea of the sublime more than ever as a species. It might help center us in our insignificance within the great scheme of biodiversity and evolution and humble us before all creation. And perhaps the ideas and appreciation of wilderness and wild nature will continue to enrich our imaginations, should we decide to keep them, expanding our capacity to accept limits, grounding us in civilized restraint.

Every neotropical bird here has left or is preparing to leave, as it has since the Pleistocene epoch, a geological period that forced migrations of species southward during its ice age, much like this current geological Anthropocene era and its record heat is ironically forcing these same species farther north. Unfortunately, they will never engineer their way out of this mess. The Audubon Society predicts that many of these species will vanish from the southern Appalachians, moving farther north or crashing altogether. Occasionally over the last few weeks I've heard hooded warblers and black-throated green warblers singing, a strange time of year for them to do this, but I expect they are the young of the year, practicing their newly acquired songs. It's magic to the ear if one is attuned so. It adds to the melancholy these mountains seem to propagate in the fall, when chill winds begin to blow and the light begins to shift in dramatic and ethereal brightness and shadow. They're likely gone now, winging their way south across the Caribbean to places like Colombia or Nicaragua. Habitat in these winter ranges is dwindling due to deforestation, and coupled with climate change, their situation is becoming all the more dire. I cannot imagine an Appalachian spring without them, just as I cannot imagine a world where this would be acceptable. Their arrival is that spectacular and uplifting, that sublime.

NOTES

1. William Bartram, *The Travels of William Bartram* (Athens: University of Georgia Press, 1998), 229.
2. Bartram, *Travels*, 223.
3. Bartram, *Travels*, 222.
4. Phillip Marshall Hicks, *The Development of the Natural History Essay in American Literature* (Philadelphia: University of Pennsylvania, 1924), 261.

Appalachian Pastoral

Scott Honeycutt

————————

The tallest tree in town is a cellular tower flocked
in an ever-garment of ageless green and steely wire.
From a hilltop, it lords over stunted oaks and poplars
like a planter out surveying his crops.

Without need for water or sun,
the camouflaged thing swallows thousands of
human voices. It populates space, posing
as a single seed grown up while it spreads out
dark branches against the buzzing sky.

Deep Fade

Madison Jones

————————

Then, I set out on the dark road out of town,
picturing you still asleep in our little room,
crossing the empty country road that leads
to the interstate, grateful at 4:45 to be driving
toward the only work I could get. The grit
from endless roadwork clatters
against the undercarriage. Each one
a frozen syllable of this uncertain hour,
spelling the time until the engine heats up,
blending with static on my favorite station:
WEGL 91.1, bouncing and crackling
through the frayed speakers. The off-air static
sounds like some distant siren, announcing
its emergency until the music's silver warmth
pours in and fills the empty pastures
through the windshield. Gillian Welch sings
"Dark Turn of Mind" as if the sound bursts
from the closed factories where fog dissolves.
The sun rises and sets into the tree line,
a little slower over each hill. The heater makes
the noise that means it is rousing. Each mile
the shadows on the road move longer, fading
with the station. I won't have long to listen
before I hit the Georgia line, lose the signal,
and hope where I'm headed will be warmer.

Hemlocks, Adelgids, and People:
Ecological Learning from an Appalachian Triad

Laura Henry-Stone

———————

A group of campers sits in a circle on the floor of the common room of a large cabin. The camp pastor leads them in a getting-to-know-each-other conversation. Drawing from the natural setting of the camp's location in the Blue Ridge Mountains of Maryland, Pastor Fred asks them to introduce themselves and tell everyone what his or her favorite tree is. Among the youths in the circle is a curly-headed girl wearing glasses and braces. When it's her turn, she names her favorite tree as the hemlock. Pastor Fred chuckles and asks, "Isn't that what Socrates drank?" The girl laughs back, having no idea what he's talking about. Later she learns the story of Socrates being put to death by being forced to drink the sap of a hemlock plant, which is of course an entirely different species from that of her favorite tree, a towering conifer of the Appalachian forests. This may have been her first lesson about why scientists prefer the use of Latin names over common names for the species they study.

Donald Culross Peattie, in his 1948 classic, *A Natural History of Trees of Eastern and Central North America*, writes:

> In the grand, high places of the southern mountains Hemlock soars above the rest of the forest, rising like a church spire—like numberless spires as far as the eye can see—through the blue haze that is the natural atmosphere of those ranges. Sometimes even its branches reach out like arms above the crowns of the other trees. But though the Hemlock's top may rejoice in the boldest sun and brave any storm, the tree unfailingly has its roots down in deep, cool, perpetually moist earth. And no more light and heat than a glancing sunbeam ever penetrates through the somber shade of its boughs to the forest floor.[1]

I had no hesitation in choosing which tree to name as my favorite tree on that long-ago day. I had already spent plenty of time in the woods with my nature-loving parents. It took me a long time to develop the patience that they had for bird-watching, but I was always up for a hike in the woods, particularly in the state and national parks near our home in the central Appalachians. When asked to describe one of my earliest memories of nature, I often choose the rhododendron tunnels that so impressed me as a child. I adored hiking along a path overhung by sweeping rhododendron branches; I still do. And in my mind, rhododendrons and hemlocks are inextricably intertwined. The classic scene of a hemlock cove along an Appalachian stream usually has rhododendrons in it somewhere too. Of course it's best when the rhododendrons are blooming, but I think that what I liked about the rhodos and hemlocks when I was young was that they were green even in the winter. Again, Peattie:

> Besides shade, the Hemlock loves rocks; it likes to straddle them with its ruddy roots, to crack them with its growing, to rub its knees against a great boulder. The north sides of hills, the sides of mountains facing the rain-bearing winds, exactly suits it. Unlike the Tamarack, it seems never to grow on level land if it can find an incline. It loves to lave its roots in white water—rushing streams and waterfalls; it despises slow water, warm and muddy, and so avoids the Mississippi valley and all its work.[2]

I was twenty-four when I first visited the California redwoods, during a cross-country road trip with my boyfriend. I was smitten with the redwoods, of course, but I also smugly decided that they weren't really any more impressive than my precious hemlocks. Both trees shared the same stateliness and grace, their delicate needles collecting the scant light in the canopy and understory. It pleased me to entertain the idea that eastern hemlocks are like redwoods. Hemlocks are the magical and mystical old growth of the eastern forests, much like redwoods are to western ones.

Approaching such a noble tree, you think it dark, almost black, because the needles on the upper side are indeed a deep blue-green. Yet when you lunch on the rock that is almost sure to be found at its feet, or you settle your back into the buttresses of the bole and look up under the boughs, their shade seems silvery, since the under side of each needle is whitened by two lines. Soon even talk of the tree itself is silenced by it, and you fall to listening. When the wind lifts up the Hemlock's voice, it is no roaring like the Pine's, no keening like the Spruce's. The Hemlock whistles softly to itself. It raises its long, limber boughs and lets them drop again with a sigh, not sorrowful, but letting fall tranquility upon us.[3]

After graduating from college on the East Coast, I followed my boyfriend to Alaska, where we lived for two years. We returned east long enough to thru-hike the Appalachian Trail together and for me to earn an MA in earth literacy. After this brief period of reconnecting with the eastern forests, we went back to Alaska for another seven years. I thoroughly enjoyed my time there exploring real wilderness and native cultures while earning a PhD in sustainability education. But as each year went by, I yearned more and more for the Appalachian mountains and forests, the place that I realized would always be home for me. I turned thirty while living in Fairbanks, midway through my doctoral studies. For my birthday present to myself, I made an appointment with a tattoo artist; I thought I had waited long enough to make sure that it wasn't just youthful impulse prompting me. Besides, I had finally figured out what image I wanted to permanently ink on my body—a hemlock branch.

I told the man on the phone that I wanted an arm band and briefly described what I had in mind, then showed up at the tattoo parlor a few days later with several photos and field guides. He sketched an image of what he envisioned on my arm, describing his idea of a watercolor on my skin, and I gave him the green light. For several hours, I sat in an almost meditative state, listening to Tom Waits's gravelly voice on the stereo and feeling the hum of the needles on my skin. Hours later, I emerged with exactly my mental image manifested on my upper arm, a delicate wreath of hemlock. I tattooed myself with a symbol of my loyalty to my beloved Appalachian forest home.

> The very opposite of a pioneer species, with its light-sensitive, drought-fearing seedlings, Hemlock must wait until other trees have created a forest. When the ground has become strewn with centuries of leaf mold, and the shade so dense that other trees' own seedlings cannot compete with their parents, the Hemlock moves in. Conditions on the forest floor are then more favorable for it than for any other tree. Painfully slow though the Hemlock's growth is, it will inevitably make its way above the neighbors. One by one they are eliminated until at last only the shade-loving Beech can keep company with Hemlock. They associate together gladly, shaggy bole contrasted with paper-smooth one; somber, motionless needles with light and flickering blades; strength with grace. The hemlock has then reached what ecologists call the climax stage—that is, a vegetational group which cannot be invaded or displaced by others unless axe or fire violently intervene, or an actual change of climate in the course of geologic ages.[4]

Now we can add invasive species to Peattie's list. In the years since we had moved to Alaska, the hemlock wooly adelgid had declared all-out war on my trees. My tattoo has also become a badge of solidarity with the now embattled tree. The adelgid is an aphid-like insect from Asia that makes a white, wooly nest on the undersides of hemlock twigs and then sucks the sap from the tree, killing it in as quickly as a year. There are no native predators and the hemlocks have no natural defenses.

We returned east to live in the Shenandoah Valley of western Virginia two years ago. We rented a cabin on a creek, a tributary of the James River, and it seemed a sign of welcome to me that down the lane along the creek was a large, healthy hemlock. But I have spent many hours hiking in the Blue Ridge Mountains, witnessing and mourning the loss of ancient stands of hemlocks to the adelgid. A hemlock cove in a sheltered valley looks like a graveyard with the partial skeletons of the trees still standing, ghostly and gray.

To investigate the status of the hemlocks in the eastern woods, I recently visited ground zero of the adelgid invasion on large stands of hemlocks on public lands—Shenandoah National Park, a place that also happens to be especially meaningful to me. Shenandoah is the forested mountain park playground for many easterners, and many of us develop a relationship with it early on. My parents honeymooned there, and we took many vacations there as a family. Likewise, my husband cut his teeth as a backpacker on the hundreds of backcountry trail miles in the park. Our first date was a camping trip to Shenandoah. Three years later, we hiked through the park on our thru-hike of the Appalachian Trail, which traverses the long, narrow park on a north-south axis, paralleling the scenic Skyline Drive.

One of the most popular spots in the park was a stand of old-growth hemlock known as Limberlost, the home of dozens of 350-year-old trees. Easily accessible by a short, well-maintained trail, Limberlost was as magical as its name suggests. This was the place to go to experience the majesty of old-growth hemlocks in the way so eloquently described by Peattie. Entering Limberlost was like entering a different world, like going through the back of the enchanted closet into Narnia. Limberlost was one of the first stands of old-growth hemlock to fall to the adelgid.

I had been dreading going back to Limberlost. I knew I needed and wanted to, but the time had to be right. I had to be prepared. So I arranged a solo trip for myself in early June and booked a room for two nights at Skyland, the lodge closest to Limberlost. I also made an appointment to visit with the park's forest pest manager, who is in charge of implementing forest management plans that address things like invasive species. He brought me up to date on the status of the hemlocks and the adelgid in the park and shared what he knew about the battle against the adelgid throughout the East. I also wanted to ask him for advice about how to treat the hemlock down the creek from our cabin. In the year and a half since I had moved there, I started noticing the tell-tale wooly white patches on the undersides of the leaves. It clearly had an adelgid infestation.

The adelgid first showed up in the United States in the 1950s in Richmond, Virginia, probably arriving from Asia on a shipment of lumber.

But it didn't reach the park until 1988. By the mid-1990s, the majority of hemlocks in the park were infested with the adelgid. Shenandoah quickly became the testing ground for public forest managers who were trying to figure out how to deal with this new invasive. They began aerial spraying of the hemlocks with insecticidal soaps. This method had limited success.

The summers of 2000 and 2001 both experienced significant droughts. By the end of 2001, the drought-stressed hemlocks at Limberlost had succumbed completely to the adelgid. By 2005, a new chemical control method had been developed, which involved injecting an insecticide called imidacloprid into the ground around the base of the tree. The tree takes up the poison through its roots into its branches, where the adelgid ingests it and dies. This method has been much more successful and is the control method that has been used in the park ever since. But it was too late for the Limberlost hemlocks as well as most of the other old growth in the park. Shenandoah has lost 90 to 95 percent of its hemlocks, including all of its old growth.

The current management goal is to save the last remaining hemlocks, primarily to conserve the genetic stock for possible regeneration in the future. Unfortunately, trees within forty feet of water cannot be treated with imidacloprid because of the danger to aquatic insects. This is, of course, ironic because hemlocks love to grow next to running water. One of the most serious ecological effects of hemlock decline is the rise in stream temperatures from the lack of year-round shade formerly provided by hemlocks. Native trout prefer cooler temperatures in their mountain streams, so this is one of the primary concerns of forest ecologists.

After a two-hour drive, I arrived in the park on a windy Thursday afternoon. The weather was perfect, sunny and glorious. I felt the release of tension that accompanies most visitors to this forested mountain retreat, the reason we all come—to escape the daily cares of life in our homes in the valleys or cities below. I checked into the lodge, thrilled that I was given a room in one of the oldest cabins at the site, built by a private individual at Skyland Resort before the area became a park. About an hour after my arrival, not yet ready to visit Limberlost, I instead took advantage of a ranger-led tour to visit Massanutten Lodge, the former home of another resort resident, located just behind my cabin. Massanutten does not have rooms for rent; it has been restored as a museum to appear as it did when its original owner lived here in the 1920s. This fascinating woman named Addie Nairn was a divorcée who bought a piece of property at Skyland to build her own mountain retreat. Within two years, she married the manager and visionary behind the resort, George Pollock, who played a key role in turning the area into a national park a few years later. I was intrigued by Addie, especially when we entered her living room where she entertained guests with intellectual conversations and good music. Then the biggest surprise of all—Addie Nairn Pollock was responsible for Limberlost. As the story goes, she paid a thousand dollars to save one hundred old-growth trees from being felled for their commercial value as pulpwood:

> Where [hemlock] grows, it has long served the mountain people. They learned from Indians long ago that the high tannin content of the bark made it a valuable curative for burns and sores. More, the earliest settlers were quick to find that its bark could be used for tanning leather, and for two hundred years and more they stripped the trees in the most wasteful manner; only the broad thick bark of the lower trunks was taken, the rest unutilized. The peeled logs were left in the forest to rot, though the old-time lumbermen sometimes had a use for "Hemlock peelers" in driving Pine logs down river to the mill, since the slippery naked logs helped to ease along the Pine. Still in the southern Appalachians the bark is used as a brown dye for wool, but to leather it gives a red tone, and serves in immense quantities for tanning. Today, however, its chief use is for the making of pulp, especially in Michigan and Wisconsin. But not in newsprint and cheap wrapping paper does Hemlock serve us best, but rather rooted in its tranquil, age-old stations.[5]

The next morning, accompanied by the spirit of Addie, I arose at six and set off on foot for Limberlost, just a mile away from my cabin and Addie's old retreat at Massanutten. Addie's one hundred old-growth trees at Limberlost actually composed a relatively small stand at the far end of a one-mile loop trail. When I saw the first stands of small dead hemlocks along the stream on the way there, I wasn't manufacturing my emotional response. Bracing myself for the sight of the ghostly snags, I rounded a corner and searched in vain for the graveyard vision that I had seen in so many other places already. But it wasn't there. As I passed one stump after another, it slowly dawned on me that the largest trees had been cut down. The gray trunks were stretched on the ground rather than into the sky. But even the prostrate trees were difficult to see, as they were being overtaken by bushy, young saplings. What I was seeing instead of a graveyard was a regenerating forest in a very early successional stage, dominated by pioneer species such as black birch. The types of birds I saw confirmed the change in the forest over the last ten years. No tiny kinglets were twittering high up in the hemlock branches but rather catbirds and towhees and various species of warblers that prefer open, scrubby areas. It was a struggle to remember the way the forest had looked, with the dark hemlock canopies spreading above rather than the gaping holes left by the hemlocks among middle-aged oaks. The place appeared almost sanitized. Park biologist Rolf Gubler confirmed when I met with him later in the day that the large hemlocks had been felled in 2003 upon the recommendation of the park's legal counsel. So Limberlost has become an unintentional experiment in forest regeneration, with the controls provided by other dead stands that haven't been felled. This fate seems somehow fitting, although I would have preferred the cathartic release I was craving from witnessing the Limberlost matriarchs still standing in their ancient homes.

What would Addie think? Fifty years after her death, her hemlocks were probably the only trees remaining in the park that were growing when she lived there. Most of the forests in Shenandoah are actually quite young; much of the land was under cultivation or had been logged for other purposes in the early 1900s. During Addie's lifetime, the forests experienced the devastating loss of the American chestnut to the chestnut blight, another invasive alien species. Perhaps this loss is part of what prompted her to save the old growth at Limberlost. Or maybe she just loved the trees for their majesty and beauty or their important role in the ecosystem, though that wasn't a word that Addie and her circle of intellectuals would have known at that time. Or maybe she was motivated to preserve the trees as her legacy; she had no children. How would she feel to know that her bequest to future generations succumbed to yet another accident of human interference? She saved her trees from the saw, but an unintentional side effect of the logging industry took them anyway.

And so I am left struggling to reconcile the uneasy relationship between humans and our fellow species. This triad represented by me, the hemlock, and the adelgid repeats itself ad infinitum around the globe. I mourn the loss of the hemlocks, but is my emotional response justifiable rationally? My scientific training prompts me to articulate logical reasons for various policy options regarding how we should deal with invasives. But logically, aren't invasive species simply a form of global environmental change? And since we humans are a part of nature, what's the problem with our inadvertent contribution to this form of change? This kind of reasoning about all sorts of environmental problems frequently leads me to the framework of sustainability, which simply concerns how we need to manage our interactions with the global environment to sustain our own human species. But this interpretation feels uncomfortable as well, as the links between physical human health and the hemlocks may be too weak to make a strong argument that we need hemlocks for our own sustainability. Am I prepared to sacrifice the hemlocks for my own species, as we already have with so many other extinct species? And anyway, isn't it arrogant to think that my species is more important than any others on the planet? These become ethical and spiritual questions that may not have logical answers. I spiral through intellectual circles, certain of very little but eager to right environmental wrongs committed by my species.

A few days ago, my husband and I walked down the lane to the hemlock on our creek, armed with a rake, shovel and bucket, and a large jug of milky-white insecticide. After quite a struggle to figure out where to buy the chemical in a large enough quantity and concentration to make amateur application reasonable, we were finally committed to treating our hemlock. I mixed the toxic stuff in the bucket with some creek water while my husband cleared an area around the base of the tree and dug eight small holes, discovering a very large, orange, black-spotted salamander in the duff. He carefully moved it aside, but we both worried about the effects of this nasty poison on all the soil critters that would become collateral damage in the battle against the adelgid. I shoved aside my misgivings, reassuring myself that our tree was the recommended forty feet from running water and we were doing everything we could to minimize our negative impacts, that the possible salvation of this one hemlock was worth the risks. I felt not only Addie looking over my shoulder, encouraging me, but also the young girl from church camp who innocently declared hemlock to be her favorite tree.

NOTES

1. Donald Culross Peattie, *A Natural History of Trees of Eastern and Central North America* (Boston: Houghton Mifflin Company, 1986), 40.
2. Peattie, *Natural History*, 40.
3. Peattie, *Natural History*, 41.
4. Peattie, *Natural History*, 40.
5. Peattie, *Natural History*, 40–41.

Hear Rocks Sing. That Is a Sign

Jeanne Larsen

———————

for the *great stalactite organ* in Luray Caverns on the long
road north. Dashboard Thai monks chant
this body of mine and I see 2, 3, 5 deer, come

the mountains, *a bag of skin*, dead on shoulder, *filled*

once *with bile, pus,* corpuscles, *fat,* synovial fluid,
piss, and *sweat,* their molecules scattered by whirling

petrochemical rings. I dodge a flayed windshield
-bound retread; the monks *drone this world*
is swept away. Around me weaving *this body will*

change, drivers cut *entirely* close, miss on near miss, a sneeze
from extinction: angry one gathering mental steel

wool, sleepy one gripping 19th wheel, or his phone. *Make*
your whole the tremulous speakers say, *body* [new CD
uncoils] *a questioning.* Black beat-up Ford *an inquiry*

passes. Rear window: 2 human *what is this* skulls, plaster
or children, *great matter,* mouths loose, [this is Shugen, young

sensei] crooning. Meal break. From diner's next booth,
kvetching, joking, ash-haired [in my cranium, still
Shugen speaks on what Wu-men said *of life and death*] man

rises. Stiff legs. 1 fake. Bill paid, I'm rolling again. The flesh
of the ridge is *ask* stripped stark, *with your 84,000* road-cuts

pores revealing old seas. Hours go. Hillside graveyard
boxwoods, clipped, spell out *PRAY FOR US*, one more
imperative. Again, Shugen's resonance, *the question*

and tires' bass line *is medicine.* The suffering and dying *ask*

with your bones are medicine—*your 300* calcareous
and 60 marrow-filled *bones*: how they intone. I undo,
1-handed, another case. Swerve way wide. Recover.

Home Farm

Julia Spicher Kasdorf

————————

The year I moved back to where I was born, 2000,
one clear afternoon driving up Route 655 toward
Great Aunt Twila at the rest home, a detour turned me

toward Jack's Mountain. Trying to get back to my road
I got turned again, so I circled in on the home from behind,
and there, across the way: thick smoke, fire trucks,

hoses on the berm at my uncle's farm—no,
the cousins have it now, Keith and Kent—where I spent
summer afternoons as a kid pushing a feed cart: *shush, shush,*

surge of electric milkers, my wood-handled scoop
trailed feed under the Holsteins' slimy noses. A spring
whisk mixed the formula for calves that sucked

from a rubber-nippled bucket, then sucked my thumb
with raspy tongues. Paste-eyed kittens lapped milk
from a basin set on sparkling barn snow in the center

of the cleanest stable in Mifflin county. *Wish, wish* thrusted
the fly spray's wand. Cousins in home-sewn skirts won
4-H ribbons for blue-blooded heifers. We scaled walls

of gold straw in the haymow. Sun slanted through dust
in the granary like the oiled light in old Dutch paintings.
"I remember when the first barn burned in '47," Twila said,

"full of hay, flames so high folks watched it blaze all night,
up and down the Valley." Here's that story: electric spark
at milking time and Grandpa, my teenaged dad and Uncle Dave

dragged out half the bawling herd before the joists come down.
The barn lost, reeking of burnt beef, firemen soaked the house.
All winter men dragged logs from the mountain to rebuild.

But in the new millennium, barns are steel; the milking parlor,
a sunken pit like the place you get your oil changed, the milkhouse
an office for the farmer's desk and computer. And cows,

their tails lopped off like boxers, lounge in long sheds, eat,
chew, lactate, then, roused by gentle Spanish-speaking men,
stroll to the milkers. Their hooves never touch grass.

Professors calibrate their feed, and to raise enough corn and beans
Keith and Kent rent fields our grandpa once tenant-farmed.
Land-o-Lakes takes fifteen tons of milk a day, and the manure

from 400 slides into a covered pit, warm as a cow's gut,
where it digests with plate scraps hauled in from restaurants
to make methane, to generate electricity to run the home place

and a few others, leftovers sold back to the grid. Liquid waste
fertilizes the crops, and solids get dried for bedding.
When milk production goes up, our power goes down, Keith laughs,

we teeter between milk and manure. Barn fire and a plan
hatched by brains in Berkeley transformed this old farm
into a place I can't understand, so I spin myths of thwarted

intentions, past disasters, in which it all turns out fine,
while upstate or west of here—places where milk checks
couldn't cover the cost of gas, tractors, diesel, fertilizer—

in fallow fields and dim hemlock forests, diamond-studded
drill bits bore through the earth and split black shale
with grit and chemicals to flush out precious *what*?

Methane, which these lazy cows just make
without much thought, the same way they make milk.

Uprooted

Jessica Cory

"Jess, this is your grandpa," my father said, the words catching in his throat.

Grandpa. As someone who had lived nearly eighteen years without one (my mother was an orphan), the word conjured up many images. I had long envisioned musty-smelling old men doling out Werther's Originals from their cardigan pockets during the holidays. Men who sat in the Crispie Creme donut shop, sipping black coffee and recounting their days in Korea. Or playing checkers with other potbellied, aging men, each awaiting his turn in the barber's chair. But those images didn't mesh well with the spry seventy-something man before me who donned a short-sleeve plaid button-up across his broad chest and thick khaki work pants covering long legs, his head crowned by a gray crew cut.

As we entered his home, careful to stay on the path laid out by the heavy-duty vinyl carpet protector that guarded the ecru Berber from dirty soles, I noticed an absence. I expected his home to look like my grandmother's had—full of breakable collectibles and family photos. But as I sat on the floral sofa glancing at the walls, I found them largely bare, save a framed Monet print and the botanical wallpaper. Not a family photo in sight. Perhaps no one had given him any. Perhaps they had and he didn't care.

I drank the ice water I was handed and stared to my right out the picture window to the landscape beyond. Trails wound through the property, beneath arbors, past water features, accented by railroad-tie steps, all flanked by hostas and more wildflowers than I could ever hope to name. Countless bulbs he had spent thousands of hours placing gently in the earth. Trails he had built and maintained by hand. By himself. Apparently, my grandfather had taken to farming these decorative beauties instead of fruits and vegetables, though I'll likely never know when or why.

My father's childhood and adolescence were spent in southeastern Ohio, running several family fruit stands. Tomatoes, potatoes, green beans, berries . . . my grandfather had quite the green thumb, which ran in the family. His people, my people, I suppose, had settled in the area shortly after the Revolutionary War and farmed ever since. Then, when my dad was thirteen, his mother, tired of being a farmer's wife and with big dreams of striking it rich in the city, gathered her brood and moved an hour north. Like many Appalachians in the early 1960s and decades prior, she felt that working in a lightbulb factory or plastics plant was a far more reliable way to eke out a living than farming. Plus, she'd surely meet a man working in those places who'd provide her and the kids with a stable income. With no outlined visitation schedule or custody agreement, not to mention the distance and means to transport six kids, my dad never saw his father again until his sister encouraged him to pay his old man a visit, when Dad was nearly fifty. I imagine now that being kept apart for many years created a chasm of silence that seemed impossible to bridge.

What Grandma may not have accounted for was that she was creating a chasm between her children and the land where their people labored as well. Neither my father nor any of his siblings ever took up farming. Instead, they worked on the railroad, in manufacturing and distribution centers, as secretaries, or as clerks at the local IGA. The closest any of them came to land-based living was my uncle Bruce, who left home at sixteen to become a horse trader. They chose jobs that paid them enough to get by, but that also required dependence on grocery stores and their employers' willingness to keep them around.

This story of my family's flight from farming is hardly unique. In fact, the decline in farming has only worsened with additional generations. In 1920, seven years before my grandfather was born, just over 30 percent of the labor force, nearly thirty-two million people, were farmers. By 1950, three years before my father was born, the numbers dropped to just over twenty-five million farmers, only 12 percent of the labor force. The early eighties painted a bleaker picture, with only seven million folks identifying as farmers, about 3 percent of the population, and the last investigation into these demographics, in 2012, showed just over three million farmers, or 1 percent of the total US population.[1]

Despite these grim demographics, I have noticed that many vendors at the local Haywood County farmer's market in western North Carolina are under forty. Some were born into the family farm business, but others chose this life because it aided their personal philosophies of self-reliance and sustainability. That said, it ain't easy.

At the Chillicothe farmer's market, held in the DMV parking lot just 1.2 miles from Cory's Wildflower Gardens, my father spends his Saturday mornings playing guitar with his friends in a local folk music society. They play for donations that are then used to fund music programs in nearby schools. Fifteen feet away, his cousin Joe and wife Terri do their Saturday morning hustle, selling onions, garlic, cherry tomatoes, and green beans in the midsummer sun beneath the sign that proclaims, "Cory Farms. 200 Years. Oldest Operating Farm in Ross County." Later in the season, they'll have corn, squash, pumpkins, and jam. And winter, when the ground is resting? They make wreaths, gift baskets, Christmas decorations, and participate in shop-local events. Their Facebook page gives their address and even displays Terri's phone number, directing potential customers to text her with any questions. An entire internet full of people having immediate and easy access to one's cell phone number and address? What other job would require such a breach of privacy?

My grandfather, though, doesn't have to deal with quite so much madness. After sixty-six years of "raising and selling plants," according to his ill-kept website, the customers come to him, sometimes from as far away as Arizona and Florida. He has hybridized a few wildflowers himself and is the only one to turn to should a customer desire one of those strains. He doesn't accept orders or ship. He doesn't take credit cards. This is a man who has learned to live by what the ground gives him. Even if he's no longer growing food to directly sustain himself and his family, his sustenance is directly tied to what the land provides.

And I must say that he inspired in my dad a love of growing things. During my early childhood, we grew tomatoes in our small townhouse backyard garden plot. Then the neighbors smashed them. Another year I wanted to grow my own pumpkin for Halloween and my father obliged. The neighbors either stole or smashed the pumpkins too. Realizing the area wasn't green-thumb friendly and was beginning to thrive with crime (after all, it may start with smashing tomatoes and stealing pumpkins, but where does it end?), we relocated back to the foothills of my parents' youth and tried our hands at another garden a few years later. After my constant sprinkling of Sevin dust and my mom's persistent weeding, our tomatoes, squash, and green beans thrived. My garden help, however, came to an abrupt halt, as I quickly moved away to finish college.

College seems to be both a way out of and, for some, a way into farming. My grandfather never finished high school, let alone college, and began farming shortly after he returned from a brief stint in the Coast Guard. However, many colleges have programs in agriculture and even some community colleges offer courses in horticulture or animal husbandry. Studying English, though, I never took any of these courses. Instead, I found a desire to farm by reading a mixture of dystopian literature that made me fear reliance on any government or corporate system and literature on the environment, which encouraged a more sustainable future.

The problem of discovering a desire to farm without any formal schooling and a generational farming gap, however, is quite a dilemma. Not everyone has a grandfather who creates his own hybrids or a great aunt who's a canning fanatic. And even if these folks are part of our families, often we're so disconnected that their advice and expertise ages with them, leaving us resourceless. Yes, we have the internet. But what if the information isn't reliable? Maybe we could learn from books, but how do we know which ones are best? In my case, perhaps I could phone my grandfather, pick his catalog of a brain about how to start farming or where he thinks it's headed with my generation. This task might be easy enough—after all, his home phone number is on his website, just like Terri's. But having only met him briefly, I'm not sure he'd remember who I am. He probably hates talking on the phone for all I know. And spending two-thirds of a fifteen-minute phone call explaining the genealogy so he doesn't mistake me for a telemarketer isn't exactly encouraging. For that matter, he may be wintering in Florida, as I've heard that's what many other grandfathers do.

Or maybe I will do it. Pick up the phone, hands slick as dew-damp hosta leaves, and utter that foreign word, *Grandpa*.

NOTES

1. Associated Press. "Farming Population Lowest Since 1850's," *New York Times*, July 20, 1988, http://www.nytimes.com/1988/07/20/us/farm-population-lowest-since-1850-s.html; National Institute of Food and Agriculture, "Growing a Nation: A Story of American Agriculture," *Agriculture in the Classroom*, 2014, https://www.agclassroom.org/gan/timeline/farmers_land.htm#top.

Thanksgiving

John Lane

———————

The Pre-Socratic Greeks accepted all oracle bubbling
of springs and the authority of lightning creasing
a great tree. If the world were close to language,
it spoke as well through what is random or mundane.

I love the stories my friends tell: a forest ranger
in the Virginia mountains struck by lightning
twenty-eight times, a park service record, swears
he can feel the bolt coming before it hits, before
the clouds build. He calls it "intuition," and a fit gift
for someone who spends so much time in pagan woods.
The world has no ear for story, preferring theory now:
clear days, and the word lost in the blue skies
of signifier, signified. A Thanksgiving day outside
Charlottesville, within the landscape Thomas Jefferson
once invented according to his reason, the Rotunda's
classic lines project outward over farm fields, yeoman farmers,
predictable as logarithms. Another world spoke from an oracle
stream on Victor's farm, among the barns he'd built, straight
around a spring box tree lightning tried to bring down.

Victor tells his orphic stories too: how he tied a come-along
to the split trunk of a father oak and cranked it back together,
wrapping chains to hold the split. It gave me hope, the way
those true pilgrims must have felt that morning, the relish open,
and the divining birds dressed, cooked over a hot sustaining
fire. But in this age, when the world has dropped away
from language: it's the stories I love listening for, a voice
down to earth again, a living tree shattered from above.

Pillars of Carbon: National Forests and the Great Appalachian Carbon Commons

Chris Bolgiano

Dashes of red paint on occasional trees were easy to miss, and we did. We crossed the border unwittingly, my young husband and I, lost in the woods on Cross Mountain in western Virginia. Part of the 1970s "Going Back to the Land" movement that brought thousands of young people into rural Appalachia, we stumbled cluelessly through the seemingly endless hundred-acre woodlot we were about to buy. The back border joined the million-plus acres of the George Washington National Forest (GWNF), the largest block of public land in the East. Soon enough, I learned to recognize the line between private and public land, between mine and ours. Over time, I've also come to see it as a boundary between capitalism and community, primeval and postmodern, history and hope.

Archives, books, and photos recall the history that eventually resulted in that boundary. The woods remember too. On our southernmost ridge, I trip over stumps stripped down by time to slivers but still blunt on top where saws cut. Whittle off a chip with a pocket knife and a whiff of Christmas tree wafts by. In the 1870s and 1880s, Shenandoah Valley farmers sought out yellow pines in the surrounding mountains to replace the thousands of barns and mills burned by Gen. Philip Sheridan in his scorched earth campaign through the valley in 1864.

On one of our slopes, a remnant of handmade fence sags down to the creek, its slats axed from rot-resistant American chestnut wood and twined together with heavy wire. An elderly friend told us years ago it was a pig fence. By the end of the 1800s, counties were passing laws requiring farmers to fence in their livestock, and American chestnut trees hadn't yet died off by the billions from an imported blight. Before that, it was common practice to let livestock forage for chestnuts and acorns across mountainsides, without fences, regardless of ownership. Hunters roamed widely too, for meat and pelts, as did women foraging for plant foods, and children carefully gathering prickly chestnut burrs.

Chestnut oaks, a different species from the American chestnut but with similar leaves, are now one of the more common species in the southern Appalachians. Most are multiple-stemmed, with as many as eight mature trees ringing one enormous mother stump. Chestnut oak bark has a high level of tannic acid, which was leached out and used to tan leather. Until tree bark was replaced by synthetic chemicals in the 1940s, millions of tons of chestnut oak bark were peeled every spring just as the sap started to run and the bark became pliable. The naked logs were usually left to rot in the woods.

Unlike many other species, chestnut oaks sprout from stumps, so they proliferated instead of disappearing from the forest. Because of the dearth of deer in the decades before state wildlife agencies began regulating hunting, the sprouts were spared from grazing. Sometimes a hole rots out in the center of the stump and fills with rain, hosting whole ecosystems of tiny creatures. Or instead, some stumps grow cushions of moss, giving hunters like my husband a comfortable seat behind the cover of the sibling trees to wait for deer. Reintroduced after the panthers and wolves that kept their numbers in check were extirpated, deer have recovered beyond the capacity of the forest to feed them. Browse lines are visible on all sides of Cross Mountain, and saplings meant for the next generation are bitten off. The woods must miss panthers in particular, whose evolution was sustained by venison. Only ghost panthers haunt the woods today.

A few miles from Cross Mountain stand several massive stone furnaces, testimony to the mining and smelting of iron ore that began at least by the 1750s. Furnaces were fueled by charcoal, made by clear-cutting surrounding forest, piling the logs into a heap, and raking up soil to dump on top to keep the fire smoldering instead of burning. Some of those charcoal hearths still leave a traceable outline. A typical furnace burned about 150 acres of trees every year.

But it was a big iron boomer, or winch, in our neighbor's woods, that offered the defining clue to the dark history of the woods. Dating probably from the early to mid-1900s, it's made from separate parts ingeniously welded together to haul timbers from down in the hollows up to the ridge. Deep ruts, not quite smothered by decades of fallen leaves, reveal the old road where a horse- or oxen-pulled cart or, later, a truck carried logs to the nearest mill or railroad depot.

By 1900, railroads were creeping up almost every hollow wide enough to accommodate narrow-gauge tracks. The previous impact of individual mountaineers on the forest—pulling out a few trees with oxen, burning patches of woods to kill ticks and encourage berries, even widespread harvesting of chestnut oak bark—had been relatively light. Virgin timber still covered the higher slopes and ridges.

And what timber it was. The primeval trees of the southern Appalachians dwarfed the loggers who cut them and even the trains that carried away the logs. Timber from a single tree sometimes filled multiple cars. In a half-century frenzy of logging from 1880 to 1930, the state of West Virginia went from being almost entirely forested to almost entirely deforested. The story was much the same down the entire southern Appalachian mountain chain to Georgia. It's estimated that less than 1 percent of the original forest survived. Fortunes were made by hundreds of timber companies, mostly owned by distant businessmen. As in the coal counties, little of that prosperity trickled down to mountain people. And they lost their way of life, too, when the forest was cut, because they depended on it for so many life-sustaining products.

Much of the timbering equipment of the time was steam powered by wood or coal and threw flaming embers out into the treetops and limbs left behind on the ground. Many large, destructive fires have been recorded throughout the mountains during the logging boom. The scars remain on Cross Mountain: charcoal rubs off on my fingertips from charred husks of trees burned a century ago. West Virginia historian Roy Clarkson described the land that became the Monongahela National Forest as "smoking sticks and bare stone."

The gravest consequence was the loss of countless tons of mountain topsoil that drowned in the Chesapeake Bay and Gulf of Mexico. Already by 1911, flooding in the lowlands, from lack of trees to hold mountainside soil, was ruining farms and fields with debris and carrying away entire towns. Congress responded to public pressure with the Weeks Act. This law authorized the Forest Service, then only six years old, to begin purchasing millions of acres of burning, eroding mountainsides from willing sellers, which at that time were largely timber companies that had exploited everything of value and no longer wanted to pay local property taxes.

Today, some six million acres of recovering woodlands in eight national forests cover the highest peaks and ridges of the southern Appalachian Mountains. These nearly contiguous national forests create something rarer than a verified panther sighting: a regional ecological core of forests that make conservation possible on a landscape scale. They also represent something virtually unique in history. By purchasing and repairing exploited forests, the Forest Service reversed the millennia-long global trend of privatization of the commons, followed by environmental degradation for private profit. In an irony of historical timing, the very destruction of the original forest has resulted today in an Appalachian commons that could save the region.

Magna Carta gets all the press, but the Forest Charter that came after it in 1217 also made political history. For the first time, it defined rights that dated back to the dimmest days of the Dark Ages across all of Europe: the use of forests by common people for foraging, hunting, and grazing livestock, regardless of ownership. These were the forest commons traditions that Appalachian settlers brought with them from Europe and adapted to the uniquely bountiful forests of the southern Appalachians. Those commons traditions are now settled firmly, in modern forms, onto the national forests.

To talk about a commons, though, is to invite dissonance. In 1968 an article titled "Tragedy of the Commons" by biologist Garrett Hardin in the prestigious journal *Science* gave the idea of the commons an enduringly bad reputation. In one of the most cited articles ever, he argued that commonly owned resources would inevitably be degraded due to rational selfishness as every herder added one more animal to take advantage of common grazing land. His admission, in his 1985 book *Filters Against Folley*, that his paper was extremely misleading and should have been titled "Tragedy of the *Unmanaged* Commons" is not nearly as well known.

Recognition of that one-word difference earned the 2009 Nobel Prize in Economics for the first woman ever to receive one, despite the fact that she wasn't even an economist. Elinor Ostrom, who died in 2012, was a professor of political science at Indiana University, given to loud clothes and, unheard of in economics, actual field work. Traipsing through shared forests in Nepal and mountain pastures in Switzerland and Japan, wading through irrigation systems in Spain and the Philippines and fisheries in Maine and Indonesia, she found that people who depend on commonly held resources could collaborate for sustainable use over centuries, even millennia.

Ostrom discovered that all successful commons have variations of several basic management principles. The way that national forests operate embody most of them. There are distinct boundaries, marked by dashes of red paint through the woods. Federal, state, and county governments provide essential services of regulating extractive uses, enforcing rules, and imposing sanctions on violators.

People who use the resources must also have a say in management decisions. In recent years, some district rangers have begun meeting with stakeholder groups, using roundtable conversations to reconcile the many, often contradictory, demands on the forest. The most formal mechanism, however, is the legal requirement that the Forest Service seek public response when it updates its land management plans every ten to fifteen years.

The GWNF plan came up for revision in 2010. A new f-word was just then entering our language that had nothing to do with sex but everything to do with exploitation. "Fracking" is short for hydraulic fracturing, a way to extract natural gas by drilling deeply down and sideways, then pumping down millions of gallons of water laced with sand, salt, and carcinogenic chemicals. Gas is forced up, along with contaminated wastewater, which is often radioactive.

Like other parts of the Allegheny Mountains, Cross Mountain is made of shale, a type of rock associated with natural gas. There was a gas lease on our property when we bought it, which soon expired. On our back border is a sulfurous spring in which I once found a pile of belly-up salamanders, sad evidence of gas in the ground. A neighbor up the road claims he can light his kitchen faucet with a match, but I've never actually seen him do it. Gas wells were drilled nearby in the 1920s and '30s, providing some local jobs and prosperity to the grandparents of the families living there now. What's left of those old wells is generally hidden behind a few planted trees.

The GWNF lies over the Marcellus shale play. When the routine updating of the GWNF plan began, the gas industry was already fracking West Virginia and Pennsylvania. CEOs of gas companies exerted unprecedented pressure on the Forest Service to facilitate fracking, even forcing a congressional hearing, something rarely if ever done previously for a national forest plan. Industry ads in newspapers extolled the jobs and cheap energy to come.

Most people around here had never heard of fracking. Through meetings at local schools, we learned that fracking was not your grandfather's gas drilling. I joined a group on a frack-finding weekend visit to Doddridge County, West Virginia, a drilling hot spot. We saw entire hills being leveled for more well pads, compressor stations, vent stations with shimmering waves of unknown emissions, and holding tanks with obvious leaks. We heard stories of illnesses, underweight babies, creeks contaminated or desiccated, first responders overwhelmed by accidents and reporters barred from reporting on them. We noticed the out-of-state license plates on vehicles of the many workers brought in by the company. Above the host house where we camped in the yard, a new well was being drilled. Two months later, it exploded, killing two workers. Corporate profits were once again fracking the forests and the people of Appalachia.

Rising from the heights of the GWNF are the headwaters of the

Potomac and the James Rivers, which ultimately supply drinking water to millions of people in Richmond and Washington, DC. Polluting these rivers at their source began to emerge as a focal point of alarm. Ordinary citizens, local governments, and municipal water managers downstream questioned whether private profits should be allowed to endanger a public resource. The industrialization of rural landscapes beloved by the people who lived in them, and many others who liked to visit, was not a popular idea. Some voices asked whether massive new development of a fossil fuel source was the best way to address the greenhouse gas problems being caused by fossil fuels.

The plan was delayed for several years as the Forest Service grappled with challenges to its authority and its mission. Finally, in 2014, the Forest Service released the final plan. It stopped oil and gas leasing altogether, for the next decade or so that the plan would be in effect.

A cloud of exhaled sighs of relief rose over the Shenandoah Valley. Several community groups joined to place a large, scenic ad in newspapers throughout western Virginia: "We thank the U.S. Forest Service . . . [and] Over 75,000 citizens . . . [and] Local, State and Federal Officials from Around the Region" who wrote against fracking. "Your Voices Were Heard!"

It was a triumph of the commons.

Two small streams seep from shallow hollows near the top of Cross Mountain and run down across my property. Each cascades in a series of rock-bottomed bowls into Reedy Run. Some of those rocks are inscribed with shells of sea creatures that lived three hundred million years ago, testaments to the indelible imprint of the past.

Reedy Run tumbles down a gap in Cross Mountain to join hundreds of other tributaries to the Shenandoah River, which empties into the Potomac River, which then empties into the watery commons of the Chesapeake Bay. And so on. The whole world is an unmanaged commons: not just fresh water, but also oceans, the atmosphere, and living space for the estimated one hundred million distinct life forms, most of them unknown and invisible in soil, which together make the world habitable. The most basic conditions for human life are produced only by natural systems.

Large swaths of unfragmented forests covering entire landscapes are particularly adept at performing a panoply of such services. Management of the Appalachian national forests offers the continuation not only of these ecosystem benefits but also of the hundreds of millions of dollars spent annually on recreation that sustains many rural communities like mine. National forests also provide the setting where age-old Appalachian traditions survive as private lands are increasingly fragmented and posted.

I don't hike on Cross Mountain, or in any national forest, during hunting seasons. Deer and bear hunting remain strong where I live, recorded with trophy photos and bulletin board entries at our local store, and with long, detailed stories over coffee. Three generations of one family have hunted deer from a particular stand on Cross Mountain. I learned this just last year, when I disrupted doe day by tramping around noisily near a frustrated but friendly descendant (I had miscalculated the date, for which I apologized).

Fishing, too, remains popular as a way to put supper on the table. I've relished many a meal by a neighbor who has fished the GWNF's stocked lakes and native trout streams all his life. He's also an expert on mushrooms and has tried more than once to teach me the difference between edible "brownies" and the poisonous brown mushrooms that look just like them. Ginseng, ramps, running cedar for holiday wreaths, medicinal herbs, ornamental ferns, and various other plant products attract foragers, old and young, with permits required for some uncommon species.

To such primeval products of the forest must be added one that the authors of the Forest Charter couldn't have imagined in the thirteenth century, but which is emerging as critical to the twenty-first: carbon sequestration.

Trees take in carbon dioxide, the major greenhouse gas, during photosynthesis and store, or sequester, carbon in wood, roots, and soil. Half of the heft of every tree is carbon. Trees are the single best technology yet discovered for carbon capture and storage, a process that scientists consider essential to combat the worst impacts of global climate change. Forests of the eastern United States play an especially important role in global climate. Most of the carbon already stored in forests across America, an amount equal to sixty-seven years' worth of the country's fossil fuel emissions, lies in eastern forests.

The Appalachian national forests are the largest, most contiguous body of publicly owned forests in the East. Whether they continue sucking in carbon dioxide, helping to stabilize the climate, or release it to add heat to the world depends on forest management.

Carbon forestry is a twenty-first-century science. In recent decades, field studies have reversed the previous belief that young trees sequester more carbon than mature trees. An international team of editors analyzed hundreds of global studies in the 2009 book *Old Growth Forests: Function, Fate, and Value* and concluded that "up to an age of 600 years, old-growth forests remain carbon sinks and exhibit the same carbon sink strength as younger developmental stages . . . [and] generally lock up more carbon than any other forest stage or alternative ecosystem." So few forests older than six hundred years remain on earth that further research is impossible.

There's a chestnut oak on the cusp of a Cross Mountain cliff that I can bushwhack down to from an old tanbark road we use as a trail. This one has a single trunk, having escaped the bark skinners because back then it was a scrawny, inaccessible sapling. Like most trees in the GWNF, it's about a century old, but hardly stately; my arms overlap to the wrists when I hug it. Even on less craggy sites, few of the white, black, red, and scarlet oaks, the mockernut and pignut hickories, the maples and birches and other tree species are much bigger. The extreme erosion and fires of that earlier era drastically reduced soil fertility. Roots and soil can hold half or more of a tree's total stored carbon. Forests regrowing on severely degraded soils need centuries of leaf fall and root growth to build up as much carbon as is stored in less disturbed soils.

The longer a tree lives, the more soil it creates and the more carbon it stores. Like most species of oaks, this chestnut oak could live for hundreds of years more. A red cedar in West Virginia has been documented at more than seven hundred years old. A forester's borer used to core a friend's sugar maple wasn't long enough to reach the center and only collected two hundred rings. In temperate, deciduous forests like these, maturing and old trees would naturally cover at least half of the landscape. Some grow slowly stouter, while others grow taller until they snag passing squalls and topple in high winds. Wind is the major natural disturbance that allows forests to renew themselves. Plant species that need sun to germinate sprout in these wind-throw gaps.

Over centuries, young forests gradually mature into the complex architecture of old growth: thick, deeply furrowed bark and large limbs; multiple layers of diverse vegetation from ground to canopy; expansive canopies that create a cooler, moister microclimate refuge against heat; large standing dead and downed trees; and, most of all, the vast underground weave of roots and the fungal threads that sheathe and nurture them, dubbed the "wood-wide web." These habitat niches are unavailable anywhere else. Hundreds of species of plants and animals are endangered, threatened, or declining in the GWNF alone, and most of them use old growth for some part of their life cycle.

For decades, I have seen history in that chestnut oak above the cliff, and resilience, and strength. Now I see a pillar of carbon, and a signpost to wisdom. The young Appalachian national forests are poised to become a reservoir of resistance to climate change, if managed to rebuild soil and stability in coming centuries. Carbon forestry means working with natural processes to avoid disruptions that cause a net loss of carbon. Trees can still be harvested, but at longer intervals, with low impact methods that avoid compacting soil, and preferably for the kind of high-quality, durable products that would show up as furniture in a twenty-second-century *Antiques Roadshow.*

Although the GWNF plan halted oil and gas leasing, it called for thousands of acres to be logged and prescribed burned every year, as do other national forest plans. Some foresters argue that the threat of drought from climate change demands even more logging and burning to reduce the fuel that might feed future forest fires. But some climate models predict more rain in the central Appalachians, and rate the oak-pine forests that cover much of the mountains as the forest type least vulnerable to climate change. Debates are ongoing, as other national forests approach the timeline for revision of land management plans.

Maybe the chestnut oak that now crowns the cliff will plummet down the flaking sheet of shale in one of the windstorms now becoming more violent, or in a future wildfire. The shards of old pine stumps on South Ridge will certainly disappear in a few more years, taking with them their perfume from the past. The pig fence is slouching toward oblivion under the weight of winter snows. The phrase "going back to the land" has a different meaning to me now, after decades of watching forest life recycle itself. Visible clues may fade, but only when trees grow ancient and soil grows deep will the national forests recover from history. Maybe then a panther might even crouch on that cliff, waiting for deer. The great Appalachian carbon commons offers redemption from the past, as well as defense of the future.

Man Talk

Gail Tyson

———

East Tennessee was a hard place to grow up. Sometimes there wasn't enough to eat.

—Ben K.

Ben hitches around a puddle, up our porch, hugs
me, greets the dog. Easing into a chair—
"You need to fill your potholes"—he argues
for crusher run—"packs down hard." Dick leans back:
"57's cleaner." Ben shakes his head.
"With crusher dust, the stones don't slide away."
Their voices rub like rock worn down by trucks,
relaxed with abrasion, with facts ground flat
like James McAdams's "stone pikes." I twist
my ring; Ben grins, "I like to rile him," slides
our conversation toward the chill damp:

"Crept in last night." Dick nods, "I lit our stove,
in case it turns off cold," and Ben admits
he can't get down, kneel long enough to light
his pilots. One hand paws his heart monitor,
one foot nudges our dog curled by his chair,

rough bluster pockmarked like a road exacting
maintenance. "I'll do that for you, Ben." Dick's
voice, soft as his flannel shirt, shelters all of us
as the wind picks up. Our neighbor
ducks his head, mutters thanks, leaves to call on
a friend too frail to take on bear season.

My evening walk takes me past the cabin
Ben built himself. He hails me, weathered hands
spread on the rail gaudy with antler pickets,
shushing Little Bit, Big Man, Clemmie, Twister,
the wailing dogs he dotes on:
"Dick made himself useful." "Bring home a bear
tomorrow and I wouldn't mind a shoulder"—
a city girl, I've learned some country ways.
"Suppose you want it smoked, too?" He's pleased,
a man still proud to rise at 4, don flame
orange, see that none of us goes hungry.

May Fourteenth

Wayne Caldwell

—————

The many years I've walked Pole Creek
Give me a right long view of things.
So I know it's hotter than it used to be
Stormier too, and you used to see
Them black-winged scarlet birds all summer.
No more. Redwings is scarce, and when's
The last time you seen a green snake?
Chestnuts—gone, hemlocks—dyin,
It's enough to make a strong man cry.
But still: within a day or two
One side or t'other of the Ides of May
Blinkin yellow flashlights start their twilight glow.
Happened yesterday, right on time,
Though ever year there's less that come.

I reckon the way this world's a-goin
When we run slap out of lightnin bugs
We'll have flat run out of hope.

Frog and Tadpole

Gail Tyson

———————

Rusted trucks clutter the filling station;
regulars stop inside for bait and daily specials,
most likely bologna on white bread wrapped in
wax paper. Frog's spotted hand rotates tattered
rags, trembles on dipsticks. Tadpole fusses
over his daddy's books;
high-octane worry flows, scalds his throat like
homemade moonshine. This full-service
confounds the rare stranger, the names—blue script
wavering on worn-soft shirts—jolt drivers
lost on their way from another era.
Two jaws work plugs of chew tobacco:
men of few words, out of time.

Protect

Forest Disturbance

Katie Fallon

Isabelle stands directly on top of the running buffalo clover (*Trifolium stoloniferum*), a federally endangered species. Her silver Nikes crush some of the three-leafed plants, while other sprouts tangle between her feet. The US Forest Service scientist leading our small group assures us that this clover *likes* disturbance—in fact, it requires disturbance to flourish—but we are nervous about obliging.[1]

Our group consists of a handful of undergraduate students and their instructors—Dr. Bill Peterjohn from West Virginia University's biology department and me from English. The course, Writing Appalachian Ecology, bridges the sciences and humanities by getting students out of the classroom and into the forest. In light of certain disturbing trends—Gallup, for example, reported in 2014 that only 36 percent of Americans believed that "global warming will pose a serious threat to their way of life during their lifetimes," and a 2015 Pew Research Center survey revealed that just 41 percent of the American public thought that climate change was harming people today—the National Science Foundation has recognized the need to improve dialogue between scientists and the public.[2] One purpose of our course is to address this chasm by training artful "translators"—that is, teaching students to write creatively about biology in the hopes that their fresh, metaphoric, reflective voices will sing the science to their readers.

Our field site, the Fernow Experimental Forest, "a 4,600-acre outdoor laboratory and classroom," was purchased by the federal government in 1915 for $5.50 an acre and established as a research forest in 1934. It lies within West Virginia's 919,000-acre Monongahela National Forest (or "Mon," as the locals call it). The Weeks Act of 1911, which authorized the federal government to purchase lands to protect headwater streams and watersheds of the eastern United States, made the establishment of the Mon and our other eastern national forests possible.[3] The Mon lies just to the west and north of Virginia's George Washington and Jefferson National Forests; in some spots, the forests share boundaries. These Appalachian forests—and their preservation—matter to all of us in the eastern United States, whether we realize it or not.

Water is life, and if you live east of the Mississippi River, chances are good that the water you drink originates deep in the mountains of Appalachia, perhaps even here in West Virginia's Fernow. Elklick Run, the creek that drains this part of the forest, tumbles into the Black Fork River in the town of Parsons, then merges with Shaver's Fork to form the Cheat, which flows north until it joins the Monongahela River in Point Marion, Pennsylvania. The Monongahela also flows north, and in Pittsburgh it merges with the Allegheny to form the mighty Ohio River, which eventually twists southward and west until it meets the Mississippi River in Cairo, Illinois, near that state's border with Kentucky and Missouri. The Mississippi, of course, flows south into the Gulf of Mexico near New Orleans.

Here, on a trail uphill from Elklick Run, it's easy to feel small. Towering tulip poplars, sugar maples, and red oaks crowd around us, reaching skyward, shading life along the path; in addition to the running buffalo clover, we find bee balm, jewelweed, and stinging nettle. May apple. Bloodroot. Joe-pye weed. Meadow rue. We bend closer to snails and pipevine swallowtail butterflies. From the canopy, songs of red-eyed vireos, black-throated green warblers, and scarlet tanagers float down to us. It seems enchanted, and to me, it's the most beautiful place on earth. Accepting our responsibility as voices—as translators, as advocates—of these headwater forests, we tread lightly, even where treading may be beneficial.

We hear the dogs before we hear the rumble of the engine. Sharp, soulful baying, like drawn-out yodels. The dusty white truck crawls up the gravel road and passes us, its driver nodding and passenger waving with just his fingertips, his forearm resting on the open window, a cigarette hanging from below his white mustache. In the pickup's bed, a larger silver cage holds at least four coonhounds; they stick their heads through portholes in the sides, long silken ears flopping, tongues lolling. Each dog wears a bulky radio collar. Bear-hunting dogs, Bill tells us, in training. Camping and campfires aren't permitted in the Fernow, but the forest is open to the public for hunting. Bear hunting with dogs isn't legal everywhere, but under certain circumstances it is in West Virginia. The dogs sniff out a black bear in hiding, rouse it, pursue it, and tree it. When the radio signal stops moving, the hunter finds the dogs and shoots the bear out of the tree. Sometimes, dogs are injured; a black bear here can weigh in excess of five hundred pounds.

No one knows for sure who first hunted this forest, but the Shawnee utilized the "big spring," a reliable water source that still runs in the Fernow today. Some of the first non-native settlers in the area were Henry Irons and his family; Irons's grave lies just off an old logging road among the silent trees. For early settlers, this forest provided clean water, food, and opportunities. In addition to wild game, hogs and cattle were turned loose to forage on the abundant fallen fruits of American chestnut trees. Timbering in this forest began in earnest in 1901, after the Civil War. Sawmills and lumber camps sprung up around nearby Parsons. Some of the timber was skidded down the mountain with horses and loaded onto train cars, while other felled trees whooshed down greased "slides," made from logs shaved into V shapes.[4]

Between 1901 and 1911, most of the forest in this part of West Virginia had been clear-cut, before the US Forest Service bought the first tract of what would become the Fernow in 1915. World War II put research in the Fernow on hold, but once the war ended, forestry studies began again, with investigations into timber management, watershed management, reforesting strip-mined land, rainfall intensity, and other areas. Today, while much of the forest has regrown, it's noticeably different from the one that was logged bare more than a hundred years ago. One change resonates perhaps more than any other: the mighty American chestnut, which made up about 25 percent of all Appalachian forests, is gone, victim of an Asian blight.

How will the forest change in the future? Global warming, disease, invasive animals and plants—it's possible to despair, even standing in the middle of what appears lush and "untouched," when in fact it's anything but.

The forest still provides—drinking water, food, recreation, a measure of solace. The truck rumbles past, a cloud of gravel dust in its wake. What must we look like to the bear hunters? We huddle around a bed of fiery bee balm, taking close-ups of hovering swallowtails with our iPhones, notebooks hugged to chests. We wave back tentatively.

"This is the Carthage of the Fernow," Bill says, smirking, stabbing the earth with his trekking pole. After a short hike down an old roadbed, we arrive at a bone yard. Standing dead trees stretch skeletal branches into the blue sky; other trees, living but withered, twist nearby. Bright tape encircles several trunks, marked as part of an ongoing study. In 2007, this patch of forest was sprayed with "drill pit fluid," one of the byproducts of hydraulic fracturing, or "fracking," a method used in natural gas drilling.[5] Like much of West Virginia, surface ownership and mineral ownership in the Fernow are two separate entities; while the US Forest Service owns and manages the surface, the minerals beneath the ground are privately held—and recently leased to a natural gas company.

I sit at the base of a red oak and lean my back against its wide trunk. The sun-warmed tree feels solid and strong between my shoulder blades, but tilting my head and looking up, I see no leaves on its gnarled branches. The oak, standing dead, has one of the thickest trunks in the vicinity and some of the tallest-reaching branches. I run my hand along the rough bark where the trunk meets the earth, where the oak's roots plunge into the forest floor. There, the rich soil that had nourished the tree for decades had suddenly turned to salt. And the tree pulled the salt into its heart.

Fracking requires a specific proprietary mixture of water, salt, sand, and chemicals. This liquid is pumped into the earth, cracking the shale and releasing the gas. Some of the mixture remains underground while some is pumped back out. This leftover fluid is often stored in plastic-lined holding ponds; sometimes, as in the case of the Fernow, it is "applied" to a section of the forest, legally. The high salinity of the fluid meant death for the trees. Carthage of the Fernow, indeed.

With the discovery of Marcellus shale, the natural gas industry is booming in many parts of Appalachia. In addition to gas and oil, it's well known that carbon-rich West Virginia has abundant reserves of coal. In 2011 we mined more coal than any state east of the Mississippi, which we exported to thirty-three US states and thirty foreign countries.[6] With our rich natural resources, West Virginia should be one of the wealthiest states in the nation; unfortunately, it's not. We consistently rank at the top of the lists we don't want to be on and at the bottom of the lists we do. Often, our economy ranks dead last.

Many of our rivers—where, again, much of the eastern United States' drinking water originates—run red and orange, choked with acidic drainage from abandoned coal mines. Other small waterways are destroyed outright by mountaintop removal, a form of large-scale surface mining that blows the tops off our ancient hills to expose thin coal seams. The resulting dirt and rock from the former mountaintop is dumped in adjacent valleys, filling in headwater streams. According to the US Environmental Protection Agency, "It is estimated that almost 2,000 miles of Appalachian headwater streams have been buried by mountaintop coal mining."[7]

Here, sitting at the base of dead tree in an otherwise verdant forest, these acts seem particularly villainous. I dig my fingers into the soil and feel it warm and dry beneath my nails. Bill stands a few feet away with a copy of a scientific paper in hand—"Effects of Development of a Natural Gas Well and Associated Pipeline on the Natural and Scientific Resources of the Fernow Experimental Forest." Our students mill around, stumbling through tangled nettle and blackberry bushes, as Bill begins to read aloud, slowly, each species of the tree that has died at this site, like a list of names at a memorial service: American beech. Red maple. Sassafras. Bill pauses after each name and gestures toward a particular dead or withered trunk. *Northern red oak.* He points to my tree. *Yellow poplar. Sweet birch. Chestnut oak. Cucumber tree. Fraser magnolia. Downy serviceberry. Sourwood.* The trees stand silently, their ghosts floating between the bare branches.

We enter a clearing at dusk, just as the sun dips below the blue-ridged horizon. We spread across the field, stooping to touch knee-high mullein in bloom and inspect the delicate whites of Queen Anne's lace. Someone finds the lower jawbone of a white-tailed deer, its bottom teeth grinning in the fading light. A wood thrush begins to sing his ethereal song as one by one my students lower themselves onto the grass, notebooks in hand. The green trees turn black. Insects hum as the thrush sings on.

In a blasphemous moment, I snap a picture of the deer jaw with my phone and text it to my friend Todd Katzner, a wildlife biologist who studies the migratory patterns of eastern golden eagles; the large, uncommon birds breed in Canada but spend the winters in central Appalachia, from West Virginia to western North Carolina and perhaps beyond. Todd organized a network of camera traps—motion-sensing cameras set on posts or trees next to bait, which in the case of Todd's project is mostly road-killed deer. When animals arrive at the carcass, the camera snaps a picture, and the biologist knows what's foraging on the carrion. This field in the Fernow was one of Todd's camera-trap sites, and the deer jaw likely bait leftover from the previous winter.[8]

Todd responds immediately with two pictures of what the camera here had recorded; in the first picture, on top of a bloody blanket of snow, a golden eagle with wings spread grasps the forelimb of a dead deer with its talons. A raven paces in the background. The second picture shows two eagles, one appearing to hover over a carcass, and one standing next to the pink of the deer's exposed ribcage.

I show my students: what this place looks like in winter, what wild things gather here. The black trees hide animals moving in the shadows. But many animals no longer cross this mountaintop. Circa 1900 the last gray wolf was killed; a few years earlier, the last elk. Until 1825, woodland bison foraged on American chestnuts, and before West Virginia's last eastern cougar was killed in 1887, the big cats leapt from rocky outcrops onto deer. Billion-bird flocks of passenger pigeons darkened the sky. The year 2014 marked the one-hundredth anniversary of the death of Martha, the world's last passenger pigeon, and 2015 marked the one-hundredth anniversary of the government's purchase of the first tract of land that would become Fernow Experimental Forest.[9]

My students settle on their backs, hands folded on their stomachs, as the wood thrush sings to the dying day. For a moment, the forest seems to echo with the snuffed songs of others, and then silence.

Our students emerge from their dew-soaked tents and assemble, groggy and smiling, for the short van ride back into the Fernow, to spend time with Elklick Run, the forest's primary waterway.

They disperse down the banks and into the creek, finding nooks to sit and listen, to write. Bill and I walk the gravel road; a mud-caked Bud Light bottle rests beneath a tangle of yellow jewelweed.

"If Boy Scouts came to do a workday, they'd fill garbage bags with bottles and cans and go home feeling like they cleaned up the forest," Bill says, "but bottles and cans don't affect the forest like climate change does." He gestures toward the uprooted eastern hemlock trees that had fallen across the creek.

In 2012 Superstorm Sandy slammed the Fernow, along with much of the eastern United States. Sandy began as a tropical storm in the Caribbean and quickly grew into a hurricane, tearing across Jamaica, Cuba, and Haiti and then up the coast, eventually making landfall in New Jersey. When the winds died down and the rain and snow subsided, almost two hundred people had died and eight million homes and businesses were without power. While coastal New York and New Jersey felt the brunt of the storm surge, some parts of West Virginia (five hundred miles from the Jersey shore) received three feet of heavy, wet snow. Many of the hemlocks along Elklick Run couldn't withstand the snow's weight and toppled, roots and all, into and across the creek.

One of the great challenges of climate change is its intangibility; we can't see carbon dioxide, can't smell or taste it as it builds up in our atmosphere. Discussions of stronger and more frequent storms are laden with words like *might*, *could*, and *perhaps*. Questions are posed on news reports: *Did global warming cause Superstorm Sandy? What role could climate change have played?* While we can't see the temperature rising, we can see the storm damage here along Elklick Run. One charge of this course is to give voice to climate change, to make our readers know where to look to see the effects of a warming planet, to illustrate the interconnectedness of the soil, the trees, the animals, the water, humans. Central Appalachia is a good place to start looking: here, at the headwaters, at the source, not only where our water originates but also where much of the climate-changing carbon is extracted from the ancient mountains.

Like the running buffalo clover, some members of the forest ecosystem need to be stepped on—footsteps conjure life in green leaves, fallen trees create pools for trout, ridge-top clearings attract eagles. The forest recovers, the scales steady. But other changes are not so easily managed: salt-sowed soil, a mountain scraped of its top, air dense with burned fuel. Here in Appalachia, we've been stepped on too—our homes poisoned, waters polluted, and mountains emptied of resources. At some point, the scales will tip, and lives resting in the balance will buckle and collapse, like a hemlock in a hurricane. My students and I may be small, just tiny voices floating up from the wilderness, but now we carry the forest in our hearts and our pens. The disturbance here has stirred us to life too, and we plan to sing.

NOTES

1.   Melissa Thomas-Van Gundy, lecture to class, July 12, 2013.
2.   Jeffrey M. Jones, "In U.S., Most Do Not See Global Warming as Serious Threat," *Gallup*, March 13, 2014, http://www.gallup.com/poll/167879/not-global -warming-serious-threat.aspx; Richard Wike, "What the World Thinks about Climate Change in 7 Charts," *Pew Research Center*, April 18, 2016, http://www .pewresearch.org/fact-tank/2016/04/18/what-the-world-thinks-about-climate -change-in-7-charts/.
3.   US Forest Service, "Fernow Experimental Forest," US Department of Agriculture, https://www.nrs.fs.fed.us/ef/locations/wv/fernow/.
4.   James Kochenderfer, lecture to class, July 12, 2013.
5.   Mary Beth Adams et al., "Effects of Development of a Natural Gas Well and Associated Pipeline on the Natural and Scientific Resources of the Fernow Experimental Forest," Gen. Tech. Rep. NRS-76, US Department of Agriculture, Forest Service, 2011.

6. West Virginia Coal Association, "Coal Facts 2012," January 8, 2013, https://www.wvcoal.com/coal-facts/coal-facts-2012.
7. "EPA Issues Comprehensive Guidance to Protect Appalachian Communities from Harmful Environmental Impacts of Mountaintop Mining," US Environmental Protection Agency, 2010 News Releases, April 1, 2010, https://archive.epa.gov/epapages/newsroom_archive/newsreleases/4145c96189a17239852576f8005867bd.html.
8. Todd Katzner, email to author, July 25, 2013.
9. Kochenderfer, lecture to class, July 12, 2013.

Sections #24 and #25 from "Tweet: A Long Poem"

John Lane

——————

24.

#I'm pleased,
pleased, pleased
to meet ya!

the chestnut-
sided warbler
whistles at

us, the passing
bikers, on
the Creeper Trail

a perfect tourist
greeter for a
second-growth

industry (logging
then bike-riding)
these warblers

prosper in
"thickets, briars,
and bushy lands"

birds like us
thrive and wane
and some fade away—

the ivory bill, passenger
pigeon, Carolina
parakeet, to name

three once numerous
in these high places
the bike-seat philosopher

with plenty of time
rolling downhill
for 17 miles

when not humming
"Petticoat Junction"
thinks of the patterns

of habitat/extinction
species expansion
pleased, pleased

to meet ya
old-growth
naturalist

John James
Audubon
you only saw

one chestnut-sided
in old-growth rambles
(no bike only pony

and tireless feet)
so take that
I've seen
ten so far
Jimmy Boy
as we descend

to Damascus
"extinction is 4-ever"
the bumper sticker

I saw in the outfitter's
parking lot
but so far the little

bird has beat the odds
and works this
second-growth

forest like a logger
but I know
extinction is

a last paycheck
a drained account
bills unpaid

larger trees
fewer briars
damn you're gone

like log trucks
and spur lines
and iron mining

we all face it even
clever tourists
bombing down

from Whitetop
on precision
recreational

machines
rented
for the day

25.

What bird sings
#aurora borealis
travel weary

on the descent
to Crabtree Falls
I hear in

dead hemlocks
the Neil Young
lyric over and over

think at first
it's from his
Cortez song

appropriate
enough in trees
lost to conquest

by white aphid
but what bird
whistles Neil

Young? Water
ouzel maybe
or yellow-eyed

vireo at the
bottom of
the waterfall

three boys
search for service
on iPhones

wait for parents
left behind
up top

Waynesville Watershed

Kathryn Stripling Byer

———————

We stare down
the flank of a mountain
that's branded
with names
of spring wildflowers.
Trillium Preserve.
Laurel Vistas.
Mayapple Manor.

Trillium
let's say,
and say over
and over again,
while there's still time
to find it alive
beside branch water.

Your Mee-Maw vs. CXP Oil & Gas, LLC

George Hovis

When she pulls herself from bed,
alone in the house again,
she does not think of you,
as normally she does,
whether you're passing your classes,
or if you've gotten serious about that new crush,
whether you'll find time to visit on your next break,
and if you've come yet to understand
that one day you, too, will have to die.

Neither does she think of her son, your dad,
who teaches at your school and,
of course, could not cancel his class
to drive her to the demonstration.
Besides, he still has two kids at home,
is coming up for tenure this year,
and could not risk being seen.

She doesn't even study the searing pain
that blossomed in her neck
and spent the last week
migrating down her spine.
Nor does she consider, as perhaps she ought,
the forecast of bitterly cold weather, and the
very real chance of hypothermia
for a woman so frail.

Today she thinks
only of the man she helped send
to the governor's mansion,
where now he lives in sin
with that woman who, they say,
works for the very company
that poisoned her well.
Those frackers.
Those . . . those . . . *fuckers*!
There. She said it.
And now maybe she can move
beyond her anger
and prepare herself to face
the 18-wheelers
and their tons of radioactive water
and accept the fact
that throughout history
the front lines of any battle
are occupied by those who
are most expendable.

Trace

Madison Jones

————

Even in this untouched scene
outside my window,
morning recalls disappearance.
Spoor and trails of meaning,
agony of hour and year intersect
and dissolve, peeling like layers
of paint on the yellow door
across the street. That wild yard
that nearly swallowed the curled
abandonment notice, staked
in the front lawn as if to tame it,
and I would stand there
early in the morning, looking out
at the unopened door, listening
to the neighbors' voices
through the wall, the squirrels
arguing in the pear tree, shaking
the fruit-laden limbs until
they snapped in the linen sunlight
dangling from the sky by a thread.

In Praise of Wilderness:
Getting What You Give Up

Thomas Rain Crowe

———————

Lucky enough to have been involved in the foundational days of the bioregional movement on the West Coast during the 1970s, I was working with and around people like Peter Berg of *Planet Drum*, Lee Swenson of *Simple Living*, poet Gary Snyder, and others. What I learned from these poets and provocateurs was that *biodiversity* is the sustaining reality throughout all of nature. It is, in the end, diversity that allows for the quality of life of all living things, as well as allowing everything to survive and to evolve, and to continue. Once the idea or the reality of monocultures takes root, everything starts becoming like everything else around it—the gene pool is weakened, and the quality of life is compromised.

Diversity, for me, is essential in both philosophical and practical ways. It is essential to the natural world—meaning it's also essential to the human world. I think it's a wonderful thing that we have different geographical bioregions, different cultures and peoples, different races, different languages, different religions and belief systems. Life would be fairly dull, don't you think, if we were all the same color and there was only one variety of tree, and one kind of salamander, and one way to think of or worship God? In this kind of mono-world, our imaginations, which are essentially fueled by the natural world and the diversity and mystery of the Universe, would go flat, dry. Entropy would set in. We would cease to be the creative creatures we are. Having had my eyes opened to this paradigm, and believing that diversity is necessary for the well-being of all living creatures and systems, it is easy for me to say now, and with conviction, that I am not willing to live in a world absent of elephants and whales!

Pulitzer Prize–winning biologist E. O. Wilson in his book *Half-Earth: Our Planet's Fight for Life* discusses the premise that a huge variety of life-forms on Earth still remain largely unknown to science and that the species discovered and studied well enough to assess, notably the vertebrae animals and flowering plants, are declining in number at an accelerating rate—due almost entirely to human activity. In response to this premise, Wilson very succinctly states: "The global conservation movement has temporarily mitigated but hardly stopped the ongoing extinction of species. The rate of loss is instead accelerating. If biodiversity is to be returned to the baseline level of extinction that existed before the spread of humanity, and thus saved for future generations, the conservation effort must be raised to a new level. *The only solution to the 'Sixth Extinction' is to increase the area of inviolable natural reserves to half the surface of the Earth or greater. . . .* But it also requires a fundamental shift in moral reasoning concerning our relation to the living environment."[1]

The most concerning phrase in the above paragraph is "to increase the area of inviolable natural reserves [e.g., wilderness-designated land reserves] to half the surface of the Earth," echoing the book's title. Half of our planet saved as wilderness or wildlands seems an awful lot, given the shrinking size of the planet due to global markets, global population statistics, the internet, and social media. But after reading Wilson's compilation of facts and figures and prescient logic, one can only agree with his compassionate analysis and fears for the future of all species, including humans. His omniscient observations and study of species extinction hit hard and very close to home as he cites our own Great Smoky Mountains National Park as his primary referent example. "It is instructive to proceed to the Great Smoky Mountains National Park, one of the best-studied American reserves, and to reflect briefly on the breakdown of the numbers of known species in each group of organisms. The actual number of recorded species in the Park, especially when all suspected but still unrecorded transient species and microorganisms are added, has been estimated to lie between sixty thousand and eighty thousand,"[2] writes Wilson.

Very impressive numbers these are, and those of us in these western North Carolina mountains are immensely fortunate to be living in such a diverse neighborhood. Yet we should be humbled by such numbers, or as Wilson writes,

> The wildlands (such as the Great Smoky Mountains National Park [here in the southern Appalachians]) and the bulk of Earth's biodiversity protected within them are another world from the one humanity is throwing together pell-mell. What do we receive from them? The stabilization of the global environment they provide and their very existence are the gifts they give to us. We are their stewards, not their owners. These wildlands of the world are not art museums. They are not gardens to be arranged and tended for our delectation. They are not recreation centers or harborers of natural resources or sanatoriums or undeveloped sites of business opportunities.[3]

Wilson's layman-friendly book is full of scientific evidence to support his predictions as well as his solutions to this very real and urgent global crisis we all seem to be ignoring at our own peril.

Wilson is not alone with his convincing data and dire predictions. Many esteemed scientists, economists, social scientists, artists, and politicians worldwide agree with Wilson's findings and predictions. Or as Wilson says in his ending chapter: "The pivotal conclusion to be drawn remains forever the same: by destroying most of the biosphere with archaic short-term methods, we are setting ourselves up for a self-inflicted disaster. Across eons the diversity of species has created ecosystems that provide a maximum level of stability. Climate changes and uncontrollable catastrophes from earthquakes, volcanic eruptions, and asteroid strikes have thrown nature off balance, but in relatively short geologic periods of time, the damage was repaired—due to the great variety and resilience of the life-forms on Earth."[4]

Here in the southern Appalachians and elsewhere, Earth's shield of biodiversity is being shattered, and the pieces are being thrown away. In its place is only the promise that all can be solved by human ingenuity. Some hope that we can take over the controls, monitor the sensors, and push the right buttons to run Earth the way we choose. But in response, all the rest of us should be asking: Can the planet be run as a true spaceship by one intelligent species? Surely, we would be foolish to take such a large and dangerous gamble. Or as Wilson says, "There is nothing our scientists and political leaders can do to replace the still-unimaginable complex of niches and the interactions of the millions of species that fill them. If they try, as some of them seem determined to do, and then even if they succeed to some extent, remember we won't be able to go back. The result will be irreversible."[5]

Gazing from my farmhouse porch out into this beautiful place we refer to as the Tuckasegee valley here in the Smoky Mountains of western North Carolina, I'm not always contemplating beauty, my mind full of pleasant thoughts; I also find myself contemplating more unpleasant things arising from environmental issues that are almost constantly in the local news these days. And I'm wondering: who is going to lead us out of this self-destructive paradigm that was set into motion with the Industrial Revolution and has continued to gather momentum in the last century and a half with the indulgent escalation of free-trade capitalism? I keep asking myself: Where are the "dirt-doctors," the "earth-healers"? Where are the great charismatic voices in government that might begin the work of turning things around? And if not in government, then in society in general—where are our leaders? It seems that there is no one in a position of power addressing the truly fundamental questions of our day: overpopulation, unchecked and unregulated economic growth, globalism, and land preservation.

If we look back, it has always been the naturalists who have led the way toward more progressive thinking about balance, sustainability, and biodiversity. It is the nature writers who have positioned themselves on the front lines of the myriad battles to save and preserve the environment. And through their writing, they have sown seeds that sprout, as ecological movements, private foundations, and governmental programs focused on the long view concerning the welfare of the country's and the planet's landscape and wildlands. Past generations have looked to the work of such writers as Ralph Waldo Emerson, Henry David Thoreau, John Burroughs, John Muir,

William Bartram, Horace Kephart, Aldo Leopold, Rachel Carson, and Loren Eiseley, while more recent generations have looked to writers like Robinson Jeffers (*Give Your Heart to the Hawks*), Gary Snyder (*The Practice of the Wild*), and—here in the South—to writers like Birmingham, Alabama, native E. O. Wilson (*In Search of Nature*), Wendell Berry of the Kentucky backcountry and farming communities (*The Unsettling of America* and *The Gift of Good Land*), and Thomas Berry, a North Carolina native who has captured the imagination of the whole environmental movement with his elevated message of spiritual ecology (*The Dream of the Earth* and *The Great Work*).

Following in the footsteps of Bartram, Kephart, Wilson, and the Berrys here in the southern Appalachians is a new generation and a new breed of gifted nature writers. "If you would learn the secrets of nature," Thoreau wrote, "you must practice more humanity than others." That credo, more or less, sums up the ethos of these "new naturalists." They are not only talking the talk; they are walking the walk. They are not only writing an engaged prose and poetry that evokes the spirit of the "old naturalists" and their tenets for a sustainable future, but they are quite literally engaged in a kind of activism that is journalistic, literary, and biographical. They are, through their work and deeds, inspiring, organizing, and participating in nonviolent actions that provide alternatives to community apathy and destruction of natural habitat.

While writers such as Bill McKibben, Elizabeth Kolbert, Paul Hawken, Amory Lovins, Stewart Brand, and Michael Pollan are writing on the subjects of nature and the environment from their homes in the Northeast, Midwest, Southwest, or West Coast, the South has also risen up to be counted as a regional voice espousing preservation and sustainability. In and around the area of the Great Smoky Mountains National Park and the hill country to the north, south, east, and west is an exceptionally dedicated, if not devout, group of 1960s nature writers worthy of national attention. In a region where the issues of wilderness designation, air pollution, water quality, extinction of floral and faunal species, and loss of traditional cultures are front and center, these remarkable writers are not only making a mark on the genre of environmental nonfiction, but they are making a difference.

This group of Southern nature writers (www.southernnature.org) who live in, adjacent to, or have connections with the Katuah bioregion of the southern Appalachians in North Carolina includes, in Jackson County, outdoorsman Burt Kornegay. Kornegay is a mapmaker and writer for a variety of state and national "field-and-stream" publications. He is past president of the North Carolina Bartram Trail Society and has been featured in *National Geographic*, *Wildlife*, and *American Hiker* as a wilderness guide who owns Slickrock Expeditions.

In Barnardsville, Buncombe County, just north of Asheville and bordering the Mount Mitchell State Park in the Pisgah National Forest, Will Harlan and his wife live off the grid in a solar home surrounded by gardens, vineyards, and orchards planned and maintained with the principles of permaculture. Will is editor and writer for *Blue Ridge Outdoors* (based in Charlottesville, Virginia), a staunch supporter of the grassroots organization The Canary Coalition (which focuses on air-quality issues in the region), and a world-class extreme-terrain marathon runner. His latest book, *Untamed*, is a history of the fight to preserve Cumberland Island, Georgia, from commercial development.

In Swain County, there is poet-turned-naturalist and journalist George Ellison, whose knowledge of nature lore and Native American history in the region is nearly encyclopedic. His books (*Mountain Passages* and *A Blue Ridge Nature Journal*), newspaper columns, nature-walk workshops, and contributions to the living folklore of the region are invaluable in educating the public about its past as well as its invasive present. Ellison's stamp appears on two of the seminal tomes of southern Appalachian natural and cultural history: James Mooney's *History, Myths, and Sacred Formulas of the Cherokees* and Horace Kephart's *Our Southern Highlanders*, for which he has written new, updated introductions.

Just next door in Jackson County along the Tuckasegee River, whitewater enthusiast, wilderness and recreation writer, and poet John Lane owns land in a remote cove off John's Creek Road in the Caney Fork community of Cullowhee. There he has reconstructed a beautiful one-room sawmill shack, which he uses as a writer's retreat and where he spends his spare time in close proximity to the headwaters of the Nantahala and Chattooga Rivers. Lane is actively involved in water and land development issues in the region and has authored a book on the Chattooga River (*Chattooga: Descending into the Myth of Deliverance River*). His book *Weed Time*, which was written in the environs of Whittier while living up Camp Creek Road, is a snapshot of place-based awareness in journal form. Lane's investigative journalism into ecological issues here in the mountains and down on the other side of the "Blue Wall" in the South Carolina piedmont is written thoughtfully and fiercely, leaving no stone unturned. While his journalistic work is clever, aggressive, and place-based organic, his poetry written about the western North Carolina mountains is equally as sensitive and lyric.

Up in Watauga County, the movement for sustainability has been enjoined by anthropologist, writer, and activist Harvard Ayers at Appalachian State in books such as *An Appalachian Tragedy: Air Pollution and Tree Death in the Eastern Forests of North America* and *Polluted Parks in Peril: The Five Most Air-Polluted National Parks in the United States*. His work on behalf of clean air coalitions in western North Carolina has been influential, if not essential, in the state's passage of the groundbreaking 2001 Clean Smokestacks Act, setting an important precedent for the rest of the country.

And in Macon County, over in the Cowee community, there's Brent Martin (*A Shout in the Woods* and *Poems from Snow Hill Road*). Martin is the founder and director of Alarka Expeditions and is the former director of the Wilderness Society for the southern Appalachian region. He has been a director for other environmental groups in the region, including Georgia ForestWatch and the Little Tennessee Land Trust of the Great Smoky Mountains. While he writes columns for *Smoky Mountain News* and the *Mountain Xpress* from his home in the Cowee community, he's often out in the woods, searching and mapping old and new terrain for potential preservation, looking for stands of old-growth forest, and following issues that threaten the wilderness areas of western North Carolina.

Also residing in Macon County in the remote Alarka Watershed, where he grows a large vegetable garden, is Lamar Marshall. Lamar originally hails from Alabama and is something of a legend there as a woodsman, trapper, and relentless activist for the preservation of wilderness. He is the founder of Wild South and its magazine of the same name. Having moved to the cooler environs of the Smokies, Lamar has taken up the cause of the Cherokee and is working with the tribe along the Qualla Boundary on an extensive mapping project to discover, identify, document and protect the Indian trails, old village sites, and nature-related survival systems (such as fishing weirs) misplaced or lost to Cherokee history. His work as trailblazer, explorer, mapmaker, and writer in the western North Carolina mountains has only served to expand his legendary reputation as someone working to preserve and protect our region.

While the amount of work to be done in cleaning up and preserving our environment here in the mountains of North Carolina, and in the surrounding areas, might seem overwhelming at times, these new naturalists and others like them are more than equal to the task. This is a focused and dedicated "wild bunch," who has taken on the heavy yoke of unchecked progress, growth, and development, and—in exemplary bioregional fashion—with strong backs and thick ink are pulling the ecology wagon here in the southern Appalachians.

We have only one planet, one mountain chain known as the Appalachians, and we are allowed only one such experiment. They all depend on the balance of a diverse biosphere. Diversity is not only preferable, it is paramount. Why continue with this world-threatening and unnecessary gamble if a safe option is available? E. O. Wilson's option is for humans to relinquish control and ownership and to surrender land into wilderness to total one half the surface of the Earth. You get what you give up.

NOTES

1. E. O. Wilson, *Half-Earth: Our Planet's Fight for Life* (New York: Liveright Publishing, 2016), 167. Emphasis added.
2. Wilson, 85.
3. Wilson, 84.
4. Wilson, 173.
5. Wilson, 173.

Take in the Waters:
On the Birthplace of Rivers, West Virginia

Rick Van Noy

———

To get to West Virginia, I follow the course of the river. The road parallels the New River as it slices through the Appalachian Mountains. At a section pushed up millions of years ago, the river narrows. There I turn right at Rich Creek and head north through Peterstown, West Virginia, the town that nearly struck it rich.

In 1928 a boy was pitching horseshoes in his backyard. As luck would have it, he found a diamond.

William "Punch" Jones's horseshoe kicked up some dirt near the stake and revealed an alluvial diamond weighing 34.46 carats, the second largest known in North America. The family was already famous for setting a record for consecutive male births—Punch was the eldest of seventeen. He kept the diamond as a curio in a shoebox during the Depression until he showed it to a Virginia Tech professor in 1944. It then went to the Smithsonian for display and was eventually sold at Sotheby's for seventy-five thousand dollars in 1984.

Geologists aren't sure where it came from but speculate that it washed downriver. Though a good mile from the current channel of the New River, Punch played in an ancient riverbed.

I learn some of this from a road sign as I travel north on Highway 219, the old Seneca Trail, long a travel and trading corridor used by the Catawba, various Algonquian tribes, the Cherokee to the south, and the Iroquois Confederacy to the north. The road crosses many rivers: the North Fork of the Blackwater, the Shavers Fork of the Cheat, Tygart, Elk, Greenbrier, Indian. I am traveling this road to learn more about a special designation that would create a national monument to honor these and other rivers, to make a section of the Cranberry Wilderness and some of the Monongahela

National Forest into the Birthplace of Rivers National Monument. It would preserve one of the largest stands of contiguous wild forest in the East and protect the headwaters of six rivers: the Cranberry, Gauley, Greenbrier, Elk, Williams, and Cherry.

I love to travel this road, but it twists with the rivers, rises and falls with the topography. Geologists say that when an ancient continent slammed into our own, it smooshed up the mountain and some of that material fell back over the vertical onto the land below, creating a series of folds and lumps. The road follows the valley and ridge topography—the elongated dorsal fin of Peters Mountain and the Appalachian Trail to the east, goosebumps to the west.

The road seesaws until I pass Indian Creek, a covered bridge nearby, and the remains of an old resort, Sweet Springs, one of the many places where people used to "take the waters" in the nineteenth century, a remedy for a range of ailments. The first five presidents all stayed there, as did the Marquis de Lafayette. I was on my way to Lewisburg, near the Greenbrier in White Sulphur Springs, another of these spas. They were popular before air conditioning, when people wanted to escape the heat and humidity by heading for the cool mountains where they could soothe their joints in the warm, curative mineral baths. The waters were said to have a quieting effect on the circulatory and nervous systems and offered a sound night's sleep. But their novelty wore off, and now only a few remain, such as the Greenbrier and Homestead, which were favored by railroad stops.

The local springs are connected with disturbances in the geologic structure of the area. Along the fractures and faults, groundwater heated by the earth's core rises to the surface.

On the drive, I enjoy the road signs: no pipeline, no fracking pipeline, no frack in karst. Permanent threat 4ever, Savethewatertable. org, PreserveMonroe.org. And yet, once solidly Democratic, West Virginia went for Trump more than any other state, narrowly beating Wyoming, Oklahoma, and North Dakota—other energy economy producers.

There were Trump signs but also ads for Jim Justice with the words "jobs, jobs, jobs," featuring men in hardhats. "Tired of being 50th?" asks one sign, a reference to the state being last in several categories: finances, education, and health. Though two-thirds of voters pulled a lever for Trump, they elected Democrat Jim Justice for governor (who switched to Republican in August 2017). In 2009 Justice, a coal and agriculture businessman, purchased the Greenbrier for twenty million dollars, rescuing it from bankruptcy.

When candidate Trump held a rally in my town in southwest Virginia, I went to see if he would say anything specific to the region. He mostly gave the standard stump speech until the end when someone asked him about coal. "Coal," he said, when prompted. "We're going to bring the coal industry back one hundred percent." Then he added, "Clean coal, I hear it works."

Most economists agree that the decline in coal jobs is due to mechanization in the mining industry and a market shift by electric utilities away from coal and toward cheaper natural gas. Telling the region that coal jobs are coming back has been likened to telling New Englanders that the whaling industry will return.

I wanted to visit Lewisburg because a summer film event there was trying to envision a future beyond coal, a new economy. The Live Monumental film tour was sponsored by Keen, a shoe manufacturer; several young people traveled the country showing films that highlighted a love for wild places and their support for national monument status. In addition to Birthplace of Rivers, West Virginia, the campaign sought to protect Owyhee Canyonlands in Oregon; Boulder-White-Clouds, Idaho; Gold Butte, Nevada; and Mojave Trails, California. The staff brought a young, outdoorsy vibe. They called their '76 GMC motor home variously "Twinkie," "Old Yeller," or "Teddy," after Roosevelt, who signed the Antiquities Act in 1906, authorizing the president or Congress to set aside federal lands to protect significant natural, cultural, or scientific features.

The mayor of Lewisburg, John Manchester, welcomed us and talked about the potential economic benefit to the town of a national monument designation, saying he could see Lewisburg as a gateway city. Matt Kearns of the West Virginia Rivers Coalition also spoke. To bring awareness to the effort, he and a friend floated, hiked, and biked the headwaters of Laurel Run to the Elk, then they did the same along the Greenbrier, the New, and the Kanawha into Charleston. They drank the water in the Elk but not from the river near Charleston. On certain days in 2014, the residents of Charleston could not drink out of taps when a chemical used in the coal industry spilled from a storage tank, contaminating the water supply.

At dinner before the movie, I met a guy wearing an orange golf shirt who played a round at the nearby Greenbrier. He seemed like an important man about town as he knew the bartender by name, hugged one of the waitresses, and people came up to shake his hand, but he didn't know about the festival, and said the Birthplace of Rivers was "controversial."

I brought that up with Mike Costello, director of the West Virginia Wilderness Coalition. He said people learned that one monument does not allow hunting and then assumed that none would. "This one will allow hunting," he told me. Matt Kearns told me that people think you are shaking with one hand but have your other hand, fingers crossed, behind your back. Rivers connect us, but they can be full of obstacles, as was this process. In a river, among the earliest forms of travel, you have to pick a way through hazards. Matt said that the only good argument against the monument was to keep people out, to keep it pristine.

Mike told me the monument would set aside a unique area on the East Coast. It would be more flexible than a national park, allowing mountain bikes for example. And conservation groups could continue the red spruce restoration.

In the morning, I wanted to see some of the proposed site. On my way up, I stopped at Beartown State Park, full of massive fragmented boulders, vertical cliffs, deep crevasses. "Hidden within the rocks is the story that really has no ending," said one of the signs on the boardwalk. White sand could be seen at the base of the cliffs. Otherwise, all green fern and hemlock. A few rocks are scooped out enough that a person could climb in, nap. The horizontal strands I saw are related to deposits of sand and silt.

"The ripple-like angular cross beds in the different rock strata were caused by current action when the rock-forming material was deposited along the shore of an ancient sea," said another sign.

Walking around the boardwalk, I heard an energetic birdsong I did not recognize. I recorded it and played it later for a naturalist friend. Clyde Kessler tells me it's a winter wren, and "you have found a bit of holy ground when you hear that song." For druids, the bird was sacred, and in England it is still known as the king of birds.

After Beartown I stop at McCoy's Market, a convenience store in Hillsboro, hometown of Pearl S. Buck, author of *The Good Earth* (1931). Near the coffee pot are six guys in T-shirts and ball caps, big burly men. I want to talk to them about the monument proposal, but I realize, as I'm looking in the bathroom mirror, that I'm wearing the Live Monumental hat, given out as swag the night before. I don't want to give myself away, nor do I want to get my ass kicked. So I take the hat off and go out to the car and grab another. When I pour a coffee and join the conversation, I get an earful about the government screwing everything up, taking away logging rights. Trust the government? Ask an Indian. The only good tree is a stump.

But the funny thing is that although these guys and I share little in common, I am enjoying their company and laughter more so than with some of the folks I agreed with last night. Whatever their cause, they have not lost their sense of humor.

One of the biggest, Joe Walker, who drives a Neathawk Lumber truck, asks, "Why change? It's perfect like it is."

For these men, coal and timber work become ingrained in the fabric of a community, much like farming. Factor that in with a natural distrust of change. Accepting change, after all, would require admitting being wrong about something, and that would require a kind of reflection and humiliation big burly men rarely engage in.

At that moment, a tall muscular guy they call "Doc" comes in saying, "I'd sure like to operate on some people." He's apparently not a doctor but retired from law enforcement for the Forest Service. They point to me and tell Doc, "This man wants to know what we think about the Birthplace of Rivers." "I think it sucks!" Doc says to a round of laughter. Besides, "the government screws up everything it touches," says the guy who worked for the government.

They tell me more, about how timber sales help with schools. About how the county is a hundred miles from one end to the other, a forty-five-minute drive, so transportation costs are high. They run mills, heavy equipment, and one has a son that works the limestone tumblers that keep the streams from being too acidic. But what causes them to be acidic? In part, acid rain. What causes that? The burning of coal.

They scoff at the idea of tourism helping the economy. For proof, they ask me how much I spent on my coffee. Point taken.

I travel on to the Cranberry Glades themselves, a forest in a bog. Some trees struggle to survive in the wet ground and acidic soil, but other animals take up burrows in the hollow trees.

The glades are a great natural bowl in the nearby mountains, four thousand feet high, a misplaced tract of Arctic tundra in southern mountains, including reindeer moss. The namesake cranberry is an evergreen shrub more at home in the far north. Over ten thousand years ago, Ice Age glaciers pushed far south, and plants and animals suited for a colder climate took hold. In the area are several flesh-eating plants, sundew and purple pitcher, adapted to take in nutrients from insects because there are few nutrients in the damp habitat.

Red spruce would have blanketed the area but it was mostly clear-cut. The slash the loggers left behind, treetops and limbs, created a tinderbox. And in 1930 Black Mountain burned to the ground, the heat so intense that the soil was consumed.

On both sides of the Highland Scenic Highway, I look down on folds upon ridges, sunlight and shadow, cloud cover as varied in depth and shape as the mountains below. I was enjoying the scenery, as were others. I saw cars from New York, Ohio, Pennsylvania. At least some sign of tourism.

The area is defined by rivers, the Williams River to the north and the South Fork of the Cranberry River to the south. A former state black bear sanctuary and haven for animals such as bobcats, foxes, and the threatened northern flying squirrel, the Cranberry Wilderness is one of the wildest places east of the Mississippi.

I ventured off the road to the north-south trail, which actually runs east-west. Only a few hundred yards in, everything seemed unnervingly still. Even the light rain, what Scottish immigrants to the region would have called a smirr, seemed hushed.

Step by step, the path seemed to grow wilder until I was standing in waist-high ferns beneath dense stands of spruce. A few spring flowers held their bright color and the rhodies were about to bust among the many shades of green. There was the sweet smell of pinesap and another birdsong I could not recognize, but I had no recording device—I'd left the phone locked in the car. Besides, in nearby Greenbank is the National Radio Astronomy Observatory, which operates the world's largest radio telescope, and a radio-frequency-free zone. The faintest signal can interfere with the telescope's detection of the music of the spheres. In the National Radio Quiet Zone, cell phones are restricted or banned.

I vowed to remember the song with some mnemonic I could look up later, some phrasing like "here Sam Peabody," Thoreau's mnemonic for the white-throated sparrow, but I didn't write the *zee zee zoos* in my journal and the music was ultimately lost. I kept looking up at the sound. Cerulean warblers can be found in West Virginia, high in the canopy, "sky blue, sky high." Once plentiful in the United States, their population is decreasing faster than that of any other eastern songbird because much of their breeding habitat has been destroyed by mountaintop coal mining.

Whatever song it was, it left me in a kind of silent awe. No wonder birds like the winter wren inspire folklore.

I kept walking, and though my phone was in the car, in some ways it was still with me, and with little effort my mind could churn through emails and to-do lists, putting me there and not here, but the river lay ahead. I trudged on, the trail growing less and less discernable, ducking under downed tree trunks and sloshing through ferns. I hiked on, stepping over coral-shaped fungi and meadows lush and majestic. Every few yards there was a spider web that caught little but the morning's mist, tiny droplets like gems in a necklace.

Then I heard a bird I could recognize, the fluted *ee-oh-lay* of the wood thrush. Thoreau wrote that the bird "touches a depth in me which no other bird's song does," calling it "a Shakespeare among birds."

Jim McGraw, professor of biology at West Virginia University, has studied how the wood thrush's migration may be assisting wild ginseng. Studying the birds on game cams and in the lab, McGraw has found that the birds pick up the shiny red fruit but do not eat them. They spit the seeds back out. But like the cerulean, their numbers are declining. That decline could affect ginseng populations that rely on thrushes for the free ride. And the plants may need to migrate as the climate warms. Ginseng is one of many plants adapted to a long-term temperature climate, so they will need to move to follow their optimal environment. Thrushes may be needed to help them get there.

In my bird reverie, I must have stopped paying attention to the cairns that marked the switchbacks, because soon it felt like I was off the trail. Coincidently, at about the time I realized I was lost I became acutely aware of a loud crash of bushes below me. Possibly bear. How close to *panic* is Pan, god of woods and wild.

I bumped my head on branches and barked my shins on down to the North Fork of the Cranberry River, where I picked up the trail and river and camped for the night. I had one ear open for loud crashing noises and was awakened once by the split-crack-woomph of a downed tree, but I slept soundly, soothed by the water.

In the morning, I hiked back to the car and stopped in Marlinton at the Dirtbean for coffee where I ran into Matt Kearns again. He was meeting with several people, including the CEO of Snowshoe ski resort, Frank DeBerry, to talk about the recreation economy. It was a good place to have these discussions: at the back of the Dirtbean they rent bikes for the Greenbrier Trail. Fat tires and a coffee to go.

At the moment, much of the county's economy comes from timber sales. But could lodging taxes provide a new revenue stream? Currently, 85 percent of tourists come in winter for skiing. Matt and others were talking about increasing tourism for the spring, summer, and fall. He saw the Birthplace of Rivers idea as part of a climate change survival plan, as a way to take up some of the slack and hedge against the warming that could decrease winter tourism.

Many people were looking for a silver bullet to bring jobs back. From Matt's perspective, there were good-paying jobs but not as many, "so we have to adapt. Instead of one company that brings a thousand jobs, maybe there are a hundred that bring ten."

I mentioned the fear and uncertainty I heard in the market of Hillsboro, their "why change?" sentiment. He and other monument supporters were doing their best to provide information. "If you like the way the area is currently being managed, we will keep that plan, but lock it down the way it is. So it doesn't change. It's the change, new kinds of extraction or drilling, we're helping to guard against." Matt said they have to work very hard to keep the same, or unwanted change will happen. For Kearns, protecting public lands was like protecting the family jewels.

I said the guys in the market thought the idea was coming from outsiders. "I chafe at the notion that I'm not from around here," said Matt. He showed me the tattoo on his arm, the state motto of West Virginia, *montani semper liberi*, mountaineers are always free.

Several days later, when I was back to routine and plugged in, the meaning of temporarily getting lost in the wilderness started to become clearer. I thought of writer Wallace Stegner's well-known "Wilderness Letter," that "without any remaining wilderness we are committed wholly, without chance for even momentary reflection and rest, to a headlong drive into our technological termite-life."[1]

Less well known is the inspiration for his devotion to wilderness. In "Overture," Stegner said it was camping by a river, the Henrys Fork of the

Snake, when he gave himself to wilderness. Among the spray-cooled and scented spruce, a "symphony of sound," "I gave my heart to the mountains the minute I stood beside this river with its spray in my face and watched it thunder into foam."[2]

By the Cranberry, I spied a few brook trout disappearing into the shadows. They predate the glaciers and are a sentinel species, threatened by warming waters. However, Than Hitt, a fish biologist with the US Geological Survey, said they could be more affected by flow. He sees some adaptations to heat, some thermal tolerance, but worried that the increased water and storms would scour the streams during their breeding season, washing away eggs and laying habitat.

By the river I drank in the river music, hiss and splash in the main channel, lower murmur on the sides, some faint gurgle in the back, and beneath it all pulsing a steady rhythm and flow, changing yet everlasting.

I returned to West Virginia to cross-country ski the last weekend in January, one of the first weekends there had been enough snow, in a winter likely to be the warmest yet, each warmer than the one before. I was up there seeking some solace from the week's news of building walls and banning people. On the road into Whitegrass, near the Dolly Sods Wilderness in West Virginia, they fly flags of many nations attached to alder birch saplings, welcoming everyone.

The cover was thin, a little sticky, and I found more than a few roots and rocks but also more and more snow as I went higher, as if traveling to some mythical land where it would be higher and deeper yet. At one spot, by a small creek and waterfall, I took in the stillness of waters, even among the rushing sound of the creek and the dripping icicles. I thought of the springs that fed it, the layers of rock cradling it, the forest surrounding it, and the far ridges beyond, which I still had time in the day to explore. Leaning into my poles, catching my breath, as I thought of my own past trips and of natural processes, a deep sense of time began to form, which also made it possible to imagine a deep future.

Paying attention to the hardwoods on the way up, the greenish mosses on the north side of the bark—to the movements and tracks of animals, invisible neighbors—lightened my spirits after a fear-filled and disappointing week. The only tweets were high up in the canopy above.

After the morning's ski and on into late afternoon, legs rubbery, I skied down to the bottom near a bubbling sand springs, artesian pressure pushing up from below. A family with young kids was there, taking a snack break, hypnotized by the waters. The kids were asking where it came from, where it went. Their curiosity was feeding their imagination, which nourishes overall well-being and wonder. The water would join with that of the creek I stood near, travel through the boggy glen of the Canaan Valley Wildlife Refuge, on to the dark forested Blackwater north and west, and eventually on down to the Mississippi valley where it would join with the mountain waters of Stegner's West.

The Birthplace of the Rivers National Monument never happened under President Obama and its future looks dim under a Trump administration. It had grassroots support but never garnered enough backing from local and state officials. Matt Kearns of West Virginia Rivers Coalition told me they hand delivered over two thousand emails, postcards, and letters to the White House, but "without the buy-in from our congressional delegation, President Obama wasn't willing to wade into our battle."

To make matters worse, a week after the film festival in Lewisburg, the region experienced the third-worst flood in state history, with the worst one occurring in 1972—a rainfall so hard that a dam built for a coal slurry pond had dislodged and ravaged the community of Buffalo Creek. After the more recent flood, the Greenbrier golf course was littered with severed trees, buried under mud. The Greenbrier Classic PGA had to be canceled.

According to Kevin Trenberth, a senior scientist at the Center for Atmospheric Research, there is about 10 percent more moisture in the atmosphere since 1970. West Virginia and the Northeast have experienced a 73 percent increase in extreme rainfall events since 1958, according to the Third National Climate Assessment, a problem particularly acute for the mountain state with miles of runoff. It's difficult news for a state whose economy has been built by a fuel responsible for a quarter of all greenhouse gas emissions.

In the lodge at Whitegrass, which always smells like woodsmoke and homemade soup, where the staff all sport wet ski boots, I asked owner Chip Chase how he was faring in the warm winter. Although he doesn't make snow, he "snow farms" by putting up fencing to catch drifts. His wife, Laurie, runs a natural food café. Skiers eat bowls of chili and chocolate chip cookies around the potbellied stove. Chip was hopeful winter would finally arrive, but "we've built a resilient little business here, so don't worry about us." In other words, they have diversified their economy.

On my ski to the very top of Weiss Knob I could see Mount Porte Crayon, named for a writer-illustrator (also known as David Hunter Strother), who published often in *Harper's Monthly* in the mid-nineteenth century and loved the nearby highlands. In his *Virginia Illustrated* (1857), he wrote of his visits to Canaan and the region's many springs, helping to popularize them. At the close of the book, he writes of hidden deep valleys overshadowed by gloomy hemlocks and a pervading sense of toil, even "oppressive loneliness." But occasionally, a brook appears, and then "a hoarse murmuring deep down in the earth." Now a feeling of awe and mystery "steals over the spirit." A little father, he sees a "broad, bold river burst suddenly, its crystal waters flashing in the sunshine, roaring and leaping," "rejoicing the lonely valley with the voice of music, and the eye of the wanderer with the freshness of beauty." In some human hearts, he writes, "the course of love is like that mountain stream."[3]

Though it never achieved monument status, we can still enjoy the wild and wonderful in West Virginia for now, when we need wilderness more than ever. There are other jewels than the ones underground, timeless ones like warbling birds and spring-fed streams. "Knowing wilderness is there," wrote New Mexico Senator Clinton Anderson in 1963, "we can also know that we are still a rich nation, tending our resources as we should—not people in despair searching every last nook and cranny of our land for a board of lumber, a barrel of oil, a blade of grass, or a tank of water."[4]

Wallace Stegner said the idea of wilderness alone could sustain us, but we need the real thing too, the actual contact with it. Up there in those headwaters, I find the source of so much—rowdy creeks running wild and free, hot springs and cold ones, a symphony of nature and a source of rivers, a bubbling richness. If not a "geography of hope," to use Stegner's phrase, it could certainly be the birthplace of it.

NOTES

1. Wallace Stegner, *The Sound of Mountain Water* (Lincoln: University of Nebraska Press, 1985), 141.
2. Stegner, *Mountain Water,* 42.
3. Porte Crayon, *Virginia Illustrated: Containing a Visit to the Virginian Canaan, and the Adventures of Porte Crayon and His Cousins* (New York: Harper, 1857), 257.
4. Clinton Anderson, "This We Hold Dear," *American Forests,* July 1963, 24–25.

Haint How To

Rosemary Royston

———

After dark, avoid
    narrow woodland trails,
    the base of dead trees,
    wherever lightning has struck,
    and (obviously) graveyards.

To keep the haints away,
    hang basil over a threshold,
    plant rue or purslane near your home,
    spin three times, counter-clockwise,
      before entering the house,
    hang chimes on the front door.

To banish haints
    at sundown, offer the ghost a snack
    of raw potato. At dawn,
    bury the potato, and your ghost
    is grounded, never to return.

Magickal Substitution

Rosemary Royston

———

i.
Bring a shovel into the house
and a grave will be dug by December.

Rest a tool against an interior wall,
illness will manifest and someone will die.

To defeat the spell, break the shovel
or tool in half. Bury in separate places.

ii.
If you're hit by a falling rock
pieces of your soul will escape, like fog.

Take the rock and find two others
similar size, shape, color.

Cast the three stones into a stream
in the name of the *Father, the Son,*

and the Holy Ghost. Or, if you prefer,
Maiden, Mother, Crone.

iii.
A blackbird perches on your windowsill,
caws its ragged caw. Death is imminent.

You must kill the bird after it takes flight.
Bury at the edge of the cemetery.

iv.
The crowing hen or rooster after dark?
Kill it too. Wipe its blood on the doorpost.

v.
If a white dog stops and gazes upon you
in the setting sun, the only way to save yourself:
drink a tea brewed with the dog's drool.

Broom Lore

Rosemary Royston

Never loan out your broom,
as brooms take an interest
in their home. When you move, leave
your broom behind. If you allow
another's broom in your house,
you've invited disaster.

Nothing evil can cross a prone
broomstick, so lay one lengthwise
across the hearth to stop anything wicked
from slinking down the chimney.

Brooms are guardians,
sweeping out the evil. Sweep at least
once a day, but steer clear
of the feet of an unmarried woman,
or she'll forever be a spinster.

Evolve

Letter to West Virginia, November 2016

Ann Pancake

———————

Dear West Virginia,

Place that made me, and made my parents, and theirs, and theirs, and theirs, and theirs. I write you from Seattle, Washington, three weeks after the election and three decades after leaving you. A note of thanks for the most recent gift you gave.

In early October, West Virginia, you placed a picture in my mind. A slender arc of deer leg, curving to an elegant hoof. Most but not all of the flesh decayed; a little fur left at the fetlock. Although the image came to me in Seattle, I knew that the leg lay in West Virginia, could tell that by the dead oak leaves on the ground. I saw the leg like I've seen, heard, felt that spring-fed reservoir of images, sounds, scents, people, stories you have given me, West Virginia, all these thirty years away. And what kind of writer would I have been, West Virginia, without you? Would I have been a writer without you?

If I hadn't grown up surrounded by land always, land around my shoulders, land up over my head, hill, hollow, ridge, creek bed, riverbank, draw, that land pushing up into my throat, word-birthing land. What kind of writer would I have been, West Virginia, without your language? The accent itself feels close to the ground, an English soft and loamy, language I can wrap around, language that will play with me, easy in my mouth, language that never binds me as so often "standard," "proper" English does.

What kind of writer would I have been (would I have been a writer?) if I couldn't walk on you and hear a story, the sounds first, then the pictures, then the narrative itself, like beats from the ground? When I cannot hear land anywhere else, not in Washington, or New Mexico, or Japan, or Pennsylvania, or Samoa, or Thailand, or North Carolina, all those mute-to-me places that I've lived, no matter how I've ear-cocked asked-them tried. When I can hear you, West Virginia, without even having my body on you. I can hear you just by dreaming myself back to you, just by imagining myself into you earnestly enough.

That deer leg in my mind, torn or cut from its body, I guess a lot of people might find such an image grotesque, macabre, but the associations are different for me. We played with deer legs when we were little, picked them up after our fathers and uncles butchered bucks. We gripped them by their knees and made them prance. Imagining the whole deer trotting in front of us, or imagining the deer taking us for a ride, or imagining being a deer myself, fast-flowing up a hollow side. Bones mean death, but they are framework too. Bones are, in a sense, where we begin.

Dear West Virginia, what kind of writer would I have been if I hadn't been raised to love you? Taught to love you by my family and by the culture, by school, and even by church, but taught to love you also (and here *taught* is too innocent a word: *seduced*? *ensnared*?) by the land of you yourself. Pull of you, draw of you, hold of how you won't let us go, and why, when almost everyone else I know is also decades from their childhood places, I'm about the only one who still calls that place home?

And through you, West Virginia, I have also learned how the ferocity of any love is hotter-fired by threat of loss. To grow up in you, West Virginia, was to be nurtured by what was also continuously being taken away, from the days I stood, six years old, in the picture window of our middle-class home in Nicholas County in view of bulldozers stripping a mountain, to the day I stood, thirty years later, with another generation of West Virginia children at the turquoise-goo toe of a seeping mountaintop removal valley fill. West Virginia, how profoundly beautiful. How profoundly vulnerable. Loving you accompanied always by witnessing, by bearing up under, your destruction. Clear-cut, strip mine, gas well, chicken factory farm, pipeline, power line, subdivision of second homes, whatever the appetites of people not of this place who don't and won't have to look at what was sacrificed for what they have to have.

West Virginia, what kind of writer would I have been without this staggering ambivalence? If I only loved you? If I didn't sometimes hate you too? Hate when our culture is narrow, intolerant, resigned, hate when it's callous about the land. Hate how it feels to be so profoundly attached to a place so compromised. Ambivalent, too, because in West Virginia, the line between lover of place and destroyer of place is not invisible like it often is elsewhere. In West Virginia, I see without obfuscation how we ruin you ourselves and in this way ruin ourselves as well. West Virginia, you expose my complicity too.

West Virginia, nucleus of contradictions, reverence and decimation, desire and repulsion, warmth and violence, ignorance and decency, murder and fecundity. From you I've learned, as an artist and as an activist, the power of the in-between. How the richest making can arise in the friction between polarities. How tension brutal-births unexpected acts of imagination.

And my long experience of witnessing your ruin has taught me, too, that tearing down clears an emptiness for opportunity. The extent of breakdown offers corresponding extent of possibility for transformation. The richest making can happen in that loose, terrifying, nothing-anymore-taken-for-granted—the way, West Virginia, you pull open my chest. I have known for a very long time, West Virginia, that you are not different from so-called mainstream America, but a distillation of it. That you are not backward, but the opposite: you are prophecy. The kind of disintegration—environmental, political, economic, spiritual—underway elsewhere in the United States already took down much of West Virginia. What we, along with other derided, exploited, tossed-aside places have already learned about creation and destruction the rest of the nation finally learns now for real.

At the end of October, a few weeks after you put that deer leg in my mind, I walked up into the woods on my father's family land. Land that's been in our family for two centuries, but where I hadn't set foot in two years. Because during those two years, that piece of you, West Virginia, which is closest to me had been ravaged too.

But in October, I told myself I had a responsibility not to abandon you who weren't responsible for what you'd undergone. I reminded myself that looking away was the reason the madness everywhere could keep spinning on. So I climbed up the bank into the woods, not to the hurt place itself, couldn't do that yet, but to the edge of the wound, there in the border area where trees still grew. I spent a couple hours there, mostly sitting at the base of a pin oak, then I headed out, stepping over logs, scuffing through leaves. I was nearly to the clearing above the road, the edge of the edge, when I looked down.

And there that deer leg lay.

West Virginia, for most of my life, you've given me images, feelings, rhythms, stories in my head, and some of those, as best I could, I tried to make into art. This time you gave me, in bone, on the ground, you made real, the imagined thing itself.

West Virginia, you've taught me, as an artist and as a human, discipline, resourcefulness, how to cobble together, improvise. West Virginia, you've taught me how to suffer loss without losing my mind. You've shown me the space opened for making after the destruction is over and even while it's still going on.

And I know this is an era to make, not maintain. A time to invent instead of sustain. Improvise. Imagine. West Virginia, you've shown me.

There that deer leg lay. I could touch it. The one you'd placed in my mind. West Virginia, nothing is impossible.

Love,
Your great-great-great-great-great-granddaughter Ann

October Woods

Jesse Graves

The first cold nights have curled
the edges of forest-floor ginger,
rouged the locust and poplar leaves,
cracked the caps of fallen acorns.
Mushrooms and polyps of lichen
thrive now, all shapes and colors
sprout from the gloaming dirt.
Turkey-tail fungus fans up across
the torsos of downed trees,
morning frost illuminating it all.

Rooted: Lessons from Landscape

Amber M. Wright

I.

One minute, I am upright, trotting over craggy ground at least two miles into a run on a local, yet fairly technical, trail. The next, I have earth in my nostrils. I taste the soil, and dead leaves funnel into my throat from my sinus cavity, a result of the floodgates releasing hot streams down my cheeks: the involuntary response to getting knocked horizontally and unexpectedly. I groan and force my head up to look around.

Inconspicuous, just lying on my stomach in the middle of the woods. I feel both gladness that no one witnessed my spill and disappointment that no one is there to offer consolation. I roll over and sit on my butt looking toward my outstretched legs, my knees imprinted with the remains of tiny twigs, mud, pebbles, and brown leaf particles.

Underneath my calves, I see peeking out from under layers of leaves the very source of my descent: thick, robust roots belonging to a trailside maple.

Fucking roots, I think, shaking my head and dusting off the dirt on my knees. I stand and pull a maple leaf from my hair and drop it. It lands atop the exposed root. I take a few shaky steps onward, making sure that nothing is broken, fractured, or sprained. I admonish myself for forgetting the foremost rule of trail running: *always look down!* I ease back into a jog, taking extra care to look directly down so that another community of roots does not surprise me again. I think about them—roots and their resoluteness—for the rest of my run.

2.

When I was a child, my dad took me to a lake near our home every weekend during the summers. There on the beach, we had "our spot," which was a pile of large rocks, riprap we had collected from around the recreation area and used as makeshift seats. They were "our rocks"—we marked them as ours. We graffitied them with a jumbo-sized Magic Marker, scratched messages upon their surfaces. "Amber's Rock." One of the rocks, a personal favorite of ours, was an oddly elongated rock my dad transformed with the marker into the head of an alligator, which also featured the rock-reptile's invitation: "Sit on my head, please!" It was evident that my dad thought he was brilliantly hilarious for his creation. I thought so too.

The one lone tree on the beach, a grandiose sweetgum that dropped its not-so-sweet, spike-covered gumballs on the ground, shaded our rock pile. The gumballs, large cherry-shaped seeds, generally scattered in a ten-foot radius before tender feet were safe from their bites. Sitting on our rock pile, I would ask my dad to tell me war stories from when he was in Vietnam, but he usually just told me I was too young to hear those sorts of things. Once, however, he mentioned that he had to traverse a minefield, and compared it to how we navigated the span of gumballs between our spot and the shoreline. Later, I waded in the water after successfully avoiding the small sand bombs and watched my dad make his way from under our tree. He was stepping wide and putting on a show when he must have miscalculated a step. He yelped, "Owha!" and took his foot into his hands. Then, losing his balance, he quickly jammed it down into the sand again: "Owha!" "Owha!" "Owha!" I watched my dad theatrically bounce from foot to foot all the way to the water's edge. I was roaring when he met me. As he splashed his sore soles in the water and soothed them by squishing his toes in the soft Mississippi clay, he said, "You think that's funny, huh?" I did.

3.

We are rooted in the regions we come from, in landscape and the history of place. Our lifestyles are dictated by what resources lie beyond our front door. Yet when we physically relocate, we resist a change in ourselves. I come from the flatlands. The Mississippi Delta, where you can see for miles and miles and miles, where the sky touches the earth and the landscape hides no secrets. Highway 61 stretching straight from Memphis into the deep,

deep delta is a book spine with perpetual expanses of farmland to the east and west like open pages. The rows of raised dirt, lines of a story. No matter how long, when I come home, the story will be the same. There's comfort in those repetitive rows of cotton, soybeans, and corn. I love coming home to a landscape that never changes, but I often wonder on my trips home how much I would hate it if I had stayed.

I would have stayed if it had worked out with my high school sweetheart. A few months before college graduation, I would have had a little diamond on my left finger, and the church ladies would be gushing with marital advice: "always submit to him" and "don't go to bed angry." We would have bought a little land, built a house, and started having babies right away. He'd probably drink, and so would I. We might take a family vacation to SeaWorld or Pigeon Forge, but besides that, the only world we'd know outside our own would just be talk. I fell in love with him at a young age and was entangled in the familiarity of life with him, a future with him. I could not, would not, have dreamt of exploring an alternative life with another or even on my own. The more we grew up, the more distant we became from the people we once were. I knew that. I noticed the changes, but I was unwilling to allow this relationship we had spent so many years growing, at times desperately, to die. I'm glad he cheated. Glad he got her pregnant. Glad they got married. I admit that these sentiments are tinged with bitterness, but my gladness is still earnest. It took a series of actions out of my control for the relationship to end, to provide me with an exit. After we broke up, he didn't even acknowledge the Facebook message I sent to him about my dad dying. When I visited his profile—not because I missed him, but to see what my life might have looked like, to confirm how much it's not at all what I wanted—he looked happy. He looked devoted, with her on his arm and children planted at his feet.

4.

There were sweetgum trees on each side of the driveway at my home in Mississippi. I used to collect the fallen seeds, picking them up by their stems, as not to get pricked by their spurs. Pretending they were cherries,

I would put them in a large ice-cream pail and bring them to my dad, who would praise me for cleaning off the driveway—he liked everything to be kept tidy. Once, when I was about five years old, I had a classmate over to the house. I invited her to pretend we were on a fruit orchard and told her we needed to collect the fallen cherries. We ended up with a full Blue Bunny ice-cream bucket each, and I was pleased my game had ended well, or at least I thought it did.

Later that evening, hours after my classmate had gone home, I was watching *Wheel of Fortune* in the living room with my mom and dad when from down the hallway we heard my brother yell in pain. We all jumped from our seats, startled. In his bedroom doorframe, my brother appeared, pulling a familiar cherry-like ball out of his bare back. He reported a dozen more were tucked into his bed sheets. All eyes went toward me. "It wasn't me! I promise!" I wailed. I had a pretty good track record. My family believed me. However, my classmate was not invited back.

5.

When I started running a few years ago, I had a lot of anger to burn through. I wasn't going to let my cheating ex-boyfriend see me get fat and depressed, so I started making laps around my university's intramural track. It just happened to be located right in front of his apartment complex. I was going to show him how okay I was by getting skinny. It made perfect sense at the time, but then I learned he had gotten engaged to the girl he cheated on me with. A shotgun wedding, a hallmark Mississippi tradition. By then, however, I decided I liked running for other reasons than what it would do for my figure: it helped me work through the pain. By this time, my dad was dying of cancer. The only thing I could do was run. I was running because he couldn't even walk anymore. I was like a tree in a storm, and my legs were my trunk. If I could strengthen them, make them solid, then no matter how much I swayed up top, I knew I was still firmly grounded.

I branched out from the track into town, and finally the long country roads that seemed they would eventually end at the base of a sunrise or sunset. I often would run during those twilight hours in the summer because it was the only bearable time to exercise in the hellish Mississippi temperatures. The asphalt would turn into gravel, then dirt. Sometimes, while jogging down a long stretch of lonely roadside, I would become a distraction for an old farm dog patrolling the crop lines for deer and coons. He would see me coming a hundred yards away and start barking in circles until I was right up on him. Then, he'd silence his alarm and sniff aggressively in my direction, until with eyes still set on the horizon ahead, I'd say, "Hi, puppy." He'd join my stride and prance alongside me for about half a mile, the end of his owner's property line. Knowing his boundary he'd promptly stop, then sit to watch me as I trotted onward. Who knows how long he gazed after me, perhaps until the sunbeams swallowed up my silhouette entirely? He knew I'd return, had to get back where I came from. I'd find him again, and we would repeat our act as I ran home.

6.

While I was in college at Delta State, my parents had the sweetgum trees at the end of our driveway removed. They told me about the trees' removal over the phone as if it was just another piece of news. I surprised them when I responded rather vehemently. "WHAT? WHY WOULD YOU DO THAT?" I choked out over the line as my eyes involuntarily welled with tears. They explained that one of the trees had been struck by lightning multiple times and looked like it was about to fall. The other might as well go too—something about its root system.

The sweetgums had grown so tall and full over the years that their branches met and intertwined with one another high above the foot of our driveway. They had formed a natural archway, my first sign of welcome when I arrived home from being away at school. I didn't go home for weeks after my parents told me what they had done. I didn't want to face the bareness that existed in place of my trees. I knew that coming home would feel different now.

Eventually, I did go home. When I turned into my driveway, there were stumps. I was flooded with grief as I guided my steering wheel toward the center of my driveway. Yet even that small action felt wrong. The trees with their outstretched, welcoming arms, evocative of my dad's who'd often be waiting for me, his arms outstretched, at the top of the drive, were gone. That was around the same time my dad's cancer came back. I sat in my car trying to understand why I was crying. I'd be doing the same thing just a few short years later when I'd come to visit home the first time from West Virginia, my new home. Then, I'd be mourning my dad's absence.

<h1 style="text-align:center">7.</h1>

After my dad had passed away, I quit my first job out of college. I decided I needed a change of scenery. My heart was set on the mountains, any mountains. I had spent a summer in the Sierra Nevada once, and the snow-capped ranges remained imprinted on my mind. One of my favorite spots was called Hidden Lakes, a remote wilderness area where I stayed overnight on a day off from camp counseling. Every time I think about looking down upon a pool of water from a lakeside cliff right before I plunged down, I'm brought to tears by the water's piercing clarity. I can still feel the roughness of a giant redwood on the John Muir trail against my cheek when I hugged its base for a photo. Mount Whitney, Half Dome, and El Capitan were all calling just like Muir had said. I wanted to return.

Since my summer in California, I also made it to the Rockies in Colorado and had started quite the love affair with those stony peaks as well. In fact, it was on a trail in Rocky Mountain National Park that I experienced my first trail run. It had started to rain while I was leisurely hiking, and I needed to beat the lightning back to camp. Gray stony walls and emerald foliage ran parallel to my stride. I hopped over rocks and puddles forming on the path, feeling invigorated by the altitude. I was brimming with a mixture of cheerful fright at the danger the impending storm presented until I joined the rhythm of the million falling raindrops and became a forest child.

I dreamed of moving west, to the mountains of California and Colorado, but I got Appalachia. To be honest, I was ignorant of this eastern range. In fact, my new boyfriend, Chad, and I secured seasonal jobs in Telluride before he got an interview for a permanent position in West

Virginia, and then another interview, and then a job offer. We traded in our plans of being ski bums out west for the security of health benefits and a housing lease that lasted longer than six months. I was disappointed, I admit, worried that we missed out on a grand adventure, but as we drove our U-Haul through Tennessee, Kentucky, and across the Ohio, the Appalachian ridges welcomed me with the promise of the unknown.

The landscape here also tells a story, one you have to engage with deeply to understand. It's not scrawled in lines of earth like the Mississippi Delta. It's etched into stone, ancient and mysterious. The mountains here are not like the grandiose walls of the West either, but they are vast in other ways. Ways I'm still uncertain about. They are prodigious, yet humble. The wind that tunnels through the valleys and ridges seems to whisper and beckon. When I walk outside in the morning, I'm often met with dense fog. It reminds me that I cannot know what the day holds. No matter that it's Tuesday or Sunday or any day that generally brings the same routine. The clouds that touch my front porch proclaim the unexpected happens every day. Sipping my coffee, while looking out on the beauty of a neighborhood ridge being revealed through dissipating fog, I meditate on the muddle of realizations stirring inside of me. I feel grief for missing my family in Mississippi, knowing that without my dad's presence nothing will ever be the same there and, yet, a sense of comfort overcomes me because somehow it will always be the same there. I feel gratitude for the sequence of life, even the painful moments that have afforded me the view I have at present, for what I've learned simply by experiencing other places, each beautiful in their own ways; I feel an itch to move on again. Never did I think I would uproot so voluntarily and for the uncertainties of adventure.

8.

I admit it's hard to do, but for the first few months I lived in West Virginia I avoided running hills at all costs. I was intimidated by the inclines and the curves of the Mountain State. The roads here are never straight. They hug the foot of a mountain or wrap like a strand of ribbon around a ridge.

In Mississippi, I knew exactly where I was going. I just never knew when I would get there. Here, I never know what is around the corner.

One evening in the winter, I was trailing a few steps behind a running buddy in a woodsy suburb. It was only a little after six, but we were wearing headlamps because it gets dark early during that time of the year. We were trudging up a steep, windy hill, the geography West Virginia is known so well for, when my light caught the green reflection of a small, flying dot. The dot was attached to a large dark mass that was darting directly across our path. As I gained ground, my flashlight beam revealed that it was a buck, at least eight points, and if my friend would have been going half a second faster she would have had been sporting hoof prints. "Deeeeer!" she warned in the same way we call "Car!" when we encounter vehicle headlights or "Hoooole!", "Roooock!", or "Rooot!" when we're out on the trails in order to warn those following behind. I bet the deer was as thrilled as we were at our crossing. A spurt of adventure on his way back home.

I have always thought that road running is a bit more predictable than trail running, that it's safer, that you can really *know* a road if you've run it enough. Unlike the trails that seem to change every day with the falling of a tree or shifting of rocks, road paths don't alter much. I felt you could foresee anything out of the ordinary. But this night reminded me that that is a myth. Even the most familiar paths can teem with surprise.

9.

I got two tattoos when I knew I was going *somewhere*, but not quite sure where or how I was going to get there. I got a compass on my right forearm in hopes that any direction I pointed would be the right one. And I got the outline of the state of Mississippi on the inside of my left ankle, at the root of my own body. Neither are very original ideas, especially the image of one's home state. They even sell jewelry, magnets, and T-shirts of the shapes of states. They're marketed to people just like me, those who enjoy advertising state pride. Chad once poked fun at state tattoos. He said, "I know state tattoos are a *hip thing*, but do people from Colorado *really* get tattoos of Colorado?" We laughed. He certainly had a point since a tattoo of Colorado would just be a rectangle!

But a tattoo is for yourself. It embodies some sort of personal significance, at least for most people. Honestly, it hurts to get a tattoo. Mine range in sizes and I have some rather large pieces considering I'm a petite woman, but the one that hurt the most was the smallest, the one of Mississippi. The tibial nerve lies underneath my home state on the inside of my left ankle. The nerve branches all throughout my leg and foot, which explains why the tattoo needle put into contact with that specific area, as a true Mississippian would say, hurt like the dickens!

10.

At my home in West Virginia, my across-the-street neighbor put out this hanging grim reaper decoration in her front yard this past Halloween. It would shake and cackle when someone entered through the fence gate or the wind simply blew through its black tattered garb. My eight-month-old golden retriever, Crosby, was not a fan of it for the first week or so after it was positioned under the giant oak tree in her yard. He barked at it relentlessly every time I let him out. I lightheartedly told my elderly widow neighbor, Myrtle, that Crosby didn't like her little ghoul at first, but he seemed to have finally accepted that it's not harming anyone.

A week later, Myrtle called me over to her fence line. She informed me that she was having the huge oak tree in her front yard removed the next day and that the work trucks and equipment would be arriving at eight o'clock in the morning; she didn't want us to get blocked in. The familiar pinch at the back of my throat triggered a catch in my voice as I stammered, "Oh, uh . . . why are you getting rid of it?"

Myrtle said, "Oh, honey. It's causing me all kinds of trouble. It drops so much debris on my roof and, and the roots are growing right through my plumbing." She added that she would still have the evergreen in the middle of her yard that her late husband had planted. Myrtle and her husband were some of the very first to build a house in what is now a densely populated neighborhood. Myrtle has seen the street we live on grow and change over the forty-plus years she's been in her home.

I collected myself enough to give my voice a more solid sound and told her I understood. "I actually have to be at work at eight tomorrow, so I'll be out of here by seven thirty in the morning," I assured her. I lied. I wasn't due in until nine, but I didn't want to see the trucks rolling down our road like grim reapers, ready to collect an old soul.

When I came home that evening, there was barely a sign that workers had been present earlier. No scattered limbs or piles of sawdust. They must have been paid to clean up the scene of the crime. Of course, to those who live on the street, the landscape was certainly different. The whole lane and sky had opened up and the only testament to the grand oak was the stump. Myrtle had already placed potted fall flowers on it as if it were a grave. Later, while sitting on her porch, now in full view from our own, Myrtle commented, "My husband Ken planted that oak tree. It took thirty-three years to grow and only three hours to remove."

Rime Myth

Michael McFee

———————

Laughing, the old gods rally
along this fall ridge
and swap their dazzling stories,

hoary breath clinging to sticks,
crisp blades of grass,
needles, leaves, the outermost tips

and tops of twigs and branches,
that feathery frozen dew
highlighting everything, casting

brilliant ice-shadows
briefly skyward,
shining like the holiest of days

before a jealous younger god
rises and burns
his way through low dense clouds,

forcing the crystals to loosen
their grip till melted,
untransfiguring the mountains,

that lofty shivery glory dead
everywhere except
some old man's uncovered head.

High Water

Mark Powell

————

There ain't no gas in the tank for that, she told him. You got money to put gas in the tank I'll be more than happy to drive you.

He was playing rec department football but you couldn't very well drive on air. So he was walking, some days he was walking. But it was almost three miles from the Group Home down to the Chickapea ballfield and by then what was the point? They played on the infield dirt and into the outfield, church league softball all around them. The sound of metal bats, the lights coming on at dusk. You got red clay in the grooves of your hands, all the lines that marked life and happiness tinted orange. You got it in your eyebrows to where it wouldn't hardly come out. His football pants were more or less ruined with mud even though he kept washing them with Clorox and hanging them on the line off the back porch. Three miles. Not even counting on you had to walk back in the dark.

DSS ain't no taxi service, son.

They were on the porch. Cory and the housemother they called nana.

What's he wanting?

The voice came through the screen door. That was her husband, the one they called Jeb, on the couch with a Natural Light and a rerun of *Dancing with the Stars*. Jeb would be gone for a week and then back for three or four days, his Peterbilt parked across the front lawn like a riding toy.

Wants me to drive him to the ballfield.

Down to Chickapea? Have his ass walk.

She had her phone out, fingering down Craigslist.

I told him, she said.

Ain't no gas for that.

That's what I told him.

He want all that exercise let him exercise his legs.

That's what I just said, damn.

Twelve years old. He could heal things but not this. His name was Cory.

Cory counted five boys in the Group Home and all of them were older. Only Martin was his friend. Sixteen years old and tiny for his age. He was self-contained at school and was learning to read, which Cory sometimes helped him with. They read *Little Critter* and *Franklin*, books discarded by the library because someone had scribbled *shit* with crayon on every page. Martin liking that owl they had for a teacher, one boy a fox, another a turtle in bifocals. You reckon why that owl don't up and eat him? Martin so simple and so small they let him play on the twelve and under team. They sat on the same stoop wearing the same kind of stained football pants and same kind of off-brand Under Armour shirts the rec department had given them.

They ain't gonna drive us.

Their pads sat on the concrete walk clear of the fire ants, face masks pulled through the neck holes for carrying.

Shit don't matter, Martin said. We all gonna die anyway.

What do you mean?

Bird flu. I seen it on the tee-vee.

The house sat up in the holler with a view of the mountains.

We could just walk, Cory said.

Nah.

We done it before.

That ain't shit we need to be doing, walking like that.

Martin picked at his face. He had pink eye again.

A few days later he and Martin dyed their hair with Kool-Aid.

Two days a week a van came to take Cory and Martin and one of the older boys to the services center downtown where they drank Sam's Cola and wrote in their dream journals. It was a half-hour ride, everything following the river, past farms and pastures and chicken houses with giant ventilation fans. Churches everywhere. Concrete blocks painted white. Picnic shelters and big two-by-four crosses with a towel dyed purple and hung over the arms. Ingles. Hardees. A place women got their hair cut and their nails done in glittery reds. Town was just one big parking lot with a Walmart and a crew of Mexicans paving a new turn lane.

The one place he liked was the Cherokee museum. A concrete building off Short Street with high lunettes and an old woman volunteering at the front desk. Now and then an old legionnaire would push-mow the grass in dickeys and a ball cap from the VFW, arms liver spotted and roped with veins. Inside were buckskin shirts and leggings in display cases meant for jewelry, arrowheads knapped to fine points, an ax-head grooved from its banding and pulled from the Tuckasegee. A black bear was mounted on its back legs, upright and reaching like a shaggy clown, and though a sign read DO NOT TOUCH, people had touched, people had rubbed the right paw for good luck so that now the paw was bare and hairless, wiped to its taxidermic shell. It seemed to Cory like a disgrace, but the bear appeared unaware with its dog's muzzle and giant yellow teeth, its eyes glossed to dark mirrors.

At the end of Group, he was allowed an hour or so to roam the town and it was here he always went. He would walk past the maps and paintings depicting long houses and encampments, and pause by the bear to pay his respects.

But it was the canoe that held him.

When you live in the mountains you dream of the sea, that vastness. The hard sand, the tide. The canoe was a dugout. Thirty-two feet of American elm. The sign estimated it dated from the early eighteenth century. If you bent close, you could still register the faint tracery of eagles and bears and wolves carved along the bow. It had been found in a river just to the south and would have traveled past Cherokee and Creek villages. Possibly it would have traveled as far south as the Savannah River. There was no reason it might not have traveled as far as the ocean, except for the most reason of all: there was no floating free of this place. The mountains held you. The mountains were greedy. They came up in green folds to move against you. The fog too. He didn't trust the fog.

One of the older boys was seventeen and a junior at the high school and it was he who had first taken Cory to the museum. After Group, he would sit behind the services building and smoke pot. Cory would come up on him and another girl who was here because she'd cut herself down to the white meat, row after row as if she were preparing a garden. The girl called Cory *little bug,* as in hey, little bug. Don't you look cute today, little bug.

Don't listen to her.

I'm gonna take you home with me one day.

Don't ever listen to her shit.

He lit the joint in his hand, but just held it until it began to eat itself and finally the girl said Hand that here and took it from him.

Little bug, she said.

The older boy took the joint back.

Where's your other self today? he asked.

Cory shrugged.

You don't know?

No.

The girl tried to take the joint back and the boy turned.

Quit it, Ella.

Hand it here.

Quit for a minute. I'm trying to talk here.

He turned back to Cory.

I thought you looked out for him.

Sometimes.

Sometimes? You know they get a check for each of us, Nana and Jeb. Which means they're actually getting paid for this shit. You know that, don't you?

He shrugged again.

That means they get paid for you too, the girl said.

The boy put the joint back up by his mouth and Cory noticed his hand was shaking.

Yeah, well, fuck them. Soon as my medicine's strong I'm gone right down that river.

The girl smirked but the older boy wasn't looking at her. He was looking at Cory.

A check ever week, he said. Just ask your buddy about it one day why don't you.

One day Cory came in to find Martin on the couch with the remote control in his mouth, not exactly chewing, but then Cory realized yeah, he was. From the kitchen he could hear nana singing with the radio *but on the other hand, there's a golden band.*

He ain't here, Martin said.

Who?

It's all right. She said he's gone to Houston.

The older boy was in the back bedroom reading a book about the Trail of Tears.

They moved out, he said.

Cory stood in the doorway.

Who?

Matt and Cobra. They were just waiting till he was gone and now he is. Houston and then Dallas or somewheres.

Jeb?

He nodded at the bunkbeds on the far wall. They looked exactly as they always had.

They're gone, he said. But they didn't take my medicine. My medicine is strong.

They walked to practice two days in a row and ran suicides and did pushups in the dirt and after the second night while everyone lined up for a Popsicle the coach came over and pulled Cory over and said Somebody needs to talk to you a minute, son.

It was a woman in a white blouse and black skirt with two pencils in her hair like chopsticks. Her heels sinking into the infield clay.

Let's walk over here a minute, Cory. Did you get you a Popsicle?

No, ma'am.

What's your favorite flavor?

I didn't get one.

Oh, well, I'm sure they'll save you one, grape or whatever.

They walked around the wire backstop over to the picnic table past where some of the parents sat in folding chairs.

I wanted to ask you about two of the boys you live with, Matthew Farris and Philip Steele.

Cobra?

Have they ever said anything unusual to you, Cory? Particularly about your housefather.

They had not. No one ever said anything to him.

One day his hair was different, peroxide blonde. The Kool-Aid just washed out at practice, stained the V-neck of the shirt he wore under his pads. Pink it turned it. Which was bullshit is what it was.

There was no sign of Matt or Cobra.

Jeb was in Cleveland.

You wash that out your head before he gets back, nana said.

Jeb was in Milwaukee.

He took Cordicil in the morning so that the day floated on a bodiless cloud, the world screened in a green haze exactly the color of the fat gel-caps he swallowed by the handful. Four or five taken with sips of blue RockStar. School started back, but instead of school they dug potatoes with a beach shovel, a flimsy plastic thing meant for sandcastles. They filled a plastic bag, Cory and Martin, some of the potatoes the size and hardness of marbles. Left them in the kitchen sink like an offering.

Then he went out and healed things.

The blue jay had somehow impaled itself on the top two cords of barbwire.

They found it after coming along the ruin of the highway embankment onto the driveway that washed out in heavy rain and had to be scraped with the box blade on the Kubota parked in the garage, an orange thing with a lawn mower seat crossed with silver duct tape.

The bird had a barb at its neck and another in its abdomen.

It flew like that, Martin said. It didn't see.

The feathers were wet and pliant and as blue as the fall sky. There was no blood, only a single drop of black lacquer he realized after a moment was blood.

You think it flew like that? Martin asked.

You would sometimes see field mice or moles strung over the barbs by shrikes, but they had never seen a bird like this. It was as big as Cory's face.

Touch it, Martin said.

And Cory did, slowly, one hand and then the other, cupping its body until it began to move and he closed his hands around it and pulled it off the wire and then it flew from his hands, blue wingbeats in the blue air.

It weren't dead, Martin said.

But they both knew it had been.

They quit football sometime in October. They couldn't get to practice, and when the woman with the pencil in her hair like chopsticks showed up at the ballfield to offer them a ride Cory decided to not go back. If anyone noticed, no one said anything.

Halloween nana painted their faces with some of her old makeup and drove them to town where the stores were giving out candy. She parked and said three hours and then walked to the Towne Tavern. Jeb was in Kansas City.

They carried plastic bags they filled with Smarties and Tootsie Rolls and little miniature Snickers and Milky Ways. In the Walgreens, they stuffed plastic masks down the front of their pants and put them on out in the street. Frankenstein's monster with stiches and a gray bolt. A pale zombie. The masks smelled of rubber, and they sweated foundation down their necks. Pushed the masks up onto their foreheads like discarded skins. Wandered off Main Street through a neighborhood of shabby duplexes with plywood stoops and porches made from raw lumber. Four of five cars on every lawn. Jack-o'-lanterns. The sort of spiderwebs you sprayed from a can.

Hey.

The voice came from a porch crowded in darkness and the lit cherries of whatever they were smoking.

Hey. Come here.

Cory and Martin stopped on the sidewalk, eating Starbursts and leaving the wrappers behind them like a crumb trail.

Come here, little motherfucker. I ain't gonna hurt you. You remember me?

They walked into the yard and stood at the bottom of the concrete steps. There were maybe ten or so people on the porch and more inside. Music. Voices. Eminem.

It was the one they called Cobra, one of the older boys who had run off after no more than a few months at the Group Home.

You remember me? Look here.

He was leaning over the balustrade with a Coors and a cigarette in one hand, the other around a girl.

This is that little motherfucker I was telling you about, he said to the girl. You remember me saying. You all right?

They were silent.

I like your mask, she said.

Martin held forth his bag, the plastic top open between his two hands.

Y'all want some candy?

The boy and girl laughed.

See? he said. Simple.

But sweet.

She looked at the two of them and made a face, lips puckered. Her skin wasn't as white as Cory had thought. It was makeup. She was a ghost.

You want to come up here? she asked.

Shit.

I'm serious, she said. You can come up here. I'm the one saying you can, not him.

I'd just as soon you punched me in the heart, the boy said, Cobra said. Here, he said, and something cold hit Cory, a can of beer that rolled to his feet.

Drink that, he said. And kill that motherfucker you ever get the chance.

Who? Martin asked.

That motherfucker didn't try but once to put his hands on me, no, sir.

He's sweet, the girl said, come up here, honey.

But they were already walking back through the dirt yard past a jacked-up Tacoma and onto the street where they opened the beer and drank off the foam, wandering beneath the streetlamps and passing the can between them.

It weren't alive, Martin said later. It ain't like you healed it.

So Cory didn't tell him when he found the dead junco a week later. It had flown into the kitchen glass and broken its neck, stiff in the brittle brown grass. But when he touched it, it flew.

The older boy who had not left was trying to start the Kubota parked in the barn.

Battery's dead, he said, and came back with the charger and an orange extension cord looped over his shoulder like a coil of rope.

But when I get it running I'm gonna roll right out of here.

He attached the clamps and ran the extension cord to the porch.

I did my fast. I cleansed myself. Three days without food and your medicine is strong. You know about the Cherokee?

Cory was silent.

You know about the Sioux?

He plugged in the charger.

Look here, he said, and took a small pistol from the waistband of his jeans and showed it to Cory.

Lakota don't mean nothing but enemy people, he said.

He went back to see the Cherokee canoe.

It wasn't exactly an eagle carved in the soft wood but the head and wings of an eagle on the boy of a man. He would have put his fingers in it had it not been for the glass case. But in his mind he did.

The woman came to school, no chopsticks this time, but she had the sheriff with her and the principal himself came to get Cory out of class. He sat in the empty lunchroom across from them and then the principal said All right, I'll leave you to it.

The woman had a yellow legal pad on the table and had written the date across the top. He read it upside down. When the sheriff cleared his throat, Cory fixed his eyes on the rounded points of his star, his badge.

Jeb was in Phoenix, or Dallas it might have been by then, drawing closer by the hour.

Thanksgiving the older boy who had not left came into the room Cory and Martin shared and woke them.

I need you for a minute. Put on a coat.

Between the house and the propane tank, flipped on its back and tipped against the asbestos siding was an aluminum canoe. Silver. The dead grass yellow and high along the edges where the mower couldn't reach, dirt beneath. When they flipped it they found grubs and night crawlers.

The older boy hosed it out.

I got the tractor running too, he said. Help me to drag it.

Dinner was turkey and dressing a woman from the church brought in a casserole dish.

The older boy wore a sachet around his neck he said was made from deer hide and held the medicine of his spirit animal.

Don't you wear that thing at the table, Jeb said. He stared at the boy. I will knock the ever-living-shit out of you need be.

Later, Cory saw him in the yard sitting on the chrome passenger step of the Peterbilt. He had a pocketknife and had been crying and every now and then he took the curly pigtails of the blue and green airbrake lines and made to cut them.

But he never did.

A dead hummingbird, ruby-throated and broken. But he raised it up.

The older boy got the Kubota running and elevated the scoop on the front-end loader, used a length of logging chain he found in the barn to drag the canoe down to the creek. Cory and Martin followed behind, a cold clear morning, walking slowly behind the tractor as it popped the rain cap on the exhaust pipe and the canoe furrowed the grass like a plow.

When he reached the creek, he kept the tractor running and unhooked the canoe, and together they lowered it into water so shallow the aluminum scrubbed the sandstone bottom, unmoving.

Creek ain't deep enough, Martin said.

No, the older boy said. Except come flood.

Cory looked at the sky.

Not a cloud in sight, Martin said, and the older boy scratched his forehead with his wrist.

No, not this minute there ain't.

That night he came into the bedroom and motioned for Cory to follow him onto the back porch with the washing machine and a rototiller backed against the steps.

Which one are you right now? he asked.

What do you mean?

I mean are you Martin or Cory?

I'm Cory.

He ain't laid a finger on Martin cause he's special, he said. But that don't mean your time ain't coming.

His breath was a silver space, a lighter form of darkness. The pistol was back in the waistband of his pants.

Jesus, he said, when he was a boy, he made doves out of clay and brought them to life. You won't find that in the Bible, not in your regular Bible, at least.

In December, the museum put up a display on medicine men and he felt the familiar forces all around him. The four cardinal directions, the seven tribes. Only the owl and cougar stayed awake for the seven days of creation and thus they were blessed with such perfect night vision it was itself a holiness.

And there was water too, all sacred and all flowing to its common gathering.

He understood then about the medicine and felt it grow strong.

He went twice more and came home to find the older boy digging out the old potato cellar in the cliff.

Go get a shovel or something and help me, he said.

That night, when Martin was asleep, Cory rose from bed, put on his coat, and walked into the yard to listen for owls. The older boy was still digging. Jeb was in Virginia, coming hard on I-81.

The owl came in the new year. A barn owl secreted in the cavity of a dead oak up on the granite ridge. He watched it hunt over the back field.

The canoe was still in the dry creek.

The potato cellar was almost dug.

It's getting near time, the older boy said.

Martin was sleeping.

When he comes back, nana said, you just keep your mouth shut, all right? Much as you can, you keep your mouth shut.

They get a check for you, the older boy said later when they were digging. You're worth four hundred and thirty-two dollars a month according to the state of North Carolina.

January and they walked up the ridge below the dead oak.

Around the tree were owl pellets, gray bundles of tiny bones swaddled in what appeared as grass twisted and thin as needles.

I'd like to see you make that whole, Martin said.

The potato cellar was dug out by the first week of February.

Cory and Martin shoplifted chocolate hearts and Cordicil from the Walgreens in town.

The woman with the chopsticks was around the school but Cory wasn't sent for again.

Now I'll build up a big fire, the older boy said. You fast. Sit for three or four days until your mind is clear and your medicine's strong. It's real near now.

One day they swallowed six gelcaps and found a dead crow with one yellow eye pecked from its head. Cory carried it in a Converse shoebox for three days before he made it fly again.

The next day they shoplifted a dispenser of hand sanitizer, Martin sticking it down the front of his Wranglers.

On account of bird flu, he said. Since you won't quit touching em.

At the services center they wrote in their dream journals and after Martin sat on the front porch with his hot chocolate and Big Sixty cookies, which was where Cory found him.

They been watching me, Martin said.

Who?

Martin pointed at the three girls across the street staring at their phones and laughing. His index finger was ringed with a cookie.

Them girls, he said.

Right there?

Right there in front of your face.

Watching you?

Taking my picture and all.

Another boy from Group came out and Martin told him the same thing.

You're full of it, he said.

I been sitting here watching em back.

You're full of shit is what you are.

When the van took them home, the older boy dragged a dead tree off the ridge into the yard where he bucked it and cut it into stove length pieces.

Jeb ain't gonna like that, Martin said.

Jeb can go fuck himself, the older boy said.

He touched the deerskin sachet around his neck.

Jeb's in my bag now.

Come high water the canoe would flow down the creek into Big Branch into the Broad River and down through the Piedmont and the Carolina foothills into the Congaree on to the tea-colored darkness of the Santee and into the common gathering of the Atlantic.

This was not magic but the simple dictate of geography.

March came and the older boy cured the wood but not long enough so that when he built the fire by the opening of the potato cellar it smoked terribly.

Don't matter, he said.

He had three flat stones carried from the creek in the scoop of the tractor and he stacked them beside the fire. He was wearing Jeb's work gloves, stiff and smelling of 3-in-One oil, but Jeb was somewhere on I-95 and nana was at either the Dollar General or the Towne Tavern, depending.

I get the stones hot and then they go inside with me, he said. That's what the gloves are for.

I doubt them gloves'll help much, Martin said.

I sweat out all my impurities and my medicine gets strong.

How long you sit in there?

Until it rains. Then I need you to put me in the canoe.

It's likely not to rain for another week.

You can use the front-end loader. Just roll me into it.

It's likely not to rain till spring.

The canoe's tied up. When you get me in, push me off hard. Make sure the paddle's with me. I'll need the paddle.

You'll need high water to float past the highway bridge.

The older boy was fingering his sachet.

And one more thing. He looked then at Cory. Can you bring me the owl?

Only the owl was dead. They found it farther up the ridge, mummified and dragged between piles of granite that cropped between the big hardwoods and the dwarf pine. Cory carried it in the bowl of his hands like an offering, down the slope and past the cellar and around the house where new grass sprouted over the lawn. He spread its wings on the concrete walk and weighed each with a rock. It appeared frayed. It had been picked at by something, though not well. Tissue had been pulled from its open beak, a pinkish cord, and some feathers were broken. Its wings were as wide as Cory's arm.

He just wants its eyes, I think, Martin said. It don't have to be alive or nothing. He just wants its medicine.

Jeb was in Cleveland and nana had a box of Franzia on the couch with her.

They made the fire and started heating the rocks.

There was rain in the forecast.

It was nearer by the hour.

The older boy wet a towel and with the towel and gloves was able to carry the rocks into the cellar. It was six or so feet deep and equally wide, maybe three feet from floor to ceiling so that even sitting cross-legged they had to hunch. The air heated and they began to sweat, the humus scent stronger, like burned earth, which it was, but also like motion, which it was not. Cory didn't know what had become of the eyes of the owl. Possibly the older boy had eaten them, but possibly they were in the sachet around his neck. Besides a pair of boxer shorts, it was the only thing he wore, his dirty Nikes left by the cellar door, a sock stuffed in each.

You cain't breathe in here, Martin said.

Breathe slow, he told him.

I feel like I'm strangling.

Breathe slow. Don't talk.

Cory and Martin walked to the house to eat a can of Spaghetti-O's for dinner. Nana was asleep on the couch. After, they fixed a cup of water and walked back and stripped to their T-shirts and underwear and crawled back inside. The older boy appeared asleep, leaned into himself, skin pinking and eyelids heavy. But his head rose when they entered.

Hey, he said.

You all right? Martin asked.

I'm at peace.

We brought you some water.

I don't want it.

You don't want even a drink?

Pour it on the rock.

When he did, the rock steamed and Martin jerked back.

Jeb be back day after tomorrow, Martin said.

I got Jeb right here. The older boy touched his sachet. I got that motherfucker right here around my neck.

That night they slept with the windows open. It was still too cool for such, but if there was anything to hear they wanted to hear it. But there was nothing but the faint glow that came beneath the closed cellar door and then at some point even that was gone.

Nana was asleep on the couch the next day when they left for school.

The chopstick woman was there again, lurking around the picnic tables at lunch but never quite approaching.

In the afternoon a storm filled the sky, coming out of the north or out of the west. It didn't matter, really. Graying light and the crackle of electricity, the promise. Treetops swayed as they walked home, the crowns twitching. They saw the birds flying and then all at once the birds were gone.

I reckon his medicine's done got strong if he's calling in thunder, Martin said.

When they got back, nana was in the kitchen singing with the radio.

I fried some chicken, she said.

The storm broke that evening, the wind pushing the rain so that it fell in one great leaning angle, so hard the earth leaned with it and what was once plumb was made slant, the fissures and gaps wide enough to enter.

It was still raining though not as hard when they walked up to the cellar.

The older boy look diminished, somehow smaller. He couldn't seem to hold his head up.

It's real near now, he said. The canoe didn't float away, did it?

I don't think so, Martin said.

Check for me, all right? Make sure the paddle's there. The tractor too. All this water the boat'll float free.

The rain beat the cellar door and his head lolled back onto his shoulder.

Jeb be here come morning, Martin said.

I know, he said.

But his head stayed where it was.

Y'all be listening for me.

They were crawling out when Cory felt a hand grab his ankle and fix like a claw. He turned around. The pistol was in the older boy's lap.

Don't you go laying hands on me, he said. You let him drag me out by himself if that's what has to be done.

All right.

My medicine's strong, he said, but it ain't fit for you to raise me up. You ain't Jesus.

I know that.

You ain't the Messiah.

I know.

Nana was back on the couch with her phone and her Craigslist.

Where's Reggie? she said.

I don't know, Martin said.

Staying with one of his friends, Cory said.

Well which is it? You don't know or he's staying with a friend?

A friend, Cory said.

Well, friend or not he better have that road scraped by the time Jeb gets back.

The owl was flying again, some owl.

Cory heard it in the trees and when it came closer he woke Martin and they got dressed. It was raining something terrible and the creek would be high. It was possible the canoe had already washed downstream but when they got there they found it still fixed in the reeds and cattails and they dragged it higher on the bank and walked toward the cellar.

We're soaked to the bone, Martin said.

I know.

We're freezing.

We're all right.

The owl was in the trees directly above them, which is how they made their way to the cellar. When they opened it, a wall of trapped air gentled its way, warm and mineral rich, like the smell of the deer Jeb had dressed once out in the barn, its legs parted and hoisted in spreaders hooked to the joists.

One of us needs to get the tractor, Martin said.

I'll get it, Cory said. He said for me not to touch him.

Martin crawled halfway in, the soles of his tennis shoes muddy and showing.

We couldn't hear it I guess on account of the rain.

Don't touch the gun.

I ain't.

It was too dark to see the blood but when Cory crawled in he saw the sachet around the stump of his neck. The pistol had fallen from his hand. He crawled back out.

Go get the tractor, he told Martin.

That thing looks like a little pea shooter but I reckon it did its job.

Get the tractor.

I thought you were.

I want to sit here with him.

Martin shrugged and headed down the wet slope into the darkness. A few minutes later Cory heard the engine catch and then the spaces between the boards of the barn lit vertically with the headlights.

The older boy was still warm and Cory couldn't tell if this was the strength of his medicine or simply the lingering heat of the stone. Either way, he didn't touch the body, only allowed his hands to hover near. It was Martin who dragged him out and rolled him into the scoop.

A light was on in the house now, bedroom light, kitchen light.

She's up, Martin said.

We need to hurry.

It'll all be different now. I reckon they'll send us away.

Come on.

The Kubota slipped down the grass, sliding until the treads caught in the soft lawn and then they were bouncing away from the house toward the creek. The porch light was on now.

He didn't want you to touch him? Martin asked.

Cory stood on the step.

That's what he said.

They lowered the scoop slowly but the body still tumbled out. Water and blood dripped over the metal teeth. When Martin cut the engine there was only silence, and within that silence the rain, the rain and the sound of their working, rolling the body down the bank. The sound of the creek running past, high and silted and foamed with trash.

You'll have to help me, Martin said. I can't get him in by myself.

He said for me not to touch him.

Well, I cain't do it alone. Get by his feet.

They lifted him head and feet like a roll of wet carpet that thudded into the canoe. The paddle was there and they placed it at his side.

Then they were dragging it forward, the cold water rushing past their ankles and then their calves and up over their knees until they were thigh deep and the current was strong enough to bow the low-hanging limbs of the trees that grew along the bank. The current was mud colored and running, pulling diapers and plastic bags and the canoe righted itself like the needle of a compass.

Push him off, Martin said, and they did, and it went, moving and banging its way through the rocks and between the banks where the new grass laid over in waves, but moving. Down past the mailboxes nailed to the two-by-four, down past the trailer that sat at the holler's edge, pulled by the current as if it might never stop. On and on until they could no longer see it and simply stood there in the rain, freezing and staring at the spot it had been until Martin wiped his sleeve across his eyes and said,

It ain't like you healed nothing.

And Cory said nothing.

Cory was silent.

Never bothering to say that just before the canoe passed beneath the highway bridge he had seen the body raise up and take the paddle in his hands, his medicine very strong and his boat floating free.

cycles and (scrambled) seasons

doris diosa davenport

————

Context & introduction. Almost twenty years ago i was gratefully and happily included in two anthologies of Appalachian writers (*Bloodroot: Reflections on Place by Appalachian Women Writers*, ed. Joyce Dyer, 1998, and *Listen Here: Women Writing in Appalachia*, eds. S. L. Ballard and P. L. Hudson, 2003). Then i moved away from Northeast Georgia for a while to find work. Then the work ended and here i am, Affralachian, back home since August 2015, retired seventy (almost) year old college professor, still seeking employment and ironically—yet gratefully—submitting to another anthology.

For personal and political, local and global reasons, these are strange, stressful times. And yes, we all must acknowledge, struggle, evolve, survive, transform, and transcend. Nevertheless, now as always, i find inspiration and truth in the eloquent beauty of this landscape, the way it speaks to my soul. This long poem is how i listen.

Thick choking blinding smoke
forests of northeast Georgia,
of western North Carolina
syfy post-apocalyptic world
occluded vision   tainted breath

A healing song for the burning earth
the tortured ground and a sweet
smell of breakfast sausage in the air
40% chance of rain smolders
under fires and old stank hatred again Goddess,
Goddess send rain.

And if this morning
in the pre-dawn non-light
there is a soft sad scurrying
under the window it is
my sorrow settling in,
preparing to slide down the road to the creek

Rain—only a few drops
a teaspoon to this long drought
yet the mountains sing
leaves shimmer & sigh

Laying here blessed in bed
in this Solstice Sunshine—
today i will walk around glowing honey-brown
and be a Credit to the Race
an Asset to the Universe.

Landscape:
scrap iron gray
comfortable faded blue
laid back green
electric orange

and i saw a mountain hunker down
shivering, heading north on
129 from Gainesville to Cleveland. Georgia.

Winter trees
nodding mountains
sleeping shadows

Like a big fluffy blanket
this cloud settles around
my house

Holding all the things
in the world in my head
is tiring yet

to wake (again) to bright sunlight
to know all is right,
for a few minutes

silence of dusk
slow sun setting
again, back home
trees call my name
i sing to the mountains
air wraps me in peace

again where i want to be
in sun drenched spring
storm pushed winds, distant
mountains darken & twinkle
this is my appointment. This
is all.

Love in the Age of Inattention

Stephen Cushman

———————

What I like best about turning a corner
and seeing a snake, seeing me, coil
is having each other's complete attention.
Nobody saying, What were you saying?
Neither not focused, eyes of both parties
never so locked. Could you hold, please?
Not happening. Same goes for meeting
a deer, a hawk, a fox, a bear. Everybody stretched
thin toward the other. You prefer animals
because you fear intimacy, she said from the bed
and glanced at her phone.

I don't mind the nostalgia

Larry D. Thacker

———————

I don't mind moonshine and fiddles
and rocking chairs and ginseng hunting
in the old sense. I have a mostly
unearned nostalgia, like most in my
generation, for all things mountain
and finely Appalachian flavored.

Just make sure the moonshiner is
reading from some LA-rendered script
when he takes off from his still on that
four-wheeler trying to outrun the law.

And make sure the fiddle's duct-taped
back together after the guy down the road
cracked it across his cousin's neck
over a lost sandwich bag of pills.

Check that the rocking chair you got
was from Cracker Barrel or Pier One
or TJ Maxx or Target or the Walmart
and make sure it was made in China,
or anywhere else other than some
"local" woodworker at the flea market.

And make sure that the ginseng you're
hunting is in accordance to a script written
by some New York producers always
mispronouncing the word *Appalachia*,
and in time to make up for dropping
dope sales heading into the winter cold.

Manage all that and, hell, I'm good with it.

Returning Me My Eyes

Bill King

———————

Down here, from my porch swing, I hear a raven
croaking somewhere overhead. And though my body
and spirit no longer align, I rise through oak
and maple, magnolia and laurel, to where
the red spruce reign. No matter why. At some
point, everyone travels only in mind, up and out,
until everything is drowned in a blue roar of sky.
And this returns me my eyes, and everything
to its place, which I see as I descend. Where
the canopy opens, white-petaled liverwort blooms
thick as stars. And there, up on the bank, pink
and purple columbine fracture stones, rolling them—
over centuries—down the mountainside.

Wings and Other Things

Chauna Craig

———————

She thought she was haunted: that shudder echoing through the living room's west wall like the bass line to her favorite show's theme song. When she muted the TV, nothing but the wind chimes on the porch clinking off beat. Then, the sound again, pinpointed now to the fireplace. Stupid, loose damper rocking with the draft. Anya twirled the knob, and it spun freely, catching on nothing, doing nothing. Stupid, hand-me-down house.

Then she recognized the sound as wings stirring air, a soft, flapping smack on brick. She hopped back from the fireplace and crouched as if something were about to erupt, horror-movie style—the cave flooding with bats, the attic a tornado of sharp-billed crows. She froze in her ridiculous pose, barely breathing and embarrassed, though she had no audience.

Her Pittsburgh grandmother would say, "Bird in the house means death." Her Morgantown grandmother would say, "Angels come in all disguises." Jason, if he were still around, would say, "Babe, it's just a bird. It won't hurt you."

That man could take care of any problem, even when she didn't like the solution. Problem: losing his job when Halliburton pulled out, capping the local gas wells. Solution: following the work to North Dakota, leaving her behind. Her Pittsburgh grandmother had said, "You don't let a good man go." Her Morgantown grandmother had said, "When God closes one door, he opens a window."

Right then everything was open. The chimney, the flue, the fireplace, the possibility that anything could fly in her face.

The fluttering continued the next morning, and Anya's spine crawled to hear it. She avoided the living room and silenced the radio so she could hear if the bird left. But what sound does leaving make? With Jason, it had been the damaged muffler of his truck. But that, too, had been the sound of his arrival.

What if the bird were injured? Trapped on a small ledge and yearning for the postage stamp of blue sky visible? Flapping her wings for take-off and going nowhere? What if the bird fell into the fireplace, panicked wings scattering ash?

Anya's stomach clenched. She gathered duct tape and a black garbage bag. She quickly sealed the fireplace, steeling herself when the beating wings resumed. The final strip of tape pressed into place, she felt relief, her world contained again.

That evening, after her shift at the sports bar, Anya settled into an armchair to unwind with a magazine, the type that told her how to pluck her eyebrows and keep a man. Her throat convulsed when she heard the crinkling of the plastic bag over her fireplace, followed by a small whoosh. The bag was moving, and Anya jerked out of her seat. But it was the wind. Of course, the wind. The draft sucking the bag back, then expanding it again, like a dark lung, the house breathing.

In the morning, the sound—again—of wings in too-small spaces.

Two chimney service companies in town, and the first one wouldn't help. The woman on the other end said, "Bird? It'll fly out on its own."

"What if it's hurt?" Anya asked. "I've heard it for days now."

"Could be nesting then."

"No. The flue is open. The damper is broken. I can't have baby birds falling into my fireplace." She imagined the blind, bulge-eyed, featherless things squirming and choking in the thick layer of ash she failed to clean after winter.

"We aren't a wildlife removal service."

Anya huffed. "I need my chimney cleaned. Can you do that?"

"Not if those birds are chimney swifts."

"Why not?"

"Migratory Bird Act. They're protected." She heard the flutter-shudder again, like muted applause, and Anya hung up.

Remember, the web page advised, *the birds are more frightened than you are.*

But that wasn't true, not yet. The birds were building a home, oblivious to Anya's intentions. The garbage bag sucked in, billowed out. The fluttering filled her ears.

Chimney swifts once nested in tall trees, but as the trees disappeared, they adapted to open chimneys. Now, with redesigned chimneys, most of them capped, nesting sites are limited, and the chimney swifts' habitat is again threatened.

She called Jason that night. "How's North Dakota?"

"Hey," he said, voice soft and—she hoped—lonely. "You remembered my number. You still mad?"

"I was never mad," she answered, deciding it was true. "It's just—you're forever away now."

"Not forever. Just until the work ends."

"And then what?"

He paused so long that she rushed to fill the space with her bird woes, telling him about the damper and the horrible, trapped fluttering sound.

"It's always something with that house," Jason said. "Sell it. Move here." And then she was mad because the market was flooded with houses since the oil and gas company pulled out, realty signs popping up on lawns like stubborn weeds. Even if she wanted to live in North Fucking Dakota, no one was going to buy this house, certainly not those squatting, seasonal birds.

"I want a *solution*, Jason. Not some pipe dream."

"Pipe dream. That's funny," he said. "Because of the gas pipeline. I'm literally following a pipe dream, yeah?"

She hung up on someone for the second time that week, swirling with a childish rage, embarrassed, and angrier for it.

Rainstorms the next morning, and Anya was happy to go to work. The damn birds would be staying in, and she didn't want to hear them.

"I should have been a nurse," she told Becky, the bartender, as she straightened the same stack of napkins again. "No shortage of business there." Slow day, only a few local attorneys and court clerks out for lunch.

Becky admired her own perfectly polished nails, waving the tips of her fingers like casting a spell. She splurged on a weekly manicure and a monthly massage in Pittsburgh. Her boyfriend, who worked in the lab at the hospital, was the only local Anya knew who wasn't perpetually underemployed.

"So go back to school and be a nurse."

"I don't like blood."

"Nobody *likes* blood. Except vampires, I suppose."

"I faint when I see it. And I don't handle suffering well."

Becky laughed and shook her head. "Oh dear," she said. "This is about Jason, isn't it?" Becky wandered to the far end of the bar, posing her rose-colored fingernails against the ruby swizzle sticks, then the orange and lemon wedges. "Sweetie," she called, "move there or move on!"

On one of their first dates, Jason had taken her for a walk in the woods. He'd grown up on the Maryland–West Virginia border, a nature boy to the core, and hand in hand they'd stood by a small creek that babbled as steadily as she did. She was in the middle of some story about the coal trains that shuttled through the center of town in the night when he let go of her hand and squatted by the bank, eyes fixed on a rock that turned out to be the tiniest turtle she'd ever seen, its shell smaller than a quarter. Jason pinched it gently in his fingers and held it up so she could see its long tail flicking, miniscule jaws snapping as its head turned back and forth. It looked like a windup toy, head and tail jerking, tiny block feet paddling the air.

"Even the babies are mean bastards," he noted, with an admiring laugh. He held the turtle to his face. "Fight on, little snapper," he whispered, and he set it in the grass, away from the bike path. They watched it turn like a slow, jerky clock hand and move stubbornly toward the dry, gravel path. Jason picked the turtle up again and carried it to a flat, sun-warmed rock beside the creek. "Stay," he ordered.

She'd really started to like him then, this savior of small creatures. They walked back to the car, and she tried not to talk too much, listening instead to the calls of birds she'd once been able to name. She inhaled the heady honeysuckle punctured with acrid pockets of natural gas.

When Anya returned from work early because there hadn't been enough for her to do, she called the second chimney servicing company. She said, "I want to schedule my annual cleaning now, get it done before fall."

They came the next morning in a white van fitted with extending ladders, crammed with buckets and brushes and tools. Two men carried into her living room large canvas tarps, a super-sized shop vacuum, and various rods and brush attachments. The short, thin one greeted her and introduced himself—Roger—and his partner Gary, a large, silent, bearded man who nodded acknowledgment and methodically unfolded the tarp around the opening of her fireplace. Anya held her breath, expecting the fluttering-shuddering, but all was quiet. Maybe the bird really had left. She hadn't had her fireplace cleaned since she'd inherited the house, so not all was lost.

"What's this?" Roger asked, pointing to the garbage bag taped so precisely to the brick.

"Drafts," she said. "My flue stays open."

"I can check that." He peeled the tape and pulled back the bag, and Anya tensed. "Tall as this chimney is, we're going to clean from the inside," Roger explained.

"Don't you have an orphan to do that?" she murmured, watching Gary, the silent one, connect rods.

Roger laughed, then asked, "Do you have any idea how many of those kids back in the day died of scrotum cancer?"

It wasn't the sort of question to which one had an answer, though Anya had a good guess as to how many of the men who worked the coal mines when they were open had perished from lung disease. Like her father, dying slowly and painfully years after his last company paycheck. Her Pittsburgh grandmother had said, "The wages of sin is death." Her Morgantown grandmother had said, "My son was a cheater, yes, and your mother deserved better, but he worked hard, Anya. He took care of you."

"We'll start with this mess," Roger advised, picking charred chunks of log from the grate and tossing them into a blackened bucket. "Whoa, look at this." He pulled from the ashes a small, dark bird, dead. He held it by a wingtip so one wing fanned open. Anya stared. She'd never imagined a bird already planted in the graveyard of her neglected fireplace. He flicked the body into the ash bucket and said, "You might have a nest." He flipped the vacuum switch, sweeping the open hose back and forth until the bottom of her fireplace revealed its flat, stone floor. "Don't worry," Roger said. "This thing will scare any remaining birds right out." He brandished a stiff black brush the size of a basketball, spidery legs in all directions.

Anya moved to the far end of the living room, feeling dizzy like the room was devoid of oxygen. How long had the corpse lain there? Not long, she reasoned. She was sensitive to foul smells. She shivered. *Goose walk over your grave?* Both of her grandmothers liked that one.

The vacuum droned again, and she moved outside where the sun was burning off the dew, warming the last puddles from yesterday's rain. She shaded her eyes with her hand and studied her chimney. It looked almost flat, two-dimensional against the sky's uniform blue. While she waited, hoping to see something fly out and away, silhouettes of birds sailed through the blue, some robins, a couple crows, and dozens of chimney swifts with their tell-tale angled wings. She knew what nested in her own open chimney, and she felt sick again with guilt and anger and who knew what else.

Her father had been a bird-lover. When she was twelve and assigned a bird identification project in Life Science, he'd taken her out in the forests and fields with binoculars and a guidebook. Her parents had split by then, and he was living in the house that was now hers, dating a mostly sweet, alcoholic woman and working for PennDOT. "Nobody's going to shut down the highways," he reasoned, keeping that job until full-time use of an oxygen tank forced his retirement. Anya marveled how by summer's end his skin turned nut-brown, almost as dark as her shadowy memories of him when he'd come home in the morning from the mine, face washed, neck and ears still black until he'd shower.

She couldn't remember all the birds they'd identified that spring, but she'd finished with a perfect score on her project and a sense of wonder for all the creatures she'd never noticed nesting in thickets and the crevices of dead trees.

Something black popped up from her chimney, but it was only the large, round brush, bobbling then flopping over the brick lip as someone fed it more line. Gary appeared in her doorway and spoke for the first time. "Is it out?" His voice was deep and loud.

She didn't know if he meant the bird or the brush, but she nodded. He signaled Roger, and the brush slowly retracted then suddenly disappeared like a threatened creature retreating into its burrow.

Anya's return to the house was unhurried, a lingering in the late spring air.

She studied the dirt patches where her mother, who'd remarried and moved to Delaware, had once planted cheery, colorful annuals. "Move out here," her mother suggested when they talked on the phone. "Try it for the summer. All the bars and restaurants near the beach are hiring." Once, when Anya had begun her rebuttal—"But the house"—her usually agreeable mother had snapped, "Screw that house."

Anya paused on the wide porch, noticing the buckle and curl of peeling paint, then crossed the threshold. The men were retracting the brush, pulling hand over hand, speculating about hockey playoffs, when something burst from the fireplace. The men ducked and Anya screamed like a demon pursued her. She fled through the front door, not stopping until she reached the curb, hand on her chest, breath hitching. She knew, consciously, that it was only the dead bird's mate, and she felt like a fool, but her legs locked and she stood, paralyzed.

Roger appeared in the doorway, gingerly carrying a folded piece of canvas cloth. He walked purposefully toward her driveway, away from where she trembled, and he squatted and let the folded cloth fall away. The dark gray bird paused briefly to orient herself then took off, wings flapping hard, straight down the street as if navigating a map. They watched her flap and flap, shrinking until she disappeared.

Roger smiled. "Stubborn bird. Stayed in the nest all that time, but we scrub the walls on the way down."

"Nest?" Anya echoed. Comforting word, but all it conjured was painful longing in her chest.

"Gary's taken care of it. Shit, which one of us screamed anyway?" he teased. She blushed, and he said, "No, don't be embarrassed. Things hit us in ways we never expect. Like that movie *Titanic*. When I left the theater, I was crying too hard to see. My wife drove us home. She never said a word about it either. Just kept her hand on my back all night."

Anya looked at his face gone soft with memory, and a sob erupted from deep in her chest. Sudden, bewildering tears. Roger's eyes widened, but she held up a hand. "I'll be fine. We'll all be fine." And she rushed, half-blind, into the house to find her checkbook.

While she waited for Roger to finish writing her bill, she pressed her palms to her eyes and asked what to do if the bird came back.

"It won't," he said. "It might return to check on the nest, but the mate's dead, and the nest isn't there. No reason to stay."

"Isn't it, uh, illegal to remove the nest of a chimney swift?"

He paused with his pen poised as if writing on air. "Do you want me to put it back?"

When Anya was a girl, when her father still lived in the house with them, they'd had a black, plastic, wall-mounted phone. When she was home alone, her father hundreds of feet below ground, her mother cruising the grocery aisles, coupons clutched in her fist, Anya liked to call her own number and listen, the receiver pressed to her ear until the skin throbbed hot and sticky. Self-hypnosis. That incessant, rhythmic busy signal, pulsing, calming her, reminding her that somebody was home. She'd tried it again after her father's death, the landline long gone, but her cell phone offered only a manufactured voice asking for a password to let her hear messages she knew didn't exist.

Anya signed her check with the big loopy letters she hadn't used since she was a teenager. "Fixed your damper," Roger remembered, as his partner carried the ash bucket with the dead bird out the door. "Let me show you."

She peered up the chimney while he pointed out the mechanical gears, the teeth that had been off track, unable to grab on and rotate the damper. "Which," Roger added, "was somehow flipped upside down. But now, when the knob's in this position, you've got a good seal. Nothing's getting in."

She didn't ask about the nest, whether there were eggs. She hadn't heard peeps or any sounds beyond those fluttering wings, but who could detect the throb of tiny avian hearts in their shells? Now it was all she heard. Like a rapid drum line at a football game across town. Or a ceremonial summons from a faraway tribe. The ocean beating the Delaware shore, the rhythmic muffler blasts on a truck a thousand miles west. Always at a distance, those calls of life. When they came too close, wings and other things in her walls, she got someone else to answer.

Snowfields

Larry D. Thacker

————

Something about how the snowfield
turns to the evergreen
tree line then to the quickened black

of the forest's repeated questions.

Lone leaves too solid now
to twist any further in the wind,
the branches turning only with squeaks and pops,

ground noisy with a liveliness of new snow, freezing
voiced under your feet,
slow tidal protest of tracks behind.

Moonless, windless snow, flurries
cold cast in every direction,

the clichéd globe of night fully taking you in, branch
scratch hugging you to the bone,

dragging thoughts to the black. There

in the questions.

Where there's anything you'd imagine, of course. As when you played as a youth without much fear, out in the dark, not *past sundown*, but *in the dark*. Stuttered now in the heavied gray, in there,

past midnight,

for the lurk is something you now know,
a thing you've hurried by a few times since a child.

And you know its hard scent, even in the darkest cold.

February Springtime in the Mountains

Libby Falk Jones

———————

Bush budding white, crocus unfolding,
sudden red sheen on gray tree branches,
two tiny spiders hatching near my desk—
these invite suspicion, even pity.
What can they know, what signals
deep in earth or sky have sounded?
Not likely the morning mist
that rises in air warm or cold,
or the inevitable babble of the nearby creek.
Perhaps the flapping of heron's wings
or partridge's scurry or bears and rattlers waking up
and liking the dry leaves I walk through daily,
or the lift of the wind, or the rain brushing
the cabin's tin roof, or the cracking open
of my heart, these long silent days and nights.
Magician or charlatan, the world whirls
faster, faster than I can breathe.

Towhee

Felicia Mitchell

———————

Inside my house,
windows cracked in late March,
a towhee calls from the laptop computer,
its voice trapped like fire in wood on my hearth
I have not yet burned.

Outside, another towhee rustles fall leaves
in its dance with spring, and I watch it—
how the bird picks at the ground,
both feet jumping as its beak forages for seed,
until it hears a call from the house
and moves back into pine.

I am complicit here,
the accidental wizard of winged messages
I send out over airwaves without thinking.
Without thinking, wasting electricity,
I can disturb the universe,
or nudge it sideways into pine,
the towhee in my yard as ephemeral as seasons
and as likely to return.

Celebrate

Settling

Jane Harrington

———

Cornelius had never seen a Cherokee Indian. One of the other Irish on the railroad—one who'd been in the mountains long enough to know—told of how they'd been forced onto the road, pushed west. *Nasty stuff,* he'd said, *a trail of tears.* The Cherokee, though, he'd just been married to the daughter of a settler when the decree went down, and their stake was hidden enough in the mountains that the government troops had missed him altogether. He'd cleared the flattest ground with fire, for a pasture and a corn crop, but he'd left wild the sheerest mountainside, the deepest ravine. And it was this that was on Cornelius's mind as he tramped between tree trunks, his boots sinking into the leaf litter.

Before he'd even lost his sea wobble, Cornelius had been asking around about land. "Even if you weren't Irish, you'd need money, Con," Shea had said, a fellow from his townland who had come over with the same handbill in his pocket. Sure, Cornelius had seen the "No Irish" signs in the city when he'd arrived, and he caught the gist of the jokes told behind their backs in camp, but this hadn't dampened his determination. Nor had the fact that money was scarce, what with sending the remittances. Julia insisted, even in the last post, that she and the children were fine, but with the stories he was hearing when others got letters—*A starvation like never before*, they said; *The entire crop wiped out*, they said—he suspected she was skipping details. So, no, he hadn't been able to keep a savings, a land fund, as he'd long planned on doing. But he had a new idea: he'd find a landowner, offer work in exchange for a piece of ground to call his own at some set point in time. Shea had laughed at that, but Cornelius had only to look around to see all the untamed acreage, to imagine tracts too rugged to be valued by their owners. He'd build something, a place for them, so they wouldn't have to live in a shantytown that moved along with the tracks.

Not that the railroad work was all bad. The tunnel blasting did spook him, no lie, that making of passages through limestone, but there were enough of the others who wanted the boasting rights from those jobs. He could hang back, work with the African men and women brought in on barges from plantations. Their owners were paid for the conscription, but with the understanding that their slaves would stay whole, not do the dangerous work. "Chattel," Cornelius had heard them called by the railroad men. Until his English improved, he had thought they were saying "cattle," which had seemed insulting enough. Sometimes he watched them being put back in shackles, being led to the river, but a shot of whiskey with his mates blurred the image, his disillusionment. *The land of the free*, the poet had promised.

Suppertime in the rail camp was good craic, always, listening to stories. Many of the workers had long been on the job. They knew their way around, knew people. That's how Cornelius had learned of the Cherokee. It was Murphy, a spirited sort from Cork, who'd taken Cornelius up onto a trestle, to where the river was a snake below. "See there," Murphy had said, pointing, "that one in the middle." Cornelius could just make out the Indian's clearing through treetops of orange, red. "Now *that's* something, that turning of the leaves," Murphy had said, bragging on his new country, as he was known to do. "Nothing like that back home," he'd said, then coughed to hide the crack in his voice before retreating to camp. Cornelius had stayed and looked out at the view, at the cleaving peaks as far as he could see. And, yes, especially in the morning, when a flaxen sky turned to mist, the mountains really did look blue. Always made him think of Julia's favorite dye, her secret. "Gets the fairies upset, Connie!" she'd scolded when he'd sneaked around to try to figure out the source (a sea snail with spines like needles, it was; he'd glimpsed it one day in her hands). A faded version of that blue, from, say, the supplest of their bedclothes dropped on the horizon—that's what those mountains looked like to him.

It's dark where they are, Cornelius was thinking now, the sky above him still light, though the sun had made its western pass over a high ridge and would be gone for the day from his view too. The house he approached was in shadow, but he could see the man rocking on the porch clearly enough. Cornelius guessed the headdress he wore to be of buffalo, though he'd not laid eyes on one of those either, not living. Vast herds, it was said, had once turned views of valleys and balds black, but all he'd seen were pelts or trophies, decorations like this one with its braided leather and beads. Yellow spots painted on the horns brought to his mind the gorse he still looked for on his treks to the worksites. (He just couldn't get used to that, no gorse growing here.) As he got closer, he saw that the man in the rocker was otherwise dressed like the rest of the men in the mountains, maybe tidier, his cuffs folded neatly above hands that Cornelius could now see were resting on a single-barrel shotgun. He stopped in his tracks. "Sullivan," he said, giving his chest a thump.

"Is your English that poor?" the Cherokee asked him.

Cornelius cocked his head, tried to make out the man's eyes in the shade, his intent.

"Are you Irish?" the Cherokee asked now.

Cornelius nodded.

"Family over there, children?"

He nodded again.

"How many?"

Cornelius looked down at his boots, his toes moving inside, little kicks against leather. He thought of his cheek pressed against Julia's just swelling belly on that night before he left, knew only that this baby had come by now or gone by now. Jinxes you, too much optimism, Julia would say, so he didn't answer the Cherokee. He'd been taking up her superstitions. Found a feather a few days before, brown and white. He couldn't remember what she claimed that to portend, but he had it in his pocket in any case.

"A charity ship is going over," the Cherokee said, getting up and leaning his shotgun against the wall. "I read about it in the newspaper. Made a donation." He lifted the headpiece off now. "Tribal dress—don't know how my father stood it," he said, placing it on the floorboards next to the gun, "but it's good for scaring off trespassers." He settled back into his rocker. "Some, anyway."

Cornelius cleared his throat, got to what he'd practiced. "Do you have land for sale in your hollow? I can pay with labor."

The Cherokee pulled two cigars from a box on the table next to his chair. He gestured to an empty rocker, and Cornelius stepped up onto the porch and sat, took a light and puffed. A cigar was a treat he'd rarely had, though he rolled his own cigarettes in camp, had to admit that tobacco was one thing that was better in this place. The two men rocked and smoked until finally the Cherokee said, "I don't own the land."

"But I heard—"

"It belongs to the Great Spirit."

They sat in silence again, curls of smoke filling the air around them, then the chirping of crickets, now a snarl and a tussle of a predator wrestling prey in the forest. Murphy had said these were panthers when they'd heard them around the camp—*painters*, he said the locals called them. There was a final screech, and then just the trill of crickets again. Cornelius rubbed his cigar out on the sole of his boot and rose to leave.

The Cherokee rose too. "Paper I own," he said. "I can sell paper." And he led the way off the porch and onto a dirt road skirting a pasture. "I could use some help with the livestock. Droving to market. Slaughtering. We'll be putting a steer up to cure soon." He leaned against the fence pickets. "Maybe two this year. When is your family coming?"

After the winter, Cornelius thinks but doesn't say. He just gazes over the Cherokee's shoulder to the cattle gnawing on grass, their faces white as ghosts, a breed foreign to him. The eyes, though, those he recognized. A cow's look of powerlessness, of resignation. Same look he found himself still having to shake from his own face whenever he stumbled across a spit of still water, a pane of glass.

They reached a creek and followed it, the trail hugging the bank sometimes, sometimes winding through trees as wide as the men were tall. The elevation dropped, steeply, causing Cornelius to trip on roots, to catch himself on low branches. But the Cherokee never faltered, his familiarity with the terrain from generations in the highlands. Same ease Cornelius had known in the boreens and bogs of his homeland, the hillocks and strands. That salt air—he hadn't realized how much it was a part of him, how his heart had kept pace with wave against rock, wave against rock. For a moment, he thought he was imagining that sound, but it was the creek, turned now to a cascade over shelves of shale, spilling at the bottom into a pool. The two men stopped when they reached its edge. Frogs leapt from the reeds and landed scattershot in the water.

"If you clear a few trees," the Cherokee said, "you'll fit a cabin in here. Have you ever built from logs?"

Cornelius shook his head. "Mud."

"That's what we did until we were shown to use the timbers. Corners are the hardest part. I'll teach you how to keyhole them. Get that right and it'll last a lifetime, they said to us. Only I guess we should've asked whose." He tapped a chestnut trunk. "I'd start with this one. Good wood. Leave a flat stump for a chopping block."

Breathing in deeply, taking in the spot, Cornelius stood on earth thick with leaves shaped like strange hands, all clawing up the mountainside. A ripple of cloud moved through the channel of sky. "What's the name?" he asked, his eyes set on one of the summits.

"Some people give the mountains names," the Indian said, turning back to the trail. "But they still don't come when you call."

Cornelius let go a small laugh now. Overhead, a lone, large-bodied bird sailed lazily on wind currents. A hawk, he decided it was. (But he couldn't see, no, not from down there, the fleshy head, the pinions spread like fingers.) He imagined a brown and white breast, gave his pocket a pat. And he followed the Cherokee.

Child in Spring Snowfall, 1934

Laura Long

———————

All vibrates this morning, the cherry
tree in soft, wet bloom, a late snow
starting to fall, the ground a sheet
of blistered light pricked by tiny

flowers, their tender
precise almost-faces glinting
silver like the fairy she maybe glimpses
down where the creek seeps into ferns,

Jack-in-the-Pulpits poke up,
and a pair of Baltimore Orioles weave
a hanging nest, swiping strings
from last year's nest. In her memory

she wanders in the woods on her way
to school, swinging a black lunch box
with a sandwich of ham from the hog
they had butchered in November,

and hung and smoked and are eating the last bit of,
the hog becoming a shadow stitched inside
their bodies, the father, the mother,
and the girl, she an only child until

now—a baby brother was born yesterday—
and now she is running fast and hard
out of the woods into a flood
of light so immense it seems

the sky is falling into the broad meadow
in giant cubes and melting inside this
April morning in 1934, a morning
still full of itself 81 years later

and flashing now in the woods
outside her window, a gray jumble
of trees with tiny buds sparking
ten thousand green fires.

Appalachian Spring

Libby Falk Jones

———

Rhododendron leaves
curl in sun—oh, it's shadows
that define the light—

Clingmans Dome Before Thanksgiving

Susan Deer Cloud

————————

Lovers at the beginning then, driving
from a friend's house in Mashulaville, Mississippi,
to Great Smoky Mountains . . .

all night through Deep South sleeps,
Spanish moss hanging like lynched ghosts
in the mists,

and entering in

you made it in time to dash up
steep dirt path to see sunrise
like a Cherokee shawl of rose and gold

weaving light around the blue peaks
and your limbs shivering
child-small in that immense place.

Morning and noon you drove
on mountainsides and down
deep valley roads,

snake twists, perilous drops,
and beauty rebirthing the sacred
not too far from where Cherokees

keep their fire in a secret woods
on the Tennessee side of all that blue.

You meandered up and up
to ice-enshrined Clingmans Dome,
stepped out on park's highest peak,

wind piercing you to the wordless bone,

white fog sea at your feet, peaks
purple bruises when the mists
tore free and sun burned through . . .

frozen trees, broken weeds, limp grasses,
and lovers at their beginning
lit to bedazzlement.

In Tennessee I Found a Firefly

Jeremy Michael Reed

———

a glosa after Mary Szybist

Tonight, I'm surprised by one alone.
Here, there, lightning flits in grass, sown.
I make my way forward in the dark.
I feel grass under my feet. On a lark,
I walk a bit further than the lightning
flash by my unshoed toes, stand, lean
forward over the hill, look beyond,
past trees older than me, vines eons
older than the flashes there in space,
even imagined ones. *Luciferin, luciferase.*

You have remained inside for now
even though that is not often how
our positions are placed. Instead,
opposite more often. Only fled
can I stand here at edge of yard,
look back at lit house as if, card
written carefully, I place in box,
put up faded red tin flag. No fox
here tonight with bird, no clutching.
When I am tired of only touching,

I find you there in the house, me
outside in night, unshod, and free.
As if the bioluminescence was lost
to me briefly, it now returns, costs
me focus as eyes return to, lift up,
catch above a single light and sup:
starhaze, when focused on, opens
into tiny, particulate dust. I pen
no letter to you. Instead, again, anew,
I have my mouth to try to tell you

what only tired movement lends
itself to telling: the way love bends
over time, the way a hushed phrase
creates flash of lightning, truth, case
by case, in shadow, frond by frond.
Partners in life cannot feign fond-
ness, softness, attention, care.
From here, I only stand, stare
at flashes in dark. I return, embrace
what, in your arms, is not erased.

How to Avoid the Widow Maker

Jim Minick

Step 1: Keep your chains sharp.

It's August, already hot in the early morning as I sharpen my chainsaws. I have several knuckles' worth of scars from doing this in the past, so I concentrate and listen to the *zzip, zzip* of metal on metal. The file eats away the dullness of each saw tooth, making it shiny and a little smaller. The truck's tailgate serves as my workbench, where each stroke of the file releases a spray of metallic dust that glitters and falls like the exploding flower of fireworks.

I rotate the chain, grip with my off hand, and grind away nicks and blunt edges. After a while, my wrist hurts from the pressure and awkward angle, the file wearing me down, so I switch hands, clean the air filter, fill the oil and gas, and then file some more.

A saw can spin what looks like a bicycle chain—except it has teeth—sixty miles per hour, and when that chain is sharp, it can cut a pole-sized pine in three seconds. I have a ten-acre tract I want to thin before the summer ends, meaning I have a lot to cut today.

Step 2: Buy the chaps and read the manuals.

The dogs whine under my feet as I finish sharpening the saws—Jake knows I'm about to head out and leave him. He's a shepherd-lab mix smart enough to stay out of the way when I'm cutting wood, but I still would rather not have him nearby, especially when I'm felling trees. Plus the other dogs are not as smart. So I pen them all in the basement.

Then I suit up—steel-toed boots, helmet with ear muffs and face shield, and grimy chaps. The safety gear is expensive—my dad and brother-in-law only use earplugs, if that—but what is the cost of good hearing or a leg? One time, a neighbor who didn't wear chaps relaxed after felling a tree and rested the still-moving chain on his thigh. He was lucky it only cut flesh and not bone. I've accidently done the same, just touching my thigh with the saw, the chap's orange outer fabric opening to reveal the white strands of Kevlar, but nothing else.

There is little safety gear, though, for a kickback, another chainsaw danger, maybe the greatest. If the upper tip of a running saw touches wood before any other part of the chain, the saw will kickback hard, like bouncing a toothed ball into your face. The brake stops this, if your left hand is positioned correctly and hits the brake before the chain hits you. And how you stand—slightly to the side, not directly over the saw—and how you start the cut—*not* with that upper part of the tip—all determine if you avoid a kickback. Meaning: read the manual.

According to a 2004 article in *The Journal of Forensic Science*, over twenty-eight thousand chainsaw injuries occur every year. Another expert claims that over forty thousand injuries and deaths are caused by chainsaws annually. This same expert, Carl Smith, a forester who trains loggers, says that placing "your hands on a chainsaw . . . is like grabbing a hand grenade without a pin in it."

Few people actually die from chainsaws, but the injuries are gruesome. I've seen the photographs. Amputated fingers and legs. Cuts across thighs that reveal bone. And even a face that had the tracks of a saw traveling upward over cheek and eye and scalp, the eye still in place, with red, raw canyons above and below.

Step 3: Know you're living and keep it that way.

Tanked-up and ready to go, my chainsaws weigh over twelve pounds each, heavy enough to make an old elbow injury ache. But not as heavy as my grandfather's first chainsaw in the 1960s, which weighed about twenty-five pounds. And not as heavy as some of the first chainsaws, which weighed over one hundred pounds and required two men to operate.

An electric chainsaw gets around some of this problem, and Carl, my father-in-law, has one that weighs 6.8 pounds. I used it to clear bamboo from his backyard, the sharp teeth bouncing against the hard green stalks before biting through. It had no brake, so a kickback seemed even more dangerous and more likely. And instead of being heavy, the thing was too light. I could use it with one hand, while I caught the cut bamboo with my off hand. That electric saw—how it bounced, how it felt like a toy—that saw scared me more than any other saw I've ever used.

An electric saw also solves the problem of hard starting that Hayden Carruth considers in his poem, "Regarding Chainsaws." Here, a man remembers his first chainsaw, "an old yellow McCulloch that wouldn't start" even after he yanked on it "450 times." He recounts how mostly the saws weren't "dangerous, that the only thing they broke was your / back." But sometimes a kickback or widow maker would "make you know you're living."

Step 4: Look up.

Widow makers make you look up. Make you listen. Make your helmet useless.

Usually a widow maker is a broken branch high in the tree that hangs on by some strip of bark. Sometimes the branch is dead wood—unbroken—waiting for a certain release point triggered by the logger's work or just the right breeze.

Or a widow maker can be a hung tree, the whole thing leaning into another tree, stuck in the other tree's crotch, the threat not from a sudden shift in wind but from the logger now having to bring down the hung tree in a much slower, more dangerous manner.

Step 5: Things happen.

With two saws, two canteens of water, a wedge in my back pocket, and all the safety gear strapped on, I head out. It's nine o'clock in the morning, the thermometer reads eighty, and sweat already soaks my T-shirt. I hike the half mile of wooded trail to what we call Zig-Zag, named for the path that elbows back and forth up the steep hillside. The forest is a mix of pines and oaks, with some hickory, locust, ash, maple, and gum.

I've already cut my firewood for the year, so what I want for these woods is simply health, otherwise known to foresters as Timber Stand Improvement (TSI). Last week, Sarah—my wife—and I spent a half day marking trees, checking for stunted growth or crooked trunks. She has a good eye for angles. We craned our necks to study the leans of their tops, plotting fall-lines, avoiding hang-ups in other trees. We knuckle-tapped bark and listened for hollowness. Or if we had to choose between healthy but crowded trees, we listened to the soundness of each. I want to release the right one that will grow another hundred years if its canopy and roots have more room.

In the woods, if you blur your vision, a stand can look like a crowd of people at a rail station, too many pressing into one opening. In a healthy forest, no tree has to shove another out of the way. But I don't want too much space, otherwise the trees will grow scraggly with branches and be prone to wind damage.

When a field begins to change to a forest, one acre can hold five thousand tree seedlings. After two hundred years, that number falls to around twenty-five mature giants. TSI helps that process along by culling the weak. This yields high-quality timber, but more importantly, a thinned, healthy forest better withstands droughts and torrents and the clouds of gypsy moths and ash borers that slowly flitter our way.

Usually, this is solitary work—just me and a tree and a saw. I don't fell trees when Sarah's off the farm, but still, I often work a mile from the house, and we live in a place that has poor cell phone service. We used to have walkie-talkies, but mine kept falling off and getting lost. So if something happens, and I'm not home by mealtime, Sarah knows to come looking. I don't want this scenario, so I've learned the best methods and work as safely as I can.

But things happen. Like the time I tripped over roots and tumbled down the mountainside. I tried to hold the saw away from my body, but the blade bruised and cut my arm and leg anyway. And it wasn't even turned on. Or the time my hand slipped and my finger grazed the whirring teeth. Somehow the chain cut no veins, lopped off no tip—just left a deep incision. Or the time before I ever used a chainsaw, when I was a kid with a broken elbow waiting in the ER. The nurse kept apologizing, saying the doctor had an emergency operation. Three hours later, he finally started putting on my plaster cast. As he wrapped the wet, white strands, he told me he had been operating on a man who, as he said, "almost ate a chainsaw." The plaster dripped from the doctor's finger as he drew a vertical line on my face, starting on my jaw, traveling up cheek, over eye, across forehead, and into my hair. "That saw ran right over his face," the doctor said. "I still don't know how he didn't lose an eye."

Step 6: Girdling.

At the top of Zig-Zag, I drop the saws and drink—better to sweat and piss out too much than to cramp up from too little. I stash the canteens and one saw behind a huge keeper oak, pull-start the 026, and approach the first tree, a cucumber magnolia. It has a massive trunk, thick as two men and riddled all the way up with woodpecker holes.

But no notch-cut here, no plunge-cut or final felling release, no need to plot the path this tree will fall. I want to kill this tree but leave it standing because woods that I'm after have unsound trees as well as sound. They stand hollow, dead or alive, snags that house chickadees, flying squirrels, and the pileated woodpecker. I try to leave about fifteen of these den trees per acre. If the coons or screech owls have smoothed out a home inside a living tree, like this cucumber magnolia, I girdle it instead of cutting it down. With the saw, I ring the trunk, going round and round three or four times, just an inch or two deep, severing all connection between root and limb. The tree will stand for several more years, housing more and more creatures as they drill and burrow and homestead its dead wood.

But sometimes I see the cavity too late.

Once I felled a locust, one of the densest and best woods to heat the house. As I chunked it into stove lengths, I came across a tufted titmouse's nest halfway up the bole. The tree had split right at the cavity, revealing the soft lining of dog hair and milkweed duff. Tan freckles covered five white eggs, each egg roughly the size of my thumbnail. The two parent birds flew around me, their crests raised and their gray feathers fluffed to scare me away. They sang their simple high note call over and over, one of the few bird calls I can whistle and hear a reply. But not today. Each egg had cracked open, the yellow yolk seeping into the nest.

Step 7: Fix your brake.

Before this August day, my oldest saw, a Stihl 026 (3.2 horsepower) had a problem—the brake would stop the chain without my wanting. I'd be in the middle of a tricky plunge-cut on a hollow hickory, afraid the whole thing might bust and topple the wrong way, and the saw brake would stop the chain—click—like that. This went on for a year at least, and it made me want to buy a new saw, because after all, the 026 was over twenty-five years old, an antique.

But that antique engine still ran just fine, and so, I finally asked Carl, my father-in-law, for help. He's a retired engineer whose job in the Navy was to keep the ship's engines running. This was in the Pacific, during World War II, at Okinawa and Iwo Jima. He knows how to fix things. In the thirty years I've known him, I've slowly graduated from holding the flashlight to doing more on my own. But this chain-brake problem befuddled me.

One of the lessons I've learned from Carl is simple courage. I doubt he'd call it that, though—it's just how he lives, with a certain confidence and curiosity. If a toaster oven or lamp or lawnmower is broken, you just dig in to figure it out. Of course, he can put it all back together in the right order without later finding a few screws still lying on the bench.

With the 026, I started the saw for Carl and demonstrated the problem—the brake handle clicked forward on its own, when normally it required manual pressure. Carl watched and chewed his toothpick and then motioned to turn it off. On my workbench, we unscrewed the saw's cover and spent the next half hour studying the problem—click-clicking the brake, watching the springs and levers with each motion. He told me his plan—to tighten the pressure on the key spring by wrapping wire around the main lever. I was skeptical. I didn't understand the physics of it, *and* it involved cutting a good portion of the hard-plastic cover plate off to make room for this new wire.

We started in anyway—what was there to lose, Carl was with me. He wrapped the shiny wire around and around the lever, threading the end through the narrow gap and pulling it taut like darning a sock. I held the flashlight and helped guide the plyers and wire (Carl's eyesight is failing), and then we pressed each strand tight against the last.

"There," he said after we'd covered an inch of the rod with wire. "Give it a try."

I pulled the starter, pressed the throttle to high, and watched the brake handle. It didn't move. The new wire added enough tension to tighten the old spring. I still had to carve out a three-inch section of the cover to make it all fit back together, but my old saw was back.

Step 8: Take a break.

After more than an hour of felling, limbing, girdling, and climbing in and out of downed trees and up and down the mountainside, I take a break when the 026 runs out of gas. I hike back up the hill to drink dry a water bottle and sit with my back against a pine. Slowly, I hear the quiet again, like the air has a different density beyond the heavy humidity, a thickness of what's missing, of what's been silenced by earmuffs and the noisy chainsaw. If I wait long enough, the birds return—ovenbirds and nuthatches and a pair of ravens chortling far away. Most birds have finished nesting by this late in the summer, but not all. I know I'm pushing their season by doing this work now, and I hope to avoid felling any trees with still-active nests. I look before every cut, but it's close to impossible to spot a vireo's nest among all the leaves.

Another deadline pushes me here, one in addition to the end of summer and the beginning of my day job as a teacher. The federal government pays people—pays me—to do this Timber Stand Improvement. Not a great sum, but enough to cover expenses, plus I'd like to buy a new saw in case the 026 clunks out again. So my due date with the US Department of Agriculture hangs there on the calendar, a square-block closer every day. Nothing will happen if I don't meet this deadline, other than I'll miss out on some money. The trees will still grow and the birds still return in the spring. But I like the challenge, the extra cash, and a healthier woods, so I empty the other water bottle and head back down the trail, this time with my other saw, the 036.

Step 9: Know your intentions and make them good.

I inherited the Stihl 036 (4.5 horsepower) from Dad when he and Mom moved to a retirement village. He bought it with his brother, my uncle Harry, now gone. The saw weighs more and has more power than my 026, so technically it'll cut more wood for a longer time, if the chain is sharp. Today, I'm trying to get a little more life out of its worn chain, but the older the metal is, the more quickly it loses its edge.

The 036 replaced another Stihl on our family farm, a bulky orange-and-white machine that I tripped over in the toolshed and whose model number I don't remember. That other Stihl cut down one of my favorite trees.

At the center of my grandparents' farm, the place where I spent much of my youth, stood a shagbark hickory over one hundred feet tall, and easily over one hundred years old. It had a massive branch that hung down to almost sweep the garage, and my dad as a boy swung on that branch, bouncing it against the tin roof. I remember gathering the hickory nuts and cracking them in the kitchen where Grandma turned them into pies. Usually, we just ate the nuts raw and plain, sweet in their own way.

One Christmas when I was around fifteen, my father and three uncles decided that the hickory needed to come down. They said it posed a danger if it fell, because in every direction but one, it would crush a building, including the two-hundred-year-old farmhouse.

My uncles and father don't communicate with gentleness. If they want you to carry something, like a chain, they might throw it at you. If they have to speak, it's often a command. My dad, the most religious of the four, only swears when he is with his brothers, and then, he only says *shit*. He is the natural leader, and the two younger brothers often team up against him.

On this Christmas afternoon, with the women inside cooking and an inch of new snow covering the frozen ground, Uncle Bill, the youngest brother, leaned a ladder against the hickory and climbed as high as he could to wrap a logging chain around the trunk. Then he threw the rest to me, and I dragged the heavy chain out into the pasture—the one direction the hickory could fall without incident, and where Dad maneuvered the Farmall C. This tractor is configured like a tricycle, the front tires narrow and close together. Put a heavy load on the back of it—like pulling this hickory—and the whole tractor can flip front-end-over-back and kill the driver. So Dad turned the C around to face the tree. His wheels skidded on some ice, while Uncle Harry and I waited for him to stop. Then we hauled the chain to the front end and hooked it tight.

Dad is a math teacher. He got down from the tractor and paced off the chain. He leaned back and estimated the hickory's height. Then he approached his brothers. "I don't think the chain's long enough." He had to yell, because Uncle Don had already started the saw.

"It's long enough," Uncle Don yelled back.

I was in one of those years-long adolescent phases where your parents are always wrong, so I sided with Uncle Don, wondered why Dad just didn't get on the tractor and start pulling.

"You got anymore chain?" Dad asked Uncle Harry, who shook his head.

"Then you'll just have to be quick," Uncle Bill yelled and grinned. Uncle Don touched the saw's throttle, and the noise ended the conversation. Dad ran back to the tractor as Uncle Don crouched at the hickory's base and cut the notch. Uncle Harry and I had nothing more to do, so we scooted away while Bill stayed close to supervise.

Dad gunned the tractor, put it in gear, and pulled the chain taut. It took a long time for the saw to cut the trunk, the blade not long enough to reach all the way through, so Don had to move from one side of the hickory to the other. Halfway through, Bill and Don stopped to argue about whether or not the tree was going to fall in the right direction. Uncle Harry wouldn't let me go close and Dad couldn't leave the tractor, but he yelled and clapped anyway, urging them along.

Eventually the tree started to tilt. The tractor slid sideways on the ice. Dad held it in line long enough to guide the direction of the fall, and then the tractor and chain and tree and Dad's foot on the clutch all did what they were going to do in that brief moment when everything is decided and nothing else matters and you realize you've been holding your breath and Bill and Don hurry away from the base as the tree knifes the air and then booms against the ground, the butt-end bouncing up three feet, the whole of it rippling from end to end, bouncing again and again, each time a little less, till it stops and Uncle Don clicks off the saw and we step forward into this new emptiness to inspect, to walk its length, to come to the top and see that it only missed the tractor by a few feet (*shit*, I think), Dad shaking his head, just sitting there, bouncing in that hard metal seat, waiting for me to unhook the chain—hickory branches scratching my back—so he could move the tractor out of the way.

Whenever I daydream myself back to that farm, somehow it's always summer and the hickory still stands. It casts shade over the whole homestead in the dusty dusk of haymaking season. And I wonder if that hickory really needed to come down, or if my uncles and father just wanted to test the chainsaw, test themselves and each other, while piling up a year's worth of easy firewood.

Step 10: Avoid the widow maker.

In our woods, I only have an hour left before Sarah expects me back at the house, so I fire up the 036 and hike back down the trail. I double-check my plan, look for nests, and start cutting: a multi-stemmed red maple, a stunted beech, three crooked oaks, and a dozen or so pines. Before each cut, I plot the fall. I figure out which smaller trees to lay down first to make an alley for the big ones to fall into. I scan for dangers—younger trees I don't want to bust up, other trees that might hang the falling ones, dead branches they might fling down. Sometimes a tree lands so hard that the spring of the larger limbs will shoot it straight back over the stump. So I clear debris and plan my escape.

I'm hungry, but I hate to leave the woods with any gas left in the tank, so I move to one more stand for the day. I've picked a chestnut oak to release from a crowd of five pines. All six trees are taller than telephone poles, all of them sound. The chestnut oak has good form and greater value than the pines, both for timber and wildlife, plus it has a better chance of surviving wildfires, so the pines need to come down. I crane my neck to check once more each tree's lean. Then three pulls on the cord, a moment of loud, open-throttle roar before I trigger down to idle.

At the first pine, I kneel to cut the shallow notch, yellow inner wood facing the direction of the fall. An inch from the notch, I make a plunge cut all the way through the trunk, blade parallel to the ground. If I leave that inch of wood behind the notch, the tree should hinge on that point, a controlled fall, it's called. I step back, check clear around me, and then I make the last cut. When the tree starts leaning, I step away to watch it fall.

Even with the saw's noise and my ear protectors, I hear the loud *whomp* when the pine lands. And I feel it too, in my chest. It hits the alley, as do the next three, one on top of the others. Then I wade into the branches to limb and chunk them so each tree will lie on the ground and create more animal habitat. But this type of cutting also can injure. Limbs and small trees bend with new weight and if I cut in the wrong place, these snap like whips. I've had welts and bruises on legs, arms, and chest that lasted a month from these released poppers. So I cut in the bows of their rainbows and stand out of the way.

The last pine is slightly uphill from the chestnut oak and leans toward a nearby hickory. I make the notch and part of the plunge cut, and then I use my wedge to try to push it around the hickory instead of into it. I learned this trick from a forester friend who on one particular poplar, made the preliminary cuts and then slowly tapped in his plastic wedges until the tree fell *around* a cherry tree we wanted to save.

With an oak limb for a make-do mallet, I hit the wedge—tap and look up, hammer and watch the space of the cut and hope the whole thing moves the way I want. But when I make the final cut of the last bit of wood, the tree doesn't hit the ground. It falls in an arch of only thirty feet to hang in the hickory's upper branches. I swear. I'm tired, hungry, out of water, about out of fuel. Sarah's waiting back at home, and now I have a widow maker. I turn off the saw and throw off my helmet. Curse some more and stare up—what the hell?

I could leave this hung tree, walk away and let the wind and thirty years of weather and rot eventually bring it down, but who wants to walk these woods and be reminded every day of your error? And then there's the possibility of the hung tree suddenly dislodging to come down onto another person or pet.

So I begin to saw the pine into four-foot pieces—as high as I can safely reach. With each cut, I have to calculate the lean, predict the trunk's movement, cut from the correct side of the bole to release pressure and not pinch the saw. And each time I have to step out of the way.

Bringing a tree down like this is less predictable, much more dangerous than a straight, one-cut and down. The tree does a slow wobble back and forth, the new butt thumping the ground when a section pops loose, creating new stress points. When the cutting becomes more dangerous, I step away to saw a five-foot-long make-do pry bar from a maple. This gives me a little more space, a little more safety to push and heave until a section pops loose to roll down the mountain. Then I limb and cut the next section, pine sap sticking to my gloves when I haul away limbs.

I'm never sure which cut will be the last to bring it all the way down, so after every one, I hurry to tuck my body behind the keeper oak. When it happens—when I push the pry bar against the pinch point and the bole splits so that the lower section rolls away and the upper half finally freefalls—I jump to my oak. The pine crashes beside me, branches snapping other branches, trunk finally booming on the ground. Even where I'm tucked in, a few of the limbs brush my helmet as the tree rushes past. And then silence.

I limb this last section and then gather my tools, the chainsaws heavier, my fingers aching on the grips. I balance a saw in each hand, the water bottles clinking against them. And I head back home to Sarah.

Apis Mellifera

Rosemary Royston

———————

Benevolent, almighty bee, who is said
only to sting the dirty or wicked. Beloved bee

who spins liquid gold, while looking after
the pure of heart. I plant lemon balm, borage

as invitation. I know to tell you of a family death
or you, too, will leave and perish.

I've seen you gather at your keeper's gravesite—
a stop along the way to a new home.

Ever grateful I am for you, your sourwood—
which, along with moonshine, helps

all possible ailments in some form or fashion
here in the blue hills of God.

Wine Is the Color of Blood

Lisa Ezzard

————

a warning on papyrus:
Words that may have gone from your mouth
without your body aware
that you had uttered them.

But it is too late.

I am already drunk
Dionysus has visited me in the night
and turned his mast to grapevines
He has unleashed my Appalachian instinct
and I am yoked to the rigorous vine,
the tough-skinned fruit of the Cynthiana
the backcountry, the mead

Men with pocketknives, skins, plant knowledge,
and the memories of rain
I walk this fat and fertile land of red clay
and mimic the gnarled vines
of the Norton
down the dirt road to the barrel room
with my wine thief
I sample the colors of eucharist prayer
for 40 days and 40 nights

I spit and feel the sharp edge on the palate,
the complex aftertaste of something tamed,
I dip into free-run and oak aged, chewy and backward,
the earth, the legs, the lingering, the dregs
and I am volatile—what lackluster effect have I added to
myself? I rack. I fine. I breathe barnyard, cigar box.
I taste bouquet, and bite.

In the well of holiness
I have left my conscious self, as
the best wine is left alone
to grow robust like an old woman's lust and
yes, this is no longer about surrender I have
become who I am.

The Grandfather I Never Knew

M. W. Smith

————————

The grandfather I never knew was said to be the unofficial town mayor
who drank moonshine and played cards every evening with the other
      farming men
at the Shell station below the house.

Deep in the woods past the back pasture was a still.

The grandfather I never knew died from a liver poisoned by Blue Ridge
      white-lightning
and left us eight hundred acres
where I would learn to put up hay, catch trout in creeks, and pick wild
      berries for cobblers.

Birdbrain

Wayne Caldwell

———

This mornin I fotched in an armload of wood—
Twelve-degree wind whipsawed my jacket, tried to make off with my cap.
Enough to make a man think about central heat.
By the back door, in Birdie's nandina bush,
Perched a big old mocker, ruffled against the wind.
Red berries, green leaves, gray bird—he shivered,
Cocked his head, and ever few seconds said "Chit."
I stood, balanced my load, figured he'd fly off,
But he kept at it like a one-word preacher.
A shootin pain inside my elbow said "Go in, you old fool."
"Chit," said the graybird, spittin out his last word for the world.
"Change one letter and you got that right," I said, and tromped inside,
Filled the wood box, dusted off my sleeves, and laughed.
I've heard them birds sound like yellowhammers, rain crows,
Train whistles and plain crows,
But I reckon that was bona fide pigeon English.
Don't tell me birds ain't smart.

Acknowledgments

———

Thank you first and foremost to Dr. Amrit Singh, Langston Hughes Professor of English and African American Studies at Ohio University. Without your initial encouragement and confidence, this project would not have been explored. To the amazingly talented and thoughtful writers in this collection, thank you for trusting me with your work. To all the wonderful folks in the English department at Western Carolina University, thank you so much for your support. Andrew Berzanskis and the many wonderful folks at West Virginia University Press, thank you for your patience and guidance; you made this journey a pleasant one. John McHone and Carrie Murray, thanks for always pushing me. And finally, to my parents and Joy McHone, thank you for your faith in me and the alone time to complete the manuscript.

Contributors

CHRIS BOLGIANO has written four books, edited two, and contributed to three anthologies. Several of her books have won awards. Over the last thirty-five years she has also written innumerable nature and travel articles for *The Forestry Source*, *Appalachian Journal*, *Audubon*, *American Forests*, *Defenders of Wildlife*, *The Washington Post*, *New York Times*, *Islands*, *Forest Magazine*, *Wilderness*, and other publications. In 2015 two of her columns syndicated by Bay Journal News Service won first and second place in the Virginia Outdoor Writers Association Excellence in Craft contest. After dozens of presentations, including some keynote speeches, she hopes she's becoming a little less boring.

TAYLOR BROWN lives in Washington with his fiancé Jess and a dog named after an Edward Sharpe song. He was raised in Granite Falls, North Carolina, in the foothills of Appalachia where his interests led him down a trail of hiking, early childhood education, creative writing, and casual musicianship. Previously, Brown has published poems and an award-winning short story, "Remodeling," in *Branches* magazine published by CCC&TI Foundation.

BEN BURGHOLZER is a PhD candidate at Binghamton University and an adjunct at the State University of New York–Rockland and St. Thomas Aquinas College. When he is not teaching or writing, he spends as much time as possible in the woods, mountains, and rivers.

KATHRYN STRIPLING BYER has published six collections of poetry. Her second, *Wildwood Flower*, received the Lamont (now Laughlin) award from the Academy of American Poets, and her subsequent books have been recognized by the Fellowship of Southern Writers, the Southern Independent Booksellers Alliance, and the North Carolina Book Awards. Her work has been frequently anthologized and published in journals ranging from *The Atlantic* to *Appalachian Heritage*. She served for five years as North Carolina's first woman poet laureate. She lived in the mountains of western North Carolina, within listening distance of the Tuckasegee River.

WAYNE CALDWELL, a native of Asheville, North Carolina, is the author of two novels, *Cataloochee* and *Requiem by Fire*, as well as several prize-winning short stories. He has won the Thomas Wolfe Memorial Literary Award from the Western North Carolina Historical Association and the James Still Award from the Fellowship of Southern Writers. He is at work on another novel and a collection of poems.

SARAH BETH CHILDERS is the author of *Shake Terribly the Earth: Stories from an Appalachian Family*. Her essays also have appeared in journals, including *Brevity, Pank, Guernica, Wigleaf,* and *The Tusculum Review*. A Huntington, West Virginia, native, and a graduate of Marshall University and West Virginia University, Childers now lives in Stillwater, Oklahoma, where she teaches creative nonfiction at Oklahoma State University and lives and writes with her Boston terrier and cat.

JESSICA CORY is a native of southeastern Ohio, now residing in western North Carolina where she teaches in the English department at Western Carolina University. Her work has been published in a variety of journals, including *A Poetry Congeries, ellipsis . . . ,* and *Menacing Hedge*, and is included in the chapbook *Women Speak vol. 3*, a publication of the Women of Appalachia Project.

CHAUNA CRAIG was born in Montana, but she's lived eighteen years in Indiana, Pennsylvania, home of the Northern Appalachian Folk Festival, and spends her weekends walking in the endless woods. She is the author of the story collection *The Widow's Guide to Edible Mushrooms*. Her fiction has appeared in dozens of magazines and anthologies, including *Prairie Schooner, Sou'wester, SmokeLong Quarterly, You Have Time for This: Contemporary Short Short Fiction*, and *Flash Fiction International*. Her stories have been honored with Special Mention in the Pushcart Prize anthology and *descant*'s Sandra Brown Fiction Prize. She teaches creative writing and women's studies at Indiana University of Pennsylvania.

THOMAS RAIN CROWE is the author of *The End of Eden: Writings of an Environmental Activist* and *Zoro's Field: My Life in the Appalachian Woods*. Both are available through City Lights Bookstore in Sylva, North Carolina—specializing in literature of the southern Appalachians. He lives in the Little Canada community of Jackson County in the Smoky Mountains of western North Carolina.

STEPHEN CUSHMAN is the author of six collections of poetry, including *Hothead* and *The Red List*, as well as two books of criticism and two books about the Civil War. He is general editor of the fourth edition of the *Princeton Encyclopedia of Poetry and Poetics* and Robert C. Taylor Professor of English at the University of Virginia. He has hiked in the Appalachians from Newfoundland to North Carolina and frequently writes and teaches on the connections between literature and the environment, often focusing on the Appalachian region.

DORIS DIOSA DAVENPORT. As an undergraduate, around 1968, i first wrote my name in all lowercase letters, as well as the word *i*. Similarly, at a time before time, in our magical community on a hill in Cornelia, Georgia, i totally identified as "Affralachian" before the wonderful creation of that term. Working against all the isms for all my life, i often use caustic humor, satire, and hyperbole to achieve my (artistic and activist) ends. i am a seventy-year-old scholar-educator/writer/performance poet; a lesbian-feminist biamorous anarchist; working-class iconoclast from northeast Georgia; with a BA in English from Paine College and a PhD (African American literature, University of Southern California). i love teaching and have taught at colleges and universities in at least twelve states, but i am presently unemployed. i recently published my eleventh book of poems, *rectify my soul*. Available for poetry performances, workshops, lectures. Contact: zorahpoet7@gmail.com.

West Virginia native ED DAVIS retired in 2011 from teaching at Sinclair Community College in Dayton, Ohio, where he taught writing. He has also taught both fiction and poetry at the Antioch Writers' Workshop and is the author of the novels *I Was So Much Older Then*, *The Measure of Everything*, and *The Psalms of Israel Jones*, which won the Hackney Award for an unpublished novel in 2010. Many of his stories and poems have appeared in anthologies and journals, including *Evansville Review*, *The Vincent Brothers Review*, *Appalachian Heritage*, *For the Road: Short Stories of America's Highways*, *Every River on Earth: Writing from Appalachian Ohio*, *Eyes Glowing at the Edge of the Woods: Fiction and Poetry from West Virginia*, and *Wild, Sweet Notes: Fifty Years of West Virginia Poetry*. Four poetry chapbooks have been released as well as a full-length collection, *Time of the Light*. He lives with his wife in the village of Yellow Springs, Ohio, where he bikes, hikes, and blogs mainly on literary topics. Please visit him at www.davised.com.

SUSAN DEER CLOUD, a mixed-lineage Catskill Mountain Indian, is the recipient of a National Endowment for the Arts Literature Fellowship, two New York State Foundation for the Arts Poetry Fellowships, and an Elizabeth George Foundation Grant. Her books include *Before Language*, *Hunger Moon*, *Fox Mountain*, and *Braiding Starlight*, and her work has been published in numerous literary journals and anthologies. Most recently her image and poetry were included in the photographer Chris Felver's *Tending the Fire, Native Voices & Portraits*. Currently Deer Cloud does a lot of roving on Turtle Island and lands on the other side of the Atlantic in quest of ancient mysteries and wiser ways too often eluding us. As a mountain woman, she feels a deep love and affinity for mountains everywhere.

A long-time poet and teacher, LISA EZZARD is a member of the Squaw Valley Community of Writers and a fellow at Hambidge Art Center in the Smoky Mountains. Her poetry book, *Vintage*, published by New Native Press, chronicles a year of growing wine grapes and making wine in the Appalachians of northern Georgia, where she is sixth generation on a family farm. She has also published in many literary journals and anthologies, including *Appalachian Heritage* and *Appalachian Adventure: From Maine to Georgia—A Spectacular Journey on the Great Appalachian Trail* (a book nominated for a Pulitzer Prize in journalism). She currently resides on an organic farm at the border of North Carolina and Georgia and is a vintner on her family farm at Tiger Mountain Vineyards.

KATIE FALLON is the author of the nonfiction books *Vulture: The Private Life of an Unloved Bird* and *Cerulean Blues: A Personal Search for a Vanishing Songbird* and two children's books, *Look, See the Bird!* and *Look, See the Farm!* Fallon's essays have appeared in a variety of literary journals and magazines, including *Fourth Genre, River Teeth, Ecotone, Bark Magazine, Appalachian Heritage, Now & Then, Isotope, Fourth River, the minnesota review,* and *The Tusculum Review.* Her essay "Rebirth," published in *River Teeth*, was listed as a "Notable" in Best American Science & Nature Writing 2014, and her essay "Hill of the Sacred Eagles" was a finalist in Terrain's 2011 essay contest. She has been nominated several times for a Pushcart Prize. Fallon has taught creative writing at Virginia Tech and West Virginia University. A lifelong resident of Appalachia, Fallon's great-

great-grandfather, great-grandfather, and grandfather were coal miners in West Virginia and Pennsylvania. Both of her parents were public school teachers. In addition to writing, teaching, and caring for injured wildlife, Fallon enjoys birding, hiking, travel, canoeing, yoga, and wine. She lives in Cheat Neck, West Virginia, with her daughters, Laurel and Cora; spouse, Jesse; beagle-ish rescue dogs, Liza Jane and Sally Ann; and (formerly) wild horses, Rosie and Ranger.

CAROL GRAMETBAUER's poems have appeared in journals including *Appalachian Heritage, Appalachian Journal, Connecticut River Review, POEM, The Kerf, The Notebook*, and *Third Wednesday*; in the online journals *drafthorse, Still: The Journal, Fluent*, and *Maypop*; and in numerous anthologies. Her chapbook, *Now & Then*, was released by Finishing Line Press in 2014. She lives in Kingston, Tennessee, where she is chair of the board of directors of Tennessee Mountain Writers. Her work was nominated for a 2016 Pushcart Prize.

JESSE GRAVES was raised in Sharps Chapel, Tennessee, forty miles north of Knoxville, where his ancestors settled in the 1780s. Most of his writing and teaching relate to the history and natural environments of Appalachia. Graves is the author of three poetry collections, *Tennessee Landscape with Blighted Pine, Basin Ghosts*, and *Specter Mountain*, cowritten with William Wright. Graves received the 2015 James Still Award for Writing about the Appalachian South from the Fellowship of Southern Writers. He is associate professor of English and poet in residence at East Tennessee State University.

JANE HARRINGTON lives in Virginia's Blue Ridge, where she works as a free-range college professor, presently teaching fiction writing and literature at Washington & Lee University. She has written best-selling books for young adults, and her literary fiction and creative nonfiction have been published in anthologies and journals, including *Chautauqua, Anthology of Appalachian Writers, Circa*, and *Portland Review*. Harrington has done extensive research in and about Ireland and is working on a novel that explores migratory connections between Ireland's west and Appalachia. She is a fellow at the Virginia Center for the Creative Arts. You can find links to some of her published work at www.janeharrington.com.

LISA HAYES-MINNEY is a former journalist, now serving as a public librarian, adjunct instructor, and publisher of a humble lifestyle magazine, *Two-Lane Livin'*, which is popular throughout central West Virginia. She was the 2015 recipient of the Linda Culp Memorial Scholarship, which she combined with her Segal AmeriCorps Education Award to help her earn her MFA in creative writing from West Virginia Wesleyan College. She has received writing awards from the West Virginia Press Association and West Virginia Writers, Inc. In addition to her own magazine, Hayes-Minney's work has also appeared in *GreenPrints Magazine, Wonderful West Virginia Magazine, Intelliguide, The Trillium, Fireside Folklore of West Virginia*, and various newspapers. She publishes *Mountain Ink* (a literary magazine featuring West Virginia writers), leads a monthly writers' group called "Friendly Fonts," and is an official weather spotter for the National Weather Service. She and her husband, Frank, enjoy organic gardening, keep honey bees, and raise free-range hens.

LAURA HENRY-STONE's bioregional home is the Appalachian region of the Chesapeake Bay watershed. Raised in Shepherdstown, West Virginia, she left the Appalachians to acquire a BA in biology at St. Mary's College of Maryland, an MA in earth literacy from Saint-Mary-of-the-Woods in Indiana, and an interdisciplinary PhD in sustainability education at the University of Alaska–Fairbanks. In 2000 she took some time off between degrees to thru-hike the Appalachian Trail with her partner. She is currently living again in her home bioregion as an assistant professor of environmental studies and sustainability at the University of Lynchburg in Virginia, where she teaches undergraduate and graduate courses such as Environmental Science 101, Sustainable Living, and Capstone in Environmental Studies. She also conducts numerous cocurricular sustainability education projects and is actively involved in transforming the general education curriculum to prepare students for the environmental and social challenges of the coming decades.

SCOTT HONEYCUTT is an assistant professor of English at East Tennessee State University. When he is not teaching, he enjoys walking the hills of Appalachia and spending time with his family.

A native of North Carolina's western Piedmont, GEORGE HOVIS moved in 2006 to the northernmost county of the Appalachian chain, Otsego County, New York, which during the past several years has become a central battleground in New York's successful campaign to produce a statewide ban on hydrofracking and to limit expansion of gas and oil pipeline infrastructure. His short fiction has appeared most recently in *Carolina Quarterly* and *The Fourth River,* and his novel *The Skin Artist* is due out from Southern Fried Karma in 2019. He has also published numerous essays on southern and Appalachian writers, including Thomas Wolfe, Fred Chappell, Lee Smith, and Robert Morgan. Hovis currently is an associate professor of English at the State University of New York–Oneonta.

GENE HYDE is a writer and photographer living in western North Carolina. He has an MA in Appalachian studies and works as an Appalachian archivist and special collections librarian.

LIBBY FALK JONES is Chester D. Tripp Chair in Humanities and professor of English, emerita, at Berea College, Kentucky, where her teaching included creative and contemplative writing and literature as well as nature writing and photography. Her poems and creative nonfiction have been published in regional and national journals and anthologies, including *Appalachian Heritage, Still, Anthology of Appalachian Writers: Charles Frazier Volume IX, The Merton Seasonal*, and *New Growth: Recent Kentucky Writing*. She is the author of *Above the Eastern Treetops, Blue* and coauthor of *Balance of Five*, both books of poems. Her landscape photography has been exhibited in various Kentucky galleries.

A fifth-generation Alabamian, MADISON JONES is a graduate research fellow at the University of Florida, where he studies ecocomposition and environmental rhetoric and works with the *Trace* journal and innovation initiative. He is the editor in chief of *Kudzu House Quarterly*, a literary and scholarly journal devoted to ecological thought. *Reflections on the Dark Water*, his second poetry collection, was released this spring from Solomon & George. His poems have appeared in *ISLE, The Goose, Shenandoah, Birmingham Poetry Review, Greensboro Review, Painted Bride Quarterly*, and elsewhere. He coedited *Writing the Environment in Nineteenth-Century American Literature*. Visit his website at ecopoiesis.com.

JULIA SPICHER KASDORF has published three collections of poems in the Pitt Poetry Series, including, most recently, *Poetry in America*. She has also published a book of essays, *The Body and the Book: Writing from a Mennonite Life*, and a biography, *Fixing Tradition: Joseph W. Yoder, Amish American*. She coedited a new edition of Yoder's regional classic *Rosanna of the Amish* as well as Fred Lewis Pattee's novel *The House of the Black Ring*. With photographer Steven Rubin, she is currently completing Shale Play, a poetry and photo project that attempts to document the human, social, and environmental impacts of fracking in Pennsylvania. She teaches poetry writing at Penn State and the Summer Community of Writers of Chatham University, and she lives in Bellefonte, Pennsylvania.

BILL KING is a graduate of the MA program in creative writing and the PhD program in literature at the University of Georgia and has taught literature and creative writing at Davis & Elkins College in Elkins, West Virginia, for the past twenty years. His work has appeared in many journals and anthologies, including *Kestrel, Appalachian Heritage, Still: The Journal, Mississippi Quarterly, The Southern Poetry Anthology*, and *A Narrow Fellow: Journal of Poetry*. He has been nominated for the 2016 Pushcart Prize for Literature by *Still: The Journal*.

JOHN LANE is the author of a dozen books of poetry and prose, including *The Dead Father Poems*. His latest, *Abandoned Quarry: New & Selected Poems*, was released by Mercer University Press in Macon, Georgia, in 2012. The book includes much of Lane's published poetry over the past thirty years, plus a selection of new poems. *Abandoned Quarry* won the Southeastern Independent Booksellers Alliance Poetry Book of the Year prize. He was inducted into the South Carolina Academy of Authors in 2014. His latest prose book is *Coyote Settles the South*, published in 2016 by the University of Georgia Press. He cofounded the Hub City Writers Project in Spartanburg, South Carolina, and teaches environmental studies at Wofford College there. Visit his website at www.kudzutelegraph.com.

JEANNE LARSEN is the author of two books of poetry, *Why We Make Gardens [& other Poems]* and the AWP-winning *James Cook in Search of Terra Incognita*, as well as two literary translations, *Willow, Wine, Mirror, Moon: Women's Poems from Tang China* and *Brocade River Poems: Selected Works of the Tang Dynasty Courtesan Xue Tao*. She has also published an e-novel, *Sally Paradiso*, set largely in the southern Appalachians, and three print novels, *Silk Road, Bronze Mirror*, and *Manchu Palaces*. She teaches in the Jackson Center for Creative Writing at Hollins University and lives in Virginia's Roanoke Valley between the Blue Ridge and the Allegheny Highlands.

LAURA LONG coedited the anthology *Eyes Glowing at the Edge of the Woods: Fiction and Poetry from West Virginia*. Her other books are the novel *Out of Peel Tree* and two poetry collections, *The Eye of Caroline Herschel: A Life in Poems* and *Imagine a Door*. Her writing has appeared in *Shenandoah, Southern Review, Still*, and other journals, and her novel was a finalist for the Balcones Prize, the IndieFab Award, and the Weatherford Award. She's received a James Michener Fellowship and Virginia Center for Creative Arts Fellowships. She teaches courses in creative and environmental writing at the University of Lynchburg. She was born and raised in central West Virginia, with her family having lived there since the 1770s—her grandfathers farmed, mined coal, and worked on the railroad.

BRENT MARTIN is the author of three chapbook collections of poetry— *Poems from Snow Hill Road, A Shout in the Woods*, and *Staring the Red Earth Down*—and is coauthor of *Every Breath Sings Mountains* with Barbara Duncan and Thomas Rain Crowe. He is also the author of *Hunting for Camellias at Horseshoe Bend*, a nonfiction chapbook published by Red Bird Press in 2015. His poetry and essays have been published in the *North Carolina Literary Review, Pisgah Review, Tar River Poetry, Chattahoochee Review, Eno Journal, New Southerner, Kudzu Literary Journal, Smoky Mountain News*, and elsewhere. He lives in the Cowee community in western North Carolina and has recently completed a two-year term as Gilbert-Chappell Distinguished Poet for the West.

A native of Asheville, North Carolina, MICHAEL MCFEE grew up in south Buncombe County, where he attended public schools, wandered in the local woods, and hiked and camped along the Blue Ridge Parkway near Mount Pisgah. He is the author of eleven books of poetry and two collections of essays, most recently *We Were Once Here: Poems* and *Appointed Rounds: Essays*. In 2009 he received the James Still Award for Writing about the

Appalachian South from the Fellowship of Southern Writers. He has taught poetry writing at the University of North Carolina–Chapel Hill for many years.

JIM MINICK is the author of five books, including *Fire Is Your Water*, a debut novel released in 2017. His memoir, *The Blueberry Years*, won the Best Nonfiction Book of the Year from the Southern Independent Booksellers Association. His honors include the Jean Ritchie Fellowship in Appalachian Writing and the Fred Chappell Fellowship at University of North Carolina–Greensboro. His work has appeared in many publications, including *Poets & Writers*, *Oxford American*, *Shenandoah*, *Orion*, *San Francisco Chronicle*, *Encyclopedia of Appalachia*, *Conversations with Wendell Berry*, *Appalachian Journal*, and *The Sun*. Currently, he is assistant professor at Augusta University and core faculty in Converse College's low-residency MFA program.

FELICIA MITCHELL, a native of South Carolina, has made her home in rural southwestern Virginia since 1987, where she teaches at Emory & Henry College. Her poems and essays, both scholarly and creative, have been published widely, and she edited *Her Words: Diverse Voices in Contemporary Appalachian Women's Poetry*. *Waltzing with Horses*, a collection of her poems, was published in 2014 by Press 53.

A native of West Virginia, ANN PANCAKE is the author of two short-story collections, *Given Ground* and *Me and My Daddy Listen to Bob Marley*, and a novel, *Strange as This Weather Has Been*, which was one of *Kirkus Reviews*'s Top Ten Fiction Books of the year, won the 2007 Weatherford Prize, and was a finalist for the 2008 Orion Book Award and the 2008 Washington State Book Award. She has also received a Whiting Award, a National Endowment for the Arts grant, the Bakeless Prize, and a Pushcart Prize. Fiction and essays have appeared in journals and anthologies like *Orion*, *The Georgia Review*, *Poets and Writers*, and *New Stories from the*

South: The Year's Best. In 2016 she was the first recipient of the Barry Lopez Visiting Writer in Ethics and the Community Fellowship. She has a PhD in English literature from the University of Washington and teaches for Pacific Lutheran University's MFA program.

ELLEN J. PERRY grew up in the small mountain town of Weaverville, North Carolina, where she continues to live today. From her sunroom, which doubles as a writing space, Perry can hear her high school marching band practicing in the summer. Her father's side of the family lived for many generations in eastern Tennessee; her mother's side settled in northern Georgia. Perry's Appalachian roots run deep, and while she loves to travel, it's always a joy to come home again to the mountains.

MARK POWELL is the author of five novels, most recently *Small Treasons*, released by Simon and Schuster in 2017. Powell has received fellowships from the National Endowment for the Arts, the Breadloaf and Sewanee Writers' Conferences, and in 2014 he was a Fulbright Fellow to Slovakia. In 2009 he received the Chaffin Award for contributions to Appalachian literature. He holds degrees from Yale Divinity School, the University of South Carolina, and the Citadel. He lives in the mountains of North Carolina where he teaches at Appalachian State University.

HEATHER RANSOM received her MA from Marshall University where she taught English until discovering it wasn't the right gig for her. She holds a bachelor's degree in English and media studies from High Point University and has worked in marketing for nearly a decade. Ransom is currently helping her husband construct a tiny, off-grid-ish house in the mountains of West Virginia where she continues to focus on her writing, activism, and other creative pursuits. Her creative nonfiction has appeared in *Written River: A Journal of Ecopoetics,* the *Chattahoochee Review,* and *Gravel Magazine*. Ransom received an Emerging Voices Award in 2014 and is cofounder of the women writer's group Society of the Lark.

JEREMY MICHAEL REED is a PhD student in creative writing at the University of Tennessee. His poems are published in *Public Pool, Still: The Journal, Valparaiso Poetry Review*, and elsewhere, including the anthology *Bright Bones: Contemporary Montana Writing*. He lives in Knoxville, where he is the editor-in-chief of *Grist: A Journal of the Literary Arts* and codirects the Only Tenn-I-See Reading Series. More of his work can be found at www.jeremymichaelreed.com.

JOHN ROBINSON is a graduate of the Marshall University creative writing program in Huntington, West Virginia, with a regent's degree. He has an interest in critical theory of poetry and American Formalism. Robinson is also a twelve-year educator for Mason County Schools in Mason County, West Virginia. He strives for a poetics similar to Donald Hall, Maxine Kumin, James Wright, Louis Simpson, Gallway Kinnell, and Robert Bly though enjoys learning from intrinsic poets and their theories in the critical writings of Denise Levertov, Robert Creeley, Louis Zukofsky, William Carlos Williams, and Richard Kostelanetz. Robinson is currently working on a creative dissertation in contemporary poetry, though outside the university environment.

ROSEMARY ROYSTON, author of *Splitting the Soil*, resides in northeast Georgia with her family. Her flash fiction and poetry have been published in journals such as *NANO Fiction, Appalachian Heritage, Southern Poetry Review, KUDZU, Town Creek Review, *82 Review*, and *Still: The Journal*. She's the vice president for Planning and Research at Young Harris College, where she occasionally teaches creative writing.

M. W. SMITH was born in Wheeling, West Virginia. He is currently the chair of the humanities department at Bluefield State College where he's been an English professor for twenty years. He has six fishing guides published with the University of Virginia Press and one book of literary theory with

State University of New York Press. He is an avid fly fisherman and resides on a family farm in Floyd, Virginia, with his wife and daughter.

LARRY D. THACKER is a seventh-generation Cumberland Gap–area native. A writer and artist, he was raised in the mountains of Kentucky and now lives in the mountains of upper east Tennessee. His first fascinations with writing happened as a result of collecting the folk stories of his family, which led to more of the same in the larger region, which led to a column in the local paper in 1991, titled "Mountain Mysteries." That led to his first book, *Mountain Mysteries: The Mystic Traditions of Appalachia*. His poetry appears in more than ninety publications, including *Still: The Journal, Poetry South, The Southern Poetry Anthology*, and *Appalachian Heritage*. His books include *Mountain Mysteries: The Mystic Traditions of Appalachia* and the poetry books, *Voice Hunting* and *Memory Train* and *Drifting in Awe*. He's presently working on his MFA in both poetry and fiction. Visit his website at www.larrydthacker.com.

After living in Philadelphia, Palo Alto, Berlin, and New Orleans, GAIL TYSON married a southerner and sank her roots in the red clay of Georgia and rocky ridges of east Tennessee. She publishes poetry, nonfiction, and fiction. Her work appears in *Appalachian Heritage, Art Ascent, Big Muddy, Cloudbank, Presence, San Pedro River Review, Still Point Arts Quarterly, The Citron Review,* and the anthology *Unbroken Circle: Stories of Diversity in the South*. Tyson splits her time between Roswell, Georgia, and a log cabin in the Cherokee National Forest, east Tennessee, which she shares with her husband, Dick, and border collie, Maggie.

RICK VAN NOY is a professor of English at Radford University. He is the author of two books, *Surveying the Interior: Literary Cartographers and the Sense of the Place* and *A Natural Sense of Wonder: Connecting Kids with Nature through the Seasons*, which won an award for Outstanding

Writing on the Southern Environment from the Southern Environmental Law Center. His writing has appeared in *Appalachian Voices, Blue Ridge Country, Orion*, and *Creative Nonfiction*. At present, he is working on a book about climate change adaptation in the South.

G. C. WALDREP's most recent books are a long poem, *Testament*, and a chapbook, *Susquehanna*. With Joshua Corey, he edited *The Arcadia Project: North American Postmodern Pastoral*. He lives in Lewisburg, Pennsylvania, where he teaches at Bucknell University, edits the journal *West Branch,* and serves as editor-at-large for *The Kenyon Review*.

MEREDITH SUE WILLIS is a writer and teacher and enthusiastic reader. Born and raised in West Virginia, she is a proud member of the Appalachian Renaissance with deep roots in West Virginia and the western mountain counties of Virginia. Her books have been published by Charles Scribner's Sons, HarperCollins, Ohio University Press, Mercury House, West Virginia University Press, Monteymayor Press, Teachers & Writers Press, Hamilton Stone Editions, and others. She teaches at New York University's School of Professional Studies and also does occasional writer-in-the-school residencies and workshops for writers. She lives in an inner ring suburb near New York City with her husband, Andrew B. Weinberger. She does organic gardening in her backyard and is active in her local Ethical Culture Society and in the integration organization, South Orange/Maplewood Community Coalition on Race.

AMBER WRIGHT was born in Wisconsin and raised in Mississippi. She earned her BA in English from Delta State University and worked in journalism postgrad before moving to Huntington, West Virginia, where she earned her MA in English from Marshall University. It was during graduate school that Wright discovered environmental literature and place theory. Her essay that appears here comes from her thesis collection.

After graduate school, she taught high school English and creative writing in Huntington and has recently moved to New Hampshire where she is working in a school library. Wright enjoys running, hiking with her husband Chad and their zany golden retriever Crosby, and watching *Gilmore Girls* marathons while snuggled deep in the couch with their two cats, Walle and Willoughby.

DAVID R. YOUNG attended Duke University and is now professor of English at Edgewood College, in Madison, Wisconsin. His stories have been published in *River Oak Review, Willow Springs, Ploughshares*, and *Indiana Review*, among other literary journals, and an essay on William Styron's short fiction appeared in 2012 in *The Southern Literary Journal*. He is the recipient of a Creative Writing Fellowship from the National Endowment for the Arts. As a boy in Cleveland, Ohio, he would travel with his family to Noble County, in the southeastern part of the state, where his grandmother had been raised. Though she had moved to Cleveland as a young woman, his great-grandfather, once a coal miner, among other occupations, and his great-grandmother lived on a small hillside farm in Noble County.

Sources and Permissions

"Dead Soldier" and "My Grandfather's Church Goes Up" from *Midquest* by Fred Chappell (LSU Press, 1989). Reprinted by permission of Louisiana State University Press. All rights reserved.

Excerpts from "The Dry Salvages" from *Four Quartets* by T. S. Eliot. Copyright 1941 by T. S. Eliot; copyright © renewed 1969 by Esme Valerie Eliot. Reprinted by permission of Houghton Mifflin Harcourt Publishing Company and Faber and Faber Ltd. All rights reserved.

"Water Tank" by Meredith Sue Willis was adapted from ideas in her novel *A Space Apart* (New York: Charles Scribner's Sons, 1979).

Portions of "Take in the Waters" by Rick Van Noy also appear in his book *Sudden Spring: Stories of Adaptation in a Climate-Changed South* (University of Georgia Press, 2018).

"Letter to West Virginia, November 2016" by Ann Pancake was republished with permission from *Souvenir: A Journal*.

CPSIA information can be obtained
at www.ICGtesting.com
Printed in the USA
LVHW061910080719
623451LV00020B/1389/P